THE SHADOW *of* WINGS

BY THE SAME AUTHOR

fiction

Marama
Marama of the Islands
Sandstorm

non-fiction

The Sultans Came to Tea
A Gift of Islands
A World of Islands
A South Sea Spell
Tales from Paradise

THE SHADOW *of* WINGS

June Knox-Mawer

Weidenfeld and Nicolson
LONDON

First published in Great Britain in 1995
by Weidenfeld & Nicolson

The Orion Publishing Group Ltd
Orion House
5 Upper Saint Martin's Lane
London WC2H 9EA

ISBN 0297 81567 9

A catalogue record for this book is
available from the British Library

Typeset by Deltatype Ltd, Ellesmere Port, Cheshire
Printed in England by Clays Ltd, St Ives plc

For my grand-daughter

Polly

whose mother was born in the islands

AUTHOR'S NOTE

The seeds of this novel were sown during the twelve years I spent in the South Pacific, from 1958 to 1970. Based in Fiji, I travelled around most of the island groups, including the loneliest of them all, the Gilberts, then under British administration, now independent Kiribati. Here I saw gruesome reminders of the Japanese occupation of 1942–3. I also talked to government officers and missionaries from the pre-war era who had lived lives of incredible isolation in these scattered outposts, cut off from their own civilization for years on end.

Memories of those early times brought up the name of the world-famous American aviator Amelia Earhart, whose plane disappeared over the Pacific in July 1937. The theory was sometimes put forward that she had ended up as a castaway on one of the uninhabited Gilbertese atolls, although massive air and sea searches revealed no trace of either wreckage or survivors.

Nevertheless the idea continued to fascinate me. My own researches indicated the outlying Phoenix group as the most likely area for a forced landing, when Earhart was unable to locate Howland Island, the pre-arranged refuelling point 500 miles to the north. In particular, Nikumaroro Island (then called Gardner) somehow fixed itself in my mind as the place where she might finally have been washed ashore.

You can imagine my feelings when, in March 1992, press and radio carried reports of the discovery of certain artefacts on Nikumaroro which could be linked to Earhart's survival. These included part of a woman's shoe in her size, a small piece of aircraft fuselage, a broken metal box, also the cap of a medicine bottle of the type she used for stomach trouble. According to Richard Gillespie of the American-based International Group for Historic Aircraft Recovery, these findings, together with subsequent navigational research, provide the true key to the Earhart mystery.

On a personal level, there has been one curious postscript to these findings. It occurred during my recording of a BBC interview with the distinguished colonial official, Eric Bevington, now retired, on quite another topic. Reverting to his early years as a young cadet in the Pacific, he happened to mention that while posted to the Gilberts, he had made a brief call at Nikumaroro to reconnoitre it for possible settlement. In the middle of this small deserted island, never before inhabited, he had come across what he described as a 'bivouac' – a rough shelter of branches for which there seemed to be no explanation. There were no other signs of habitation. This was September 1937, exactly two months after Earhart's disappearance. The war came and he never returned to the island. In fact, he had only been reminded of the incident by the recent reports of other discoveries.

It was the final spark needed to bring to life in my mind a story of what-might-have-been in this haunting and haunted far corner of the world.

ACKNOWLEDGEMENTS

Among the many accounts of Amelia Earhart's life, including her own books and letters, I would like to single out the excellent definitive biography by Mary S. Lovell, *The Sound of Wings*.

I must also thank Terry Berringer of the Royal Commonwealth Society Library; Dr C. J. Morgan of the Australian National University Department of Pacific Studies for her help in tracking down the wartime records of the Sisters of Notre Dame du Sacré Coeur in the Pacific; and June Grimble for her memories of a Gilbertese childhood.

By strange coincidence, a letter out of the blue from the late Katherine Tottenham in 1986 also served to set me on the Earhart track.

These acknowledgements would not be complete without a tribute to my editor, Allegra Huston, for her longterm commitment to the book, and to Elizabeth Blumer at Weidenfeld for seeing the book through. I am also grateful, as always, to Janet McCormack for transforming my original pages into an immaculate typescript.

Finally, a very personal thank-you to my husband for sharing with me the turbulent experience of living under 'the shadow of wings' for the last three years.

PART ONE

CHAPTER ONE

July 3rd, 1937

Somehow the sunrise had given me new strength. Flying on endlessly through the darkness, with only the sea below, there were moments when I felt I might not be able to last. It took all my will-power just to keep my eyes open. But the sight of that first faint streak of gold on the horizon was a miracle.

Never mind the cramp in every joint of my body after eighteen hours in this four-foot by four-foot cockpit. Never mind the throbbing roar of the engines that fills my head till I think it will burst. Never mind the figures on the dials in front of me that remind me how the last tank of fuel is running lower with every turn of the propellers. Suddenly I feel we're going to make it. Only another hour and out of the blue will come floating the tiny speck of Howland Island and we'll have done it. More or less, anyway. The chance to get some sleep – blessed sleep – to stretch our legs on firm ground, to eat a proper meal instead of a dry scrambled-egg sandwich, that's all we need to get us across to Honolulu and then the final lap to California and home.

Our last glimpse of land was around 3 am, when we picked out the Gilbert Islands through the cloud. Fred climbed through from his navigation post at the back to call out the names for me – Kuria, Aranuka, Nonouti – an incantation to the gods of Micronesia to deliver us safely across the ocean. In the moonlight, the string of tiny atolls looked like stepping stones from nowhere to nowhere. Now with the sun up, it's awesome to look down on the vastness and the emptiness of the central Pacific, nothing moving across that shimmering expanse except the shadow of *Electra*'s wings, a first-day-of-creation kind of feeling, up here with the angels.

Maybe that last gulp from the coffee thermos is the reason for this euphoria. I catch a glimpse of myself in the mirror, but I can't see it. When I raise my goggles I find only the drawn face and staring eyes of a stranger. And then another wave of nausea, which I've been getting in the early mornings. I'm swigging from the little bottle of gastric medicine, but it doesn't seem to do much good.

At first I thought it was the petrol fumes. But maybe it's just that I'm not as tough as I used to be. Thirty-nine going on forty isn't young any longer, especially for a woman flier.

The sound of the engines has a syncopated downbeat about it when you're tired. That new jazz song of Bunny Berrigan's keeps floating through my mind in time to it:

'I've flown around the world in a plane . . .'

Around the world. It sounds so simple. Turn back the reel of film in my head and what do I get? A blurred succession of takeoffs and landings, jungle clearings, dusty desert strips, concrete runways gleaming in the rain. All those different signboards – Natal, Dakar, Khartoum, Karachi, Rangoon, Singapore, Port Darwin, Lae, New Guinea. And each time the press of the crowd to try to touch me, the flash of cameras, the reporters' questions fired so fast there's hardly time to answer. 'Miss Earhart! what's it like up there?' 'How do you keep awake?' 'Are you gonna make it, Amelia?' Then there are the speeches to go through at the receptions afterwards, before falling half-dead into strange beds, to be off again at first light to check on the plane with Fred and the mechanics.

'Working like a grease-monkey,' they always tease me. But for me it's the heart of the adventure clambering around the great silver bird, feeling the powerful frame smooth under my hands, ready to explode into life at the turn of a switch.

At Lae Fred and I spent hours packing and repacking equipment, belongings, clothes, to take up the smallest space possible. In the end we jettisoned the tiniest non-essential items to allow for the maximum weight of fuel. Even my good-luck ivory bracelet went. I feel strangely uneasy without it. At least I've kept the lei of paper orchids they slipped around my neck at Luke Field. It's hanging right here beside me, slightly tattered, just to remind me that if I could get over that disastrous takeoff, I can get over most things.

A tap on the shoulder brings me back to the present. Fred is leaning across the fuel tanks, trying to make himself heard above the engines. Usually he passes a message on what we call our bush telegraph – a bamboo pole with a cleft top that was Fred's idea.

'Try the goddamn radio again.' His voice cuts harshly through the vibrations. 'We've got to get through this time.'

Immediately fear digs its claws into me again. The silence from the speaker has been a nagging anxiety ever since the early hours. *Itasca*, the coastguard cutter anchored off Howland, should now be making regular contact with us to guide us on course. Is it because our own calls haven't got through to them yet? Or worse, they're responding to us but so far we've not been able to pick up their signal – and, of course, they wouldn't know.

It's coming up to 7.40, nearly an hour since I last tried to raise them. I suppose I kept thinking the longer I left it, the more likely I might be to get an answer the next time round. But we can't wait any longer. I switch on to autopilot and pull my log book open at the last scrawled page.

> '2.45 am. Cloudy and overcast. Try first call to *Itasca* but maybe there's too much static to get through.
>
> 3.45 am. Listening out every hour and ½ hour on 3,105 kcs.
>
> 4.54 am. Weather partly cloudy. Still do not get anything back.
>
> 6.15 am. About 200 miles out. Bearing needed urgently on the hour. Try whistle into mic. after message.
>
> 6.45 am. Asking again for bearing. About 100 miles out.'

Fred is behind me again. 'By my calculations we've got to be nearly on Howland. But there's no sign of it, or the ship. Tell them our last tank won't hold out much longer.'

Obediently I press down the key and speak into the microphone, trying to sound calm.

'KHAQQ calling *Itasca*. We must be on you but cannot see you. Gas is running low. Been unable to reach you by radio. We are flying at altitude one thousand feet.'

I hold my breath and wait. But no voice breaks through, not even the faintest tap of a Morse Code signal. I turn and shake my head at Fred but he is back at the side lookout, crouched over his charts. This may be all we have now. The radio system has failed us and it is partly my fault. It was my idea to leave the drift antenna behind. The fixed loop system was so much more convenient and every bit as efficient, they told me. The truth is I never took too much trouble getting into all the technical detail of transmitter frequencies and so on. Even my Morse is limited, Fred's too. That was for the sound people to worry about, along with the weather forecasts. It seemed to me that flying was all that mattered. Maybe it still is.

I'm sweating inside my leather jacket. For a moment my vision seems to swim as my eyes rake endlessly over the controls, the sea below, and back to the crumpled map beside me. Somewhere down there is Howland, a scrap of land less than a mile in length, a needle in a haystack. The navigational charts of this area are notoriously unreliable. A hair's breadth out of line could mean a miss by ten or twenty miles, and all Fred's star tracks and sun shots would be in vain. I want to climb higher to get a wider range but can't because of a cloud bank just ahead.

A scrap of paper comes over my shoulder, dashed across with Fred's scribble. 'Try circling. Call again.'

I watch my hands make the appropriate movements as I turn the plane. This time I say a silent prayer as I open the microphone. '7.58 am. We are circling but cannot hear you.'

Miraculously, out of the static, a faint signal clatters through – the letter A repeated. Then there's the blessed sound of a human voice. 'Go ahead on 3105,' it says.

For a second I have a clear picture of the young operator crouched over his transmitter in a crowded radio room. Fred has scrambled into the seat next to me. His hand is tight on my arm, which is shaking. I catch the sour whiff of whisky on his breath.

'Tell them we need more to get them on the direction finder.'

I take a deep breath. 'KHAQQ calling *Itasca*. We received your signals but unable to get a minimum. Please take bearing and answer 3105 with voice.'

We wait. My heartbeats only intensify the silence. A minute goes by, then another. Time is running out. But there is nothing more. Both of us know we are on our own again. Fred's eyes meet mine, bright blue slits of exhaustion. We have to try something different.

'Fly north,' is all he says as he climbs past me.

For some reason my own instinct refuses this. In a moment of panic and revolt, I turn south. Now I am hunting for Howland along a right angle, crossing the equator instead of running parallel. Somehow it feels like falling off a tightrope, now we have lost that invisible line of contact between Lae and Howland. But surely there must be a safety net. Surely they'll be waiting for us, watching for us, ready to pick us up as soon as we come down. For come down we must, either here and now when we may be closest, or using our last drop of fuel to make for some other landfall.

It's a quarter to nine. Time for another go on the radio. Now my voice sounds frantic, almost out of control, however hard I try to slow down.

'We are on the line of position 157–337. Will repeat this message on 6210 kilocycles. Wait, listening on 6210. We are running north and south.'

Only static fills the cabin. Now there is a new enemy, the sun itself. The angle of its rise throws a dazzle across the water that blinds me. All

I can do is keep going. I always said I would turn back to the Gilberts if there was trouble, but now they're too far behind us. I reach for the map but Fred's reading my thoughts, right there behind me.

'We'll try for one of the Phoenix Islands. And this time do as I say, for Christ's sake.'

Once again I watch my hands. They seem to belong to someone else, efficiently doing the things they've learned to do to prepare for an emergency landing, while my mind races. The wheels must come up to give us a better chance of floating, the undercarriage retracted to protect the plane if it's on the jagged coral or a reef. Please God, I hear myself say. There must be an island somewhere out there, one of those storybook desert islands with palm trees where the castaway is washed ashore and survives on coconuts until the rescue ship arrives?

It seems unbelievable, but right on cue I catch sight of a smudge on the furthest horizon, a low greenish blur that doesn't seem to be moving. It's exactly 10.30 and I grab the radio key.

'Land in sight ahead,' I tell whoever's out there.

I feel the power fade, just as the image fades. I have seen a mirage at sea before in this kind of weather, but to see one now is the cruellest twist of fate. Almost at the same moment, the roar of the engines drains away. There is a spluttering, then silence, with only the whine of the wind rushing past, the worst sound of all. The last tank is empty, I tell myself. Or could it be an airlock, even now? My fingers are trying to turn the sharp handles of the petcocks. They must be bleeding. Drops of crimson are falling onto my trousers. Mesmerized, I watch the altimeter needle whirling as we lose height. Everything else seems to be happening in slow motion.

The engine coughs into life again – a dying cough, but it means a vital few minutes more in the air. Now I can ease the stick back again, dare to take another look outside. The sky has darkened to violet. There's the shudder of an electric storm out there, the sea roughening. How high do these waves reach, I wonder. Five feet? Ten feet? And is it true that the British refuse to set up a commercial airline over this part of the Pacific because it's so infested with sharks?

Fred is in the tail of the plane, struggling to get at the life raft. I try to imagine us launching it from a sinking plane, the door held fast by the force of the water, wrestling to inflate it with these CO canisters that never seem to work even on dry land.

Now he's coming forward again, trying to yell something to me. 'Crosswinds!'

Even as I catch the word, the whole plane lurches violently to one side. The thousand gallons of gasoline that weighed us down all around is virtually gone. The turbulence catches us up like a leaf, throws us down again. From behind there is the crash of glass, the sound of someone screaming, just once. I won't believe that it's Fred.

Then I'm going forward like a stone, my head flung against the panel. The violence of the impact dazzles, then there is darkness. But only for a few seconds, not long enough . . .

My leather helmet must have been some kind of protection. Incredibly, the plane is still in the air, but only just, dipping seawards now like a gull, all power gone. Pulling myself up in my seat, I turn to look for Fred. Through the gap in the tanks a terrible picture prints itself on my brain. The steel case of his equipment has fallen from its shelf, and shattered the glass top of the navigation table. Fred is lying face downwards among the pieces, one long jagged splinter against his throat. Blood lies in a pool around his head, running over the top of the table on to the floor. There is no way he can be alive.

The pain of realizing this meets the pain inside my head, and suddenly everything fuses. I sit quite still waiting for my own end, unable to move. The plane lurches downwards like a broken lift.

Strangely, there's no sense of my whole past flashing across my consciousness. Only a split-second picture of George with that good-luck grin on his face as he waves goodbye. Please don't blame yourself, George. I told you, didn't I, that this was my decision and mine alone, my one last adventure. I only wish you knew how much I loved you. There never seemed to be time to say it properly.

A terrible sadness sweeps over me, blotting out the terror. Then the sea comes up to meet me, smashing into the belly of the plane. The world fragments into blankness. My brain sends one last message to itself.

'Thank God I won't die burning . . .'

CHAPTER TWO

November 1969

Laura had always thought of herself as a good air traveller. She had been on long plane journeys half a dozen times over the last five years – to Africa, India, Hong Kong – ever since she began working for the BBC. Now here she was, jerking awake in her comfortable first-class seat in a positive sweat of terror.

She must have made some kind of exclamation. The man sitting next to her looked up from the papers he was studying.

'Are you all right?' His expression was solicitous in the dim overhead light.

'It's nothing,' she said, the words catching in her dry mouth. She wondered if he could hear the galloping of her heart. 'Just a dream. Actually, more of a nightmare.'

'There was a spot of turbulence just a while ago. Maybe it disturbed you. It usually happens over that part of the Pacific. It'll be calm now all the way to Fiji, you'll see.'

He smiled reassuringly, a very white smile in the smooth brown of his face, and went back to his papers. A charming man, she thought, some kind of diplomat perhaps, in his early fifties. He had boarded the plane at Honolulu, and looked more Polynesian than Fijian.

It seemed important to Laura to remember her dream. Yet it had been so brief – little more than a single image flashed onto the blank screen of her mind between sleeping and waking.

It was a picture seen from the air, a bird's-eye view of a tropical island ringed by a coral reef. In the middle of an empty beach stood a man motionless and alone, a European. Instinctively she knew it was her father. Her childish image of him, a tall thin figure in a khaki sun-helmet, was unmistakable. So was the sense of apprehension she had always felt just at the sight of him.

Everything about the scene seemed untroubled. That was what was so strange. The sun shone clear and hot in a sky of enamelled blue. In the distance were the thatched roofs of a village and under the palm trees lay two or three upturned canoes. Yet somehow the air was full of menace. It came from the fishing net her father was carrying over his shoulder. She could see that inside it was not a fish but a bird, a white bird flapping its wings in a desperate attempt to free itself.

In her dream, Laura was only a powerless onlooker. But she felt the creature's panic as the strong threads of the net snarled its feathers. It was this horror of being trapped without reason, and without escape, that had forced her awake in her seat. Even now, just letting the dream run through her mind, the sense of claustrophobia was impossible to shake off.

She shivered. How could one feel claustrophobic surrounded by nothing but sea and sky?

'You are cold?'

Before she could protest, her companion was passing her a blanket from the rack above.

'The temperature drops at night, even inside a plane.'

Laura felt embarrassed, not liking to be thought of as the sort of female who constantly demands attention. She straightened her shoulders.

'That's very kind of you.'

'I'm Edwin Vunilau, by the way.'

She recognized the name at once. For the past few weeks she had been holed up in the cuttings library at Broadcasting House. Vunilau was a key figure in Fiji's independence preparations, one of the hereditary nobles with the title of Ratu and a highly respected government minister.

'Fijian by birth, Tongan by ancestry,' he went on. 'And Scottish by absorption.' He was grinning slyly, waiting for the reaction.

'Scottish?'

'I'm afraid one of my ancestors developed a taste for Presbyterian missionaries.' The line, delivered with Noël Coward finesse, was obviously part of a polished social repertoire. Laura was intrigued as well as amused.

'And you?' he asked in the same soft undertone. 'You're flying on to Australia? Or taking a holiday in Fiji in search of all these paradise beaches?' He chuckled. 'The romance of the South Seas, Tennyson's lotus-eaters, and all that.'

'I was born in the South Seas,' Laura replied, a little stung at being treated like a tourist.

'Is that so?' He clicked his tongue in delighted disbelief. 'Not Fiji?'

She shook her head and smiled back at him, feeling he was no longer a stranger.

'Not quite. A tiny atoll called Taparoa. One of the Gilbert and Ellice group.'

'I know it, of course. I go on tour there sometimes.' He was looking at her hard now. 'But what were you doing in the Gilberts?'

'I'm sorry, I should have introduced myself. I'm Laura Harrington. My father was a district officer out there.'

They were still talking in hushed voices. The fact that everyone around them seemed to be asleep gave their exchanges a curious intimacy. Now, with sudden formality, Ratu Edwin held out his hand – an extremely elegant hand, Laura noticed, long and slender with a blue signet ring on the little finger.

'How do you do, Miss Harrington.' He hesitated. 'You are the daughter of the famous doctor, then? I didn't know he had one.'

Laura caught the new note of reserve in his voice. 'I'm not surprised,' she said quickly. 'There's been no contact between us since I was a small child. When the war came I was sent home to England and brought up by his sister. There'd been a rift between them for years and my father seemed to want to keep it that way. He's never been back to England, never even wrote to us. As you know, he's made his life in Fiji.'

'And your mother?'

'She died before the Japanese came. So I barely remember either of them.'

'You'll be seeing your father, though, even after all these years?'

Laura felt that old twinge of trepidation. 'I can hardly avoid it. Anyway, I shall need to talk to him about his books. He's the leading authority on Pacific history, isn't he?'

Ratu Edwin raised an eyebrow. 'So he would have us believe.'

'I'm making some programmes for BBC Radio,' Laura explained. 'About changing times in the South Seas, with Fiji's independence coming next year.'

The Australian businessman in the next seat stirred uneasily. 'We're keeping people awake,' she whispered. 'I think I'll try to sleep myself. We'll be landing in a couple of hours, isn't that right?'

'Maybe less.' He nodded towards the tiny window and the handful of stars beyond, so close and brilliant in the darkness they seemed to be clustered along the tip of the wing. 'That's the Southern Cross. Your Taparoa is somewhere down there, right below us. Just think of that.'

But Laura was no longer thinking of islands. Thankfully, the dream too had faded. Closing her eyes, she summoned up a picture of Jack. She tried to imagine meeting him again in maybe just a day or two. But it was always the moment of first seeing him that sprang into her mind, even though it was almost a year ago. There he was, standing in the foyer of Broadcasting House, a clear-cut figure in his black pinstripes among the casually-dressed lunchtime throng. As she came out of the lift towards him, he seemed to be studying something overhead.

'Mr Renfrey?' She was holding her absurd clipboard clasped in front of her. A symbol of authority, or some kind of shield against the curious shock of that confrontation? His face was like an actor's, open and mobile, with broad cheekbones, the hair longish and tawny gold, the eyes dark. But it was something else, the way those eyes had fixed on hers, summoning her out of the crowd. It was as if each had instantly said to the other, 'I know you.'

In fact what he said was, 'Hello. I was trying to translate the famous legend.' He pointed up to the gold lettering in Latin above the marble archway. 'I only got as far as "This temple of the arts and muses is dedicated to Almighty God . . ." '

She laughed. 'I've never even got as far as that, apart from the Anno Domini 1931 bit.'

And so the mundane took over. Sitting on opposite sides of a microphone in one of the small self-operating studios, she asked him the usual questions. She was recording a series of interviews with people who had come from distant corners of the world to live in England. The programmes would be called 'A Long Way From Home', and Jack Renfrey talked about his upbringing in the South Pacific, where his family owned a large copra plantation. He had come to London five years before to study law. Now he was a qualified barrister, with a lowly place in the chambers of an eminent QC in the Middle Temple. But he hoped to be going back to Fiji to get some experience of government work as a Crown Counsel.

His face softened as he told her this. 'There's no place like home. London can be a lonely place, even in the swinging sixties.'

Laura nodded. 'I can imagine.'

With one part of her mind, she was evaluating the material she was recording. Of course she'd mentioned her own childhood in the islands to him, something that made her feel especially involved in this particular interview. But once again, it was that other link between them that was pulling her in. All the time she was aware of the teasing, unspoken messages running between them.

'You've never been back to the Pacific?' he asked her afterwards, outside the studio door.

'Sadly not. There just doesn't seem to have been the chance. And it's pretty expensive to get out there.'

'But your father's still there, of course. You don't visit . . .' He stopped. Thinking that he must have noticed something about her expression, Laura was grateful for his sensitivity.

'It's a pity I have to be back in court. I'd love to have had more of a yarn together. Perhaps we can meet up before I'm off again?'

'Yes, let's.' She warmed to that word, 'yarn'. It was a real South Seas expression. But 'off again' was also registering. He wouldn't be here for much longer.

'I don't have your home number, do I?' he went on.

Out of the corner of her eye, Laura saw Martin emerge from a nearby control room to join them, a stack of tapes under his arm. 'You can always get me here,' she said in an offhand way. She felt Martin's hand on her shoulder.

'This is Martin Collins, senior producer, Features.'

'Sorry I wasn't able to be in studio with you,' Martin told him. 'Something came up. But I'm sure it'll be great. Laura's an old hand.'

She felt her shoulder squeezed. It was not a phrase that endeared itself to her, having just turned the corner into her thirties. She knew the tone of bantering charm was purely for the benefit of the outsider.

'Any good?' he'd ask her languidly, once the victim had left. 'Have to come down by at least half. There's far too much on tape already.'

At this particular moment, though, Martin was still the gracious host, radiating enthusiasm and authority in equal measure. The hand was removed from her shoulder and was now pushing back his glasses, then smoothing over the bald patch behind the famous black curls, two habits that had particularly begun to irritate her.

But Jack Renfrey was looking at her, smiling. 'She's the perfect interviewer. Makes it all so easy.'

'Good, good.' Laura's ear caught that fractional diminishing of warmth which meant signing-off time. Now I have to get back to more important things, Martin was saying. 'If there are any problems,' he went on, 'I'll be making contact with you myself. You'll be getting the usual fee, of course. Not exactly lavish, but radio's the poor relation, I'm afraid. And many thanks for sparing the time.'

'Thank you for having me.' A hint of cheekiness peeped out from beneath the schoolboy good manners.

Once again, unnecessarily perhaps, Jack shook her hand. Again she felt that secret current between them, like electricity. Inwardly she laughed at herself. Maybe she had been reading too many scripts for *Woman's Hour*, something she still did from time to time, even though she was now working mainly as a presenter of feature programmes, Martin's little kingdom. In any case, she was not really free to indulge herself in flights of romantic fancy. Martin's displays of jealousy could make life difficult if he even suspected her of a new liaison.

'Why am I not allowed to be jealous of Susan?' she had asked him only a few weeks ago, when they were in bed together.

'That's different. You know we agreed right at the start to keep this relationship of ours absolutely separate from my marriage.' He kissed her shoulder. 'And besides, it's so precious, isn't it? Let's not spoil it.'

It had been precious, especially three years ago when they had first become lovers. Martin had simply taken her over, made her feel that the creative side of his life revolved around her alone. As for her, still very much the provincial newcomer, she had fallen in love not just with Martin but with the whole romantic role of secret mistress. The little flat he'd found for her in Wigmore Street was perfect, so close to Broadcasting House that work and pleasure dovetailed as neatly as an edited tape. Quite often they had three or four hours together before it was time for him to drive home, far too fast, for a late dinner in Richmond. The unsuspecting Susan, it seemed, was busy with entanglements of her own at the Conservative Party office where she worked. Sometimes, too, there were weekend visits when last-minute work cropped up.

People at the BBC guessed at the relationship, one or two anyway. But there was little danger of dénouement. The boundaries between home and work were well respected and such internal affairs, as they were dubbed, were not exactly unheard of. So the rules of the game were observed, and everyone said Laura deserved her success as a broadcaster because she was so good.

So why had she risked all that to see Jack again? Perhaps the risk itself was something of an attraction, like the kick of adrenalin flowing when you suddenly had to improvise on air. It was certainly asking for trouble, that first time, to have dinner with him at the Veneto, the little restaurant in a side street near Portland Place where so many BBC people went. But then she was a free woman, wasn't she, as far as the rest of the world was concerned? And it ought to be harmless, meeting up again with someone who was a contributor to her current series.

In fact, it was far from harmless, as both of them knew. Nothing serious was established between them on that evening – nor could it have been. She had made her involvement with Martin Collins quite clear. But the potential for damage was undeniable. It was there not just in the physical pull between them, but in the strange sense of affinity that lay beneath the surface, a whole range of sympathies that would take time to explore and establish. And time, perhaps fortunately, was in short supply.

'You're not inviting me in, then?' he asked as the taxi drew up outside her flat.

'You know I can't.'

'Surely you must have other people coming to visit you?'

'You're not other people,' she said, half to herself. She had a sudden picture of Jack in the sitting room Martin had papered with a William Morris pattern last Easter, his pictures and books side by side with her own, the red velvet chaise longue she had hankered for drawn up to the fire. In that moment she recognized the strength of her tie with Martin. These might be the freedom-loving sixties, but nothing could change the loyalty that was part of her nature.

Jack's response was somehow typical. He simply leaned forward and passed the driver a five-pound note. 'Anywhere,' was all he said.

He closed the glass panel. The cab moved off again. Then, pulling her to him, he turned her face to his and kissed her. It was a long and private kiss that totally ignored the life going on around them, the traffic surging past, the people on the pavements. She was wearing a fur-lined Afghan coat against the winter cold, and he drew this round them, slipping his arms beneath to encircle her more closely. The whole moment was wrapped up in the mingled scents of leather upholstery, the musky black lamb and his cologne that had an edge of something exotic. Sandalwood? Coconut oil?

The taxi stopped at a traffic light. Drawing away, Laura saw Jack's face caught in the light, staring at her. The rapt expression she saw there, the look of disbelieving joy, was reflected, she knew, in her own face.

The lights changed. The world had changed. The taxi lurched on, the driver's back solid and unmoved in front of them. Jack leaned forward to tap on the glass. Through the partition, he said something Laura didn't catch.

'Where are we going?' she asked him.

'You'll see. It's quite close.'

He didn't kiss her again but sat leaning forward, looking out. His hand was so tight around hers that it hurt, as her fingers pressed against the jade and silver ring Martin had bought her in Hong Kong.

'It's no good,' she heard herself say. 'You've got to see that.'

He did not reply. She retrieved her bag from the corner of the seat, trying to restore her emotions to some kind of order. One of her gloves had fallen to the floor. She picked it up, then glanced out of the window and recognized the narrow entrance to the Middle Temple.

Jack was out before her, still holding her hand, and pulling her out on to the pavement.

'No need for any more, guv,' she heard the driver call out. Before she realized it, the taxi was gone.

They were outside one of the tall Georgian houses that lined the courtyard. No one else seemed to be about. He drew her into the doorway with its overhanging lamp, a list of barristers' names in old-fashioned black script on the wall.

'These are my chambers.' He brought out a keyring. 'Old Timpson-Smith has a flat on the third floor and he let me have a couple of rooms that were empty, right at the top.'

'I'm sorry, Jack,' she began.

'Coffee will be served in the penthouse suite, ma'am.' He gave a jaunty bow, but Laura felt him trembling as he took her arm.

'I'm sorry, but I thought you understood. I thought you'd be dropping me off home again, after . . .'

'After our nice little goodnight kiss.' He said it teasingly, but his face was tense.

'After I'd been hijacked without warning.' She tried to be teasing in return. It was a mistake.

'Hijackers make demands.' There was anger in his face now. 'I'm sorry to disappoint you.' He stepped away from her and put his key in the lock. 'Freedom is all yours, Miss Harrington.'

'So you're not even going to see me home?'

'See me home,' he mocked, over his shoulder. 'What a typically well-brought-up English expression! And I thought you were women's lib personified, a genuine independent woman of the world.'

She turned away. Now she was trembling, partly from the cold, but also with an illogical sense of affront. She tried to trace in her mind the quick flare of his temper.

Halfway up Regent Street she was telling herself it was all her own fault. How could you expect some bush lawyer from the wilds of Fiji to know how to behave, let alone stick to the code of ordinary good manners? Back at Wigmore Street, as she let herself into her flat, she had resolved she would certainly not be seeing Jack Renfrey again. Put it down to experience, she told herself, the kind of cliché that had been pressed into service more than once before. She remembered with amusement her broken engagement at the age of twenty-one.

The next day a huge bouquet of tropical orchids and gardenias arrived in her office. 'Forgiveness please!' read the note. 'The hijacker repents.'

She had torn it up by the time Martin walked in. The flowers were sitting in two water jugs, being arranged with much admiration by one of the secretaries.

'Your South Sea admirer?' he said, wrinkling his nose at the overpowering scent.

'I'm afraid so,' she laughed. 'Not many people say thank you for an interview so expensively, do they?'

She caught him looking at her quickly. 'I gather he's off back to the islands this week,' she went on. 'So I hope the tape's okay. Did you have a chance to listen?'

'It's all right. A bit long-winded. It'll fit in quite nicely next to the nurse from Borneo.' He yawned. He'd lost interest, switching on the playback machine to do some editing, after carefully hanging his new black suede jacket on the back of the chair.

In fact, it was three weeks before Jack Renfrey was due to fly back to Fiji. He told her so next day on the phone before she replaced the receiver, and the next evening when he tried again. 'This is silly,' he said the third time, a rainy Sunday when she was at home writing a script. 'Let's just meet for a quick lunch tomorrow. I can hardly misbehave between cases. And there's a good pub just opposite in the Strand.'

That was her next picture of Jack, a tall figure in a billowing black gown as he hurried towards her across the marble concourse of the Royal Courts of Justice. His wig, tilted forward over his eyebrows, made him look like some dashing eighteenth-century rake. He pulled it off and stuffed it with his gown into the barrister's blue duffel bag he carried slung over one shoulder.

'I'm sorry I didn't make it in time to hear the case,' Laura said, hurrying to keep up with his long strides down the steps outside.

'Oh, you didn't miss much. All I had to do was keep a note for my honoured master, make sure his briefs were nicely tied up with that pretty pink tape. If you see what I mean.' He was grinning at her and seemed to have cast aside the intensity of their last encounter. 'It was only a running-down, anyway.'

'What's a running-down?'

'It's what's going to happen to us if you don't keep up with me in all this traffic.'

They dodged between the cars, making for the ancient pub on the other side of the street. Inside, it was full of smoke and noise and the smell of wine, a kind of courtroom in recess, every corner packed with legal flotsam and jetsam, counsel and clerks, clients and reporters, and eager hangers-on from the public galleries. Some of the barristers still wore their court bands under their collars, tucking into their sausage and mash like babies in bibs. On Jack, the starched white against the black of his jacket only set off his golden good looks. There was a note of incongruity too. Robert Redford as a Victorian parson, she decided, settling herself on a stool at the far end of the bar.

But Jack seemed to be looking at someone else as he sat down beside her. Suddenly she caught his eyes in the gilt-framed mirror behind the bottles. 'Guilty,' he said, turning to hand her a glass of Bordeaux. 'It was a good way of staring at you from another angle. The trouble is I want to stare at you all the time.' He took a large gulp from his own glass. 'You're not really beautiful. You're not strictly pretty. But you've got a face that stands out in a crowd because it's so alive, and yet so still. Watchful too. A cat's face. But you must never wear a hat.'

He leaned forward and removed the upturned Breton hat she loved, so exactly right with her button-up jacket. 'That hair must be seen.' He ruffled her fringe. 'The dark brown is absolutely vital for everything else, don't you see? The pale skin, those very blue eyes.' He studied her severely. 'So just remember.'

It was the only time he touched her that day, except for the moment when they said goodbye.

'Hopeless, isn't it?' he murmured with mock passion, brushing her cheek with a kiss. 'Just ships that pass in the night. That's all we are, dear Laura. Ships that pass in the night.'

After that it was a line they used each time they met, a coded message that said everything but promised nothing. The B-movie drama of it made them laugh and they laughed together a great deal. That was something that made their meetings possible. And it seemed impossible that they should not meet while they could. Now the situation was clear, they could relax together – on the surface, at least. Laura's determination to resist the powerful undercurrents between them set up an inner tension that only heightened her pleasure.

Each encounter remained stamped on her mind, vivid and separate as icons. They were leaning against a shopfront in Carnaby Street, pressed by the crowds of sightseers and would-be hippies while Jack tried on a Beatles cap he had bought her. They were in a record shop buying the Bruch Violin Concerto for Jack to take back with him while, idiotically, the music being played was from *South Pacific*.

> 'You've got to have a dream,
> If you don't have a dream,
> How're you gonna have a dream come true . . .'

And then they were standing in front of the Gauguins at the National

Gallery, drawn deep into the real Polynesia, the brilliant colours of decay, the heaviness of the air, the languid resignation of paradise lost.

'It's true,' Jack said. 'There is that other side to the islands. Sad and sinister places sometimes, as well as unbelievably beautiful. But you'll see for yourself.' His eyes held hers. 'You'll be coming back for a visit before very long, isn't that so?'

Laura shook her head, smiling. 'It doesn't seem likely.'

The evening before he was to fly to Fiji, she knew she should tell him about Martin's decision. But somehow she couldn't bring herself to do it. What was the point? It would only distort the balance, spoil what should be an easygoing farewell drink.

They met in the same bar in the Strand. Jack talked about his family's plans for the plantation, with British rule in the Pacific coming to an end in a year or so. She talked about the series she was about to begin on the National Trust. There wasn't much time. Martin was expecting her at the flat at seven.

'Let's walk a little way,' Jack said as they came out. There was a tube station quite close. As they came towards it he stopped and faced her. He had only to touch her shoulder for Laura to feel herself weaken with longing. It was a containable longing, simply the overpowering need to be held close to him as she had been that night in the taxi.

She sighed as Jack's arms came round her. This is ridiculous, she told herself, to be clinging together like teenagers in the middle of a crowded pavement.

'For God's sake, Laura,' he whispered. 'Can't you see I'm in love with you?'

He turned up her face and kissed her hard on the mouth, blotting out words, blotting out thought. At the same moment, common sense flooded into her mind. This is all wrong, a voice said inside her head. I must be mad. Swiftly she pulled away, feeling like a rumpled schoolgirl as Jack caught up with her.

'It's true, isn't it?' He was holding the silk paisley scarf that had slipped from her shoulders as they kissed. 'And you're in love with me.'

'I have to go. Martin's waiting for me.' Laura made a huge effort to retrieve what little dignity was left to her, but the catch in her voice was harder to control. 'I should have told you before. He's asking his wife for a divorce. We're going to be married.'

The change in Jack's face went through her like a physical pang. I feel guilt, she told herself. It should never have come to this. It's all my fault. 'I'm sorry,' she said. 'Really sorry.'

Jack looked at her still, but his eyes were blank. A muscle tightened along his cheek. It was hard to imagine his smile. Silently he held out the scarf. In one quick movement she took it from him, then reached up to loop it round his neck.

'A keepsake.'

'You'll need a taxi,' he said. 'It's starting to rain.'

At the same minute one came along. He opened the door for her and she got in.

'Take care then.'

'And you, Jack.'

What else was there to say?

The door banged behind her. Raindrops lingered on the window glass.

'Where to?' asked the driver.

She leaned forward to give the address. When she turned back to the window, Jack had disappeared.

As the cab moved on, she suddenly caught sight of him striding fast through the crowd. That was her last picture of Jack, a blurry snapshot of a fair-haired man in a raincoat, shoulders hunched, hands in pockets, a bright yellow scarf blowing out behind him. He did not turn to look for her. Then he was gone.

CHAPTER THREE

'Is there anyone meeting you?' Ratu Edwin asked.

A pale dawn light was filtering in through the cabin windows. The ever-cheerful Qantas steward had cleared away the coffee cups and at any moment the plane would be starting its slow descent through the clouds.

'I shouldn't think so,' Laura replied. The same question had been running through her mind for the last half hour. 'It's a bit early, isn't it?'

'Not as far as my people are concerned.' He shook his head indulgently. 'Fijians love any excuse for a party. I expect it's been going on for most of the night.'

Ahead of them the 'fasten seat belts' sign flashed on. You could feel the rise in adrenalin as everyone fumbled to comply. The engines had changed to a different note, which was joined by the crackly surge of a Mantovani waltz, the kind of background music selected by airlines everywhere to steady the nerves of their passengers for the impact of landing. Laura always found it queasy-making rather than soothing. It went with the sickly taste of the barley sugar that never did stop the painful popping of her ears, or the lurch of her stomach as the plane lost altitude.

This time she was aware of a different kind of tension. Why had she heard nothing from Jack? She had written to tell him she was coming as soon as her itinerary was confirmed. That had been four weeks ago, plenty of time for an exchange of letters by airmail. She had also told him, very briefly, of her break-up with Martin. But then, she reminded herself, it was almost a year since they had said goodbye in London, almost a year without contact of any kind. He might well have changed the post-office box number he had given her as his address when they had first met. He could even have moved away from Fiji. Still, that seemed unlikely. Only recently she had come across his name in a copy of the *Pacific Islands Monthly*, one of the magazines the BBC information library had sent her. Jack Renfrey was now prominently involved in drafting the legislative changes for Fiji's new constitution, and that was hardly something he could drop at a moment's notice to take off for New Zealand or Australia.

On an impulse she turned to Ratu Edwin. 'Do you know someone in Fiji called Renfrey?'

'Of course. One of our oldest white settler families.' He smiled to himself. 'Or almost white, I should say. We're all a bit tangled up in the islands, as you'll discover.'

'It's Jack Renfrey I knew. I met him in London last year.' She made her voice as casual as possible.

'Ah, yes. Young Jack. One of the colony's legal lights. Drinks and plays a bit too hard. If he'd only settle down he could have quite a future in the new government.'

Ratu Edwin was still smiling, looking at her sideways. 'The trouble is,' he went on in his slow, velvety voice, 'he has to choose between politics and taking on the family estate. Did he talk to you about that?'

'A bit.'

'And then again, there's Australia.'

'Australia?'

'I believe he has various contacts there. Some of them very attractive ones, so I'm told.' He paused discreetly. 'He's rather a restless young man, especially since he came back from England.'

He glanced at her again with that quizzical lift of the eyebrow, but Laura refused to be drawn. She smiled brightly.

'I think we must be nearly there.'

The plane gave a jolt that reminded her of the old lifts at Broadcasting House. For a moment she almost wished herself back there, surrounded by familiar faces and drawn into the buzzing activity of all the other worker bees inside that huge stone hive, ceaselessly manufacturing honeycombs of sound.

The jolt changed to a slow glide downwards. She looked down and forgot her uncertainties. There was always a thrill about the first glimpse of an unknown destination, but Fiji's main island, Viti Levu, was a view to take your breath away. Purple mountain ranges hung with mist stretched into the distance, as unreal as the backdrop in the old film of *Lost Horizon*. Dark green forests rolled down towards the secret arteries of deep-running rivers, then swiftly gave way to the tawny lowlands of the western side, where rain was rare. Thatched Fijian villages melted into the landscape. Here and there the tin rooftops of scattered townships glinted in the sun, following the coastline with its sandy bays and loops of white surf. And then beyond, as far as the eye could reach, there was the sea, more brilliantly blue than one could ever have imagined. They were close to it now, skimming lower all the time, so that the great plane seemed to be racing its own shadow over the surface of the water.

She heard Ratu Edwin's voice in her ear.

'Nandi airport is just coming up. You know that the capital, Suva, is on the other side of the island, three or four hours' drive away?'

She nodded.

'There's a plane connection, but not till this afternoon. I've a car waiting for me, and I'd be only too delighted to give you a lift if you haven't made other arrangements.'

Once again Laura was touched by his thoughtfulness.

'I'd have loved that, Ratu Edwin. But I've booked myself into the airport hotel, to unwind for a bit. Besides, it'll be a chance to have a look round this part of the island before I go on to Suva. But thank you.'

'You'll promise to keep in touch?' He brought out a card from his pocket. 'You can always find me here, either at home or at the office. I'd be happy to be a help in any way.' He laid his hand over hers for a second and looked at her intently. 'Any way at all. Don't forget.'

Was there an undertone in his voice? He seemed about to add something, then stopped and turned his attention to settling the Prince of Wales knot in his regimental tie. Laura leaned back against the jarring impact of the wheels touching down. There was a long screech as the plane braked hard across the concrete runway. It came to a sharp halt and the voice of the stewardess broke through the chatter.

'If you could please remain in your seats, ladies and gentlemen.'

The door at the front was opened and two enormous Fijians in white overalls clambered aboard. For one absurd moment Laura thought they were hijackers. Then she saw that the guns they carried were flit-guns. Honestly, she reminded herself, this is the South Seas, not the Middle East.

'Our Department of Agriculture is very strict in Fiji,' Ratu Edwin murmured from behind a large red silk handkerchief as the cabin was enveloped in a pungent-smelling haze of insecticide. 'Who knows what bugs we may be carrying on us. Better be careful when you go through Customs!'

He giggled like a small boy, wide-mouthed and helpless. The two Fijians were grinning too as they bundled out of the plane. Laughter seemed to come easily in this part of the world, Laura thought as she stood in line inside the modern airport buildings. Even the officials behind the desks were smiling, the bearded Sikh in an orange turban who chalked his scrawl on her luggage, and the balding Melanesian with a missing front tooth who inspected her passport.

'You're a Kai-viti?' he said, twinkling up at her through horn-rimmed glasses. 'Fiji-born?'

'Not quite. But near enough.'

He brought his stamp down with a flourish. The ink in the pad was drying out so he repeated the performance.

'Maybe you'll decide to stay this time.'

Laura laughed. 'If only!'

It was just a passing exchange but it gave her a glow, something to help her confront whatever hazards lay ahead. Taking a deep breath, she pushed her way through the barriers into the crowded reception area. Fiji, it seemed, was already well and truly geared to the tourist industry. A flood of song poured out from the loudspeakers, rich island voices wrapped around the throb of electric guitars. Every wall was plastered with huge enlargements of wish-fulfilment views – golden paradise beaches, coral reefs swarming with exotic fish, desert-island huts under the palm trees, and everywhere the sun-bronzed bodies of carefree visitors, indistinguishable in colour from the happy islanders bearing trays of drinks to tables shaded by blue-striped umbrellas.

Laura turned from these images to the reality around her. Throngs of pink and peeling tourists were pushing forward to make their return journeys to Sydney and New York, weighed down with cameras and baskets of souvenirs. Tempers frayed, children squalled and voices were raised. Someone had mislaid a vital document. Someone else had been given the wrong seat. Beneath all was the lurking anxiety that this might be the flight that did not make it at all. According to the law of averages, surely there had to be one unlucky plane from time to time.

Out of this sea of harassed humanity, a carefree face emerged.

'You need a car, marama?' A fat Fijian taxi driver, a yellow hibiscus tucked behind one ear, a homemade cigarette behind the other, had already taken charge of her suitcases and now stood waiting for instructions.

'I think so. Can you hang on just for a minute?'

She moved away a little and looked around for a familiar face. After thirty-six hours of travelling, she was so keyed up with exhaustion and excitement that it was hard to think clearly. The floor was swaying under her feet the way it always does when one steps off a jet, and her ears were buzzing. She tried to concentrate her mind on an image of Jack, as if that would magically summon him forth from the crowd.

Somehow she had been certain he would be here. But there was no sign of him.

Over in the far corner she caught sight of an extraordinary tableau surrounding the distinctive figure of Ratu Edwin in his cream linen suit, ensconced in an armchair in a kind of VIP enclosure, roped off from the rest of the concourse. Before him were gathered some twenty or thirty Fijians seated cross-legged on mats. The man in front, who wore a garland of leaves over his bare shoulders, was crouching to offer Ratu Edwin what looked like a small wooden bowl. Laura watched him raise it to his lips. There was a ripple of hand-clapping, a low murmured chant from the bowed heads. An aged person with a mop of white hair began what was obviously a speech of welcome. Ratu Edwin turned his head slightly and Laura knew he had seen her. But his grave expression gave no sign of recognition. It was a ceremonial mask of authority that had nothing to do with the Westernized traveller she had come to know on the flight. Suddenly Laura felt as if she and the people around her did not exist, and all the comings and goings of an international airport were totally irrelevant to the real life of Fiji. What chance have I, a passing observer, of penetrating the secret heart of this place, she asked herself?

As she turned away, a wave of loneliness went through her. It was chilling suddenly to find herself in a country where no one knew or cared about her existence, Jack Renfrey least of all.

'You need the car then, marama?' a patient voice reminded her. The driver was still waiting, still smiling.

'Oh, yes. Thank you. I'm going to the airport hotel.'

She slung the tape-recorder more firmly over her shoulder as she followed him across the concourse. The precious machine was a friend, her reason for being here, a faithful companion that would go with her everywhere over the next few weeks. Always, before, Martin had been at her side on these recording trips, organizing, taking charge, cutting through problems. It felt strange to be on her own.

So what? Stop being unsure of yourself, said the other Laura. This was a solo adventure. At last she was free to explore whatever and wherever she liked. Once she had got her bearings and made her contacts, everything would begin to fall into place. Besides, hadn't she planned it this way? The Pacific trip was to be a marker of her new independence, a way of rediscovering her identity now she was free from Martin's shadow. Stop thinking about him, she told herself. Above all, stop thinking about Jack.

She walked through the sliding doors, out of the noise and confusion, the unreal chill of the air-conditioning and the glare of fluorescent lights. It was very quiet outside, the sun only just showing above the trees. With a shock of delight, she felt the first touch of the tropics on her skin. It was like walking into a soft embrace, the air so warm and moist and rich with different scents. There was a sheen on the lush greenery lining the pathway. Crushed scarlet flowers lay underfoot, fallen from the flame trees around the parking area. Inside the car the pungent smell of local tobacco took over as the driver squeezed into the seat in front of her.

'Where's the sea?' she asked him.

He chuckled. 'The sea is everywhere, marama.' He waved his hands towards the horizon.

Now she could see the pearly glimmer of the bay swing through between the silhouetted shapes of the palm trees. She wound down the window and, like a child, sniffed in the salty air that always brought back the charmed excitement of seaside holidays. But this time the smell struck a deeper chord, the faint resonance of a time she had thought she could barely remember. So the past is still there, she thought wonderingly, those faraway first few years of my life. Everything I experience now may help to bring it back. Because the strangest thing of all is the feeling that I am coming home again.

'This all new, marama. Very fine place, yes?'

The driver was pointing to the hotel, a white stucco complex of neo-colonial buildings at the end of a sandy drive. Sprinklers flung water in lazy arcs over the carefully tended lawns. An elderly man in a battered straw hat swept leaves from under the trees with a broom of dried twigs. Laura liked this easy combination of old and new. She liked the huge Fijian drum, carved out of solid wood, that stood in the doorway, and the swathes of black and white checkered barkcloth that lined the walls inside. She even liked the corny message on the porter's T-shirt that read, 'Bula means welcome!'

She paused as she signed in at the desk. The blonde New Zealand receptionist in her crisp white blouse smiled a professionally crisp white smile.

'Any problem?'

'I just wondered if there were any letters waiting for me?'

The girl flicked through the pigeonholes behind her, then turned back with another version of the smile, a slightly sympathetic one this time.

'Fride not. You'd like breakfast sent along?'

'Thank you. Just tea and toast. And some juice.'

It had taken a day and a half to fly half-way around the world, and there had been so many stops and time adjustments that it was impossible to relate to normal schedules. Laura checked her watch with the clock above the desk. Ten minutes past seven. The reception area was busy with early-morning arrivals and departures. At the information bureau, a languorous-looking half-caste beauty in a long pink shift was dispensing flower leis to people as they passed. To some she cooed, 'Have a safe journey,' to others, 'Have a good day.' Slipping the garland over Laura's shoulders, she simply smiled conspiratorially.

'You travellin' alone?'

'That's right.'

'You have good time then.'

'A good sleep is what I need,' Laura told her with a grin.

The Adonis in the T-shirt was striding ahead down the corridor with her luggage. Brown muscled calves gleamed with coconut oil beneath his red cotton kilt, which was riotously patterned with yellow pineapples.

'This your room, marama.'

He opened the door for her with the bunch of keys slung round his waist. At the sight of the cool white bed under its canopy of white netting, she felt instantly weighed down with weariness. Sunlight streaked in through the slatted blinds, glancing off the low glass table with its bowl of fruit, the white cane chairs and terracotta floors. With a sigh, she turned back to the young man, now busy stacking her cases into a neat pyramid next to the dressing table.

'You like, marama?'

'I like, thank you.'

He took the coin with careless elegance, not looking down at it.

'Now you will rest, marama.' Bare feet padded out and the door was closed.

Laura walked across to the window, and saw that each room had its own verandah, neatly framed by a low wall. Beyond it, she caught a glimpse of people in swimsuits lying around a bright turquoise pool. It was almost a pleasure to close up the blinds and blot out the glare, to slip off her shoes and feel the polished tiles underfoot as she went to the bathroom. Jet-lag, she thought, mixing herself an Alka-Seltzer, such a strange-sounding word. And strange was the way you felt, your body clock ticking away backwards, pulling at every fibre of your being so that you ached all over. Laura's mind ached too, longing to switch off after the tensions of so many takeoffs and landings.

On an impulse she swallowed a sleeping pill with the rest of the Alka-Seltzer. The pharmacist had said they were mild, but she hadn't taken one on the journey in case of side-effects. Turning to the bed, she took off all her clothes except for her slip, too tired to wait for breakfast. With a groan of relief she slid between the sheets. In the silence, the air- conditioning stuttered and hummed, hummed and stuttered again. Its rhythm was soothing. Close to her, there was a scent she could not identify. Of course, she had hung the lei on the chair next to the bed. But the scent wasn't frangipani, it was something more subtle. She remembered the fragrant bark shavings strung between the petals. Sandalwood. Jack's cologne. A twinge of regret surfaced for a second. Resolutely she pushed it away and let sleep draw her down into the dark.

It was the sound of drumming that woke her. The natives are restless, said the caption in her head, the kind of knee-jerk joke she associated with Martin. Drowsily she made the connection. The Fijian drum in the entrance hall was also the gong for meals, and guests were being summoned to lunch. She must have slept for a good five hours. Her headache had gone, or nearly, and she was feeling hungry.

Under the shower, she checked off in her mind the various things that had to be done. She had to confirm her flight to Suva tomorrow and her hotel booking there. The BBC had given her the names of various contacts at the Fiji broadcasting station, but she still had to fix times for interviews and recordings. And there was her father.

Again came that warning shadow she had felt on the plane. It was bound to be a difficult encounter, but it had to be done. An interview with him was essential to the series. But first, she must break the news to him that she was here at all. A thirty-one-year-old daughter turning up out of the blue might be not just a problem but a disaster. On the other hand, in his old age he might welcome the chance to renew the relationship after such unhappy beginnings, so long ago. As for herself, she had to admit she was curious as well as apprehensive.

Wrapped in a large black towel, she looked at the phone by the bed and instinctively recoiled from it. She would ring him tomorrow. Today she needed time to adjust. Above the phone was the air-conditioning switch, and she reached to turn it off. It was almost cold in the room now and she was longing for the warmth outside.

She went across to open the blinds, then caught her breath in irritation. Someone was sitting on the verandah wall, a man with a beard, wearing dark glasses and a frayed panama. He was leaning back in profile, his bare legs in khaki shorts comfortably drawn up, a glass in his hand as he surveyed the view of the gardens.

What a nerve, she thought to herself. Typical Australian tourist, no compunction about invading someone else's privacy. Indignantly she pushed open the door.

'Excuse me.'

At the same moment, the man turned towards her.

'Good afternoon, Miss Harrington.' He removed his hat with a flourish but did not get up. Sitting there, he surveyed her with a grin.

'Jack! What on earth?'

Even as she spoke, she still could not believe it was him. She pulled the towel more tightly around her as if that would control the thumping of her heart. She saw the silk scarf knotted around his neck, and in that moment she was back in the cold and wet of London, saying goodbye to him in the Strand as the crowds pushed by. How bright his hair looked here, its coppery glint caught by the sun as it fell forwards over his forehead. The beard was rougher, lighter somehow, as if it belonged to a stranger, and she didn't think she liked it.

'I've been waiting for you to wake up. About time too.'

The intimacy of his voice touched a different nerve, as if this was a conversation carried on from their last meeting. He gestured towards the tray. 'Started on your breakfast.'

'So I see.'

Finally, he came over to her. Standing close, he took off his glasses. Nothing could protect her now from the penetration of those brown, heavy-lidded eyes that seemed to search out her hidden self as if by right.

'Laura.'

Gently he touched her shoulder. She stood quite still, waiting. But he did not reach out to hold her. Instead he put his mouth to hers, a little parted, in a long kiss that was more an exchange of breath than an exploration.

When they drew back they were unable to look away from each other, held in an almost painful intensity. Laura wanted words now, to ease them through to what would happen next.

'I wouldn't have recognized you. It's a completely different Jack Renfrey.'

'Maybe that's no bad thing.'

Instinctively they had moved inside the room. The light outside was too bright, too hot. It belonged to those other people, the ones with walk on parts, moving inconsequentially around the pool and the gardens.

'Have you had lunch, apart from my breakfast?'

'No. But I think we could do with a drink.'

She noticed the faint beginnings of lines, traced white against the tanned skin between his eyebrows and around his mouth, signs of vulnerability that touched her. She saw his crumpled safari jacket had a top button missing.

'Do you like Black Velvet?' he asked her.

'I don't think I've ever tried it.'

'And you're the swinging Londoner,' he teased.

'Anything. I'm so thirsty.'

As he gave the order over the phone, she walked towards the bathroom. 'I'll just put some clothes on.'

'Why?' His voice was low. He pulled out one of the cane chairs for her and sat down in the other. 'You look perfectly respectable – perfectly lovely – in your towel.' He touched her hand, almost shyly.

Silence fell between them. Both were waiting, aware of the imminent arrival of the waiter. They began talking at the same time.

'You got my letter?'

'I'm sorry I didn't write back.'

There was a pause and they laughed.

'I only got it yesterday,' Jack said. 'I've been away.'

'On holiday? Or are you a beachcomber these days?'

'I've been up at the plantation. My father hasn't been well. I had to take over for a bit. And you've come to . . .'

'To make a programme series.'

'Is that all?'

'To see my father, I suppose.' Her lips felt dry. It was growing warmer in the room without the air-conditioning.

'And me?'

He had taken hold of her hand now and was holding it very hard. At the same moment there was a tap on the door. Jack stood up quickly as the waiter came in, and placed the tray on the table between them. Jack brought out his wallet, but the young Indian in the white jacket handed him a slip of paper.

'It will be on your room bill, sir.'

The door closed behind him. Gravely Jack handed Laura a tall glass, gleaming black topped with creamy foam.

'Guinness and champagne. The best way to celebrate.'

He was staring down at her with an expression she recognized at once. It was the same look of tender elation she had seen on his face as they kissed in the taxi that very first time.

'Welcome home, Laura,' he said.

CHAPTER FOUR

The Black Velvet was the mistake, she thought afterwards. On an empty stomach, the delicious potency of it was lethal. The urgent desire to be made love to by Jack had somehow spiralled out of control. It had all been too intense, too frenzied. Gradually, a gentle muzziness had descended, blurring the edges of sensation. Now they lay still, entangled in a kind of dreamy limbo.

'I'm sorry,' Laura said after a while. 'It was my fault.'

'Darling! What are you talking about?' He turned her face to his, among the rumpled pillows.

'It's such an important thing.' Her voice shook. 'It should be . . .' She hesitated, looking for the right words. 'Properly over.'

'Laura! Of course it's important. But you talk as if making love was some kind of obstacle race.' There was a look of concern in his eyes. 'Is that how it was with Martin?'

She was silent, her face buried in his shoulder. With horrible clarity, she thought of her flat, the ticking of the bedside clock, the taste in her mouth of the ritual glass of whisky, the tension at the back of her neck, the whole cut-and-dried pattern of sex with Martin before the hour was up and it was time for him to dress and drive home.

'That man has done you damage,' she heard Jack say, half to himself. He studied her tenderly. 'Do you trust me?'

She nodded, not trusting herself to speak.

'Think of music. Remember the Bruch? Nothing is ever resolved until the final movement. All those pauses, changes of mood – but they're all part of the whole, never to be rushed. Not when it's something so rare as this. Something so precious,' he added. He bent his head, as if suddenly shy of talking, and stroked the inside of her arm with a succession of tiny, gentle movements. Somehow that touched her beyond anything else.

'Besides.' He looked up at her with a teasing smile. 'The

combination of jet-lag and strong drink, not to mention the shock of my sudden appearance – what do you expect?'

She pushed back his hair where it fell forward over his forehead. 'Jack. In London you told me you loved me. And now . . .'

'And you?' he broke in. 'Did you ever tell me?'

'I think I do,' she said slowly. 'But I want to find the right words.'

'These words! They only get in the way!' He threw back the sheet and sat up, away from her, on the edge of the bed. 'Isn't it enough?' He stopped.

'Enough?' She felt cold all of a sudden.

'That you're coming to stay with me.' He pulled her close to him again. 'At Vailima, for as long as you're here. What will it be? One month? Two months? Longer?'

'I've got six weeks.' The fear had gone. But the mention of time drew her up in a different way, somehow dulling the radiance of the here and now. Quickly she banished the thought. 'Where is this Vailima? Is it the plantation?'

'Of course not. A man must have a place of his own.' He kissed her shoulder and got to his feet. 'Now let's get out of this ghastly place.'

'But I've only just arrived!'

'You're not coming with me?'

She jumped out of bed, laughing, and began looking round for her clothes. 'Of course I'm coming.'

'I hope you're not totally cut off from civilization,' she told him. 'I do have work to do, remember. In Suva, for a start.'

They were rattling along the coast road in an ancient Land Rover that Jack said could take them anywhere on the island, through bush and beach and mountain flood, if necessary.

'So do I. But not right away. Not for a few days.' He looked round at her intently and her bones seemed to melt.

'I'm glad.'

It was mid-afternoon and very hot. Jack drove fast with one hand on the wheel, the other arm resting on the open window. Every now and then he tapped his fingers against the roof in time to the tune he was humming. Once or twice he sang the words, Fijian words, in a soft light tenor that was surprisingly sweet.

'It's a song about lovers. I'll play it for you on the flute.'

The fields of rustling green sugar cane had disappeared behind them, along with the tin-roofed settlements of the Indian workers. Now the villages they passed had houses of thatch and bamboo that looked in the distance like haystacks. Pigs and chickens rooted under the shade of breadfruit trees. Children appeared on the roadside with shrill cries of greeting, their pink soles flashing in the dust as they ran on ahead, trying to keep up. Some women, brown and buxom in faded cottons, looked up and waved as they pounded their washing on the rocks of a little stream. Laura wanted to call out to them but she didn't yet know the Fijian greeting. Sometimes the people had produce to sell to the cars passing by.

'Shall we buy some?' Laura asked as two smiling girls held out crabs on strings with fresh leaves knotted between. Next to them stood a small boy, a huge green papaya balanced at shoulder level in the upturned palm of his hand. But Jack had nothing in the Land Rover that would hold the crabs and stop them scuttling about all over the place. As for papayas, he said, they grew wild at Vailima.

Seeing Laura's look of concern, he patted her knee. 'Don't worry. They'll be taking everything to market tomorrow, just down the road. Besides, what we need is something to eat right now. Or perhaps you've forgotten we've had no lunch?'

'I haven't forgotten. And I'm absolutely starving.'

A few miles further on, he pulled up outside a couple of weather-board shacks that looked as if they belonged to a ghost town in an old-fashioned western. One sign said 'Wing Lee Stores'. The other, 'New Empire Caffe'.

'Great place for curry,' Jack said. 'Won't be a minute.' He disappeared inside, leaving Laura to the scrutiny of two tousled youths and a hungry dog. Alongside them a very old transistor radio was playing. After a moment she decided to go in search of Mr Wing Lee and something to drink.

'Bula!' one of the boys called out, leaning against the verandah rails with a broad smile. He stretched out a toe to turn up the volume on the radio.

'Bula,' Laura responded, above the thud and crackle of pop music. Emerging again from Mr Lee's musky emporium with two warm cans of Coca-Cola, she saw that Jack was back in the Land Rover. As she passed the boys, one of them drew two fingers across his throat and called out softly something that sounded like 'Ka-shine'.

'What does that mean?' Laura asked Jack, somewhat alarmed.

He laughed. 'He thinks you're very beautiful. Better even than a shiny new car. It's the latest slang from Suva.'

'And the throat-cutting?'

'He'd be ready to die for you.' He cocked an eyebrow at her, in the way she remembered from London. 'Well, who wouldn't?'

As they drove on again, he took off his panama and dumped it over her eyes. 'You'll need this more than me.'

'Where are we going?'

'Picnic time.' He nodded at the pungent-smelling package on the dashboard.

The inside of the Land Rover was sweltering now, gumming Laura's cotton dress to the back of the seat. She looked out at the dense thickets of mangroves that screened the view ahead. Suddenly they opened up and with a flash of delight she saw the sea again. The open bay stretched ahead with the sweep of an enormous amphitheatre. Creamy breakers curled in over miles of empty beach, the palm trees rising behind in the same curving line as far as the eye could see. They turned down a sandy lane. The only sign of habitation was a large shabby bungalow that seemed to appear out of nowhere.

Jack pulled up and Laura was startled to hear a gruff voice call out from behind a hedge of purple bougainvillea, 'This part of the beach is private, y'know!'

'It's only old Sharkie,' Jack told her. 'Mr Mumby, that is. Once he had a narrow escape from a shark when he was a copra skipper, hence the name. Now he's settled back on his piece of land here. They're an old part-European family, the Mumbys.'

Laura had not heard the expression 'part-European' before. Instinctively she found it patronizing, yet the wrinkled, coffee-coloured person in baggy shorts who appeared at the gate seemed to match up to it accurately enough. The face was as English as the name. But those sharp black eyes could only have belonged to an islander, a Fijian grandmother perhaps from the early days of colonization.

'Oh, it's young Jack!' He stretched out a hand. 'Sorry! But with so many riff-raff tourists around nowadays!' Gold teeth glinted in a whiskery smile. 'No trouble with the village boys. They always keep to the other end.'

'That's all right, Sharkie.' Laura noticed Jack's voice slide companionably into the same seesaw accent. 'We stopped for a picnic. This is Miss Harrington. She's Dr Harrington's daughter, come over from England.'

For a moment the old man's jaw sagged. The cloudy grey eyes studied her with an expression of disbelief.

'Daughter? Didn't think Harrington had family.' Imperceptibly he seemed to withdraw, just the way Ratu Edwin had.

'You know my father?'

There was a pause. Mr Mumby swatted a fly away with his rolled-up copy of the *Pacific Islands Monthly*. 'Know of him, of course.' He seemed unwilling to continue. 'He was doctoring in these parts after the war. We had a housegirl once worked for him.' His voice trailed away. 'Famous now of course, with his books,' he added with an effort at politeness.

Mrs Mumby came bustling down the verandah steps, a welcome interruption. She was carrying a large jam jar.

'Just been making my guava jelly, Jack my boy.' She handed it to him, then stood back smiling at Laura, her freckled arms folded over a flowered smock. 'Jack's Great-Auntie Liza gave my mother the recipe years ago when they were neighbours up on Vanua Levu. In the old days.'

As she talked, Laura could picture the close web of settler families stretching from island to island in the various retreats they had made for themselves over the past hundred years. This was Jack's world too, she reminded herself, this strange castaway life, so idyllic and yet so vulnerable. No doubt his family lived on a grander scale than the Mumbys, but the ties of the past were strong and Jack himself was a product of that past. Out here, the dashing young barrister she had known in London seemed irrelevant, almost a figment of her imagination. Did it seem like that to Jack too? Was it as if he'd created a role for himself, and now here she was, just part of a play that belonged to another time?

But Jack had taken hold of her hand as he stood talking, and that warm grasp was reality. Mrs Mumby caught her looking at the name on the gate.

'Malua,' she told Laura. 'It's a byword in these islands. Means "why-worry", sort of "tomorrow-will-do".' She smiled with a touch of ruefulness. 'That's about us, I'd say.'

'Come in for a yarn next time,' Mr Mumby called as they left. 'This independence thing – could be trouble if the Indians get the upper hand. Some of the young Fijians are a bit hot-headed too, the educated ones. Need people like you to watch out for us, Jack.'

'It's always the same,' Jack said when they were out of sight, walking towards the beach. 'These old-timers. My father's a bit like that too, living in the past. The irony is that it's the very people they brought over from India to work the plantations a hundred years ago who are causing the problem today. Simply because the Indians now outnumber the Fijians.' He broke off, taking her hand again. 'Hell, Laura! You've probably swotted all this up already. Besides, now's not the time for a political lecture.'

'Another day!' She had already made a mental note to come back and talk to the Mumbys with a tape-recorder. But at the moment her mind was on something else.

'It doesn't sound as if my father's a very popular person. What did he mean about the housegirl?'

'Oh, just gossip,' Jack said lightly. 'Bush telegraph, they call it. And with an eccentric like Harrington, someone who lives alone and doesn't conform to the usual colonial rules . . .'

'He never remarried?' Laura put in.

'Not as far as I know.'

'And so?'

'After all, I hardly know the man. Except that he was kind enough to put me on the right track when I was looking up some constitutional history. It's just that he's got some kind of reputation for himself.'

'What sort of reputation?' she persisted. A pulse in her mind was quickening, as if she was getting close to something important. With her experience of interviewing she knew the signs.

'Well.' Jack sounded unwilling. 'I have found out a bit more since I got back from London. After meeting you, I suppose. There were stories about his involvement with some of the local women. Nothing new in that. But apparently one of them got beaten up and tried to take him to court. Nothing came of it. He's known to have a bit of a vicious streak, though. And he's said to have dabbled rather too deeply in Fijian custom for some tastes. Superstitions, magic, all that stuff. In his younger days I expect, probably background for his books.'

'And now?'

'Now he's an old man, a bit of a guru as far as visiting anthropologists are concerned. And there are plans for making him a Fellow of the new university, I hear. So maybe he's a reformed character nowadays. You'll be seeing for yourself soon enough.'

'Be careful!' she said suddenly. They were walking over a stony part of the beach and Jack was about to put his bare foot on a jagged piece of coral. She had a sudden sensation of herself as a very small girl nursing a badly grazed foot. There had been a lot of pain, and she could remember the agony of stinging antiseptic dabbed on by her mother.

'See, I still have the mark,' she told Jack, showing a small scar beneath her heel.

'A coral cut goes poisonous in no time, I can tell you.' He ran his finger over the scar. 'What else do you remember? About your father, for instance?'

'Very little, really. After all, I was only four when I left. Not so much a picture, more a feeling. Anxiety, fear almost. A lamp being knocked over on the table when I couldn't finish my milk. It always made me sick – I suppose it was the powdered kind. A shadow across the bed where I was lying with my mother.' She stopped, not wanting to go deeper.

'What about your mother?'

'Fair hair, cut short like a boy's, that made curls round your fingers. She seemed to be crying a lot. And she had a limp. I remember the old canvas shoes she wore, and sort of pyjamas, never a dress.'

She paused again, feeling the pain of sadness this time.

'Not a happy picture then?' He slipped his arm round her waist.

'No. But now I'm back in the islands, I remember some of the nice things. Being carried on someone's shoulders to look up for coconuts. Playing with the Gilbertese children if my father wasn't there. Making pies with this stuff.'

They had come to the sand now, soft as brown sugar. Jack laid out a straw mat he had brought from the Land Rover and Laura opened the package of food, Indian rotis rolled up like pancakes with a marvellous sharp-tasting potato curry inside. They both ate greedily, then drained the warm cans of Coca-Cola.

'This was what I used to have for lunch at my junior school,' Jack said. 'We were allowed to go down to the Indian café in the town with our pocket money – something my mother never knew, thank goodness.'

'Was she very strict?'

'Bloody-minded, you could say.' Jack grinned. 'She's the one who had me packed off to boarding school in Australia. Said I was running wild, going bush. Then I came back with this dingo accent of mine!'

Laura laughed, and lay back with her head in his lap. More than once, she had turned over in her mind this very image, the two of them together on a sun-filled beach, the world to themselves and time standing still, just for a little while. It was the stuff of a hundred film scenes and television commercials, the oldest romantic cliché of all. How very different it was to be inside it, living it with every nerve of her being. She treasured the gritty touch of sand against her skin, the glittering light filtering through her closed eyes and under the rough cotton, Jack's body which she could now summon up like a secret code, the pale brown solidity of it, bright with the sheen of sweat. He is mine, she said to herself, and now he knows every part of me too. Just for a second she felt the fever of the morning flare between them again. Now she was content remembering, going back to that first inkling of the truth as they faced each other across the hall in Broadcasting House.

And yet, I so nearly lost him, said her inner voice. We must be more careful of each other from now on.

A sudden breeze flicked up the paper wrappings. Jack crumpled them into the bag with the cans, then bent and kissed her. She tasted spice on his tongue and felt again that tremor of longing.

'You haven't told me yet what happened with Martin,' Jack said, reading her thoughts. 'When I left you, you told me he was getting a divorce. You were going to be married, remember?'

'I remember.'

She sat up against him, smoothing back her hair as if that would smooth the past into some sort of order.

'Then tell me.'

'I'll tell you quickly because it's over now and nothing to do with us. But I need to tell you.' She took a deep breath. 'You were right when you said Martin had damaged me. In fact, he nearly broke me, but something held the pieces together. You, perhaps. Or the thought of you.'

'He changed his mind?'

'His wife discovered she was expecting a baby. As he explained, it would have been impossible to leave her under the circumstances. It was bad timing that I got pregnant too. I had the test straight away. Martin said it was lucky I'd found out so soon, because it meant that the abortion would be a simple matter. He knew a specialist who did these things privately. He gave me his name, and the name of a psychiatrist in Harley Street.'

'A psychiatrist?'

'You have to get a professional opinion, that to go through an unwanted pregnancy would seriously affect your mental health.'

She felt Jack's hand tighten around hers, but she kept her eyes fixed on the slow incoming waves. A sea bird of some kind was stalking along the shallows, absorbed and indifferent.

'It wasn't difficult to convince him. I was fairly distraught. My GP was a friend and he paved the way for me. Then all I had to do was to press Martin's hundred pounds into the hand of the specialist, pack an overnight bag and present myself at a rather seedy nursing home in North London. That was it.' She paused. A picture of the specialist, Mr Goldstein, was suddenly vivid in her mind. 'He was quite a nice man, really. Bald, with glasses. Had a way of putting his hand on my knee and staring at me while we talked. Afterwards he told me I shouldn't dwell on it, concentrate instead on finding myself a reliable husband. That was when he put me on the pill. Just in case,' she added lightly.

But Jack wasn't smiling. 'Did you have a bad time?'

'Not really.' She bit the inside of her lip to keep her face still. 'It was grotty more than anything else, and humiliating. But pathetic too.

There was this white covered bucket under the operating table. The anaesthetist gave me a wink. I remember that. When I woke up, the girl in the bed next to me was being wheeled off for the same thing. She was howling her head off.' Again, she tried hard to control her expression. 'I didn't cry. I was too angry, with myself mostly.'

'And Martin? Afterwards?'

'I made sure I never saw him again. Not even at the other end of a corridor. I had a month's sick leave – appendicitis complications. I went to stay with a good friend in Scotland. When I went back to Broadcasting House I was attached to another department. It was the one promise Martin kept. And then I got myself this assignment, which was lucky.'

'I knew he was a bastard as soon as I met him.' Jack was staring past her now, his mouth set in an angry line. 'But you . . .'

'Yes, I was naive, I know. Ignoring all the signs, thinking you can change someone just because you've set your mind on it. It's a failing of mine. One day I'll learn.'

She leaned forward, away from him, her chin on her hand. But he wrapped his arms around her.

'I don't understand,' he said. 'With your looks, your talent, why were you so determined to latch on to this one particular relationship? Instead of reaching out for something new, I mean. Moving on in your work, for one thing, instead of slaving away for someone like Martin Collins while he collects all the credit.'

'It goes back a long way, I guess. You could call it lack of confidence.'

'Well, it doesn't show.'

Laura sighed, rubbed her cheeks against his shirt. 'Thanks. But all my life I seem to have been looking for security, looking for a family, I suppose. It's hard to forget your mother sending you away.'

'Perhaps she knew she was going to die. And getting you onto that ship was the only hope she had that you'd be safe.'

Laura nodded. 'People do these things, don't they? Like handing over a baby for adoption. But there was no way of explaining it rationally to a child of my age. All I ever felt was an awful blank.'

'You still had a father.' Jack was wrestling with the strangeness of it all, trying to make sense of it.

'A father who decided he wanted nothing more to do with his child,' Laura said bitterly. 'I suppose after the war he decided it was something he just couldn't cope with, so he set himself up in his new life in Fiji and that was the end of it.'

'But you told me you were living with his sister. Surely they must have been in touch.'

'They hated each other's guts. Something to do with the money left them by their parents. Apparently, after university, he'd gone off to the Pacific with her share as well as his own. At least, that's what she told me. Not that she told me much.'

'Were you happy with her?'

Laura laughed. 'Imagine a house out of *Wuthering Heights*, stone floors, cold rice pudding, a list of tasks on the kitchen dresser every morning. Poor Aunt May! She did her best for the miserable little refugee wished on her out of the blue. But she'd never been married, and she hadn't much idea what to do with me. Things were better when I went to boarding school. She got a bit of maintenance out of my father for that.'

'So he *did* write.'

She shook her head. 'Just notification to my aunt of my mother's death. When she told me, it was so unreal I couldn't even cry. There was an annual cheque in the bank after that. And after a few years even that stopped. But then I escaped, got myself taken on as a cub reporter by one of the Yorkshire papers. When I'd had a bit more experience, I went to London to work on a women's magazine. Then I applied for a job with the BBC.'

Laura got to her feet, dusting down her skirt. She felt quite light-headed at having unburdened herself of so much autobiography. 'The story of my life. You have it all, Mr Renfrey.'

'Not quite all, I don't think.' He stood up and rolled together the mat and the bag. Then, with his other arm around her shoulders, they walked back down the beach the way they had come. 'There must have been love affairs, even minor ones. Before Martin, I mean.'

She shrugged her shoulders. 'I was terribly unsure of myself, you know. Didn't even know what kind of clothes to wear.' She relented. 'But there were boyfriends from time to time, one of the young reporters. He actually wanted to marry me but I broke it off.'

'Poor fellow.' Jack was amused. It was so safely tucked away in the past. 'Why was that?'

'Oh, I don't know. Something seemed to be missing. It was so dull, so predictable. More like following a knitting pattern than a love affair.'

Jack burst out laughing. 'Laura! What do you know about knitting?'

'Aunt May taught me,' she said indignantly. 'I'll do you a scarf sometime, just to show you.'

'Not much good for Fiji.'

'You can keep it for coming to London.' She touched the silk paisley round his neck. 'And I can have this one back again.'

Silence fell between them, unspoken thoughts ranging just below the surface. Warning, Keep Off, the messages seemed to say to Laura. She concentrated instead on the present, the pleasure of Jack's body close to hers as they stood side by side, looking across the bay. There was firm sand here at the edge of the sea, wet from the outgoing tide, and a ripple of movement as hundreds of tiny crabs scuttled away to hide themselves under the surface. Something stirred in Laura's mind, something else she had to share.

'Jack! I had the strangest dream in the plane. A man was standing on a beach like this, all alone. It was my father. He had a bird caught in a net. That's all. But I just couldn't forget it. Why was it so frightening?'

She looked at his face, striving to impress on him the power of that picture. But he was staring at the waves.

'Better ask someone else. The local people are great ones for dreams in this part of the world, second sight, magic, all that. Every island has one decent sorcerer. Or a sorcerer's apprentice at least!'

She turned to him and reached up to hold him tightly by the shoulders. 'One thing I know for sure. Something important's going to happen to me out here. I feel myself being pulled towards it.' She laid her head against his cheek. 'Perhaps it will make sense of my life, tell me who I am.'

'Hasn't that something already happened?' Jack's lips were close to her ear and his voice was tender.

'Yes, my love, yes. But . . .' She pulled away again, looking over his shoulder at the boundless shimmer of the ocean. 'I think I need to go home while I'm out here.'

'Home?'

'Back to Taparua, where I was born. I want to see it.'

Jack looked doubtful. 'It's a hell of a long way. And it's not at all easy to get there.' He pushed back her fringe with a gentle finger. 'I thought your programmes were about Fiji. The Gilberts is a different place altogether. Darkest Micronesia, the islands that time forgot.'

She hesitated. 'Perhaps when I've seen my father . . .' She was thinking of the phone call she had made before leaving the hotel. A servant had answered to say the doctor was out, so she had simply left Jack's number with a message to ring her there. 'When I've seen him . . .' she began again.

'You'll know better,' Jack finished for her. 'And now it's time to take you home. It's still quite a drive.'

*

In fact, Vailima was only an hour away, but in that time the landscape changed completely. Gone was the sunshine of the open coast. Dusky clouds had rolled up out of nowhere and ahead rose the towering slopes she had glimpsed from the plane, dense with greenery. Giant ferns and thick knotted vines hung so close to the road that they brushed against the Land Rover. Then the road itself was left behind as Jack followed a hairpin bend over a tiny wooden bridge.

A steep lane wound upward through thickets of bamboo. Through the open window Laura felt a different air, cool and earthy. It was late afternoon and a purplish dusk was closing in. They passed a villager making for home, a basket and bush knife in either hand, behind him the humpbacked silhouette of a woman laden with firewood. Jack raised a hand in greeting as they waved to him. In the tiny hillside settlement, watchful figures looked out from the shadows of the eaves, lit by the flare of cooking fires. Laura had the feeling she was penetrating secret territory, already marked as a stranger.

'This is the old Fiji,' Jack told her. 'The people are darker, smaller, descended from the original inhabitants, you see, and they still keep themselves to themselves. They remember the old customs too.'

'Cannibalism?' Laura asked.

'Up till a hundred years ago. That's something they don't like to talk about, though. See that mountain ahead?' He pointed to a long black outline that ran across the greenish horizon like the backbone of a giant dinosaur. 'That is where the Spirit Path runs, from east to west. That's the track the souls of the dead must travel before they jump off at land's end. Then they make their way to the afterworld, beyond the horizon.'

Laura studied Jack's face in profile, caught in the last gleam of light, under the bronze helmet of his hair. She felt that she hadn't even begun to know him.

'How did you learn all this?'

'Hell knows. Back when I was a kid, I suppose. We used to come up here on holiday. A whole gang of us boys used to chase through the bush on make-believe boar hunts, so we heard all these stories from the local people. There was an old Australian forestry chap living up at Vailima then. That's how I got the place. Years later I heard he'd retired and no one else seemed to want it. I put in an offer and here I am.'

They had come to the top of the hill where the forest levelled out in a wide clearing. On the edge, in the dusk, Laura saw a rambling wooden house that reminded her of a Swiss chalet with its pointed gables and railed verandahs. To her surprise there were lights in the windows. But Jack simply said, 'Good. Matti's still here.'

At the same moment the door at the front sprang open like a cuckoo clock, and a small stout Fijian woman came out to greet them, lamp in hand.

'Bula, turanga! I waiting here. I see the car come.'

'Matti comes from the village,' he told Laura, introducing them. 'She keeps things in order here, especially me. Right, Matti?'

But Matti had already bounced back inside. 'Kana come soon,' they heard her call amidst the clatter of pans.

'I hope you're hungry again,' Jack said. 'I am.'

'I'm always hungry.'

Laura was suddenly overcome with shyness, standing in the middle of Jack's sitting room while he disappeared to bring in the bags. How jumbled and comfortable it was, with its book-stacked walls and battered cane chairs, the Fijian mats on the floor and the Victorian oil lamps with their warm, wavering light. There was a record-player in the corner. She felt a pang of recognition as she saw the familiar Bruch cover on top of the stack of records alongside. The ceiling was low and sloping and all over it were pinned curling reproductions of French Impressionist paintings. Perhaps he liked to look at them as he lay on the bulging horsehair sofa with its pile of old cushions. She was studying the Van Gogh sunflowers when Jack came silently up behind her and rested his arms on her shoulders.

'You approve?'

'It's a marvellous place.'

'Wait till you see the view in the morning. And when it's cold in the evenings . . .'

With a flourish he pushed aside the bamboo screen. Behind it was an old-fashioned brick chimneypiece and the remains of a log fire. That charred, ashy smell had been puzzling Laura ever since she came in, reminding her of England.

On the other side of the room, Matti was putting food out on the table, her dandelion-puff of black hair glinting in the lamplight.

'Come on.' Jack pulled Laura to sit down in front of enormous plates of sausages, bacon and baked beans. In the centre reposed two white rubbery objects, each edged with a lace-like frill of black.

'*Oeufs chantilly*, Matti's specialty. She thinks eggs should be fried for half an hour, and nothing will dissuade her.'

He turned and winked at her. Matti lifted her chin to acknowledge the joke, but her wrinkled face remained impassive as she stood with folded arms, stomach thrust out in her flowered muumuu, watching them eat. Jack had kicked off his shoes – 'Bad Fiji habit' – and now Laura did the same. For a moment their bare feet brushed together under the table. He grinned at her conspiratorially, looking like a small boy.

'Laura,' he said softly. She felt her throat constrict with longing and weariness too. As she sipped the last of her wine, she was aware of Matti's eyes on her. In an undertone she said something to Jack in Fijian.

'Matti says you look tired. She's going to make up your bed for you.' He leaned towards her. 'I'm afraid that means the spare room. Matti's a stickler for etiquette. Oh, and that reminds me, I forgot to show you our plumbing arrangements.'

He got up and reached for a torch on the shelf by the door. 'Follow me. And don't mind the frogs.'

The dank little wooden hut at the end of the path seemed familiar, reminding her of the earth closet at the bottom of the garden at Aunt May's. 'It's only for the gardener, remember!' Aunt May had instructed her. But more than once she had used it secretly, just for the thrill of perching amongst the ivy-covered walls.

When she emerged, she saw Jack's tall outline against the night sky, and took his hand. There was a hoarse croaking in the undergrowth as the occasional frog sprang away from the circle of light. Above them the stars were so huge and close they seemed to give off an illumination of their own. She shivered. The air was heavy with a scent she could not identify.

'Azaleas,' Jack said. 'They grow wild up here, and orchids too.'

Laura stumbled over a root, and he held on to her tightly.

'Poor girl. You're absolutely worn out. Why didn't you tell me?'

'Just sleepy. It catches up with you.'

'Matti said how pale you looked. Straight to bed with you now.'

Gratefully, she leaned against him as he led the way up the steps back into the house again, and through to another, smaller room. Oh, the bliss of it, she thought – to have someone take control. And if that someone loves and trusts you, and you him, there is nothing more to worry about. All she had to do was let him slip on her dressing gown and fold her into the high little bed wedged between his desk and his bookcase, piled with soft pillows.

'My mother sleeps here when she visits,' Jack told her. 'So Matti keeps everything in order.' Matti herself was in the doorway behind him, bearing towels and an extra blanket, making clucking noises like a mother hen.

'Thank you, Matti,' she said softly. Jack put a glass of water on the table and a little nightlight, which touched her more than anything. Carefully he tucked in her mosquito net.

'Will you be okay? I have to take Matti back to the village.'

Laura nodded, half-asleep. The sense of security and peace was overpowering. Jack's voice faded away.

'So don't worry if you wake up while I'm gone. I'll only be half an hour.'

But Laura didn't wake up. She didn't hear the car drive away or come back. It was early morning when she stirred again. The light through the net was ghostly grey at first, then tinged with gold as sunlight edged through the tiny window. She sat up and smiled to see the pillowcases, doubtless embroidered by Matti as instructed by her mission-school teachers so many years ago. One read 'Jesus Loves You', the other, less cheerfully, 'Rest in Peace'.

Jack would still be sleeping, she thought. She had a sudden picture of him sprawled amidst the sheets, his head flung sideways as he had dozed next to her at the hotel. She slipped out of bed and saw her face in the mirror smile back at her, bright-eyed and smooth from sleep. She flicked her hair back with her brush and pulled the cotton wrap around her. Then, barefoot, she crossed the passageway to Jack's door, moving almost without thinking, like a sleepwalker.

'Jack.' She could feel her heart tumbling around in an absurd way, her mind filled with a dozen different images of how she would wake him and touch him. 'Jack.'

But there was no reply. The door was half-open and the bed inside empty, the bedclothes thrown back with Jack-like impatience. She walked on into the sitting room, but there was no sign of him. Of course, he would be in the kitchen making coffee. But he was not there either. Puzzled, she went out on to the verandah, expecting to see a familiar figure walking back to the house along the garden path.

But the garden was deserted, a paradise wilderness gleaming with rich life in the brilliance of the morning sun. Up against the verandah rails, the orchids Jack had described were tangled together in a mass of purple and white. Dark red ginger flowers stood tall behind, like flaming swords in the undergrowth. And there were the azaleas, the pale pink flowers still beaded with damp, the sharp scent drawing up a dozen brilliant butterflies from bush to bush. Laura watched a hummingbird thrust its beak deep into the petals, its minute body vibrating with energy before it darted away again.

Then, turning, she saw the view, a shimmering sequence of valleys falling away between the slopes of the hills, a faraway river twining towards the horizon like those streams in the background of early

Italian paintings. Away in the furthest distance she could glimpse the sea, a thread of silver against the blue, and perched upon it the shape of a single island. At that moment, the whole idyllic perfection of the Pacific broke upon her imagination and took her by storm. From now on she knew it would keep its hold on her heart, like no other place she had ever known.

This was Jack's world and hers, and he it was who had brought her back here. She felt an immense gratitude, a longing like an ache to give herself to him in any way he chose, and then to possess him completely in return. But for the moment, there was a mystery. Where did he go so early in the morning?

As if in a dream, her feet continued to take her along the path. Away from the house the trees grew thickly together, and the ground began to slope away. There was the sound of water, and out of the tangled grass, a glimpse of steps where the sound was loudest.

She saw him before he saw her. A waterfall flowed from beneath the steps, cascading over rocks into a large pool lined with stone. On the edge sat Jack, naked as the morning, his head sleek as an otter's, his legs thrust out into the rush of the falling water. She knew he was waiting for her. Even when he looked up and raised his hand to her she felt there was no haste. She reached him and without a word he drew off her wrap. Together they slipped into the water. How cold it was, but how warm Jack's body as he pulled her into his arms. He leaned back against the wall, and gently, slowly, she rocked herself down on to him, so that at once they were clasped together and he could enter the deepest part of her. Moving with them, the water held them close as a third lover. In an instant of the most violent sweetness, she felt herself released and at the same time taken. She had only to call out to him, 'Now, yes, now,' and it was over. Or rather it was just beginning, an endless-seeming moment of knowledge that went on expanding and rippling from the dark centre where they had found each other.

Jack's face was hidden between her breasts. When he looked up at her, it was with such an expression of lazy bliss that she laughed.

'Honestly! You look just like a cat that's had the cream.'

'Well, haven't I? And don't you look just the same?'

The sun was stronger now, pouring down through a gap in the foliage and warming their shoulders. Jack scrambled out of the water. He held out a towel for her but she shook her head.

'Let me just lie here, floating.'

Jack looked down at her. 'You look more like a water-lily than a cat. But come on!' He reached down and pulled her out, protesting. 'Put this towel round you at once or you'll catch cold.'

'What about you?'
'I brought two.'
'How did you know I'd find you?'
'I knew.'
On the steps Laura turned round for another look at the pool.
'Did you make this place?'
He shook his head. 'It's been here for ages.' He pointed towards the shape of a broken roof, half-hidden by trees. 'The first Governor of Fiji had a rest-house built up here for himself to get away from Suva in the hot season, and this was the viceregal swimming pool. He called the house Vailima. He was a great Stevenson admirer – you remember Samoa? In fact there are only four streams up here, not five, but I thought the name should be kept.' He squeezed the water out of her hair and kissed her on the back of her neck. 'What more could you want?'
'Nothing, Jack. Nothing.' She sighed, looking around at the shifting pattern of sunlight and shade where the trees hung over the water. 'It feels like the first morning ever up here, doesn't it? A sort of Eden.'
'Complete with Adam and Eve.' He kissed her again, this time on the mouth.
'And the serpent?'
But he was walking ahead of her, talking to her over his shoulder. 'I'm going to cook us some fish for breakfast. Matti brought it up yesterday. And I want to play us the Bruch record. Our music.'
She caught up with him, breathless, clutching the towel around her, the discarded robe over her arm. For a moment they stood facing each other on the verandah.
'I do love you,' she said.
At the same moment the phone began ringing inside the house, a shrill summons from another world. Jack hurried in. When he reappeared, his face was tense.
'It's your father,' he said.

CHAPTER FIVE

On the drive into Suva the following day, Laura tried again and again to remember the exact tone of that voice on the phone. The shock of the moment had blunted her normally sharp perceptions. A dry, pedantic kind of voice was how she recalled it now, rather high-pitched and with a stammer on certain words. Her father had sounded older than she had imagined.

'What age would you say he was?' she asked Jack.

'Somewhere in his early seventies, I should think. Looks older, though, as if he's been through the mill one way or another.'

'So he must have been around forty when I was a baby. He left it rather late in the day to get married.'

She was chattering partly to cover up the tension that grew with every mile. Jack put his hand over hers.

'Relax. He's not going to eat you. Who knows? It may even be an emotional reunion – hugs and tears and all that.'

Laura sighed. 'I don't think so, somehow. He didn't sound exactly overjoyed to hear me. More wary than anything else.'

'Well, at least he's had time to get used to the idea. You did write to him from England, didn't you?'

'A couple of weeks ago. But that's just it. He's had time to prepare himself, the way elderly people have to. Even so, all he could say was that he was extremely busy, but he could spare me a couple of hours over lunch. Just as if it was a business appointment.'

'Which it is in a way.' He patted the tape-recorder on the seat between them.

'That was the moment when he seemed to loosen up. When I explained I hadn't come all the way to Fiji just to meet a long-lost father.'

Jack shook his head. 'Funny old cove. Still, you can charm a snake out of its skin. I remember what it was like being interviewed by you.'

They reached the outskirts of Suva, and passed the tiny pastel-painted bungalows of the suburbs. A crocodile file of Indian schoolgirls, all starched white dresses and glossy black plaits, wound its way along the pavement, lunchboxes in hand. Laura could see over the rooftops to a forest of masts and funnels, where the waterfront lay.

'Are you sure you don't want me with you?' Jack asked.

Laura stroked his neck. 'That's nice of you. But I have to do this on my own, at least the first time round. Just drop me off there. I'll get a taxi back into town to Broadcasting House.'

'Well, when you've finished that's where I'll be. Just ask for Government Buildings.'

He nodded towards a stately stone edifice on their left, with the Union Jack drooping from its topmost pinnacle. A clock tower like a miniature Big Ben showed the time at 11.55. In just five minutes, Laura thought, she would be face to face with her father, and the shadow would become flesh-and-blood reality. It was all she could think of as she twisted her damp fingers in her lap. The sights of Suva pointed out by Jack had glided by like images on a cinema screen – the seething marketplace piled high with the colours of fruit and fish, the contrast of gleaming banks and office blocks alongside old-fashioned weatherboard bars and cafés. Past and present jostled together along the pavements too, bushy-haired Fijians from the villages, glamorous Polynesian girls in mini-skirts and stiletto heels, red-faced businessmen in crumpled tropical suits and sunglasses.

'That's Albert Park, where everything happens from Queen's birthday parades to cricket matches,' Jack went on. 'The Botanical Gardens. The Grand Pacific Hotel. Government House up there on the hill. Queen Victoria on her pedestal, slightly pockmarked I'm afraid.'

Part of Laura's mind was automatically registering these mementos of Fiji's colonial heyday. But her innermost self was elsewhere, locked in the grip of private emotions. It was not just her father she was encountering, she told herself. It was her mother too. Every memory of the dead woman would be precious to her. For the first time in her life she would be able to talk about her, ask questions, hear what kind of person she had been. A blank page in her life, perhaps the most important page of all, would be blank no longer.

They were driving out of the city now, along the edge of the sea, the roadside tangled with mangrove thickets, the skies heavy with low-hanging cloud. Suva weather, Jack called it, the sultry greyness threatening a downpour that often never came. Laura rubbed the back of her neck. The headache that had come on earlier was still there. It made thinking difficult and she felt this was a time she would need all her wits about her. She closed her eyes and tried rehearsing questions in her mind. But it was no good.

For a moment she found herself wishing she had never made contact with her father in the first place. Then she would have been free, free to travel and observe, free above all to shed the past and luxuriate in the miraculous present which had brought her Jack.

At the same moment he reached across and touched her cheek.

'It was a good day yesterday, wasn't it?'

She covered his hand with hers. 'A good day.'

Every minute of it was still so vivid in her mind. After breakfast they had walked into the sweet-smelling forest, explored the ruined shell of the old government rest-house, picked orchids to put in a huge pottery bowl made in the village, cooked fresh fish from the river. Later she'd taken her tape-recorder to the village and talked to the headman, whose English was good. That night, lying in Jack's bed ('Be my sweet heart' was the message on his pillowslip, Laura noticed), they had lit candles and played the Bruch concerto, then Jack had played the flute – his penny-whistle, as he called it – and sitting tailor-fashion had taught her the song he had been singing as they drove the day before. It was a melancholy little ditty in pidgin English, and it ran through her mind again now.

> Time you go long way no see,
> Sun and moon trouble me.
> Me sorry too much long you
> I think you no love me no more . . .

There was no time for singing now. With a jerk, the Land Rover pulled over to the verge. The sea was very close here, rolling in sullenly against the low stone wall. Just ahead was Suva Point. At the top of a sloping headland stood a house that overlooked the whole sweep of the bay.

'Your father's house,' Jack said.

He got out with her and they looked up at it together. From here it seemed to be the usual rambling colonial bungalow of white-painted weatherboard, beneath the rusty red of an iron roof. But somehow the place had an identity all its own. The tall peaked gables rising out of the trees gave it a Gothic touch. So did the fretted rails and archways of the long verandah below. Although the air was so warm, the window shutters were half-closed, as if the house was staring back at them with secretive, heavy-lidded eyes. From somewhere above came the call of a strange bird, harsh-sounding, almost human.

'It's a mynah,' Jack told her. 'He's taught it quite a vocabulary, I believe.'

'Perhaps it'll help out with the conversation.' Settling the tape-recorder on her shoulder, she attempted a smile. It was absurd how nervous she felt. Jack gave her a quick hug.

'You'll be fine. But take it easy going up. There are sixty-three steps, I counted them. See you later.'

'I'll be there.'

She walked across the grass, still looking up at the front of the house. But there was no sign of anyone on the verandah looking out for her. The steps were steep and curving, patched here and there with orange lichen. Huge scentless hibiscus grew wild on either side, yellow stamens thrusting out of the scarlet throats of the flowers. The rank smell of overgrown vegetation in wet earth drowned everything else. Someone must have planted some kind of garden here in the early years of the century, but Dr Harrington obviously preferred to let things take their own course. Here and there, in the corners of the steps, stood pieces of old carvings that were surely from his own collection, a phallic stone broken and scarred, a bowl shaped like an upturned turtle, archaeological relics from his travels in the Pacific. Right at the top, she was startled by a granite face peering out at her, meshed in weeds. She saw it was the squat head of some discarded idol. As she stood looking down at it, getting her breath back, a tiny gecko flickered in and out of the grimacing mouth. Laura felt something turn over inside her.

Set between two central pillars of the verandah was the front entrance. At one side, an old ship's bell hung from a lopsided chain. Laura was just about to reach up to pull it when, noiselessly, the double doors were opened. A woman stood there, tall and grave, in a long flowered muumuu. Her smooth black hair was pulled back in a tight knot from a handsome face that reminded Laura of an American Indian.

'Doctor is expecting you,' she said softly. She did not smile. Laura knew at once that the woman was as nervous as she was, as if intent on carrying out her instructions without fault.

As she was shown inside, she felt this impression even more strongly. With folded hands, the woman walked stiffly ahead, her manner so different from the other island people Laura had met so far.

'I'm a little early,' Laura said, trying to put her at ease. At this, the woman stopped and turned with a smile that lit up her whole face.

'You are Lora,' she whispered.

Laura's surprise was so intense that she found it difficult to speak. It was the first time she had heard the island version of her name. But how did the woman know her name at all?

'How do you . . . ?' she began.

Quickly the woman laid a finger on her lips and hurried on again. They had passed through a long passageway, the walls hung with prints of Pacific history and other curiosities, a whale tooth on a cord of sinnet, a tribal sword edged with razor shells. Now she was led out on to a wide verandah running the length of the back of the house.

'Doctor is here.'

The woman indicated a closed door at the far end. A printed notice hung from it. 'Keep Out,' it said, and in Fijian, 'Tabu Eke'.

Laura stopped in her tracks. This was an even stranger introduction to her father than she had imagined.

The woman stepped up to the door and tapped lightly.

'Miss Harrington here, Doctor,' she murmured.

There was the sound of movement inside. A voice called back, sharp with irritation, in a language Laura couldn't place. She heard a bolt drawn back. The next minute the door was opened, not fully but just a foot or so.

Standing behind the woman, Laura had a glimpse of a tall thin figure with white hair. It seemed to be almost dark inside the room, apart from a single red bulb which threw a dull glow on the man's haggard features.

At seeing Laura, he at once stepped forward.

'I'm sorry,' he said formally. 'You must wonder what's going on. This is my darkroom – I've just been developing some new photographs. A tricky business.'

He paused, staring at her intently with narrow grey eyes that were so light in colour they looked almost silver. In response, Laura found herself acting entirely on instinct. Without even thinking, she had crossed the gap between them and put her arms around him. His shoulders felt rigid and incredibly thin.

'I can't believe it, can you? After all these years . . .' Her words tumbled over each other, then died away in confusion. There was a stillness about him that froze her embrace. It was as if he were holding himself deliberately in check.

'I'm sorry,' he said again. Suddenly recovering himself, he thrust out his hand and briefly took hold of hers. 'It's just that you're so like your mother – not the hair but the face. A shock, I'm afraid. I hadn't . . . hadn't imagined it.'

The stammer she had noticed was tripping up some of his words. There was another pause while they stood facing each other. Laura realized her whole body was beginning to shake.

'May I sit down?'

'Of course. Forgive me.'

Still with the same wooden manner, he led the way inside. Laura wondered for a moment if he had had a stroke. But his movements were energetic as he strode towards the far side of a large sitting room.

'The sofa's the most comfortable,' he said. Once again, he flung some words at the servant, who turned and left them. Laura noticed he sat down with his back to the light, in a leather wing chair that was scuffed and peeling. For the first time she registered the clothes he was wearing, a faded bush jacket and shabby khaki trousers. She was trying to retrieve some memory of his face, but those lined, sardonic features were too changed by age. Yet she was reminded of someone. It was that portrait of Somerset Maugham, she suddenly remembered, the cruelly truthful one by Graham Sutherland. And all the time she was searching for some kind of emotion, some warmth of feeling between the two of them. So far it had eluded her.

'I'm afraid you'll find this place of mine very primitive,' he went on. With a bony hand, he indicated the rest of the room. Politely Laura glanced around, noting the clutter of a lifetime in the islands, in particular the fine old bark-cloth hanging on every wall, the patterns now faded to a tawny brown on the thin parchment-coloured material, coded messages from the mysterious past of the Pacific.

'They're magic symbols, you know,' he said suddenly, as if following her thoughts. 'Primitive hieroglyphs, but with a kind of power, like cave paintings. Suns and moons for prosperous seasons, the square boundaries to keep out evil spirits, circles and verticals for sex and fertility.'

'Do the people still make them like that?' Laura asked.

'They're forgetting now.' Harrington stared past her, his pale eyes hooded as if lost in thought. 'Everything in the islands is about forgetting.'

'As you forgot me?' She spoke without thinking, suddenly weary of small talk. 'Forgot me for more than twenty-five years.' She leaned forward, forcing him to return her gaze. 'Why did you do it?'

For a moment his eyes met hers. In the silence, she struggled to read them, willing him to answer her. But the pause was broken by the sound of the door opening behind her. The woman was bringing in a tray of drinks, carefully setting it down on the table at Harrington's side. He got to his feet and turned his attention to the various bottles and glasses.

'What will you have? Gin and fresh lime? A dry sherry? I always have Pernod myself.'

'Gin and tonic, if you have it.' It was an automatic answer. The mixing of ice and spirits, the opening of bottles, seemed a ritual he was anxious to prolong. While his back was turned, she did a strange thing. Her tape machine was tucked away half-hidden alongside the sofa, a new tape already set up. Quickly she reached down and turned on the switch. There was no time to check recording levels, but there was a good chance that the inset microphone would pick up at least part of their conversation. I might never see my father again, she told herself. I must have some record of what he may be going to tell me. Evidence was not exactly the word in her mind, but something like it. And I have a spare tape for the interview, her practical self reminded her.

Harrington turned round with her drink. Her fingers were slippery round the cold glass. She took a quick gulp to bolster her courage.

'You never wrote to me,' she continued.

Harrington sat down, not looking at her, his shoulders hunched. He put his Pernod on the table at his elbow and passed a hand over his eyes. 'It was too painful,' he murmured. 'I had to make the break. After Millie died, everything was over. All that part of my life – I had to put it behind me, start again here in Fiji. Anything to do with you was a reminder of her all over again.' He looked up at her sharply. 'I simply closed the door on it. The war, you know. It forced one to take harsh decisions.'

'What about my mother?' Frustration was making Laura angry. 'You realize I know absolutely nothing about her, not even her name until this minute. It's not right.' Her voice faltered. 'To have totally lost her, the person who gave me life.'

His face had become a mask.

'What do you remember about her yourself?'

Somehow Laura felt she was being tested. 'Almost nothing, as you can imagine. Except the misery of being parted from her. The ship I was put on was a terrifying place. One of the other mothers looked after me, but that only made me miss my own even more. Then when we got to New Zealand, your sister was at the docks. After the war she would take me home, she said. I thought she meant home like Taparua. Can you imagine, Yorkshire in winter? But at least I had an auntie, I said to myself, Auntie May.'

She watched his face for some reaction, wondering if he wanted to hear about his sister. Did he even know she had died some years ago? But he brushed the name aside.

'I knew you'd arrived safely.' He swirled the cloudy yellow liquid round in his glass, and drained it quickly. 'Your mother,' he went on, still in the flat voice of an inquisitor. 'Did she tell you stories? About herself?'

Laura searched her mind, as she had done so often over the years. 'Not about herself, nothing I can remember. Just fairy stories. There was one about the fish that could change itself into a princess. That was a Gilbertese story, I suppose.'

Harrington nodded. 'One from the Tabituea people. There are many legends like that.'

He was rolling a cigarette in some curious procedure of his own, twisting the paper in his long yellow fingers, tucking in stray shreds of the coarse local tobacco. Then, carefully, he rubbed the end of it on a small block of solid white substance placed in an ashtray on the arms of his chair. As he smoked, the pungent smell of something like menthol was released. Laura found herself hating that smell, while at the same time wondering what its effect was on the smoker. Her father's hand was trembling almost continuously, she noticed. It was like his stammer, part of a wire-like inner tension that she could only guess at. There's an expression of cruelty in the shape of his mouth, she thought, the way it was drawn down at the corners where the deepest lines were etched. Or was it just unhappiness, the pain of having to recall the loss of a woman he had loved, even after all these years?

'You did love her?' she asked, feeling a sudden pity for him.

He unfolded himself from his chair and walked across to the window. The light picked out a rusty tinge in the thinning white hair where he must have dyed it with henna in years past – a touch of vanity she found as disturbing as the rest of him.

'I think I would have gone mad without her. I'd had a bad nervous breakdown – that was the polite way of putting it.' He was speaking with his back to her, staring down at the sea. Suddenly he turned, his face working with emotion, the first she had seen him show. 'Have you any idea of the loneliness of the Gilbert Islands? I lived for three years without seeing a fellow white man, apart from an oddball missionary who travelled through the group every six months or so.'

'The distances between them look immense,' Laura said, searching for the right words. 'The map seems to be mostly sea.'

'The sea. That awful sea,' he broke in. 'Cutting you off from everything and everyone. Millions of square miles of it, and the scraps of land just atolls no more than a hundred yards across.'

'What about your job? Didn't that bring you into contact with people?' She wanted to lead him back to her mother, but she sensed she had to be careful.

'I should never have taken it. Too much of a loner. I did what I could. But running that little hospital and the dispensary, presiding over all those meetings of the village elders, it was hardly food for the mind. So I worked my head off on my own things, my studies, my writings. As for getting close to the Gilbertese, anyone will tell you it's an impossibility. Physical company, the closeness of a woman – the lack of that became torture after a while. There were village girls, of course.' He frowned, drawing on his cigarette. 'But that was a mistake! I even advertised in one of the Australian papers once for a desert island companion, and got one.' He smiled grimly. 'She went back by the next boat to Sydney, thank God.'

He was talking to himself now, Laura thought, reconstructing a time in his life he'd almost forgotten.

'And my mother?' she asked. 'You still haven't told me. What she was like. How you met her. How she died.'

He stood in front of her now, quite close, looking down at her with a sly, almost cunning expression. She was aware for the first time of the threatening presence of the man. It puzzled her, too, that any sense of belonging to each other seemed totally absent. Could rejection do this, erase all instincts of natural feeling between father and daughter? Or was she over-reacting, having secretly hoped for some kind of rapport at least, even affection?

'I can see you don't intend to leave me alone until you have all the facts. That's what comes of being a journalist.' His voice had a razor edge to it now. The hooded eyes were all at once piercing and distended. 'Very well then. This is how it was, in brief. Then we can talk of other things.'

'Other things?' Laura was confused. She had almost forgotten the tape-recorder, still noiselessly turning at her feet. 'Oh, the interview. Of course, afterwards.'

Harrington was sitting opposite her again, rolling another cigarette. When he spoke, it was as if he was reciting something learned long ago, something that no longer had any real meaning for him. The emotion of a few minutes before was erased.

'I met Millie when I was on sick leave in Suva. She was travelling round the islands on a yacht with some friends, crazy young Americans like herself. Hippies, you'd call them today.'

'So she was an American,' Laura interjected. 'What part did she come from? Did she have family there?'

'Not that she spoke of. In fact, she didn't talk about her background at all. Neither did I. That made two of us, lost souls, free spirits, whatever you like to call us. She was certainly a romantic about the South Seas.' He gave a mocking half-smile that Laura found offensive. 'That's why she accepted my proposal, I suppose. She jumped at the idea of setting up with me on a paradise island.'

'The wedding was in Suva?'

He shook his head. 'There wasn't time. I had to get back to the Gilberts. A missionary at Tarawa married us.' He cleared his throat. 'Five years later there wasn't even time for a decent funeral service.'

A pang of anguish ran through her. This was what she had come to hear, but now she could hardly bear to listen any more.

'What happened?' She had to ask the question, otherwise she had the feeling he might have closed the conversation there and then.

'Malaria. I had no drugs left. The Japanese were on our doorstep. She died just two weeks before the last evacuation ship came through from Fiji. I was in the final party to get away from the Gilberts.'

For the first time Laura could understand her father's bitterness, the terrible guilt he must have felt about his own survival.

'You had to leave her there,' she murmured.

Harrington looked up at her, startled. 'What do you mean?'

'Her body,' Laura said awkwardly. 'She was buried on Taparua?'

He turned away again. 'A makeshift affair, I'm afraid. The Japanese planes were bombing us every other day.'

'I would like to see the grave,' Laura said in a low voice.

'There is nothing to see. One coral boulder is very like another.'

'You've been back there yourself?'

'Never. Why should I?'

'I'm planning to go out there while I'm in this part of the world,' she went on. 'If only for a day or two.'

She thought she saw a tremor cross that lined, impassive face. 'I understood that your programme research was to be confined to Fiji,' he said sharply.

'It is. But for personal reasons, sentimental reasons . . .'

'Sentimental!' he broke in. 'There's nothing sentimental about those islands. And you've obviously no idea of just how inaccessible they are. One tiny plane once a fortnight only as far as Tarawa, and that's usually packed to the hilt. Taparua is another thousand miles away, right on the fringe of the group. To get on a copra boat going that far could take months, apart from the problem of getting back again.'

He got up abruptly and began pacing the room, hands thrust into his pockets. 'It's just the kind of daydream your mother went in for. Poor woman. Not exactly practical. And that selfish streak.' He shot a glance at her. 'I hope you haven't inherited that. She was selfish to a degree, I'm afraid.'

'In what way?' Laura asked coldly.

'She would set her heart on something, something she could never have, and refuse to see reason about it. I regret to say it was often a real struggle to get her to obey me. Even though it was for her own good.'

'Obey you?' Her heart jumped. She sensed a clue that was intensely important, and tried to hold his gaze. Eye contact was the key to truth in any interview. The pity she had felt earlier for him was gone, replaced by something quite different. But he moved away again.

'In my treatment of her illness, for instance. Keeping to the correct regime and so on.' He stopped his pacing and stood by the side table, pouring himself another drink. 'Perhaps I should never have taken her to the island in the first place.'

There was a silence between them. Then he shrugged his shoulders. 'But that's old history. The past can never be changed.'

'Except in our own minds. The way we recall it.'

'Nothing will bring your mother back.'

'Photographs,' she said suddenly. It was something she had meant to ask him right from the start. 'Do you have some I could see? Maybe there is one I could have to keep.'

There was another pause. He shook his head.

'There are no photographs.'

Laura could hardly believe it. 'None? But you must have kept one or two of her. You take so many. You're famous for your pictures of island life. They're in all your books.'

'Nothing personal. Besides, when I left Taparua it was hardly a time to pack up my souvenirs. Everything was left behind – papers, pictures, books. All destroyed by the Japs, I expect.'

'You didn't keep just one of her?'

'I've told you. And you?' He stared at her. 'She gave you nothing to take away? No picture of herself?'

Laura hesitated. Was this the right moment?

'No picture. But there was something, a keepsake for luck. Just a small thing she put round my neck when I left.'

He frowned. 'I don't remember anything. It was Timu, my orderly, who took you on board at the end.'

'I still have it.' Quickly she unsnapped the clasp of her bag, got up and went over to him. She had shown it to no one, not even Jack. Such a fragile thing, she hardly ever brought it out of the box she kept it in. Now she held it out to him, the tiny oyster shell with its two halves still intact.

'It opens. Be careful.'

He took it from her on its cord of frayed sinnet. Holding her breath, she watched him prise it open with long fingers. Only when the lock of hair fell out did his expression change. He drew back from where it lay on the table between them, staring down at the twist of reddish gold as if it were something live. Then, slowly, he picked it up and rubbed it between finger and thumb. His expression was both rapt and repelled.

With a sudden movement he dropped it again, sweeping it on to the floor together with the shell. As Laura bent to retrieve them, the blood pounded in her head. Looking up, she saw something like rage in his face. For the first time, she felt afraid.

'Now you're s-satisfied, I suppose.' She caught the words over his shoulder as he turned to a switch on the wall. An old-fashioned fan hanging from the ceiling stirred into action, filling the silence with a regular stealthy creak like the sound of footsteps overhead. As he came close to her again, she saw sweat on his forehead. The clammy air in the room was pushed around in slow, repetitive circles.

'I'm sorry.' She stepped back, trying to speak calmly. 'I should never have come.'

Staring back at him, she was aware that he was making a desperate effort to regain control of the situation.

'It's just that . . .' he began. 'I mean, no one else can understand the workings of a marriage. Not even the child of that marriage. If you wanted to uncover the cracks in that relationship, I suppose you've succeeded. That's what I meant.'

'I've said I'm sorry.' She was searching for some kind of dignity in this wretched encounter. 'I only wanted it explained, the way things happened. Now I can understand.'

Even while she was speaking, she knew that nothing had been truly explained. Nor was there any question of understanding the strange contradictions and the suppressed violence of this man who was her father. Perhaps she never would.

'So now there is no need to go back, is there?' he said. 'To Taparua.'

Before she could reply, the door was opened behind them. 'Mister Goldman is come,' the woman told Harrington in her husky, sing-song voice. 'Lunch ready in one half hour.'

CHAPTER SIX

The transformation in her father's manner was dramatic. Almost immediately, as the visitor was shown in, Laura saw him become another person.

'This is an old friend of mine,' he told her, introducing the stocky, bearded man, a distinguished anthropologist from an American university.

Laura began making small talk. She had not expected company. But in a way it was useful to observe her father in his public persona as the academic guru and respected author dispensing wisdom and charm to the inquiring pilgrim.

'Perhaps now would be the moment to record our interview,' he suggested smoothly. 'Maurice will no doubt have some observations of his own to contribute.'

'A few footnotes, perhaps. Nothing to compete with your father,' Goldman replied, sampling his sherry. Behind his pebble-glasses, he studied Laura with new interest. 'This programme, it is for the BBC World Service?'

'Radio Four initially. But I expect it will go out on the World Service later.'

Goldman nodded with a satisfied air. 'Then it may be an excellent opportunity to mention my new book, on Polynesian kinship patterns.'

'Why not?' Laura said politely. She was hardly listening as she bent down to examine the machine. It was still running, with about another twenty minutes of tape still left. Returning with it, she saw her father watching her like a hawk.

'It was switched on earlier?' he asked, his eyes on the controls.

'No, no. I've just put it on for testing. It seems fine.'

Briskly she set up the hand mike and put the machine down on the coffee table between them.

'If you could just sit round it,' she said. 'Perhaps we could start with you, Father. How would you sum up the kind of changes you've seen in the Pacific over the past forty years?'

'Nearer fifty, in fact.' With practised ease, Harrington began to talk. Laura felt her nerves quietened by the familiar ritual of question and answer, as they covered the effects of the war on the local people, the changing role of the colonial administration, the kind of future that lay ahead with independence. Maurice Goldman was altogether less fluent, rambling on in his German-American accent about the commercialization of native customs now that the impact of the tourist industry had taken hold.

Laura nodded and encouraged in her usual way. But at the back of her mind another kind of tape was running, replaying the fragmented images she had acquired with such difficulty. Something of her mother – Millie – should have emerged by now, if only a ghost-like presence of the past. But it hadn't. Nothing seemed to fit. It was like trying to piece together two different jigsaw puzzles that had been jumbled up. Only one thing rang true, and that was an underlying sense of secrecy and fear. It was not just her mother's physical suffering that haunted her, but some psychological twist that remained uncovered.

Afterwards, around the lunch table, Laura continued to make mechanical conversation. In her father's face, she read relief that their confrontation was now almost over. Asking her about her work in London, he had taken on the manner of a proud father, leaning over to pat her hand from time to time. Though she tried to conceal it, she drew back from his touch. She knew that it was not just a scene being enacted for Goldman's benefit, but also a way of re-establishing his authority over her. No longer was he in the witness box, the gesture said. Once again he was in charge of his life, the threat of reopening the past successfully dealt with and removed.

'She has brains, this girl,' he told Goldman. 'Takes after her old father.'

'And her mother?' Goldman asked with genuine curiosity.

Immediately Harrington's expression closed up again. Turning to the servant, he snapped out some rebuke as she handed round the dish of kedgeree.

'My mother died when I was a small child.' Laura was about to go on, but Harrington interrupted.

'Always kedgeree on a Friday. But today it's not sufficiently seasoned. I apologize.'

Bread-and-butter pudding followed, also excellently cooked. Laura, who had expected traditional island specialities, had the feeling he was reliving the habits of university days. All the time she was aware of the servant's eyes on her face as she moved around the table. Once or twice, Laura looked up at her and smiled. But each time the woman lowered her gaze, her face impassive, as if to forestall any further contact.

'What is the name of your servant?' Laura asked her father when the woman was out of the room.

'Katua,' he replied shortly. 'A lazy creature. But she's been with me so long there's no changing her.'

'She's a Gilbertese.'

'How did you know?'

'The straight hair. The cheekbones. That reserve of manner.'

'You remember from so early an age?' Goldman put in.

'Not consciously. But something sinks in, I suppose.' She saw Harrington's wary look. 'And I have been reading up this part of the world over the past few weeks.'

'Perhaps you will make a journey to the Gilberts while you are here?' Goldman's question hung in the air.

Laura shook her head. 'Too far. Too difficult, my father says. Also, I have a deadline for getting back to London.'

It had become clear to her that any plans for such a trip must be kept to herself. There was no rational explanation for this decision, but instinct spoke more clearly.

Katua was at her side again, pouring coffee into one of the fragile Oriental cups laid out on a silver tray. As she handed it to Laura, she put a finger on her wrist, a butterfly touch but a deliberate one. Glancing up at her, Laura saw her raise her chin to point towards the back of the house. The gesture was brief but unmistakable. When she left, it should be that way.

She had a sudden urge to leave at once. The atmosphere of Harrington's house was claustrophobic. Fervently she hoped they would never meet again. And yet, and yet – the sense of unfinished business lingered powerfully. But first she needed time on her own to think, time to talk to Jack. And she had an appointment at Broadcasting House to keep.

She glanced at her watch. 'I'm sorry I have to break up the party. Is there a telephone I can use? Jack has given me a taxi number.'

'Jack?' Harrington's voice was sharp. Then he remembered. 'Ah yes, Jack Renfrey. I spoke to you there yesterday. You met him in Suva?'

'In London, just briefly. He's been showing me the sights of Suva today.'

Once again Laura felt the vital need to hide the truth. As far as

Harrington was concerned, Jack was simply a friendly guide, acting as liaison in her arrangements. His expression relaxed again.

'Clever young man. I know the family well, his father especially.'

'You must visit their estate on Vanua Levu,' Goldman told her. 'A perfect example of the old settler hierarchy, a modus vivendi of two totally different cultures, so to speak. Excellent material for your programme.'

'I must ask Jack to try and arrange it.' She pushed back her chair and stood up. 'So, if you'll excuse me . . .'

Harrington waved his hand towards the adjoining room. 'The telephone's in my study. You might see one or two things of interest in there.'

In the study she closed the door behind her, simply so that she could lean back against it and take a deep breath. She felt cold suddenly, the perspiration chilling her back under her dress. The ordeal was nearly over.

As she lifted the telephone, her eyes fell on the one thing that had the power to take her back immediately to Taparua. The moths. How could she have forgotten them? She stared at the wall above the desk with its framed collection of outsize tropical specimens, so horribly familiar to her as a small girl. In that instant, she was standing perched on a chair in her father's office, her face pressed against the glass-fronted cabinet that held them.

'You mustn't,' her mother had told her so many times. But there was an awful fascination about those rows of fat dead bodies, each one pinned through the centre, the speckled wings outstretched and still. Why did he kill them, she had wanted to know? But her mother had only pulled her away, so violently that the back of the chair had fallen against the glass. A splinter flew out, catching her on the cheek. At the same moment the tall figure of her father had appeared. The fear she had felt was even stronger than the shock of seeing her own blood staining her father's handkerchief as he whipped it across her face, catching the cut with the starched edge, once, twice and then again. She could never forget the stinging pain of it, but far more frightening to a child was the rage that had produced it. She remembered her mother bundling her away, and then the scene faded.

The phone was still buzzing in her hand. Mechanically she dialled the number and ordered a car from the Indian voice at the other end.

As she replaced the receiver her eyes wandered around the rest of the room, so full of her father's presence. The heart of the spider's web, she said to herself. It was an irrational image. Why it sprang to mind she couldn't explain. But there was a sense of patient cunning and cruelty, too, that somehow belonged to this musty lair of his, stocked with the carefully preserved acquisitions of a lifetime.

Alongside the moths hung other displays under glass, Pacific butterflies, insect life and dried plants, all carefully numbered and inscribed in her father's microscopic hand. There were also some stuffed sea-birds, perhaps the half-forgotten explanation for her dream on the plane. Ranged on the shelves below were what looked like medical specimens of some kind. Drawn against her will, Laura moved over for a closer look. With a sick feeling she saw they were items of pathology, no doubt curiosities from his surgical operations in the primitive dispensaries of island villages, things like gallstones, a coiled-up piece of intestine, an amputated finger even, all suspended in murky-looking jars of preserving fluid.

Laura shuddered. What kind of man would want to keep such things after all these years? When she came to the jar containing a tiny embryo curled up like a snail, she could bear it no longer. Turning away, she found herself looking into the face of Harrington as a young man. It was an image no larger than a postage stamp, set in the centre of a long row of other Cambridge graduates of some long-ago summer. But even in the anonymity of a group photograph, Lawrence Harrington stood out from the rest, with his blond Greek god features and brooding stare. Was this how her mother had seen him, even several years on, a personality so compelling that she would agree to share his life on one of the loneliest islands in the world?

From ceiling to floor, the walls on either side were lined with books. Harrington's library of Pacific history was famous, and Laura could see why as she ran her eye along the rows of biography, exploration, botany and anthropology, the titles faded and obscure on the peeling leather bindings. On an impulse she lifted out a slim volume with no name on the cover. As she opened it a wriggling silverfish fell onto her sleeve. She brushed it away with distaste. The insects are eating the past away, she thought, taking their revenge on the human predators in their midst. Then, with a shock, she saw the photographs, ugly sepia reproductions of naked men and women in sexual poses, the kind of scholarly pornography that obsessed the explorer Burton in Arabia. This was some mouldering treatise on the customs and taboos of the Tokelau islanders, the margins scattered with notes in her father's hand, the magenta ink spreading its stain from page to page.

Quickly replacing it, she scrubbed at her fingers with a tissue from her bag. The whiff of damp and decay seemed to have impregnated every corner of the place. Not so much revulsion as panic swept over her. It was as if she had become a prisoner in this room, a specimen of 'daughter' to be added to Harrington's collection.

She turned to the door and found her way barred by a shadow.

'Father.' Her voice shook on the word. The tall figure was standing on the threshold as if he had been there for some minutes.

'You've been inspecting my archives. You found them interesting?'

'Very.' She was suddenly short of breath, as if she had been running.

At the sound of his voice, there had been a faint rustling movement from the far corner of the room. Now the sound came again. Harrington glanced past her with that sardonic half-smile.

'You didn't realize someone was in here with you?'

He walked to an alcove on the far side of the room and pulled aside a green baize hanging she had failed to notice. Startled, she saw a bird peer out at them from the bars of a large cage, a dark glossy creature with bright eyes and a yellow beak. Seeing Harrington, it began to flap its wings in an agitated fashion, making short broken cries that were almost human, the sounds Laura had heard from beneath the house.

'His name is Nevermore,' Harrington said. 'You remember Edgar Allan Poe? "Quoth the raven, Nevermore".'

'Nevermore.' The bird repeated the word solemnly, in a caricature of Harrington's reedy voice.

It was comical in a way. Yet to Laura it seemed curiously eerie too, another example of her father's obsessive need to exert control.

'A tropical branch of the raven family,' he went on. 'Mynah birds, in fact, are one of the cleverest species in the world. In India they're supposed to have supernatural powers, being reincarnations of priests and holy men.' He brought out a piece of sugar from his pocket and poked it through the bars. But just as the bird reached out with its beak, he withdrew it again. 'First you must say your mantra.'

The bird twisted its head to one side, listening while Harrington spoke two or three words, this time in Gilbertese. There was a pause. Then, like a wind up toy, it opened its beak and repeated them, once, twice, three times, hoarsely at the back of its throat.

'What is that?' Laura asked.

'Just a local saying. Something to ward off bad luck when you're going on a journey.' He glanced at her slyly. 'It should get you safely back to London.'

Laura had the distinct feeling that he was referring to some other journey. She wondered whether the mantra might be some traditional message of spite, the kind of casual spell you put on an old enemy.

From its cage, the bird was still repeating the same words, as if the mechanism had got stuck.

'That's enough!' Harrington pulled a string and the baize cover rattled down over the bars again. He had not given the bird the sugar, Laura noticed.

'Is he never let out?' she asked. Laura was now quite certain of a deep-rooted mental imbalance in the man, something she couldn't yet define but which frightened her nevertheless.

'Once a day. The door of the cage is left open. He always flies back in again. The prisoner needs his prison, it seems.'

He came back to her, standing close to her face.

'Why are you staring at me?' she asked.

Her whole body felt weak, as if some vital source of energy was being sapped away, and when he suddenly, outrageously, reached out to her, she was powerless to move. The touch of his fingers on the nipple of her right breast was so light, so momentary, she might almost have imagined it. She stepped back as if she had been burned. Once again, just for a split second, she was a child again, her father bending over her, and it hurt.

'No!' The nightmare broke off. The flash of recall was gone. The reality was the old man standing so close she could smell the menthol on his breath.

'Why are you so frightened of me?' He was looking at her calmly. 'I was only teasing. We used to be so close when you were small.'

She was still rigid with shock, backed up now against the doorway. 'How can you?' she replied in a whisper. 'How could you?'

He shrugged his shoulders. 'You were the one who wanted us to meet again. Why all the fuss?'

'You think I don't remember?'

His face changed. He gripped her by the wrist.

'What are you accusing me of?'

Before she could reply, he shook off his grasp. 'Frigid like your mother. I should have known.'

'My mother is the reason I'm here.' She flung the words back at him, beside herself now with fury. 'And the reason I'm staying.'

She didn't wait to see his reaction. Turning sharply, she left him there. Back in the dining room Goldman was still sitting at the table, sipping his coffee, turning the pages of his notes. She realized she had only been out of the room for five minutes. In those five minutes, her whole sense of herself had changed for ever. She felt violated, pierced to the quick, and yet she felt a new strength that was almost ruthless.

'Do you feel all right?' Goldman asked her. 'You look pale.'

'I'm fine,' she said coldly. She snatched up her tape-recorder. 'But I must go. The taxi will be waiting. Goodbye, and thanks for the interview.'

'Car is there, marama.' Katua's voice came from the back verandah. 'I show you down.'

As they left, Harrington entered the room again. Once more the host, he rejoined Goldman at the table. 'You'll keep in touch then, Laura?' he called after her.

Laura did not reply. She was hurrying after Katua down into the back garden where the path led out to a narrow lane. She had a glimpse of the taxi waiting.

Halfway down the path, both women stopped. Oleander bushes had grown wild on either side, shielding them from the house. Katua put her hand on Laura's arm.

'He will come out on to the verandah, look to see us.'

Laura took hold of the woman's hand. 'How do you know me?'

'When you are just a small baby, I take care for you. I was young girl then. My father is Timu. He brings me from the village to work in the house.' Katua spoke rapidly, in an undertone, squeezing Laura's hand tight. Laura saw fear in her face, but determination too.

'My mother was sick?'

'At first too weak. Then she get well again, only she cry, cry all the time.'

Laura felt her heart contract. 'Go on.'

'Every day we women take her 'long beach when it is cool.' Her face broke into a sudden smile, her eyes bright again, looking into Laura's. 'But your father give medicine. Your mother get sick again, sleepy sick lying in her bed.'

'You were there when she died?'

Katua shook her head. 'War come. I have to go away. After, they tell me you leave on the ship, and later your father too. But your mother . . .' She lifted her shoulders helplessly. 'That poor lady. Maybe the Japs kill her.'

'My father said she died before the Japanese came.'

Again Katua shrugged. 'Nobody knows.'

'Timu, your father,' Laura said urgently. 'He is still alive?'

'Still on Taparua.' She began to hurry on. 'You see him there.'

'And you?' Laura was suddenly aware of the risks Katua was running. 'How did you come here?'

'Doctor send for me. There was no other thing to do. Here in Fiji I have his baby. Since then, two more. If I do not obey, my father lose his job.'

Both of them looked towards the house. They saw no sign of Harrington. Once again, Katua gripped Laura by the arm, and led her over to the tall mango tree which dominated the garden. Rotten fruit lay everywhere, drawing flies to its sickly-sweet smell. Katua pointed behind the tree where a large bonfire still smouldered.

'Yesterday he burn all these things, papers, pictures, letters. But I think maybe you see something?'

Laura bent over the charred remains. 'Nothing.'

But Katua had seized the rake lying nearby. Turning over some scraps of paper, she suddenly stopped. 'Look. Some picture.'

Bending down, she picked up what looked like an ancient wallet that was still intact. Laura took it from her, hardly daring to breathe. Both women leaned close and saw, tucked into the front, the picture of a woman.

'It is your mother,' Katua said gently.

A call broke in from the verandah. They started apart.

'He is there. I have to go back. Go quick.' She kissed Laura on the cheek. 'Your mother with you now.'

Laura held on to her for a moment. 'Thank you. Thank you, Katua,' she murmured, before breaking away and running towards the gate, the wallet thrust into her pocket. Only when she was sitting in the taxi, only when Harrington's house was out of sight, did she take it out again.

She found herself staring down at the blurred figure of a woman, tall and slender in crumpled slacks and shirt. It was only a snapshot, taken in bright sunlight, faded now to a dull brown. She could see palm trees behind, and a wooden house on stilts. But it was the face that held her, such a small sad face like a little boy's under a crop of fair curls. The wide-apart eyes were screwed up against the dazzle, as if puzzled by some unanswered question.

Laura's heart turned over with pity. Where was I that day, she wondered? Had I already been sent away? Or was I not even born? For the first time she felt tears come.

'Millie,' she murmured. She pressed her lips to the face. 'Mother.'

CHAPTER SEVEN

Out of the turmoil of her emotions, other questions began to surface as the car sped back to Suva. Why had her father tried to destroy the photograph? More important, why had he lied to her about its existence in the first place? And what other records of her mother's life had he put into the fire?

But there was no time now to think about any of this. Almost immediately, it seemed, the driver was pulling up outside a white stucco block just across the road from Government Buildings.

'Broadcasting House,' the young Indian said, turning in his seat.

Laura was sure he had seen her crying in his mirror. Perhaps he was used to passengers who gave way to their pain in the privacy of the back seat. In any case, she was grateful to him for not starting up a conversation during the drive.

'You okay, memsahib?' was all he said as she paid him off.

'Yes, I'm okay. Thanks.'

In fact, she was still in a state of shock. That moment with her father in his study had touched a nerve from childhood nightmares. But overshadowing even this was the horror of the thought that her mother had suffered something far worse. Whatever it was, she was almost certain that in some way her father was responsible. His pathological need to cover up the past lay at the root of her suspicions. What threat did it hold for him?

She thought of Jack. She felt a longing to be alone with him, to pour out all that had happened over the last two hours, feel his arms around her as he listened. But first she had to regain some kind of control over herself. Perhaps it was just as well she now had to turn her mind to practical matters.

Quickly pushing her hair into place, she presented herself at the reception desk. The warm smile of the buxom young Fijian woman had a wonderfully calming effect. Yes, Mr Curtis was expecting her.

'He's the guy who deals with tapes and all that stuff. In Recording, the door at the end of the corridor.'

It was good to find herself back again in the familiar atmosphere of a radio station, even one in the middle of the Pacific. At first glimpse the Fiji Broadcasting Commission seemed like a microcosm of Broadcasting House, London – red and green lights on the studio doors, the air of controlled panic as people with tapes and clipboards hurried past, and snatches of voice and music floating into the corridors. As she walked she picked up an Australian quiz show, a BBC drama serial, a bubbling song in Hindustani, the sonorous tones of a Fijian newsreader, and a Tongan choir rehearsing the *Messiah*. The place was a kind of aural melting-pot, an *Alice in Wonderland* mix going out on separate wave lengths to a thousand scattered islands and half a dozen different races.

'But we're all Fijians officially,' Bob Curtis told her. 'Fijian-born, Fiji passports – with independence coming that's the important thing. We'll be a nation then, remember, not one of your downtrodden colonies.'

He twinkled at her, teasing her, a tubby brown-skinned man with a grey crew cut and darting black eyes that seemed to sum her up shrewdly.

'That's exactly what I've come to find out about,' Laura answered.

'Good on you. At least you'll be able to tell them the FBC's not just a microphone under a palm tree.'

The sign on Mr Curtis's door read 'Head of Engineering'. Inside it was less imposing, a cramped little control room with windows looking on to studios on each side, old-fashioned dubbing and editing machines in every corner, and stacks of tapes that reached to the ceiling. A Coca-Cola with a drinking straw and a takeaway box of curry stood amongst the papers on the desk.

'You had some lunch?' he asked politely.

'Yes, thanks.'

He'd taken his shoes off and was padding neatly about his domain in bare feet, like a sailor.

'So. You've got some recordings to be sent on to BBC. How's the work going?'

'I haven't had time to do all that much yet.' Laura handed him the tapes from her bag. 'This is a visit to one of the hill villages, near where I'm staying. And some stuff I did on the first tape at the airport hotel to cover the tourist side of things.'

'I expect you'll need new batteries in your machine, a check-up and so on. I see there's something still on it.'

Laura watched him deftly rewind the tape.

'That's something I've just done,' she said quickly. 'I've been talking to Dr Lawrence Harrington.' She hesitated. 'He's my father.'

Curtis's reaction was familiar. 'Didn't know he had a family.' There was the same wary expression on his face, too, as he glanced up at her. 'I don't know him personally. But he's certainly a famous name in these parts.'

For some reason Laura felt she could trust this man. 'The thing is, Mr Curtis . . .' she began.

'Bob, please.'

'The thing is, Bob, the first part of the recording is a private conversation. I'd like to have a copy of it, to keep for myself, you understand.'

'I understand.' Without further explanation he handed her a pair of headphones. 'I'll dub it off for you if you make the cut.'

'Thanks. I need to listen back anyway – I'm not sure if it was picking up some of the time.' She looked at him directly. 'I had the machine on without his knowing.'

Curtis raised an eyebrow but said no more, turning to busy himself with the other tapes. Laura sat down in the chair he'd pulled out for her in the corner. She took a deep breath, pressed the start button and closed her eyes.

As soon as she heard her father's first words, faint and blurred as they were, Laura knew this was a moment printed on her mind for ever. For one thing, ridiculous as it sounded, here was proof that the whole encounter had actually taken place as she remembered it. It was not just a bad dream, growing monstrously in her imagination with every passing moment. The strain of talking face to face with her father meant that the exact sequence of question and answer was already confused in her memory. But here it all was – or most of it – preserved for ever on that narrow ribbon of brown plastic spinning its way between the two small spindles in front of her.

Inside her head, her concentration tightly focused, she was hearing not just words but the way those words had been put together. A professional listener could pick up so many nuances from a fractional hesitation, or the tiniest change in the tone of a voice. Where her father was concerned, they might point to the vital difference between what was true and what was false.

She bent closer and caught the tremor in his voice as he spoke of the pain of recalling memories of his wife. Now it seemed to signal nervousness rather than grief, she thought. 'Malaria,' he said. 'Two weeks before the evacuation ship came through.' There was a gathering of speed as if he wanted to skim over this part of the story so that he barely touched the surface.

But the violence with which he'd dashed the oyster locket to the floor was unmistakable, the hatred audible in his very movements. And in his angry opposition to her plan to return to the islands, the emotion rang true. For an instant she thought she heard something like panic in his voice.

The conversation came to an end, fading away as Maurice Goldman came into the room. A few minutes later, the formal interview with the two men began. With shaky fingers, Laura stuck a yellow marker onto the tape. She took off her headphones and turned to Bob.

'From here on can go to London,' she told him. 'The first part is just for me. If you could put it onto a separate reel, that'd be fine.'

'You'd like a copy?' Bob asked with that look of his that seemed to say rather more. 'If it's important. I don't need to listen to it, just put it on the machine,' he added.

She nodded. 'That's kind. It is important.'

He returned his attention to her tape-recorder, tapping through the controls with the same deft touch. 'So, what's next on the agenda?'

'More interviews, planters, politicians and so on. Then I have some things to sort out on my own account. Family history, you might say.'

Bob Curtis paused for a minute, looking thoughtful. 'I shouldn't put too much into exploring these roots of yours. Can be more trouble than it's worth.'

Laura was startled. 'How do you mean?'

He was laughing. 'Look at me. My great-grandfather was hanged for assaulting the ship's captain on the way over from Samoa to Fiji. Much good it would do me to go digging up that kind of past. Especially as the Curtis family are a pretty respectable lot nowadays.'

'I believe you.'

Bob had his eye on the glass door leading to the corridor. 'Look out. Here's Dave Luana – Fiji's answer to Mick Jagger. I think he wants to get you on his chat show.'

The face of the young man who came sauntering into the room was submerged under goggle-sized dark glasses. When he removed them, his good looks were striking. Even the psychedelic sweatshirt failed to cheapen the classic Polynesian face, with its broad cheekbones and dark brooding stare. More the young Brando than Jagger, Laura thought, as he shook hands languidly.

'So you're the BBC lady, come to do a Big Sister check-up on the little FBC?'

Laura smiled. 'Hardly.'

'Laura is the daughter of Dr Harrington,' Bob told him.

'The great white guru of Pacific history.' Dave's tone was politely sardonic.

'Dave here is a prophet of the future,' Bob told her. 'Deeply into the new Marxism, overthrow of the feudal system, colonial governors, hereditary chiefs, the lot. You should hear his independence song. Gone straight to the top of the charts in Fiji. Hot stuff, man.' He winked at Laura.

'Perhaps I could have a recording for my programme,' she said to Dave. 'Do a few minutes' interview.'

The brooding gaze brightened. 'Great! But first I need you to talk to me. I put on this afternoon programme live – *Dave's Desert Island Discs*.'

Laura laughed. 'I've heard that before.'

'There's no copyright, is there?' Dave's eyes glittered. 'The title should belong to us, we're surrounded by desert islands. Anyway, it's only a gimmick. You don't choose the records, I do. All you have to do is chat to me.' He treated her to a smile of huge charm. 'A lady of your gifts, should be no problem.'

'Interviewers make the worst interviewees, you know,' she warned him.

'Well let's give it a whizz.' He placed a hand on her elbow. 'I'm on in five minutes. It's the next studio.'

'Maybe you'll rustle up some response for your own programme,' Bob called after her as they went through the door. 'You may hear from some people out there who want to talk to you.'

The words threw a switch in her mind that had nothing to do with her programme. If I'm to start searching for the truth about my mother I need all the help I can get, she said to herself as she sat down at the microphone. Opposite her Dave greeted his listeners with his theme song, lined up on the cassette player at his elbow.

'Wake up my people!
Independence Day is near!
Put on your dancing skirts
Go out and cheer!'

The whine of electric guitars died away. As he introduced her, Laura felt suddenly apprehensive. She talked about her broadcasting career, her travels to other countries, her impressions of Fiji. More records were played and all the time she was looking for the right opening. When it came, the palms of her hands were sweating as if it was her first moment on radio.

'You've been meeting up again with your famous father, I hear, Dr Lawrence Harrington?'

'Yes. It's been a fascinating reunion.' She skipped a beat. 'But I'm really much more interested in finding out something about my mother.'

'Your mother?' Dave asked, neatly on cue.

'Yes, I know so little about her except that she was an American. She died when I was very young, just after I was evacuated from the islands during the war.'

'Your father must have told you something about her?' He sounded genuinely puzzled.

'He has,' she said smoothly. This was where she must be careful, guard every word she said. 'But he's so busy with his current work – university plans, and so on – he's rather put the past behind him. So I've decided to explore it myself.'

'How will you set about doing that? Do you have any other contacts here in Fiji?'

'There's Jack Renfrey, someone I knew in London. He knows everyone. He'll be a great help,' she said almost without thinking. 'Then I'll try to get out to the Gilberts, back to my home island. See if there are people still around with memories of her. I also want to experience for myself what it was like for a solitary European woman to settle in such an isolated spot. More isolated thirty years ago than it is now, of course.'

Dave was glancing up at the clock, making wind-up movements with his hand.

'Her name was Millie.' It was an inconsequential final remark, but Laura threw it out like a lifeline. It might just catch someone's memory, somewhere out there.

'So maybe you'll make another programme before you go back, one about your own family,' he said quickly, drawing a line under the conversation.

'Maybe. It would be something to keep at least. Something to remember her by.'

She heard the emotion in her voice. Dave looked up, startled.

'Thank you, Laura Harrington. And the best of luck with your quest.' He released the turntable on 'Sergeant Pepper's Lonely Hearts Band'.

'That was great,' he told her above the familiar Liverpool voices that reminded her of Jack and Carnaby Street. 'And we'll make a date for that chat for your programme.'

'We certainly will. As soon as I'm back from my travels.' To his surprise, and hers, she kissed him lightly on the cheek.

'And thanks, Dave. I enjoyed it.'

'Enjoyed' was the wrong word. But she was aware of the restorative adrenalin still racing through her as she made her way out. Next door, in the main studio, Bob Curtis was busy recording the Tongan choir. He gave her a thumbs-up sign as she collected the new tapes and the machine he'd left ready for her. 'Off the Record – Laura and Lawrence Harrington', he'd scrawled across the box containing her conversation with her father. Carefully she placed it separately from the others in her shoulder bag. It felt as if she had a hand grenade in there, or a small dangerous animal that might draw blood if she put her hand inside without thinking.

CHAPTER EIGHT

Outside, the cloudy sky had cleared. Walking across the lawns to Government Buildings, she felt the full heat of the afternoon sun strike down on her. It was that time of day in the tropics when everything looks strangely still and deserted. Even the clock in the tower seemed to have stopped, like a freeze-frame in a film. But when she stepped up to the main entrance, she saw that two minutes had gone by. Perhaps it was just that the world moved at a different speed here, slowed down to the minimum of effort required to do anything at all.

A Fijian policeman in a white fringed kilt and scarlet cummerbund stood to attention as she walked through the imposing doorway. She was about to ask him for directions to the Legal Department when a voice she recognized immediately hailed her from the other side of the hall.

'Miss Harrington! Laura Harrington!'

In front of the lifts stood the tall figure of Ratu Edwin, one hand raised in statuesque greeting. His pinstripe suit was in the Fijian style of jacket and wrap-around sulu. The polished bronze face wore its usual mischievous smile.

'I've been trying to track you down, elusive lady,' he told her. 'But now here you are, and a bird in the hand is worth two in the bush, as they say.'

At once, Laura felt reassurance in his presence. She had forgotten the old-fashioned English of his speech, no doubt a relic of public-schooldays, and how endearing it was.

'I was going to telephone you myself,' she replied. 'You said if I ever needed any advice . . .'

The lift doors opened and several people walked out, glancing at Ratu Edwin and his companion with interest. Now there were just the two of them, stepping inside together.

'I'm on my way to see Jack,' she told him. 'Jack Renfrey.'

'So I imagined. Can you spare me a few minutes first?'

'Of course.'

Her eyes met his. That sense of affinity she had felt on the plane was still there.

'Something disturbing's happened to you since we were on that plane,' he said in a low voice. 'I can read it in your face.'

'More than one thing.'

With a click the doors slid open.

'My office is just here, on the left. A bowl of grog should refresh us both,' he added with a comically secretive wink.

It was a tall room with long windows overlooking the Albert Park, photographs of cricket and rugby teams on the walls, and one of Ratu Edwin himself in animated conversation with the Queen. In the corner, tucked away amongst the filing cabinets, an elderly Fijian sat cross-legged behind a huge wooden bowl. Laura watched him dip a coconut cup into the murky grey liquid inside and move across on his knees to proffer it to Ratu Edwin. Graciously Edwin waved him in her direction.

'It's kava, "yangona" we call it in Fiji. Made from the root of a pepper plant. You've tried it before?'

'Never.'

'Take it at a gulp. That's the proper way.'

Obediently Laura drained the cup, aware of the kava-server's severe gaze. There was a cool sting at the back of her throat, something like a minty flavour. For a few seconds, her mouth felt numb.

'Is it medicinal?'

'Therapeutic, I should say. Relaxes the nerves. No serious conversation is complete without it. That's why I have it in my office. We're rather good at combining ancient and modern in Fiji. Maybe you've noticed.'

'I saw them serving it to you when you landed at the airport.'

'That's the formal ceremony, for special occasions. It goes with the speeches and the presentation of sacred whale's tooth – then the songs and the dances, of course.'

He smiled, somewhat wearily, as he accepted his own cup with a clap of his hands. Laura watched him drink to the dregs then slide the shell back across the mat with a kind of spin-bowler's flourish that was obviously de rigueur in aristocratic circles. She felt suddenly shy. Ratu Edwin's whole manner was a disconcerting mixture of Western panache and Polynesian dignity. What interest could this extraordinary personage have in her private affairs?

The kava-server retreated from the room and they were alone again, sitting on either side of an immense desk. Ratu Edwin turned a gold pencil between his fingers, his eyes on her face as if reading her thoughts.

'I won't keep you. But I remembered you telling me on the plane that you wanted to go back to the Gilberts, back to your home island if possible. I'm afraid I discouraged you a little, saying how inaccessible they were.'

She nodded. 'I know. Everyone says the same thing.'

'You may take heart to hear that visits do occur at least twice in a blue moon. Only yesterday I was informed that I am expected to make a visit there myself. Next week. I'll be based at Government headquarters at Tarawa, but if you could be there at the same time, I could try and arrange a boat on to Taparua for you.'

A wave of gratitude ran through her. 'That's really kind of you. It would make all the difference. And I do need to go back there, now more than ever.' She hesitated. 'I've seen my father, talked to him just this morning.'

His expression sharpened as he leaned across the desk towards her. 'What happened?'

'It – it was very upsetting. I feel . . .'

There was a tap on the door. A young Fijian clerk came in with a sheaf of papers in his hand. He glanced politely at Laura before handing them to Ratu Edwin.

'The Minister of Lands is due in a few minutes, Ratu.'

'I hadn't forgotten.'

The young man went out, and Laura and Ratu Edwin stood up together.

'You'll let me know your arrangements?' he said. 'And if you need a booking on the plane out to the Gilberts, I should be able to arrange it for you. In case there's any problem.'

'I can't thank you enough. Can I contact you? As soon as I've sorted things out?' She found herself blushing.

Ratu Edwin smiled. 'Jack Renfrey may be coming with you?'

'I hope so. I'm staying with him at Vailima, you see. He knows about . . .' She broke off, smiling back at him, then went on. 'Well, about everything really. I need him with me, don't you think?'

Ratu Edwin simply held out his hand and bowed gracefully. 'A travelling lady always needs protection. Especially one who is young and beautiful.'

'Tomorrow,' she told him. 'I'll be in touch tomorrow.'

'Oh, Laura,' he called after her. She turned. It pleased her somehow to hear him use her Christian name. 'Jack's office is just three doors along.' Again, she caught that teasing look. 'I'm sure he'll be waiting for you.'

Jack was holding the phone in his hand and frowning as she went in.

'That was a mistake, wasn't it?' he said sharply, putting down the receiver.

'What was?' She was halfway across the room to him, not even sure whether he had been speaking to her or to someone at the other end of the line.

'Telling the world there was some kind of mystery about your mother's death, and you're haring off to the Gilberts to solve it. I heard you on that ghastly programme of Dave Luana's. The whole thing sounded so cheap. You might at least have talked to me first. Now the *Fiji Times* are on to me, to fix up an interview with you.'

'But Jack!' She was so taken aback she could hardly find words. 'This is important. Something's happened.'

'How do you expect people here to take your programme seriously? It's their story you're supposed to be covering, not some kind of family soap opera. Then I'm dragged into it, if you like. Have you any idea what kind of place this is for gossip and scandal? As for your father, heaven knows how he'll react.'

'My father!' These were the words that lit the fuse. 'My God! If you only knew . . .' She turned on him furiously as the words tumbled out. 'The man is a monster. You don't know what I've just endured, what I've found out about him, and my mother. My mother . . .'

Despite herself, she felt herself crumple. Fighting sobs, she struggled on. But Jack's face was shocked. The next second he had drawn her into his arms.

'Darling! My darling! Whatever happened?'

He led her towards the nearest chair and crouched down in front of her.

Half ashamed of herself, Laura put her hands up to her face.

'If he's upset you like this, I'm going straight up to see him. What on earth's been going on? You must tell me, slowly, calmly.'

Jack's voice sounded a long way off.

With a great effort she gathered her wits together. Then, with his hand in hers, she sat up straight in the chair and began to explain. The hardest part was to convey to him this awful conviction that the truth was being kept from her, that what had really happened to her mother had been wiped away for ever.

As she talked, she watched Jack's expression. It was a lawyer's expression, dispassionately concentrating on sifting the evidence that was being presented to him. She saw puzzlement cross his face, then distaste, and finally sheer disbelief. She had come to the moment of the final encounter in her father's study.

'He touched me, here.' She laid her hand on her right breast. 'I could hardly believe it. And then I had a kind of flashback to myself on the island, the way he had touched me as a child. I believe I was abused by him sexually, regularly. The worst thing is, he still has . . . still . . .' She found herself stumbling. 'Still has those feelings about me. It's horrible, Jack. I can't explain.'

'My God.'

Jack smoothed back her hair, staring into her eyes. Then he stood up abruptly. Pushing his chair away, he passed his hand over his face several times, as if awakening from a bad dream.

'I can't believe it,' he said finally. 'It just doesn't make sense.'

'But Jack!' she cried. 'The man himself doesn't make sense. He's a psychotic case, someone who can't tell good from evil, who has no control over himself.'

'And you believe he treated your mother cruelly?'

'Worse than that,' Laura said softly.

Jack turned back and bent over her, his hands on her shoulders. 'You seem to be saying that he might actually have killed her.'

She took a deep breath. 'That he might somehow have been the cause of her death.'

'But Laura.' He sat down facing her. 'Listen. Don't you think you've been letting that imagination of yours run loose? After all, it's been a traumatic experience, this reunion with your father.' He leaned forward and pushed her hair behind her ears. 'Okay, so you took a violent dislike to the man. A lot of women hate their fathers, for one reason or another. And I grant you, Harrington is an oddball, highly eccentric to say the least, even a bit of a sinister figure perhaps, living out there on his own in that peculiar house. But honestly, to label him a murderer and a child molester sounds like fantasy to me.'

'Then why does he have to conceal the past, if not to protect himself? Why did he have to get rid of this, for instance, the minute he knew I was coming?'

Angrily she pulled out the photograph from her pocket. Jack took it from her. She saw him study it with a look of pity, tenderness even.

'She looks like you.' He handed it back to her. 'It's so sad. Can't you understand that he may want to bury all those memories? Then you come along and start raking everything up again.'

'Don't worry,' Laura said, half to herself. 'I've only just started.' Her head close to his, she looked up at him with all the urgency she could summon. 'You'll help me, Jack, won't you? You'll come with me?'

'Come with you where?'

'Back to the Gilberts.' Her voice quickened. 'I haven't told you the rest. His servant comes from Taparua. She told me her father still lives there. It seems I'm meant to go, somehow. Just a few minutes ago I met Ratu Edwin. He's offered to arrange transport for us.'

'I'm afraid the "us" is out of the question, Laura.' He had moved away from her and was standing behind his desk, turning the pages of one of the files laid open on it. 'I can't possibly get away for weeks on end. Especially now.'

'What do you mean, especially now?' Disappointment was a physical thing, dropping through her like a stone. To be let down by Jack at this moment was more than she could bear.

'That's one of the things we need to talk about.' His eyes were still on his papers. 'I heard from the Australian government this morning. They want me to go to Canberra for an interview about a job in the legal department.'

'When?'

'Next week. I had this idea that you could come with me. See how you like the set-up there. Then maybe . . .' His words died away. He was staring at her now with his lover's look, sensual and secret. At a stroke, all uncertainty vanished.

'Jack.' She went over to him and put her arms round his neck, raising her mouth to his. It was a long kiss that had nothing to do with where they stood or what they were saying, locking them into that dimension they had miraculously invented for themselves. With an effort, she drew away. 'I want it too. I want us to be together, to stay together. It feels absolutely the right thing for both of us. But first . . .' She touched his cheek gently. 'But first I have to do this other thing, for my mother and for myself.'

'And I have to do my thing. So that's that.'

To her surprise his tone was petulant. His mouth tightened into an expression that was almost sulky, the thick tawny hair falling over his eyes. This was a Jack she had not yet encountered, though she remembered hints of it in London, Jack the spoilt only son of rich and adoring parents, the legal prodigy and social charmer.

'But surely things won't change between us,' she said, bewildered. 'Even if we do have to go our separate ways for a short time.'

He shook his head obstinately. 'I see it as a turning point, Laura. Once I'm out there I may have to stay for quite a while. And we've only just found each other again. How can we be apart for weeks, not even a backward glance? I know how easily you can block me out of your mind, Laura. Either we stick together or we don't. Can't you see that?'

She was silent, trying to absorb what was happening between them.

'Here you are, planning to go on this wild goose chase,' he went on. 'In search of what? Proof of some supposed misdeeds of thirty years ago? And now you tell me you've dragged poor old Ratu Edwin into the plot.'

Something in her sparked at that. 'That's rubbish! It's an offer he made himself, out of pure friendship!'

'Friendship!' Jack's voice was scornful. 'You hardly know him.'

'Besides, it's not just about my mother's death. I want some evidence of who she was. I've spent my whole life wondering, and without it I'm not sure I know who I am myself. Don't you realize that I still know virtually nothing about her, not even her maiden name, or anything about her family at all?'

As she spoke she saw Jack's expression change.

'Listen, Laura. You want evidence. Let's go and look for it, here and now.'

'What do you mean?'

'If you can see your mother's death certificate with the details of who she was, when she married, how she died, then will you be satisfied?'

Laura hesitated. 'What do we have to do?'

'Come with me.' He was putting his jacket on. 'We'll go together to the Registrar's Department. They have archives there going back to before the war. It shouldn't take long. I know the clerk there.'

With his long, impatient stride, Jack was out of the door and half-way down the corridor before she understood what was happening. He wanted the mystery solved – now. Hurrying to keep up with him, she found herself going down in the lift again and out into the grounds. She had imagined the registry archives to be in some dusty vault in the basement, but instead they were walking into the gardens of Government House, towards a modest white-painted chalet under the trees. Young people who looked like students sat around the long tables on the verandah making notes from the files and books in front of them. The clerk behind the desk turned out to be a Gauguin-like girl in a loose cotton dress patterned with red hibiscus flowers, her hair twisted into a multitude of tiny plaits.

'No problem,' was her response to Jack's request. 'Take about ten minutes.'

While they waited, neither felt like talking. Jack leafed through the colony's Law Reports on one of the library shelves. Laura found herself turning the pages of some nineteenth-century missionary diaries. Was her mother able to cope as these Victorian wives had to, she wondered, facing childbirth in such primitive and dangerous places, and then the day-to-day, year-by-year isolation among strangers? At least they had husbands who cared for them, she thought. Whereas Millie Harrington . . .

With a start, she came back to the present. The clerk was beckoning them over to the verandah.

'I have the records. Perhaps you'd like to sit out here to study them. It's more pleasant, isn't it?'

She bestowed a ravishing smile on Jack, then left them together at one of the long tables that was shaded by the purple bougainvillea growing outside. They sat down side by side, a battered-looking bound volume between them. Laura found it difficult to focus on the page that lay open between them, her heart was beating so fast. Leaning forward, she watched Jack's finger run along the various entries on the yellowing certificate. Under 'Name of the Deceased', someone had printed in fading red ink, 'Harrington Millie'.

So Millie was all the name she had. Laura had expected something more. 'Millie' was so insubstantial, childish even. To her intense disappointment there was no note of a maiden name either. The date of birth had also been left blank. Wife of Lawrence Harrington, the details continued, District Commissioner, HM Colonial Service. Died Taparua, Gilbert Islands, 9 January 1942. Cause of death was the final entry. Two words were roughly printed here – malaria/tuberculosis. Somehow this double diagnosis confused her. It was as if one had been added to support the other, and neither was strong enough to stand alone.

'He told me malaria,' she murmured.

'I expect the TB was a chronic condition.' Jack sounded deliberately matter-of-fact. 'Probably weakened her in the end.'

Then her father's signature jumped out at her, in the same red ink, under the next-of-kin heading. At the bottom of the document, his signature appeared again, twice, against the words 'Medical Practitioner or Coroner', and then as 'Government Registrar and Magistrate'. She drew back in dismay.

'I don't understand.'

'Well, it's obvious, isn't it? Your father was the island doctor, and as the DC he would also act as sole representative of the law.'

'So no one else's word was necessary?'

'Word?' She heard the note of irritation in his voice.

'Confirmation that it was all true. I mean, my father could have written whatever he liked. No one would ever know.'

Jack slammed the book shut. 'Oh come on, Laura! This isn't an Agatha Christie whodunnit, for Christ's sake.'

Two students at the next table looked round with interest.

'Sorry, darling,' he went on in an undertone, putting his hand over hers. 'But honestly, you do seem to be looking for dark deeds where none exist. You must understand, this is how things were in the Pacific, still are in some places. I can vouch for it. One official on his own has to double up on half a dozen different duties.'

'I know that. But I hadn't realized till now what that might imply.' She tightened her fingers around Jack's. 'Did I tell you? He couldn't even say where exactly her grave was.'

'Well, how could he? When the Japanese invaded, they completely tore up the place. They built fortifications, bunkers, gun emplacements, the lot. It was full-scale war out there, you know, once the Americans arrived on the scene.'

She sat motionless, not really listening, staring down at the closed volume. The certificate had solved nothing. In a curious way, it had made her more certain than ever that this was not the end of her mother's story.

'Do you see things more clearly now?' Jack asked.

'Not really. Less clearly than ever, in fact.'

With a sigh she got up and walked over to the end of the verandah, away from the people at the other tables. The stone wall was warm under her arms as she leaned out towards the scent of the purple flowers. Instinctively she put her hand over the wallet in her breast pocket, then she brought it out, staring once more at the photograph of the fair-haired woman in her crumpled trousers and shirt.

'Something happened to her. I just know it. It's as if she were still part of me, giving me the will-power to go back and find out.'

'Laura.' Jack was leaning over her shoulder, his body warmth encircling her like some protective shield. 'Isn't the present more important than the past? What if we lose each other, just because . . .' He hesitated. 'Just because of this obsession with the memory of your mother. Obsession is the word, you know. A morbid obsession, even. It's bad for you, Laura. Isn't it time for you to give it up?'

'How can you ask me that?' She spun round to face him. As she did so, the wallet fell to the ground. Picking it up, she saw for the first time the torn flap of leather at the back where there had once been a separate compartment. Carefully she felt inside and brought out two or three folded scraps of paper, charred around the edges. Excitement quickened through her as she spread them out on the ledge in front of her. But almost at once she saw they were mere fragments of her father's past, nothing to do with her mother – a bookseller's order from Oxford, a torn-off grocery bill from Sydney, a local newspaper cutting. Her shoulders sagged.

'Darling, what did you expect?' Jack asked her. 'An old letter? A confession of some kind?'

He glanced at the cutting. It was simply a list of high tides, shipping arrivals and so on, with a date scribbled across it. July 1937.

'You see. These are the kind of scraps that end up in anybody's wallet living in the islands. Surely you don't need to keep them.'

Without waiting for an answer, he crumpled them into a ball and threw them into a wastepaper basket in the corner. The wallet with the photograph he placed carefully back in Laura's hand.

'Let's get out of here,' he said.

Laura felt suddenly exhausted, only too willing to follow him down the steps and along the pathway that led into the Botanical Gardens. After a moment they sat down on one of the Victorian iron seats under the oriental palms. She seemed unable to summon up the energy to make any more decisions.

'Before you make your plans,' Jack said slowly, 'I have one last suggestion to make. Will you talk to my father?'

'Your father?'

'He knows Lawrence Harrington better than most people. More important, he was the person who picked him up on Taparua when the Japanese invaded. It was my father's boat that made that last rescue mission. When he came on board, your father told him about his wife's death just weeks before. I've heard my father tell the story a dozen times. It's part of his wartime reminiscences. So will you listen to him? Then perhaps you'll see that there's nothing else to find out.'

He took her hands in his. 'Your mother wasn't the only one, you know. All kinds of people lost their lives around that time. There are some deaths that have never even been recorded. My father will tell you all about it.'

'You want me to come out to the plantation to talk to him?'

'I want you to come anyway. I want you to meet my family, Laura, get the feel of the life there. Forget about the past for a change. Could you do that?'

'I'd like to try. I'd like to very much.' She felt a new kind of energy, a sort of hope. 'You know I love you, Jack,' she said suddenly. 'Don't you?'

'I know it. And I love you, bloody little idiot.'

He pulled her to her feet. 'We can have time on our own there, just for a day or two, long enough to decide what we're going to do. I'll take you on a mini-cruise, on the launch. Not a far-flung one. But enough to see the real Fiji, maybe get some more material for your programme.'

'And make love in a moonlit bay just like the songs say.'

'I promise!'

Laura was suddenly hungry, ravenously hungry for the taste of that pure happiness again. 'Let's go home and pack then.'

He kissed her, not caring about the nearby party of tourists who were admiring the tropical ferns. 'Let's go to bed.'

PART TWO

CHAPTER ONE

It was the stillness of the river that caught Laura's imagination more than anything else, the stillness and the dense canopy of shade thrown by the overhanging trees and vegetation on either side. The sparkle of the estuary with its crowded landing-stage had vanished behind them as if such a scene had never existed. Now the little boat was gliding through a tunnel of green into the hidden world of the Viti Levu interior. Even the throb of the engine was an intrusion here. When it suddenly spluttered into silence, Laura jumped.

'Now you know why we call these things put-puts,' Jack told her. 'This one's pretty well past it I reckon, don't you, Jo?'

'Your father say to send the launch down for you.' The grey-haired Fijian at the helm sounded apologetic. 'But the marama go across to Levuka this morning and she take it first.' The old man shrugged his shoulders as he tugged at the cord that operated the motor, without success.

'What do you do if you're out at sea when this happens?' Laura asked.

'Close your eyes and pray,' said Jack laughing. 'Then start to bail out. Crossing the reef is the tricky bit. There's only one chance to go with the right wave along some parts of the coast. But don't worry. We only use this old tub up and down the river. Eh, Jo?'

As he spoke, the engine started up for a second then died away again. The faint whirring of cicadas from the long grass seemed to mock the sound. From further up-river came the cry of some water bird, followed by a screech that made Laura jump again.

'Parrot,' Jack said. 'Lots of them in these woods. I had one as a pet when I was a kid. Poor old Koki. I used to tease the life out of him.'

'Mister Jack was a bad small boy,' Jo remarked reprovingly. He had discovered a screwdriver under some sacking and was busily poking about among the innards of the engine. 'Always he want to play with the boats, falling in the river. Too much trouble.'

'What I really wanted was a ride on the No-Come-Back. But that wasn't allowed, of course.'

'The what?'

'It's the Fijian name for the bamboo rafts they make to take their stuff down-river to market. It's not worth the effort of poling them back upstream, so they simply let them loose at the other end and hitch a ride back or walk. It only takes an hour or so to make another one, so what does it matter?'

'These bush people!' snorted Jo, who came from a village on the coast. 'Too much lazy people!'

He pulled at the cord again and gave a cry of triumph as the engine finally sparked into life.

Jack took up the cry. 'Vinaka, vinaka!' He scrambled over to clap the old man on the shoulder. 'That's an extra pack of tobacco you've earned, don't forget.'

Watching him crouched next to Jo, his old canvas bush-hat tilted over his eyes, Laura wondered not for the first time at Jack's chameleon-like ability to merge into his setting. Effortlessly, the London barrister could turn into the poetical recluse of Vailima who was also a pillar of colonial government. Here at Nailangi, he had become the Boy's Own explorer, with more than a touch of the pioneer planter now he was on home ground again. Who are you really, Jack Renfrey? she asked silently. Why was it only when they made love that she felt she had reached the innermost man, who was so vulnerable he could sometimes weep for happiness in her arms? Then he was gone again, eluding her, teasing her sometimes from behind one of his different facets and moods. She remembered a moment when he had told her he loved her.

'So now you feel you have your foot on the neck of the tiger, I suppose,' he had added immediately afterwards. A joke with a warning note, she thought to herself.

'Don't be ridiculous,' was all she said. 'Why should I?'

Perhaps this element of separateness was part of the fascination. There were times when it was as if he had lent himself to you, rather than giving himself without reserve. Then there would be the moment, as now, when he looked round at her with such a private tenderness that every doubt melted away.

'Do you like our river, then?' he asked her.

'It's magical.'

'Wait till you see the house. Not far now.'

Many other women must have fallen in love with him, Laura

thought. There was an immediate sexual charge to that smile, the way the eyes widened, compelling you to respond. She had told him so much about her own relationships, though so far he had been casually dismissive about any of his own – almost too dismissive. She sensed a barrier, as if something had been put aside that should not concern her. Oddly enough, she accepted this. Why try to probe, she told herself, when their happiness together was so real?

At this moment she felt the same careless ease about everything, a letting-go of anxieties and obsessions, even the decisions that would have to be made before next week. Perhaps it was something to do with the river. There was a hypnotic effect about that glassy green surface, drifting past her so slowly, as it always had done and always would. Occasionally a fallen coconut would float by, or a stray palm frond. Once or twice a fish bubbled gently to the surface, then sank back again. Even when a human figure appeared on the bank ahead, it seemed to Laura to be part of the same dream-like sequence.

'It's old Hatty Parkin.' Jack raised his hat to the person standing behind some broken-down fencing under the trees. Laura had a glimpse of an elderly European woman in long skirts, who raised a battered trilby in a regal return of Jack's salutation. She could see cattle grazing in a clearing behind. At the foot of the bank a young Fijian boy was tying a punt to a rickety landing step.

'She lives there?' Laura asked.

'It's the Parkin sisters' estate. Her family were settlers from New Zealand and she's the only one left. Hardly ever goes off the place nowadays. So I usually stop and have a yarn with her when I'm over, take her a bottle of Johnnie Walker.' He shook his head affectionately. 'Last time she played me a whole stack of her old records, even had me doing the Boston two-step.'

The boat was coming towards a bend. As she turned to wave, Laura saw that Hatty was still standing there, hand on hip, gazing out at the river in the way that old ladies in England watch from their windows to see what's going on in the street. Then the solitary figure was gone, lost against the darkness of the forest. She found herself remembering the elderly couple she had met at the beach house with Jack. Once again, she had the sense of a whole network of settler families rooted in remote places, bound together by scraps of gossip and news, a shared telephone line and a mail delivery waiting at the local trading post. Jack knew them all, or knew of them. They were his people, as Jo the boatman was and the Chinese storekeeper at the landing stage who'd wanted Jack to stay for his usual game of dominoes, and Matti the cook up at Vailima.

On the far side of the bend, another greeting awaited them. The gloom of the trees fell away. The river here was broad and clear, glittering suddenly in brilliant sunshine. They were turning in towards a stone jetty with elegant curving steps leading up from the water. Standing stiffly to attention at the top she saw figures in white uniforms with scarlet cummerbunds. Dark faces were framed in scarlet turbans. Then the figures came running, and the faces broke into smiles. One of them called out in Hindi as the little boat drew up alongside. Jack laughed and called something back.

'These are the three pillars of the house of Renfrey,' he told Laura, jumping out to hand her onto the jetty. 'Vijay, Tulsi and Krishna.' The older man saluted, military style. The others nodded shyly, darting forward to pick up the baggage.

'Sahib inside,' Vijay murmured. 'Resting today.'

'Resting?' Jack looked surprised.

'Little bit sick yesterday. Dr Mac came down and give the tablets.'

'The old boy's had a few turns with his heart,' Jack told Laura. 'But I thought the trouble had settled down.'

Still holding her hand, he hurried up the steps. Laura caught sight of sloping lawns rolled to perfect smoothness, English-style flower-beds under widespread trees, a setting to match the pillared porch of the large white house at the far end.

'*Gone With The Wind*,' she said in some astonishment.

'Clever of you. My grandfather modelled it on one of the plantation houses in the Southern states. You'll be hearing about him, no doubt, and all the rest of the family.'

On the porch, the wide double doors stood open. Inside, the air was cool and dim, fragrant with the scent of beeswax. Striped linen blinds at the long windows threw a chequered shade over the parquet floor and the old-fashioned mahogany furniture. A huge bowl of yellow and white roses glowed on the marble side table. A scribbled note in an unmistakably feminine hand was propped up against it, headed 'Jack', with an exclamation mark. Laura was aware at once of the invisible presence of Mrs Renfrey, a lady to be reckoned with, she imagined.

'I'm sorry my mother's not here,' Jack said, examining the note. 'She says she'll be back this evening. She's queen bee of the Fiji Red Cross in these parts. It's their annual jamboree at Levuka, I gather.'

'You gather correctly,' came an amused voice behind them.

A tall distinguished-looking man with a neat silver beard stood in the doorway. He put down an airmail copy of *The Times* and removed his glasses. 'This is Miss Harrington?'

Laura found herself responding instantly to the smile that was so like Jack's. The expressive eyes were even darker, almost black.

'And you are Jack's father.'

Max Renfrey nodded and took her hand, holding it in his for a moment. He made no effort to disguise his admiration.

'I must warn you,' Jack said as they followed him into the library. 'My father's a famous flirt.'

'Was, Jack, was. I'm afraid decline and fall is fast setting in.'

'Vijay told me you'd not been well. What did Dr Mac say?'

The three of them sat down and Max smiled wearily. 'Well, he was more than a little hung-over when he called. Been up at the Gillies' place to celebrate a silver wedding. But after the hair of the dog, so to speak, he got round to giving me a thorough check. Said the usual things.'

'Which were?'

'The heart was under strain, blood pressure up and I must start on some new pills.' Max Renfrey stretched out long legs in shabby brown mosquito boots. 'Damn stuff makes one feel like lead. But your arrival has revived me more than a little.' He took up a small silver bell by his chair and rang it twice. 'Meanwhile, tea, I think.'

At the same instant the door creaked slowly open. Two stout island girls in starched black and white, their hair tied up in red ribbons, came in bearing trays piled high with silver tea things. One of them knelt by the low table to pour, daintily replacing the lace cover, fringed with shells, over the milk jug. The other passed round plates of cucumber sandwiches and a Victoria sponge cake before taking her place on the mat by Max's chair. An ornate feathered fan had been produced and was being wafted from side to side to dispatch any unwary fly. Laura found the whole ritual entrancing, well aware that she was being intently studied from beneath lowered eyelids.

'The Indians may run the front of house,' Max said, 'but our kitchen is pure Tongan.' He smiled at the girl beside him and patted her hand. 'This one is fourth generation to be with us.'

'It's a family tradition,' Jack explained. 'All because of old Jacob there.' He nodded towards a not very skilful portrait that seemed to have been coloured over an early photograph. Even so, the stern, wooden-looking features had a life of their own.

'His eyes seem to be following me,' Laura said.

'Don't let them follow you too far,' Max told her. 'The story is if the eyes move there'll be a death in the family.'

'Anyway,' Jack put in quickly. 'Jacob Renfrey came out to the Pacific to make his fortune and very sensibly married a niece of the old

King of Tonga. Of course, she brought her own servants with her to the estate and their descendants have stayed on ever since.'

'It all sounds highly romantic.'

'Far from it, starting from scratch in the bush in the 1860s. You bought your piece of land from the chiefs for a few rifles, built yourself a leaky old shanty to start with, kept on the right side of the local tribes – they were mostly still cannibal in those days, and always fighting. But Jacob himself was a pretty tough old bird from all accounts. Started life tin-mining in Cornwall, then went out to Australia in the gold rush. But the South Seas got him in the end.' He grinned happily at Laura. 'Doesn't it always?'

'Who wants to hear about all this?' Max sounded apologetic. 'My wife finds it extremely boring, I can tell you. No doubt Laura does too.'

But Laura was already studying one of the other pictures, a middle-aged man with more than a hint of Tongan blood in his dark good looks as he posed for the camera on the steps of the house.

'Jacob's son?'

Jack nodded. 'My grandfather, Frederick Renfrey.' He pointed to the fair-haired buxom woman next to him. 'He married the daughter of the German consul in Samoa. The two of them decided to introduce some culture into the wilds of Fiji. Having built the house, they needed the furniture to go with it. So all this Victorian stuff was brought up-river, family silver, pictures and so on. A whole library was carried up through the bush, can you imagine?'

'The piano too?' Laura laid her hand on the somewhat battered Bechstein grand that dominated the room.

Max Renfrey groaned. 'I was given my first lesson on that by my mother at the age of seven. It was part of the daily ritual, like changing for dinner and taking turns to read aloud in the drawing-room afterwards. My two sisters were best at that. But they'd had enough of plantation life by the time they grew up.' He shrugged. 'I hardly see them now. They're both rich widows, living in America.'

Laura turned to look at an oil painting of a small boy in a sailor suit. 'And this is you. The only son?'

'And more than a little spoilt, I'm afraid. Like someone else I know.' He smiled a little ruefully in Jack's direction. 'My father owned one of the local shipping lines. I spent more time on trips round the islands than I did at my lessons. They sent me away to study in Dresden and then I came back to learn about growing copra. That brought me down to earth, still does.' He sighed and rested a hand on Jack's shoulder. 'This fellow will show you round the place, if you're not too tired. As for me, I think I'm due for a nap, if you don't mind.'

Laura saw that his face was suddenly drained of colour.

'Are you all right, Mr Renfrey?'

'Just a bit weary, all of a sudden.' Standing next to her, he took her arm and said quietly, 'I know you want to hear about your father, about the time I brought him off the island, in the war. Jack's told me.' He glanced at the two girls, busy with their trays. 'We need to be on our own. Sundowners on the verandah, I think, in a couple of hours.'

CHAPTER TWO

'Do you really want that guided tour?' Jack asked. He was leading the way through the hall to a side door. Two horses stood waiting in a shady courtyard, held by Tulsi.

Laura nodded. Distraction from thoughts of the conversation that lay ahead was what she needed most. 'It'll be lovely to ride again. Haven't done that since my Yorkshire days.'

Jack grinned. 'Don't get too excited. These are only going to walk us round. So just sit back and relax.'

'Your father's a lovely man,' Laura said as the two elderly mares ambled along the familiar tracks. Riding side by side, she and Jack brushed close to one another as the pathway narrowed between the seemingly endless groves of coconut palms.

'I think he's fairly enthusiastic about you.' He glanced at her, smiling, under the brim of his hat. 'I've told him you're coming to Canberra with me next week.'

'But I haven't . . .'

He held up his hand. 'We won't talk about it now. Not till you've had a chance to listen to my father. Besides, remember what I said? That it was time to live in the present for a change?'

Laura was about to reply but changed her mind.

'So what do you think of plantation life? Is it what you imagined?'

'Much grander.'

He laughed. 'And you haven't even seen my plane yet.'

'Your plane?'

He was watching her with a look of schoolboy triumph. 'It's only a little four-seater Drover from Australia. It's under cover about a mile up-river. We've cleared a runway out of the bush, so we can get up and down to the coast in no time at all. My mother's idea, really. She's set her heart on starting up a tourist complex, a riverside hotel, safari trips and so on.'

Inwardly Laura groaned. A new picture of Jack's mother had just emerged – the hard-as-nails Australian businesswoman rather than the good-works châtelaine of colonial society.

'I can't say I'm all that keen,' Jack went on. 'Though when Mother gets the bit between her teeth there's no stopping her. Says it's important for the economy, jobs for the local people and all that.'

He caught sight of Laura's expression and changed the subject.

'Anyway, that's just pie in the sky. This is the stuff that really matters.' He waved an arm towards the palm trees rolling away on either side. There was something of a cathedral atmosphere, Laura thought, about the heart of a plantation. The topmost branches arched overhead in fan-vaulting patterns above the long aisles of blue-green shade. Here and there in a clearing, a bonfire of coconut husks smouldered away in a sweet-smelling haze that hung on the air like incense. In the distance she could see the thicker smoke of cooking fires rising above rows of corrugated roofs.

'That's the labour lines – not as grim as it sounds. Our people are well looked after. Every now and then they take their earnings home to the islands they come from, but they nearly all turn up again. They've knocked off for today. I'll just have a word.'

Sprawling groups of men in singlets and sulus got up from the grass as Jack stopped to talk. A pack of spindly puppies sniffed round the heels of Laura's horse and a fat baby came tottering out of the nearest hut. The mother gave Laura a shy smile as she scooped him up again, disappearing round the side where the other women were cooking the evening meal.

At the end of the lines stood a huge wooden shed. The doors were open and Laura peered inside as they rode past, catching sight of the mountain of husked coconuts that would soon be crushed into copra. The wooden floor was as glossy with oil as a ballroom.

'You should see the dancing they put on here,' Jack said. 'Next time you come we'll have one of our party nights.'

In the corner loomed something that looked like a giant's cooking stove. It was the new copra dryer, Jack told her. Better than the old way of doing things.

'When I was small I remember the nuts used to be spread in the sun on mats. The first sight of rain, we had to rush round dragging them all inside again.'

'We?'

Jack's face lit up.

'It was one of my great thrills to be allowed to help when I was quite small. Getting up before dark, watching my father shave by the oil lamp, then being allowed to beat the lali drum to get the workers up. The war was a hard time for planters. My father had to oversee everything himself.'

'And now?' Laura asked.

'There's a manager and a deputy manager, New Zealanders. They have their own bungalows, see to all the cargo side of the business. My father still likes to keep an eye on things, though, especially the trees. It's me who's the outsider. Just here for the odd weekend.'

'But you might find yourself taking over one day, I suppose?' Somehow Laura felt this was the most important question of all.

He screwed up his eyes, looking away over the labour lines.

'Something I would like to do is to turn this into more of a village. You know, thatched roofs, a school for the children, the women making the traditional things – pottery, mats, baskets, and selling them in the market.' He turned in his saddle. 'What do you think?'

Taken by surprise, Laura found herself face to face and suddenly close to him, so close that a kiss seemed imminent. But at that moment the figure of Vijay appeared, running down the path towards them.

'You forget this.' The young man was panting, grinning as he handed up a small covered basket.

'Well done, Vijay.' Jack took the basket and turned his horse in the opposite direction.

'So where are we going?' Laura asked as she followed behind.

'There's a special member of the family I want you to meet. Everyone calls her Auntie Atu. She's not on Mother's visiting list, which is why my father didn't mention her to you. But she's very dear to me.'

He pointed ahead through the trees. A gingerbread cottage of reeds and thatch had come into view, the low doorway hung across with some kind of flowering vine.

'What does that remind you of?'

'Hansel and Gretel,' Laura said immediately.

'Exactly. When we were children, my sisters used to bring breadcrumbs for the ducks on the river – it's only just below. I used to scatter mine on the path as we went along in case we got lost.'

It was no witch who appeared at the door, but a young woman who looked exactly like the two Tongans with the tea-trays and was evidently delighted to see Jack and his basket. When the horses had been tied up to the picket fence, she beckoned them down the path with its neat edging of white conch shells and clumps of marigolds and tiger lilies.

'She is sitting outside, round the back.'

As they turned the corner, Jack held Laura aside for a minute.
'Go gently. She's almost blind.'

But the immense old lady, enthroned in a tall cane chair, was already calling out to them. Although she was very much older, the first sight of her reminded Laura at once of the famous Queen Salote in her open carriage at the Coronation. As a teenager she had never forgotten the pictures of the Polynesian monarch waving through the rain at the adoring London crowds.

'You look like . . .' she began, as she was introduced by Jack. She hesitated. Auntie Atu lifted her curly white head attentively, hooded eyes turned up at her, waiting. Risking a Tongan faux pas, Laura went on, '. . . like Queen Salote.'

The moonlike face creased into a stately smile.

'That is a very kind thing to say. Also, it is true. The Queen was a relative, you see. We both have the same great-grandmother, who was was also called Salote. It is after your Queen Charlotte, you know that? From long ago, when Cookie came to Tonga?'

'Cookie?' Laura was bemused.

'Captain Cook,' Jack explained. 'And no doubt you've guessed that Auntie Atu is my great-aunt, the daughter of the princess who married Jacob. When she became a widow she came to live here at Nailangi. But she likes to be independent, as you can see.' He sat down with his basket at the old lady's feet. 'I didn't forget to bring you something.'

'My fish?'

'Fresh from the coast.'

Auntie Atu leaned forward in her loose-flowing robe. All dignity was forgotten as she put her small plump hand into the basket. The next minute, a tiny sprat was extracted, popped whole into her mouth and chewed delicately before slipping down like an oyster. Laura watched the process spellbound.

'Auntie Atu used to be an expert at catching fish, too,' Jack said. 'Remember the clams I used to dive for, Auntie? One day I was certain I'd find a pearl inside. You always told me to be careful opening them. If there was a pearl, the clam would spit it out at me. But there never was.'

The sun had begun to slide behind the trees and the air was growing cooler. A clap of Auntie's hands brought the girl out with her shawl. The brightly-fringed mat at her feet was rolled up and the old lady took Jack's arm to go inside.

'We have to leave you now,' Jack told her. 'My father's expecting us.'

'Laura will drink a glass of lemonade first,' she decreed. 'So that she can see my house.'

Inside the little parlour, sipping the sweet drink, Laura had a confused impression of chequered tapa-cloth hangings and Victorian mirrors, German cuckoo clocks and lace antimacassars on maroon velvet chairs. Along the central beam coloured portraits of King Edward and Queen Alexandra hung, side by side with a multitude of moustachioed Tongan nobles in faded sepia. Auntie Atu had settled herself on a Hawaiian day-bed piled high with mats and cushions. On the wall above her head was suspended a Biblical text framed in bamboo which read, 'Prepare thyself for thou knowest not the hour when thy Master cometh.'

'Tomorrow is Sunday,' she announced. She drew on a small brown cheroot the girl had prepared for her. 'You will be attending church, Jack? Down at Raki?'

'Tomorrow we have to travel on, Auntie.'

'Travelling on a Sunday!' The old lady clicked her tongue, but Laura could see she was only pretending to be shocked.

'Are you Wesleyan?' she asked Laura.

'I'm afraid not.'

The soft little hand reached out and patted Laura's hair and face. 'Is this girl pretty, Jack? I only see in a blur, these days.'

'Laura is very pretty indeed. Eyes that change colour like the sea. Dark brown hair, very thick. A small hollow in the middle of her chin that smoothes out when she smiles.'

'Jack!' Laura protested in a low voice. But he simply went on looking at her, as if studying a painting.

'She also has a most pleasing voice,' Auntie Atu added. 'Not like that young woman from Australia who was visiting a little while ago. She was with her mother, you remember. I told you she had a strange name – Kam? Kim? Bad voice, bad manners. And that perfume of hers! Like a poisonous plant, it was so strong.'

Laura watched Jack's face freeze. 'Father will be waiting for us,' was all he said.

To cover her dismay, Laura pressed her cheek to the old lady's. The papery skin had the faintest scent of its own, like dried flowers. 'May I come again?' she asked her.

'Jack will bring you. Does he play his flute for you?'

'Sometimes.'

'Tell him to make a song for you. All Tongans do that. Queen Salote's husband wrote one for her when he was courting her, did you know.' She paused to take a breath. 'She is like a dove that soars. But one day I will claim her.'

The thin voice died away. 'You will travel to Tonga?'

'Not this time.'
'Then here is a souvenir instead.'
Laura found a fan put into her hand, one of those round, delicately-woven things fringed with red feathers.
At the door Auntie Atu told Jack, 'Say my lolomas to your father. Your mother . . .' She shrugged her shoulders and bowed her head.
'I don't understand,' Laura said as they rode away, 'why your mother doesn't visit the old lady.'
'It's Coloured Blood, isn't it.' Mockingly Jack put the words in capitals. 'Mother prefers to pretend it doesn't exist. After all, it's not her side of the family.'
'And the Australian visitors?' Laura was careful to keep the neutral tone in her voice.
Jack was looking ahead. She saw no change of expression on his face. 'Guests of my mother's. They came upon the house when they were out riding. Mother had told them my old nanny lived there. You can imagine.' He broke off.
'They were not exactly respectful?' Laura suggested.
'It wasn't really their fault,' Jack said defensively. 'I only heard about it afterwards.'
'They must have been embarrassed when you told them the truth.'
'I haven't seen them to tell them.'
There was an abrupt pause. The topic was obviously closed. Laura felt she would rather die than ask who this Kim was. She had that sense again of a barrier not to be crossed.
'I don't usually ride this way back,' Jack said, breaking the silence.
'Why not?'
'See just to the right there, under the big ivi tree. That's the old family cemetery. I thought you might be interested. I used to think it was rather a spooky place.'
'I'm not surprised.'
It was that brief interval between daylight and dusk. A greenish sky threw into relief a low wall of river boulders. Someone long ago had planted red ginger between them, the Pacific flower of mourning, and now the tall crimson spears were choked with long grass, as high as the old iron railings that encircled them.
'They started off burying the family pets here, and I suppose they just carried on with the idea.'
She could tell from his voice that he was trying to make light of a place that secretly moved him as much as it moved her. Some of the graves, she noticed, were obviously those of children, though the lettering was so furred over with lichen it was impossible to read the

names. Besides, the light was going fast. She waved her fan against the mosquitoes that were already darting around. There was the steady swish of the horses' tails and high up in the mango trees behind them the squeaking of fruit bats, rousing themselves for the evening.

'All we need is the garlic,' Jack said, joking still.

'Do you still have family burials here?'

'Auntie says she's booked her place.' He pointed with his hat. 'Up there on that little rise. Father too, so he says. It's where the sun comes up first in the morning.'

'And you?'

'Why not? There's many a worse place.' He replaced his hat. 'Come on then, darling. Enough of mortality.'

But Laura was staring down at the half-hidden crosses and crumbling cherubs.

'I envy you this,' she heard herself say, almost without thinking. 'It's like the house and the portraits.'

'What do you mean?'

'Just that you know exactly who you are and where you fit in. You've known it ever since you can remember, I suppose.'

'I suppose.'

'Lucky you.' She was unable to keep the bitterness out of her voice.

'Laura, darling.' He brought his horse alongside hers and put his hand on her shoulder.

'It's just that I've had to invent myself right from the start, if you see what I mean. Not knowing anything about any family before me, not even having anyone to tell me. It's like a piece of china that's been broken, and I'm the only fragment left.'

She pulled herself round, searching his face. 'Can you understand? It means you have no sense of yourself in time, of the things you might have inherited from others. Not just my mother, but my father's side too. Even his sister would never talk about the family background. He was a black sheep, so I was treated like one too.'

'Darling,' Jack said again. The tenderness in his voice made her tremble. He touched her cheek gently with the back of his hand. 'At least you have me.'

'Do I?' She drew away again. A feeling of uncertainty had taken hold of her almost like sadness. Perhaps it was the place, the melancholy spirit of it.

Briskly Jack took hold of her reins with his. 'Come on home. Come and talk to my father.'

The horses moved on together, out of the trees and down the

pathway to the house. Laura could see the soft yellow flare of oil lamps along the verandah.

'So much more friendly than electricity, don't you think?' Max Renfrey said when they joined him. He was already ensconced at the far end, a drink in hand, his feet up in his long planter's chair. 'My wife disagrees with me. But as she's just telephoned to say she's going to be another hour or so, we can bask in the glow for a little longer.'

Settling her next to him in one of the old-fashioned basket chairs, he handed her a long glass containing a pale green drink and a great many ice cubes.

'That's a Grasshopper, planter's special. Vodka and crème de menthe, topped up with soda. See how you like it.' He raised his own glass to her. 'The sun's been down a good ten minutes, so I've already started on mine, I'm afraid.'

Laura took her first sip. 'It's rather good.'

Jack looked round from the drinks trolley where he was pouring himself his usual whisky. 'Are you sure? My father has some curious tastes.'

'Quite sure.'

She and the old man exchanged smiles. She realized he was trying to ease the awkwardness of this encounter and she was grateful to him, recognizing the kindness beneath the lazy charm.

'You enjoyed your tour?'

She nodded. 'Especially meeting Auntie Atu.'

'I'm glad Jack took you there. She's an amazing lady, so many family memories. We have long chats together at her place, though I can never get her to come down here.'

He paused. Out of politeness, Laura began to tell him of her other impressions. All the time she was wondering how soon she could bring the conversation round to that wartime episode in the Gilberts.

After a minute or two Max Renfrey leaned forward and put his hand over hers. It was a surprisingly roughened hand, reminding her of Jack's account of those early-morning plantation rounds with his father.

'You don't have to be polite. I know you want to talk about your father. Jack told me on the telephone you'd had a rather unhappy confrontation with him.'

'Worse than unhappy. It was like meeting a stranger. A stranger who frightens me.'

'I think Lawrence Harrington is a stranger to most people,' Max Renfrey said slowly. 'To himself also.'

'You know him quite well?'

'I hadn't met him until that day in February 1942 when I picked him up. Since then he's been living in Fiji, so naturally our paths have crossed. He was doctoring this side of the mainland in the fifties and of course we had interests in common – Pacific history, anthropology and so on. He used to discuss his books with me sometimes. But he wasn't a man I ever felt close to. There was always a coldness about him – *is* always, he hasn't changed – something secretive.'

'That time in 1942, Mr Renfrey.' Laura fixed her eyes on his. 'Can you tell me about it, everything you remember?'

'Dear girl, you must not be so intense. And please try to call me Max.' He got up and mixed some more drinks. 'For you?'

'Just a small one this time, please.'

'Now.' He settled back in his chair. 'First tell me something. You do not believe what your father told you about your mother's death. Why?'

'For one thing, he told me so little.' Laura tried to muster her thoughts. 'Also, I just felt there was something false about it. And then the death certificate filled in by him with no witnesses. But there were other things, too – a photograph of my mother he'd lied to me about and tried to destroy. And a Gilbertese servant who tried to tell me he was hiding something from me.'

'As, of course, he was.'

Laura's heart seemed to contract. 'What do you mean?'

'I mean you were right not to believe him.' He leaned forward, his hands clasped in front of him, keeping his eyes on hers. 'Listen, Laura. This is exactly how I remember it, as it happened at the time. It was two months after Pearl Harbor. The Gilbert Islands were the first target for the Japanese invasion in that part of the Pacific British territory, a feather in their cap if they could take them. There was no question of the colonial government defending them – they were far too remote, too small, too unimportant. The handful of Britishers living there managed to get away in time – most of them, anyway, chiefly women and children.'

'That was the ship they put me on, the mission ship?'

Max Renfrey nodded. 'The *John Williams*. I was delegated by government to try and pick up the rest and get them back to Fiji. I had a good old sailing launch in those days, and a marvellous Fijian skipper. We made landfall at nearly a dozen of those tiny scraps of land in spite of awful weather, and Taparua was our last call. We couldn't go ashore. There was no time. Japanese shipping was only a short distance away and they were already bombing the main islands. But we took a boat off through the reef and into the lagoon. The local people were on the lookout for us on the beach. Then we saw an Englishman wading out towards us. It was your father.'

'And my mother?'

'There was no sign of her. Harrington was in pretty bad shape. It was low tide so he'd had a long walk out. He practically fell into the boat when he got to us. White as a sheet and looking half-starved. He seemed to be in shock, shaking in every limb. I understood why when he told me what had happened. Apparently his wife had died just two weeks earlier.'

Laura turned her face towards the forest. When she looked back at him Max's expression was a blur. 'I don't understand. If she had left with me two months before, surely she could have lived.'

'He told me she had been too sick to make the journey. They still hoped then that the Japs wouldn't get as far as Taparua. Besides, they'd been told there would be another evacuation ship round in a few weeks' time. Harrington had to stay on till the last moment, and he said he thought your mother would stand a better chance by then.'

'It was malaria,' Jack put in. He was leaning against the verandah rail, his eyes on Laura.

'That was his story first of all. Then when we were alone in my cabin, sharing a bottle of whisky, he told me the truth.'

'The truth.' Laura repeated the words dully. It was as if her brain was unable to take in the fact that this moment had come at last.

Max paused. Then he said gently, 'Your mother committed suicide.'

'No!' she called out in protest, even before she had time to properly absorb the words. 'Oh, no.'

Jack had come to sit beside her, holding her hand. 'How did she do it? Did he say?'

'And why?' Laura said, her voice barely louder than a whisper. With her father's face fresh in her memory she felt she already knew the answer.

'Apparently she had become very depressed, irrational almost. She was very weak anyway – lack of proper food, frequent bouts of malaria. She was convinced she would fall into Japanese hands. Everyone had heard stories of Jap atrocities against women prisoners. She knew that at least her child had been got to safety. So she must have decided to take her own life. She just walked out into the sea one night, on the windward side where the breakers are enormous. She was never seen again. Harrington only knew the next morning when a fisherman told him he had caught sight of her but it was too late to stop her. Her body was never found.'

'So there is no grave.' In Laura's mind, she heard her father's voice again: 'One coral boulder is very like another.' It had sounded so heartless. But perhaps he had been trying to tell her something else.

'Why didn't he say all this when I was with him?' She looked up at Max pleadingly. 'Surely I had a right to know. Why didn't he tell me everything?'

'Because he had resolved to tell no one, and your father's resolve is unbreakable. That is his nature. He only let it out to me in that first moment of weakness, I suppose. The man was distraught.' Max leaned towards her, searching for the right words. 'He was the survivor, you see. In the eyes of the world his wife's death would be judged as his failure. The shame of it, the awful stigma, would be fastened on him forever, and he just couldn't take it. The private guilt would be bad enough, I imagine. Anyway, he told me he would report the death as due to malaria, hastened by chronic TB. It was wrong of him, I know. But how could I judge him after what he'd been through?'

Laura was silent for a moment. 'Did he ever talk to you about it again?'

'Never. He pledged me to say nothing about it to anyone and I never have. Until now.'

She was struggling to keep control of herself. 'Thank you for telling me,' she managed to say. 'It's good of you. And it – it makes a difference. In a way it's the answer, I suppose.' She paused. 'The answer to all the puzzles.'

'You can accept that, Laura?' Jack's voice was gentle, but he was looking at her intently. 'That there was no puzzle? Only a secret?'

She bent her head. There was a knot at the back of her throat that made it difficult to speak. She was conscious of Max's eyes on her too, watchful and sympathetic.

'It's something that's rather haunted me, I have to confess,' he said. He lay back in his chair. 'Even now I go over it in my mind from time to time wondering if . . .' He broke off. Just fleetingly a look of uncertainty passed over his face.

'Wondering if?' Laura pressed.

'Nothing really.' He shook his head.

'Did he say any more to you about my mother? About her condition at the time?'

Max's eyes were closed, as if to summon up in his mind the details of that encounter of almost thirty years ago.

'Morphia,' he said slowly. 'I remember he mentioned morphia. It seems your mother had been taking it from the dispensary. He found her injecting herself with it once or twice. I suppose it dulled the mental pain as well as the physical hardships.' He frowned. 'To be honest I think Harrington himself had got hooked on it, or some similar drug. He had all the symptoms. But whatever it was, he broke himself of it, made a completely new life for himself in Fiji.'

Laura was intensely aware of the cool evening breeze on her skin, and she could feel herself shivering. She got to her feet.

'How do you feel?' Jack reached out to touch her on the arm.

'If I could just go up to my room for a little while,' she said. 'I need to be on my own, I think, just to sort it all out in my mind. It's so awfully sad . . .' She heard her voice break and she turned away. 'My mother, my poor mother.'

'Will you be all right, darling?'

She nodded. Somehow she sensed calm ahead. Now that there was a meaning to everything she could learn to accept the sadness. There was no room left even for outrage. Her father's cruelties were bred in him, and her mother had chosen her own way out. Now she must turn her back on unhappiness too. Unlike her mother, she was lucky. Her real life was only just beginning.

'Do you want me to come up with you?' Jack asked at the door.

'Not just yet.' She turned to him. 'Could you do something for me, though?'

'Anything.'

'Could you telephone Ratu Edwin and tell him I won't be going out to the Gilberts after all? Just say there's no need now. He'll understand.'

Quickly she pressed her face to his. 'Come up soon, Jack.'

CHAPTER THREE

It seemed to Laura a happy omen that the Renfrey yacht should be called the *Tongan Queen*. Broad in the beam and tall at the mast, she had all the regal charm of her namesake as she swayed towards them on the incoming tide.

This was the classic way to travel the South Seas, Laura thought, waiting with Jack on the little wooden jetty down at the point. Around them stretched a perfect Pacific morning, shimmering and cloudless along the whole length of the horizon. Once again she felt that magical lift of the spirit, and at the same time the sense of being at home in such beauty that she had experienced looking out to sea from Vailima. Free as a bird, she said to herself, watching a silvery tern wheel up and away from the tangled shadows of the shoreline.

The schooner was alongside now. Close up, the sunlight bounced off polished brass, scrubbed decks and fresh white paint. Two barefoot Fijians sprang back and forth with ropes, calling out to each other in a kind of operatic duet for tenor and bass.

'All mod cons. Passenger accommodation for six,' Jack told her, leading the way on board. 'Single cabins, alas. There wasn't space for a stateroom. Still, we do have some delusions of grandeur.'

He pointed to the flag that fluttered from the stern. On it Laura could make out the Renfrey initials entwined around a laden coconut palm.

'My grandfather had it designed in Germany.' He laughed. 'A bit on the vulgar side, but the Americans love it.'

'Americans?'

'Just occasionally we rent her out to small holiday parties. That's where Charlie comes in. He's part-owner, as well as our tried and trusty captain.'

The young man in navy shorts and shirt who came from the bridge to greet them was something of a surprise. Laura had expected the grey-bearded skipper of seafaring legend. But this Charles Sullivan was another kind of romantic cliché altogether – crinkled blue eyes, a piratical earring glinting out of a shock of blond hair, a muscular handshake and a broad white smile as he introduced himself. With those looks, he will be tiresomely conceited, Laura decided. But she liked the self-mocking way he made them laugh, breaking into a movie-style parody of his role.

'So where are we bound for?' he demanded with a sweep of the arm. 'What landfall awaits us on yonder horizon?'

All the time, Laura could see him glancing from Jack to herself, as if assessing the two of them as a couple. There was obviously more to Mr Sullivan than appearances suggested.

'I want to show Laura a piece of paradise. The real thing,' Jack said. 'So what about a sail through the Yasawas?'

'Sounds fun. The boys have stocked up with supplies for two or three days at least, including a rather good case of Australian chardonnay.'

Now that he'd dropped the joke American, the voice was pure public-school, Laura noted. The diffident not the arrogant kind, with just the faintest burr of Irish in it. His father, he said, had been in the Colonial Service in Fiji. Young Charles had gone back to England with his family, but the island life had pulled him south again.

'Two days is all I've got off, I'm afraid,' Jack said. 'But that's time enough for Laura to see there is such a thing still left in the world as a real-life desert island. Sawai, for instance.'

'And we can drop her off there if she's had enough of us by then.' Charlie was looking at her quizzically. 'But of course the islands are home ground for you too. Your father's still out here, I believe.' He hesitated. 'Though sadly, not your mother.'

'No. Not my mother,' she replied quietly.

'Jack told me,' he said.

'Only one problem,' Jack put in. 'Tomorrow we have to call in at Korolevu. Some people staying there I have to see.' He hesitated. 'Make my excuses to, actually.'

Charlie raised an eyebrow. 'Anyone I know?'

'The Maguires,' Jack said briefly. 'I won't be stopping long.'

'Right-o.'

Charlie's tone implied that he knew rather more than was being said. Fortunately, so did Laura, after what had happened at Nailangi the previous evening. Jack's mother had arrived back at the estate. Stella Renfrey was exactly as Laura had imagined, a blonde-rinse woman in her middle fifties, very thin, very smart and very much in charge.

'You couldn't have picked a better time to visit us,' were almost her first words when Laura came downstairs to dinner. 'The Maguires will be here. It will be so nice for Kim to meet some fresh company.' She turned to Jack. 'I have a feeling she and Laura will get on splendidly. After all, they're both in the communications business, didn't you say?'

She must have noticed his blank expression. 'Surely you haven't forgotten Kim's coming over with her parents this weekend?'

'No one said anything about it to me,' was Jack's reply. 'Father made no mention of it.'

Mrs Renfrey glanced irritably towards the empty chair at the head of the table. 'Your father forgets most things these days. Can't even remember what time we have dinner.'

'Whatever,' Jack went on, his face set. 'There's no question of our being here. I've arranged to take Laura round the islands in the launch.'

'Well, if that isn't downright rude!' snapped his mother. For a moment she'd forgotten to modulate that corncrake accent. 'Besides which, it makes me look a perfect fool.'

'I'm sorry, Mother. But we're leaving in the morning.'

Silence fell while the servants brought round the first course, chilled avocado soup, one of Laura's favourites. After a few sips she sat very still, staring at the setting of highly polished silver and cut glass in front of her. Her fingers tightened around the starched napkin in her lap. The day had been hot, but now it felt very cold. Mrs Renfrey had ordered the air-conditioning to be turned on as soon as she entered the room. The old-fashioned canvas punkah hung motionless from its cords overhead.

'Such a messy affair, blowing dust everywhere,' she remarked in an effort at normal conversation while the servants were in the room. 'Even worse than these wretched oil lamps Max is so keen on.'

She motioned to Tulsi to switch on another of the overhead lights. These were glaring chandelier affairs which threw everything into relentless detail, including the sharp lines scored into Mrs Renfrey's over-tanned face.

In between courses there was a welcome diversion as Max hurried in, still fixing a rather dashing bow tie.

'So sorry. I've been taking a look at the old mare. The vet will have to see to that back leg next time he's around.'

Mrs Renfrey said nothing until the steaks and salad had been served. Then she turned sharply back to Jack.

'At least you can call at Kovolevu and explain.' Another thought struck her. 'Surely there's no reason why Kim shouldn't come with you on your sail? You'll be a foursome then, with Charlie. Much better. And then you can all end up here.'

Laura caught Jack's glance across the table, the lift of his eyebrows. It did something to help, but not much.

'Can we leave the subject now, Mother?' The anger in his voice was only just under control. 'I have a guest of my own here this evening, remember.'

Gratefully Laura heard Max asking her about the programmes she was making. She told him that she wanted to record something about plantation life. Stella Renfrey's contribution was to assume that Laura worked for television.

'Of course we shan't be able to see them out here,' she kept saying. 'It'll be years before Fiji gets round to TV. Who knows, though,' she added, brightening. 'You might be able to give us some publicity. Our tourist complex. The plans are well advanced, as no doubt Jack has told you. We expect it to be the most desirable tourist destination in Fiji.'

'I'd certainly like to hear about it,' Laura said, striving for politeness, 'and it's BBC Radio I work for, so I should be able to send you a tape.'

'You'd like the story about the workmen refusing to dig out the foundations for the hotel,' Max put in. Was it just mischief she saw in the glance he gave his wife, or something more deliberate? 'They'd only been on the site for an hour when they made off down to their village and never came back. Said two goddesses came flying out, furious with them for breaking up their home. I told Stella that part of the river was tabu – they say it's where the first ancestors landed – but she wouldn't believe me. So no hotel, I'm afraid.'

'On the contrary,' Mrs Renfrey replied. 'That kind of legend will be a real draw when the place goes up. Maguire's are interested in the contract, did I tell you?' She bent across to Laura. 'That's Kim's father, Tom Maguire, one of the richest men in Australia. You know the name, I expect?'

'No, I don't.'

'With Kim helping with the PR side of their travel operations, it makes it quite a family affair. And now her mother's set up Maguire Fashions – leisurewear, that kind of thing – to tie in. Absolutely brilliant. You'll love them all, I'm sure.' She swallowed a final forkful of the pavlova dessert. 'And now, coffee, everyone?' She looked around the three of them. 'A hand of bridge, perhaps?'

Jack pushed back his chair. 'Laura's looking tired. She's had quite a day.'

'Of course. Silly me.' As Laura got to her feet, Mrs Renfrey followed suit. 'I'll just pop up with you and see you've got everything you want. Can't rely on these men, can we?'

Jack and Max stood up. Brief goodnights were exchanged before Laura was ushered out.

'I hope your room is comfortable,' her hostess said, following her up the stairs.

'Perfectly, thank you.'

'Rather a long way from Jack's, as you've no doubt discovered. But I'm afraid I'm rather old-fashioned about things like that.'

'So am I.' I must not be goaded into losing my temper with this woman, Laura told herself.

At the top of the stairs, the two women stood facing one another. Stella Renfrey laid a hand on Laura's arm, scarlet enamelled fingernails gleaming against the soft inner skin. From her expression, Laura could see her searching for a new approach.

'You're a woman of the world, Laura. Even though your own background has been, well, rather unstable to say the least, from what I hear.' Her voice was lowered, confidential. 'But you'll understand perfectly when I tell you that Jack has already committed himself. Privately as well as socially.'

'I don't know what you mean.'

'He probably hasn't mentioned it to you, but three months ago he and Kim were going to announce their engagement. Then her parents insisted she should wait until her twenty-first birthday. That's in just a few weeks' time.'

Laura stepped back, so that the hand on her arm fell away. She was concentrating all her willpower on concealing any sign of shock.

'No, Jack didn't mention it.'

'Those two.' Mrs Renfrey sighed fondly. The close-set eyes still pinpointed Laura's. 'They've had their ups and downs, of course. The path of true love, et cetera. She's rather young for her age and Jack likes his independence. But all being well . . .' She paused, then moved nearer to Laura again. 'So I'd rather you didn't try to rock the boat. For Jack's sake.'

Laura took a deep breath. 'Mrs Renfrey, this is absurd. Why don't you speak to Jack and let him tell you himself how things are between us? On the other hand, he may well consider that his private life is his own affair. In which case we should perhaps forget we ever had this conversation.' She turned away with finality. 'Goodnight, Mrs Renfrey.'

Laura's bedroom door was just behind them. She took no small pleasure in closing it quietly but firmly in her hostess's face. Pulling off her clothes, she stood under a very hot shower without a lucid thought in her mind. Rage buoyed her up until, half an hour later, she and Jack were having their first quarrel, she in the Chinese wrap he had bought her in Suva, drying her hair at the mirror, he pacing the room, smoking one of those thin black cheroots his father liked so much.

'I know you're upset. And I'm sorry. I should have known the name would crop up.'

'Crop up!' Laura exploded. 'According to your mother you're going to marry the wretched girl.'

'That's rubbish. Something the two families have been trying to engineer ever since we met. The perfect business deal from my mother's point of view.' He twisted the stub of his cheroot into the pot of pink orchids on the dressing table, not looking at her. The line of his jaw was clenched tight, the muscle twitching beneath his ear the way it did when his anger was about to boil over. 'My mother . . .' he said, under his breath.

The childish relief she felt almost blotted out everything else. But not quite.

'You should have told me about her. So that I was prepared for the onslaught. At least I was honest with you about Martin.'

'And how!' He turned to confront her. His face was white. 'Cut me down for even daring to approach you. And all the time playing with me, like a cat with a mouse, running through all those little female tricks just for your own amusement. And your own vanity too, I suppose.'

Laura was appalled. 'Is that how you saw it?'

'Funny you never asked me that question before. You were far too concerned with your own feelings, of course. Sorry, Jack. I'm going to marry Martin. Now run away and play on these South Sea beaches of yours.'

His mimicry of her voice stung her more than anything else. 'That's not true!'

'How else could I take it? You made the choice and I heard no more from you. Nothing for more than a year. Thirteen months and three weeks, to be exact.' He was standing behind her shoulder now, looking at the two faces in the mirror that stared at one another like strangers. 'Did you really expect me just to sit around and pine? I'm hardly the celibate type, am I? You'd surely agree about that.'

'So you picked up a girl called Kim?'

'I met the family when they were visiting my mother, and she made a play for me. She's very young, very attractive, and likes her own way.

She obviously wanted to have an affair, and I didn't see any reason not to. I suppose I was looking for something.' He hesitated. 'I became pretty fond of her.'

She sat motionless, the towel in her lap, still watching him.

'And then suddenly you come on the scene again, as if you're doing me a favour,' he went on, with a cutting edge that frightened her. 'A letter out of the blue, expecting me to drop everything just because you were suddenly at a loose end. Available after all, you might say.'

The 'available' caught her unawares, made her stiffen. But the voice behind her went on inexorably.

'That's typical of you, isn't it? Thinking only of yourself. Totally wrapped up in your own daydreams. Just as you've been wrapped up in these ridiculous obsessions about your mother.'

She sprang up and hit him at the same moment the words were out of his mouth. It was a single reflex action of outrage, the wet towel catching him hard across the face with all the force she could summon.

'You dare to talk about my mother. Even now. After what happened to her.'

He had his hand up over his eyes. She heard him swear at her, softly and savagely. It excited her at the same time as it shocked her. She realized she must have hurt him a little, even with such an amateurish attack.

'If only you'd told me,' she cried, fighting back remorse. 'Told me about her, that day at the airport. I would never . . .'

Never have got involved again, was what she was going to say. But the words wouldn't come. She knew it was a lie. Nothing could have stopped that headlong rush into joy, that total surrender regardless of the consequences. You might as well ask someone dying of thirst to turn away from the hand offering a long glass of water.

Jack's eyes were holding hers now. In them she saw the same images that were flooding through her own mind – the hotel bedroom, the pool at Vailima, the scent and taste of each other's skin, the annihilating moment of possession.

'Never?' he repeated.

With a sudden movement he snatched the towel from her hand and looped it around her shoulders, pulling her hard against him. They did not kiss. Instead he bent his head and put his tongue gently against the hollow of her collarbone, a favourite place.

'There was no choice, was there?' she heard him say. 'There never will be. I knew it as soon as I had your letter.'

Slowly he moved the towel against her back from side to side as if he were drying her. Her face against his, she said his name softly. It was almost like fainting, the slight dizziness as she closed her eyes, giving herself up to ecstasy again.

The sound of footsteps broke in from another world. Voices were passing in the passageway, servants' voices, then Jack's parents, talking together as they went to their room.

'You mustn't stay,' she whispered. She pulled away from him. The separation was painful. 'We have to wait until tomorrow.'

'Tomorrow.' He held her hand to his face. 'Darling Laura. We do hurt each other, don't we?' His eyes searched hers. 'That thing with Kim, every time I thought of you, remembering London, I knew it was pointless, pretending that anything else could be the same. There never was any real commitment between Kim and myself. You must understand that.'

'And now?'

'When I got your letter, I told her about us. But now I have to see her and make certain she understands. It's only fair. She has other irons in the fire, you see. She's that kind of girl.' He smiled ruefully.

'Then you must do it straight away. Tomorrow.'

He shook his head. 'Tomorrow is ours. The morning after we have to stop at Korolevu for fuel. I'll see her there at the hotel, explain about the weekend – and everything else.' He pressed her hand. 'Do you mind?'

'Will it take long?' Laura asked, teasing.

'Don't be silly,' he said, irritation in his voice.

The footsteps went past again. Jack waited for a moment before quietly opening the door.

'And after that, Sawai,' he said in her ear as he kissed her, lightly this time, quickly. 'Remember the island I told you about, the one with the cave?'

'I remember.'

Then he was gone.

CHAPTER FOUR

Now here was the name on the map in front of them, attached to a solitary pinprick right on the edge of the folded crease of blue Pacific. Standing in the wheelhouse next to Charlie, Laura bent closer to study the tiny print of the other island names of the outlying Yasawas.

'Sawai is the very last in the group,' he told her. He pointed to another dot in the middle of the chain. 'That's as far as we'll get today, Kamba Lailai.' He turned to peer out across the seemingly endless glitter of the open sea.

'See over there, that little smudge on the horizon?'

Laura screwed up her eyes obediently. 'I thought it was a cloud.'

'That's what they always say. I expect the old exploring ships thought so too at first. Imagine the moment when they actually realized it was land ahead. Food and fresh water, and local maidens to woo.'

'There were always local maidens if Charlie's stories are to be believed,' Jack said behind them. 'But you need to be a blue-rinse American widow to get the full repertoire. The Virgins' Leap – that's the island where they all jumped off the highest cliff rather than succumb to the embrace of an invading tribe. Then there's the Giant's Cave, inhabited by a ten-foot feathered monster who lives on human flesh. Not forgetting the shark god who stirs up a hurricane if you forget to throw him some kava overboard.'

'They all come from Meli and Sam here.' Charlie grinned as he tipped his head towards the two Fijians busy in the galley. 'And they got them from their grandfathers. So none of us are to blame.'

There was chortling from below. 'Teatime, boss,' called one of them as three brimming mugs were handed up through the hatch.

Laura took hers out on deck and climbed up to sit cross-legged on the cabin roof. The dark brown liquid thick with condensed milk and spiced with rum bore no resemblance to any tea she knew. The potent taste of it belonged only to this particular moment, the sting of salt spray on her face where the sun had caught her, the lazy throb of the ship's engines beneath her, the long plume of foam trailing in their wake, white against the blue. Despite the breeze, it was very hot. But heat was now her natural element, part of the low-grade fever of being in love. Physical passion did this to you, she thought. But it was something more, an invasion of the inner self that raised the psychological temperature in the oddest way. Every impression was heightened, and yet everything was off-balance and out of focus. There was only one true centre of gravity, depending on where Jack happened to be, how close or how far away.

Still daydreaming, she heard the sound of the ship's conch shell being blown by Meli, a hollow hooting that was eerily like the double call of an owl. It was a signal that they would soon be putting in to land. But Laura stayed where she was. She wanted to be alone when they dropped anchor. She remembered reading Robert Louis Stevenson. 'The first love, the first sunrise, the first South Sea island, are memories apart and touch a virginity of sense . . .'

With the movement of the yacht through the water, the island itself seemed to tack and sway as it came closer, still curiously two-dimensional like a floating piece of scenery. It struck Laura that nothing could be further from the popular idea of a desert island as a palm tree perched on a sandbank. Kamba was a kind of Caliban's retreat, a ruined castle of crags and peaks, curtained with thick-hanging vine and fern. At its base was the half-moon of a tiny beach. The rocks that encircled it had been eroded into a gallery of modern sculptures, mysterious monuments to the forces of wind and tide.

This side of the island was already in shadow. Slowly the sky behind it was flooded with colour as the sunset took fire, that extraordinary Pacific conflagration of the most intense scarlet and gold, banked high with purple clouds. The sun itself was almost extinguished. Behind her she heard Jack say, 'Look out for the green streak. It's lucky to see it.'

They watched together as the sun slipped out of sight into the sea. At the same instant a thin phosphorescent line flew along the horizon, like electricity along a wire. Then it was gone again. Simultaneously, the ship's engines died away.

'I saw it,' Laura said. She leaned back against him and felt the silence hold them together.

Only the rattle of the anchor chain broke the spell. Soon after, the little rowboat was let down over the side to take them ashore as the three of them, with the two Fijians, set up camp on the beach. They were staying at Kamba overnight, Charlie announced. They could sleep under canvas or on board as they chose.

First there was supper, an improvised barbecue over a driftwood fire, roasted walu fish and grilled plantains, with the traditional *Tongan Queen* brew of pineapple juice, fresh lime and rum. The light from the flames gleamed yellow-gold over the circle of faces, hypnotic against the dark, drowsy-making. Laura felt as if the salt in the air was actually sealing her eyelids together.

She was roused by Jack's touch on her arm. He said nothing but gently pulled her up by the hand. Charlie glanced up from the guitar he had brought ashore, then went on strumming, head bent low over the strings, the voices of Meli and Sam in soft counterpoint on either side. The singing drifted away into the lapping sound of the shallows against their feet.

'There's a better beach on the other side,' Jack told her. They were walking with their arms around each other along the edge of the sea.

'I suppose you arranged for the full moon as well?'

'Don't you remember ordering it, just a couple of days ago?'

Always afterwards, it was the moonlight that eclipsed everything else in her mind, imprinting itself indelibly on every moment of their lovemaking. Jack had joked about it in his Noël Coward voice as they stood facing one another, suddenly self-conscious, on the far side of the point.

'You look so lovely in this damned moonlight, Amanda . . .'

But this was not the soft glow of English moonlight, Laura thought. Here at the equator, the moon hung so huge and close above the Southern Cross that the light flooded down from it with a power and brilliance that were almost threatening. This moonlight turned everything into something else. The sand beneath them glittered like ground diamonds. The long pointed leaves of the pandanus bushes were blades of polished steel, and the fruit on the wild tamarind looked as brittle as baubles on a Christmas tree. Even the sea had the sheen of metal, seemed not to be moving at all. Only behind them was darkness where the cliffs rose up, overhanging the beach. From here, a line of tall palms threw their own curious shadows, slanting bars of black across the white so that, lying together, the two of them seemed to be enclosed in a cage of moonlight.

There was a strangeness about their lovemaking too. Laura felt it at once, a relentless quality that was almost cruel as they exacted from one another only the most extreme of pleasures. There were no words between them. When Laura heard herself cry out, it was the sound of someone she did not know. The moon seemed to be staring down at her so that her nakedness felt unnatural. Lying quite still on her back alongside Jack, she felt as if she were studying them both from a distance. It was like looking at a still from an old black-and-white movie, or the stone effigy of a medieval man and wife in an English church.

'I think we have been punishing one another,' she murmured. She could feel the sweat chilling between them.

'It's only because we care so much,' he said quietly.

'As if we're frightened we might lose each other, all over again?'

It was half a question, but neither of them responded to it. For herself, Laura sensed that the shadow of an outsider had fallen across them. Somehow, even at a distance, the girl Kim had the power to make them uneasy with one another, almost strangers.

'Nothing's perfect,' she heard Jack say. He stood up abruptly. 'Even in paradise.'

She smiled a little. It so perfectly echoed what she herself was feeling at that moment. But it seemed he was talking about something else.

'These damn sandflies,' he grumbled, brushing himself down. 'Worse than mosquitoes.' He reached down and took her hand. 'Come on, or we'll be bitten to death. Besides, they'll be wondering where we are.'

She shivered. 'I'm cold. We'll go back on board to sleep?'

He nodded, slipping his jacket over her shoulders as they walked together the way they had come. 'It's best.'

The yacht stayed at anchor that night. The sea remained calm. The others were also back on board, but all was quiet. The only sound was the regular rustle of the current against the side of the vessel. Lying alone in her little cabin, Laura found it hard to sleep. She was thinking of the Australian girl, wondering how she would react to the confrontation. Would she simply accept that it was the end of the affair? Or would she lose her temper and make demands?

Finally, in the dawn chill, she pulled the thin blanket over her and fell asleep, so deeply asleep that she only half-heard Jack's voice as he put his head round the door, nine hours later.

'Don't disturb yourself. We're going ashore now.'

'We're at Korolevu already?' She was flustered, trying to collect herself. 'I didn't hear a thing.'

'We came round by sail. Sam's coming off with Charlie and myself to bring some stuff on board. Meli'll be here to look after you.'

'Jack?' She raised herself on one elbow, pushing her hair out of her eyes. 'When you see Kim . . .' She broke off, reaching for his hand. 'It may be difficult.'

'Just leave it to me, Laura. Please.' She could feel how tense he was, even as he bent to kiss her. 'Only be about half an hour.'

Half an hour. Drowsily Laura looked out through the porthole and watched the three men climb up on to the jetty with its sprawl of tourist shops and hotel fronts. When they were out of sight, sleep pulled her back again for another ten minutes. Then there was the sound of crockery and a tap on the door as Meli brought her fresh rolls, fruit and coffee.

'You okay, marama?'

'Just a bit sleepy, Meli, thanks.'

She took her second cup up on deck, still in her crumpled cotton pyjamas, her hair pulled back in a tortoiseshell clip. It was peaceful to be alone, she thought. Not all that hard either to shut out anxiety, lying back in one of the old canvas chairs, the sun hot on her face, listening to Meli moving about below and distant voices on the shore.

Suddenly one voice cut through all the others, a woman's voice, unmistakably Australian.

'Hi there!'

Even as she opened her eyes, Laura knew what kind of picture to expect. It was one she had turned over in her mind often enough in the past twenty-four hours. The only difference was that the girl walking along the jetty at Jack's side was very much prettier than she had imagined, tall and slim with a mass of curly ash-blonde hair, long legs glossy with suntan under crisp white shorts.

'Sorry to wake you up!' the voice went on cheerfully. The next minute she was in close-up, swinging herself up the ladder and over the rail.

'I'm Kim,' she announced. The smile was wide with small perfect teeth, the large blue eyes fringed with mascara. A strong musky perfume cut through the morning air, reminding Laura of Auntie Atu's remarks. Gold hoop earrings caught the sun. So did the elaborate charm bracelet that jangled over her wrist as she held out her hand.

All these details were automatically registered by Laura as she sat forward to return the greeting. It took steely will to smile back. Worst of all, she had a clear picture of herself still scruffy from bed, unmade-up and shiny-faced and in need of a shower.

'Hello. I'm Laura.'

She found herself concentrating on the fact that the girl was carrying no luggage. She must be coming simply to see them off, to show there were no hard feelings perhaps. Laura couldn't help admiring the kind of confidence it took to make such a gesture, and the coolness too. Then she caught sight of the expensive leather suitcase in Jack's hand as he came up the steps behind her.

'Kim's joining us for the trip,' he said.

His eyes held Laura's. She could read the signals of reassurance. 'Sorry about this,' the look was saying. 'There was nothing I could do.'

'There was this phone call from Jack's mother saying you were coming. So there I was, sitting all on my own at the hotel, expecting to be picked up to go to Nailangi.' Kim's face mimicked pathos as she glanced from one to the other. 'My parents went on ahead last night,' she told Laura. 'So kind Jack took pity on me. Said I could come along too.' There was the tiniest pause. 'You don't mind, Laura?'

The words seemed to hang on the air, posing a larger, unspoken question.

'Of course not.'

Laura got up and went across to the rails, staring out at the coastline but seeing nothing. Jack had disappeared below with the suitcase.

'He's told me what's happened between the two of you.' Kim had come to stand beside her, looking not at the view but at Laura. Laura refused to meet her look.

'It seems it's something he's taking seriously.' She spoke in an undertone. 'You too?'

'Me too.'

'I always knew Jack really needed someone more experienced than myself. More mature is what I mean.'

It was the bite in the 'mature' that made Laura turn to face her. Close to, she could see perspiration stand out on Kim's glossy upper lip. The mascara was not quite perfect either. There was a smudge where it had been rubbed with a handkerchief. I should feel sympathy, she thought, but I don't. Behind the smiles this girl is nervous, but she is also ruthless. It was the ruthlessness of an extremely spoilt child about to be deprived of a favourite toy.

'Anyway,' Kim went on lightly, 'we've certainly had fun together, Jack and I. He's a marvellous lover. Five-star I'd say, wouldn't you?'

The question took Laura's breath away, not just the nerve of it but the crudeness. She turned away again, feeling revulsion.

'I don't award sexual ratings to someone I love.'

'I'll bet you don't.' Kim laughed. 'How very typical Pom. What I'm getting at is that there's no reason why we can't be civilized about the situation.'

'Civilized! I'm all for that.' Charlie was standing at the top of the gangway. He tossed the word back at them with a grin that was meant to defuse the unmistakable moment of confrontation. How much had he actually overheard, Laura wondered. 'What's more uncivilized than a threesome, after all? I've never been all that good at playing gooseberry.'

He put a hand on Kim's bare shoulder. But his eyes were on Laura. The expression on his face was playful, hopeful? It was hard to tell.

'I'm going to get dressed.' Laura made quickly for the stairs down to the cabins. She had to talk to Jack, find out what exactly had happened at the hotel. But Kim was close behind her.

'Don't I get accommodation too?' she called to Jack. He was holding open the door of the cabin next to Laura's.

'I've put your things in here, Kim. We should be back at Nailangi by midday tomorrow. So it's only for one night.'

'And then?' Kim cocked her head up at him with that maddening winsome smile.

'Laura and I have to keep going, get back to Vailima.' He spoke briskly, as if to a difficult child. 'We've got a lot to do to sort ourselves out for Canberra. As I was telling you.'

Once again, Charlie's voice broke through the tension. His face appeared above them in the hatchway.

'Meanwhile, the world is our oyster. Martinis are ready mixed on the observation deck. Sullivan Tours Limited is about to take you on its famous magical mystery trip to the underwater caves of Sawai.'

'Sawai!' Kim breathed. She took Charlie's outstretched hand, then turned and bestowed her radiant smile on Laura. 'You'll love it. Jack took me there last year. It's a fabulous place.'

Jealousy was a poor word for the sensation that gripped Laura at that moment, totally unawares. It was violently physical, a spasm of cold sickness in the stomach that made her want to throw up. Nothing she had ever felt in the past, over Martin's marriage for instance, had been like this. Why should she find herself at the mercy of such raw and humiliating emotion about a relationship that was now over? Over for Jack maybe, an inner voice replied, but obviously not for Kim. Slowly the sickness subsided. Danger was what she now sensed, a warning signal that sent waves of adrenalin through every nerve of her body as she showered and dressed.

Yet it was strange how, sitting together in the hot sunshine sipping the razor-edged iced martinis, a different mood slowly descended on all four of them. At first, it seemed to Laura a painful travesty of everything she had ever hoped for from the expedition. Even this outward picture of a hedonistic foursome cruising the South Seas was a charade. How could Jack ever have brought such a shallow and irritating creature as Kim to an island that meant so much to him, she asked herself? And then plan to take her to the same place? Perhaps it only indicated that the island held no special memories for him as far as Kim was concerned. Besides, men were famously unsentimental about the connections of time and place, or so it always seemed.

Something of what she was feeling communicated itself to Jack. Quickly he leaned forward and pulled her cotton wrap closer over her shoulders.

'Don't get burned. You don't need a tan in Canberra. It's city life there, not beaches.'

He smiled his private smile. That helped. So did the martinis. And all the time there was the subtle narcotic effect of the open sky and sea, the ever-changing brilliance of amethyst and turquoise, island shapes drifting like mirages along the far horizon. Sometimes a porpoise lifted out of the water nearby, and once a shoal of flying fish glittered upwards in a magical arc before gliding back under the waves again.

Then Charlie was making them laugh with his outrageous stories of his tourist passengers. One of them, a wealthy widow in her seventies, had tried to make him promise to take over the running of her Texas ranch, 'all perks included'. But Charlie shook his head ruefully.

'Sounded too much like hard work for me.'

Little by little Laura felt the painful emotions die down. A numbing sense of well-being took over instead. Delicious food had appeared from the galley, prawn curry, crab salad, grilled breadfruit and fresh mangoes to go with the cold chardonnay. Afterwards, cushions were brought out along with a huge Hawaiian mat. There was an innocent sensual pleasure about the way the four of them lay sprawled together in the patch of shade under the awning, bare feet and shoulders brushing close. The faint sound of guitar chords drifting up from below was all part of the same spell, the Fijian malua or why-worry that was the secret password to everything in the South Seas. Perhaps this was how one of those orgies started, she thought idly. The intimacy of a truce between enemies. She closed her eyes and gave herself up to the rocking movement of the boat through the water.

When she awoke Jack was standing over her, shaking his head and smiling.

'All you ever do is sleep. Just like a Siamese cat. Come on, we're nearly there.'

She sat up. The engines died away and once again she heard the grating rattle of the anchor chain going down. Everything had changed. A tall headland rose up out of the water, quite close, a sandy cove beneath. Sawai. On board there was a sudden sense of purpose.

'This is where we swim,' Charlie commanded, emerging from the wheelhouse. Like Jack, he had already changed into faded denim bathing shorts.

'Not just to get ashore,' came Kim's voice from behind. She was childishly excited, tying back her hair in a silk scarf to match her yellow bikini. 'It's the way we get into the cave, going underwater.'

Immediately Laura felt the dread she had known at school sports, holding her breath before taking the plunge into the deep end with the rest of the team. Kim was the girl who always won, who mocked her relentlessly for her fear of being trapped below the surface. Saying nothing, she ran down to change. The brief sarong she wound round herself was a kind of freedom, at least. She always wore it instead of a tight-fitting swimsuit. Besides, being honest, she had to admit she had no inclination to compete with the vital statistics of a model twenty-year-old.

'Cheat!' Kim called out as she reappeared.

'Wrong again,' Jack called back to her. 'It's what all the island girls wear to go swimming. Besides, I chose Laura's myself.'

'And beautiful she looks in it too,' said Charlie in an undertone next to her.

They followed the other two into the water together. The swim to the shore was a gentle one. Within a few yards the beach shelved up to meet them and they were stepping out on to the smooth stones.

'Hang on!' Charlie stooped to retrieve something. 'Look here!' He held aloft something that looked like a bath loofah. 'Marvellous place for things like this.'

Kim recoiled in mock horror as he tried to press it into her hand. 'What on earth is it?'

'Sort of sea urchin. What the Romans used to make that purple dye of theirs. Bet you didn't know that!'

He took a leap on to a rock higher up, pulling Laura up with him. With the sea urchin still in his hand he struck a gladiator's pose, laughing and holding her close.

He's trying to help, fooling about like this, she thought. The entrance to the cave was visible now, dark and narrow, just above them. He can see how nervous I am. She was grateful for the reassurance of his body next to hers, thinner than Jack's and paler with patches of sunburn across the shoulders.

It was Kim's cue to take Jack's hand.

'We'll go first. I've done it before. Nothing to it really. Just take a deep breath and hold on to the person with you, till you come out inside.'

Jack, who knew Laura so well, looked back at her, an anxious shadow on his face.

'You don't have to do it, you know. If you don't like the idea.'

'I want to,' she said obstinately. 'I want to see inside.'

'Charlie will hang on to you. You're only underwater for about twenty seconds. Then you're out in the pool.'

For Laura, the panic began the moment they stepped up into the cave. The water at their feet looked horribly dark and still, and the rock wall beyond seemed impenetrable. There was no sign of the others. They must be already on the other side.

'Just two or three feet underneath, there's a gap,' Charlie told her. 'That's the way through. Then once you're inside, the light is wonderful, almost blue. And there's a ledge in the rock you can walk through to another grotto, further in.'

Laura nodded, trying to imagine it, her heart beating hard.

'Here, put these on.' He took the goggles he had tied round his waist and pulled them on for her. Then he took her hand in his as they climbed down into the water. 'We can go through side by side almost. It's wide enough. Just keep hold.'

It was no good. Laura was a strong swimmer, but the moment she dived and saw solid rock around her, just inches away, the panic exploded. Claustrophobia was something that threatened her in any enclosed place. But this was different. As in a nightmare, the water above her was a glass lid holding her down. She had an overwhelming sense of having lived through it all before, in some other time, some other place. A picture formed in her mind like a bubble, a picture of a woman struggling underwater, fighting to reach the surface. Without framing the thought, she knew it was her mother.

Almost at once she felt willpower return. Desperately she tugged at Charlie's hand, trying to pull him back. He turned and through the goggles she saw the alarm on his face, distorted like some stupid horror film. Instantly he responded, pushing them both backwards as hard as he could.

The next moment they were out of the water, out of the cave, back in the daylight again. He took hold of her by the shoulders.

'Are you all right?'

'Not really.' She was gasping for breath, shuddering, and very cold.

'You look awful. Come on. Climb up here into the sun.'

Above the cave entrance there was a pile of flat boulders. Gratefully Laura collapsed onto the warm stone, feeling relief flood over her.

'Sorry.' She shook the water out of her ears. 'I should have known.'

Charlie's arm was still around her shoulders. He stroked her gently.

'Don't be silly. Lots of people feel like that down there. I did myself, the first time. It's a strange place.' He looked at her closely. 'Laura! It's not that important, for God's sake.'

'I know. It's just that I wonder how I would cope with real danger, on my own?'

'I think you'd surprise yourself,' Charlie said quietly. 'There are different kinds of danger, you know.'

She moved away a little so that his arm was no longer around her. She leaned back against the stone, rubbing her hands through her hair. 'You're very kind to me.'

'It's the girl that's really upset you, isn't it?' She looked up at him and saw he was studying her face, frowning. 'Why on earth she had to come . . .'

'Jack could hardly leave her there, could he?' She couldn't help sounding defensive. 'How else would she get to Nailangi?'

'As long as Jack knows how lucky he's been, finding you. Miss Kim Maguire . . .' There was scorn in his voice. He broke off, staring across at the little yacht bobbing beyond the line of the breakers. 'She's a very determined young woman, you know. You need to watch her.'

'Don't worry. I can look out for myself.' She laughed. 'Most of the time, anyway.'

'And when you can't . . .' He stopped. 'Remember, I'm around.'

'Yes, I know,' she said, touched. 'Thanks, Charlie.' She looked at her watch. 'They'll be worried about what's happened to us, won't they?'

'Jack will.'

He said no more. She got to her feet.

'Can we go back on board now?'

She began walking down the rocks. At the same moment they heard the sound of the conch shell, a loud double blast floating across the water.

'Meli wants us back.' He leapt past her to lead the way down. 'It must be something urgent.'

Together they reached the water's edge. But before they could start to swim out they saw a little rowboat being lowered over the side. Within seconds Meli was alongside them, helping them in.

'Not trouble with the anchor, I hope,' Charlie said. 'Not caught in the coral again, is she?'

Meli shook his head, bending over the oars. 'A message over the radio. Mr Renfrey wants you to call him at Nailangi right away. You or Mr Jack.'

'Did he say what it was?'

Meli's face was creased with concentration, and curiosity too. 'Something to do with Ratu Edwin Vunilau.'

Laura was startled. Something told her the message involved her.

She climbed up to the deck, and slipped on the robe Sam had ready for her. Charlie was already crouched over the keyboard in the tiny wireless room, a towel round his waist, pulling on the headphones. After a minute or so, a voice came through from the other end, faint and tinny. She strained to hear what was being said, but it was impossible. She only saw Charlie's expression of anxiety change to puzzlement.

'I don't understand. Where is she to go?'

He listened again, his eyes on Laura. His expression was almost disbelieving.

'You want me to tell her?' And then, 'Yes, I understand. We'll be reporting back to you this evening.' He paused, still looking at Laura and said, 'I'll tell her now.'

Slowly he replaced the headphones and clicked off a couple of switches.

'Laura.' He stood and took her hands in his, his face intensely serious. 'Max Renfrey has had an extraordinary message from Ratu Edwin. It's for you, but Max wanted me to break it to you first.'

Laura found it difficult to be patient. 'Yes?'

'Apparently Ratu Edwin is at Funafuti island, on his way to the Gilberts. He's just been told a very strange story.'

'My mother?' She suddenly knew it was what she'd been waiting for all along.

Charlie nodded. 'Yes. A story about your mother.' His grip on her hands tightened.

'What . . . What did he . . . ?' No other words would come. Her mouth was dry, her mind whirling.

'Without raising your hopes too much . . .' He paused, his eyes holding hers. 'It seems there's a possibility your mother might still be alive.'

CHAPTER FIVE

'Alive?'

It was Jack's voice repeating the word from the doorway of the wireless room. Laura and Charlie, standing over the switchboard, had their backs to him. So absorbed were they in what was happening they had not even noticed that he and Kim were on board again. Turning, Laura saw the expression of astonishment on his face.

'Surely you're not going to believe that? After what my father was telling you just two days ago? Where has this extraordinary message come from?' He was speaking to Charlie now, with a note of anger in his voice.

'It was your father,' Charlie said. 'Ratu Edwin has been on the phone to him with a message for Laura. Apparently there's an old man he's come across in the Ellice Islands who knows something about her mother.'

'Such as?'

'Max didn't know the details. Except the man was on Taparua when the war broke out. He used to work for Laura's father. He wants to talk to her.'

'Jack!' Laura moved across to take his hand, barely able to control her excitement. 'It must be Timu, my father's medical orderly. You remember, his daughter keeps house for my father. She told me he might be able to help.'

'Laura darling, you must calm down.' His face was dark as he put his arm round her. 'These people are so unreliable. Rumours run through the islands like wildfire.' He frowned. 'I'm afraid it was that broadcast of yours. I knew it at the time.'

'What do you mean?'

'Someone out there heard your name, heard you talking about your mother, and passed the word on to this Timu. I expect he just wants to tell you some stories about the old days. Silly old fool, raising your hopes for nothing.'

'And Ratu Edwin?' she broke in. Anger was rising in her too, anger and disappointment at his reaction. 'Do you really think he's in the business of spreading rumours?'

'But he's just the same, can't you see? All these people love to tell you things they know you want to hear. It's the way they are. And obviously there's nothing definite to go on, otherwise he would certainly have told my father.'

The exasperation in his voice died away. He drew her to him and looked at her closely. 'I've been worried about you, can't you imagine? What happened at the cave? You're shaking like a leaf. White as a sheet, under that sunburn.' He pressed his face to hers, then glanced across at Meli. 'Get her some hot tea, for Christ's sake. And put some brandy in it.'

'I don't want tea or brandy.' She pushed herself away from him. They were losing time. 'Ratu Edwin is waiting for us, at Funafuti. How long will it take to get there?'

She saw him looking at her with dismay.

'Laura! There's no question . . .' He broke off, trying to contain himself.

'About two days. Three at the most.'

She had almost forgotten Charlie was there. He sounded his usual laconic self. 'Turning north from where we are it's open sea all the way,' he went on. 'If there's a following wind, we could put some sail up too.'

Jack turned on his heel. 'I think we need to talk,' he said to Laura over his shoulder.

In the passage outside, Kim was fastening up the dress she'd obviously changed into in a hurry. Her hair was wrapped in a towel, her face excited.

'What's happening?'

'Better ask Charlie,' was all Jack said. He had hold of Laura's arm and was leading her down the stairway. The door of his cabin was open. Rumpled clothes and scattered belongings lay everywhere, as they always did with Jack. She found herself sitting next to him on the unmade bunk. She steeled herself for another confrontation.

'Please, Jack. Let's not quarrel. Not now.'

'There's no need. It's quite simple.' He was facing her, his eyes intent on hers. 'There's no question of us going to the Ellice Islands. I have to be back at Vailima tomorrow to catch the flight to Canberra the next day.' He paused. '*We* have to be back at Vailima, that is. You're coming with me, remember?'

Laura bit her lip. 'I'm sorry, Jack.'

'Sorry?'

'Everything's changed now. I have to get to Funafuti as soon as I possibly can.' She tried to speak slowly. She was struggling to convey to him the absolute certainty she felt. 'I just have this feeling now, that I'm getting close to her.'

'But, Laura.' He seemed lost for words. 'You can't really believe your mother's still alive?'

'I can't know it for certain. But perhaps Ratu Edwin's come up with the last chance there is to know what really happened. I have to take it, don't I? You must see that.'

He sat silently, looking away from her and frowning. After a moment he said quietly, 'Listen, Laura. You've already gone through so many explanations as to how your mother died. First you believe your father was responsible in some way. Next you see the certificate with date and cause of death. And then you hear from my father an account of her suicide. In the face of all this, because secretly you're still looking for something more, you grasp at any straw that comes along.'

'That's not true!'

He turned back to her, his face set. 'Laura, it's become an obsession, this search of yours. And the tragedy is, it's a hopeless search. I tell you that for the last time.'

'What do you mean, for the last time?'

He sighed. 'I'm tired of it, Laura. I have my own life to get on with. I thought it was to be our life, together. But it obviously holds no interest for you.'

'Jack, please. You must see my point of view.'

He began to pull on a clean shirt that was lying on the bed. 'And you must see mine. You promised me about Canberra. I was counting on you.'

'But I may only be gone a week or so,' Laura protested. 'Then I can fly out to join you.'

'Life's not like that, I'm afraid.' He shrugged. 'Once you're back in those islands, one thing will lead to another. You may decide to stay there for good, for all I know.'

Not for the first time, Laura thought how childishly stubborn he could look, his lower lip jutting and eyes turned down.

'Don't be ridiculous, Jack. There's no question of that. It's just that . . .' She hesitated. 'I want you to be with me. Couldn't you come?'

'Well, that's the last straw!' He stood up abruptly. 'And what about me? This interview's a turning-point for me. You're not honestly suggesting I give it up, are you? To go off with you on yet another wild goose chase, just to prove some theory that only exists inside your head?' He was looking at her directly now, distancing himself in his anger. 'Honestly Laura, I sometimes wonder if you're not as crazy as that wretched father of yours.'

She heard her own sharp intake of breath. The words stunned her. Besides the outrage she felt something else, an undercurrent of fear about herself that she hardly dared to acknowledge.

'How can you say that to me?' she whispered.

She could see from his face that he instantly regretted it. To cover himself, he searched for fresh ammunition.

'I suppose you've worked out how you're actually getting there?'

Staring out of the porthole, she said, 'Fiji Airways run a flight, don't they?'

'Once a fortnight,' he flung back at her. 'A lot of use that'll be.' He crossed to the door, then stopped. 'Oh for God's sake! Charlie will take you there. He's obviously only too ready and willing.'

'What about you? How will you get back to Nailangi?'

His answer was to slam the door behind him. After a moment Laura got up and went into her own cabin. She felt bruised with the impact of so many different emotions. The hardest thing to absorb was the idea of breaking up with Jack. Were they really in the process of losing each other, as he claimed? Perhaps she was being unreasonable, expecting him to drop everything to go with her. Or perhaps it was just hurt pride on his part, the kind of bluff he liked to resort to when he was faced with a reversal. He made it sound like an ultimatum. But how could you put a full stop to a love affair which had already been tested in so many ways and survived?

As she lay down on the bunk, the same questions circled endlessly round in her head. But all the time there was a quite separate sense of elation. Her instincts might be right, after all. Out of the darkness surrounding the past, a door was opening. A new trail lay ahead and her guide on that journey, as she had somehow always known, was to be Ratu Edwin.

She had been lying there for a moment or so when there was a knock on the door. She sat up, half expecting Jack, but it was Meli bringing her tea. The quick dark eyes surveyed her discreetly as he put down the tray.

'You had some shock, marama. Maybe good news?'

'Maybe, Meli. I have to find out.'

'Take it easy, eh?' His face brightened. 'So we go north, all the way to the Ellice?'

As he spoke, they heard the sound of the engines starting up.

'What's happening, Meli? What's Mr Jack doing?'

'He been on the radio to Nailangi. The plane coming down from there to pick him up.' He nodded at her thoughtfully, with the hint of a smile. 'Mr Charlie is boss now, eh?'

'That's right.' She returned the smile with an effort. 'But what about the plane? Where will it put down?'

'Just the next island, marama. There is a place for landing there. Half an hour, it will be here. Now I must pack Mr Jack's things.' He looked at her expectantly.

She nodded. 'I'll be up in a little while.'

It was something she dreaded, saying goodbye. Perhaps she should stay down here in her cabin. But when, a little later, the engines came to a halt again, she knew she had to see him leave.

Up on deck, everything seemed to happen very quickly. The yacht had come to a standstill inside the lagoon of a large island that lay just fifty yards ahead. Jack was perched in the stern, watching the rope ladder go down. Kim would be going too, of course. I knew that, Laura told herself. So why should she feel any shock at seeing her standing there at the rails next to Jack, her shining leather case at her feet, her face alight as she looked up at him, talking. Of course. If she was losing Jack, she was losing him to the girl. How could she not have realized it?

As if on cue, Kim turned to greet her.

'Well, this is an unexpected luxury, being flown over to Nailangi. By private plane too.' The smile widened, a smile of victory. 'I hear you're having to miss out on your Australian trip.'

'I'm afraid so, yes. For the time being, at least,' Laura was careful to add.

'Never mind. I'll keep an eye on Jack for you.'

No one spoke for a moment.

'I'll be in Canberra myself for a bit. We're setting up a branch of the business there.' The high-pitched voice prattled on relentlessly. 'I expect we'll take the same flight over, won't we Jack?' She glanced round at him, but he was helping Sam put the luggage in the boat.

'I think Jack understands why I can't go,' Laura said.

'Well, of course. You had no choice.' Kim kissed her quickly on the cheek. 'Best of luck, Laura.' She laughed as she turned to go down the steps. 'Bit like one of those old detective stories, isn't it? Nobody knows how it's going to end.'

Climbing down gracefully, she disappeared into the boat. Jack was still standing at the rail. Laura willed him to look round at her, but when he did his face was without expression. On an impulse she went to him and put her arms round his neck.

'I'm so sorry, Jack.' She pressed herself close to him, then drew back to see his response. But he seemed far away from her already, his eyes on the island. Laura felt despair, as if everything was moving too fast. 'Where can I contact you? I need to let you know what happens.'

'My father will tell you.'

Then, for a second, she saw a kind of contraction pass over his face as if, deep below the surface, something was falling apart. Quickly he gripped both her hands in his. 'I don't know where I'll be staying yet. The Attorney General's department is my contact . . .'

His words were swept away in the loud buzz of an approaching aircraft. At the same moment the shadow of wings moved across them as it flew between the setting sun and the shore. Laura looked up at the little yellow Drover. It was so low now she could see the outline of the pilot's head and his raised hand in the cockpit. The shadow moved on, the noise fading away as the plane disappeared round to the other side of the island.

When she turned back, Jack was climbing down into the boat. Sam took up the oars and Kim looked up at her, waving. But Jack sat with hunched shoulders facing the shore as they were rowed away.

'Sorry. I've been down in the engine room.'

She was aware of Charlie standing just behind her.

'Sam's going back to Nailangi with them?' she said. She was making a tremendous effort to sound normal.

'Jack insisted. They need him there to run the river launch, for Mrs R.'

'You'll be able to manage the boat with just Meli?'

'You bet we'll manage.' He winked at cheerfully. 'I've taken you on as extra crew. You can cook, can't you?'

'As long as it's omelettes.' She smiled. 'You can't imagine how grateful I am to you, Charlie.'

'What for?'

'Offering to take me to Funafuti, of course.'

'All part of the Sullivan service,' he said lightly. 'Hope you enjoy it. The weather forecast is rather exciting.'

They watched together as the rowboat reached the headland. Charlie held out his binoculars to her but she shook her head. In the distance she saw Jack raise his arm towards them in a brief salute, his hat in his hand. It was enough. She had no desire to see a more detailed picture of the two of them. Then they disappeared round to the other side of the island.

'We'd better see them take off,' Charlie went on. 'I shouldn't think it's the ideal runway. More of a clearing. The Americans made it in the war for emergency landings.'

'Oh, God. If anything should go wrong.'

She spoke under her breath, but he looked at her sharply.

'You'd blame yourself, would you? Honestly, Laura. Don't you know the man yet? Jack's always doing this kind of thing. Loves the risk. He'll never change.'

'I think I'm the one who's taking the risk this time.' She put on her dark glasses although the sun was nearly gone. 'Don't you?'

He had his binoculars up. 'Could be. I did warn you.'

Silence fell between them as they stared out over the water. Then Charlie pointed. 'There she goes.'

A glint of yellow appeared above the trees, skimming the topmost branches. Laura held her breath. Slowly the little plane gained height, then dipped a fraction over the sea before settling itself on its course. Within minutes it was a speck in the sky no bigger than a butterfly, fading into the haze.

Laura's fingers loosened their grip on the rail. 'First-class pilot, that Australian chap of theirs,' Charlie was saying. 'Mind you, Jack's not bad either.'

'Jack.' She repeated the name to herself. Charlie surveyed her quizzically.

'God, you do love him, don't you? Trouble is, I think he's just as crazy about you, underneath everything.'

'Don't,' Laura said in a low voice. With that final glimpse of the plane, an awful deadness had taken hold of her. Even tears wouldn't come. There was only the cold realization that between them they might just have lost the most valuable thing they had ever been given.

'Supper,' she heard Charlie say, as from a distance.

They ate in the little dining saloon below, or rather Charlie ate. After a few mouthfuls of Meli's stew, Laura shook her head and pushed the plate to one side.

'Sorry.'

'He's not much of a cook, I'm afraid. I said you'd have to take over in the galley.'

'It's just that I'm not very hungry.'

In fact, for the first time she was feeling a twinge of seasickness. The *Tongan Queen* seemed to have developed a new rolling movement as she set out towards the north.

'Is this the bad weather you were talking about?' she asked him.

'Could be a bit choppy from now on. The Pacific doesn't always live up to its name. Are you a good sailor?'

'I wouldn't know – yet!'

'Never mind. There's a bottle of champagne left in the stores in case things get really bad. Nothing like it for seasickness. Better still if you drink it lying in a hammock.'

He smiled across at her. They were still sitting at the table, the old-fashioned lantern throwing dappled patterns of light and shade across them as it swung from its hook overhead. Spreading out a map between them, he'd put on an incongruous pair of spectacles that made him look almost schoolmasterly.

'Don't you want to see where we're going?' he asked.

'Of course.' She moved across to sit beside him and stared down at the jumbled patchwork of islands and reefs strung out across the expanse of blue. 'It's just that I hardly dare look, now I know I'm getting so near.'

'That's our port of call, Funafuti, where Ratu Edwin is, right in the middle of the Ellice group.' He pointed to another chain of atolls, slightly higher up. 'That's the Gilberts.'

She caught her breath, bending closer. 'And Taparua? It's not usually marked on the ordinary maps.'

They both searched among the scattering of tiny print.

'There it is.' His finger rested on one of the dots a little way out from the main island group. Laura felt a shiver across her shoulders.

'Will my mother be there, do you think?' She spoke abstractedly, not really expecting an answer.

Charlie glanced at her. 'Hardly. Your father would have known, wouldn't he? Unless . . .'

'Unless?'

'Unless he's been keeping the truth from you for some reason.'

'The truth! Why should it be so hard to actually get at?' She sat with bent head, her hands clenched tightly round one of the paper napkins, twisting it to and fro between her fingers. 'What do you think happened to her, Charlie?' She looked up at him in sudden appeal. 'Tell me, please. What do you think?'

Gently he took the napkin from her, enclosing her hands in his. 'Something quite different from anything you've been led to believe so far, I'd say. The Pacific is such a strange place, Laura, still so cut off in places, so secretive. Anything can happen out here. Anything does.' He kept hold of her hands. 'You'll know yourself quite soon. I'm sure of that. Ratu Edwin is not someone to be easily misled. You're lucky to have his support, official transport included, no doubt.'

He laid her hands back in her lap but his eyes remained steadily on hers. 'So after Funafuti, you won't need me any longer.'

'I don't know what I would have done . . .' she began.

'Please don't start thanking me again.' He had turned away to fold up the map. 'It's an adventure, isn't it? I like that. Besides, I'll no doubt be picking up some passengers there. There's always someone on the lookout for a boat to Fiji.'

At the name she looked up involuntarily at the clock on the wall.

'Jack will be back there by now. Back at Nailangi. Will he be going straight on home do you think, to Vailima?'

Will he be taking Kim with him, was her unspoken question.

Charlie got to his feet abruptly.

'For heaven's sake, Laura. Does it matter? Surely the important thing is what's happening to you, here and now, what's waiting for you, just ahead.' He cleared away their plates, and put away the map. 'It's such an extraordinary situation, this possibility that your mother may still be alive. I mean, how prepared for it are you, coming face to face with some unknown elderly woman after all these years?' He sounded almost impatient with her.

'Not prepared at all,' she said slowly, staring back at him. 'You don't understand anything. Can't you see? I'm deliberately blocking myself off from thinking about it. I've been led up so many different paths, turned everything over in my mind so often, wasted so much emotion. And then when I heard about her suicide, I shut down completely. Even now I just daren't hope – not until I've seen Ratu Edwin.' She stood up. 'I don't really want to talk about it any more.'

Before she could get to the door, the whole cabin gave a sudden lurch to one side. Taken by surprise, she lost her balance and would have fallen if Charlie had not been behind her to catch her round the waist.

'Captain to the rescue again,' she heard him say as she leaned back against him. There was that familiar self-mocking expression on the face close to hers.

'Laura. You must know how I feel about you.'

'I think I do.' She touched his hair lightly. 'But dear Charlie, you do see. My life's in enough turmoil already, without making it even more complicated.'

She moved away and he sighed. Then his expression changed. 'You needn't worry. I'll be good.' He looked across at her with that charming self-deprecating grin he'd given her when they first met. 'Scout's honour, brotherly love, that kind of thing.'

He broke off as there was a knock at the door and Meli's head appeared. His face was anxious.

'Glass is falling, Skip. Look's as if there's a rough spell coming up.'

'I'll come and take over.' He turned back to Laura and put his hand on her shoulder. 'Better try and get some sleep.'

CHAPTER SIX

Sleep was not easy for anyone that night. The wind had risen and all through the hours of darkness Laura was aware of the straining and creaking of timbers on every side as the little yacht braced itself against the weather. At six o'clock she decided she would be better off moving about, rather than lying entombed in a stuffy little cabin where the walls seemed to be tilting at different angles each time she opened her eyes.

Fumbling, she pulled on a pair of jeans and a sweater. It was just light, but the tiny porthole was so drenched with water it was impossible to see out.

Holding tight to the stair rail, she felt the whole vessel swing down sideways and up again. At the top she stopped and took a deep breath. This was a Pacific Ocean she had never seen before, yesterday's blue mirror replaced by a world of heaving grey. Rain drove into her face and the deck was slippery as ice under her bare feet.

'Careful, marama!'

She looked across to the far end where Meli was wresting with the ropes of the jib sail. Just yards away a roller of green water came crashing over the bows.

'Where's Charlie?' she called into the wind.

Meli jerked his thumb towards the wheelhouse. Inside she found a haggard-looking Charlie struggling to keep the boat on course, head to sea.

'Been on watch most of the night,' he told her. 'Meli's turn now.'

'I'll go and make breakfast,' she said.

He reached out and put an arm round her shoulder. 'Don't worry. It's only a bit of a gale. If it's a hurricane it usually makes for Fiji. Should be moving out of it soon.'

Meli appeared to take over and Charlie stumbled gratefully into a makeshift bed by the hatchway. When Laura took him some coffee she found him curled up fast asleep, wedged between damp pillows into the corner of an equally damp mattress. She pulled a blanket over him but hadn't the heart to wake him. Meli, however, one hand on the wheel, devoured almost the whole of the omelette she had managed to make, together with a hunk of bread, three mugs of strong tea and a bar of chocolate she had found in her bag. Surprisingly, she felt hungry now and ate something herself.

'You're very good mate, marama!' he called between mouthfuls. 'Now you go back to rest.'

But Laura preferred to stay on deck. Zipped into an anorak, she squeezed down between the hatch cover and the rowboat and sat looking out at the waste of angry sea. The glossy image of a Pacific paradise had been thrown away like an out-of-date magazine. This was the underside of the idyll, something the people who lived in the islands undertood so well. Never before had she realized how utterly lost you could feel between one glimpse of land and the next, how menaced by the cruel indifference of that empty horizon. It was something her mother must have felt day in and day out, in bad weather and good, trapped on her tiny atoll, a stranger in a strange land. It could even be the kind of world she still inhabited, Laura thought suddenly, still shut away in it for some mysterious reason for the rest of her life.

She closed her eyes tightly. All her willpower was concentrated on a single thought, as if she was praying. Except that this was not so much a prayer as a message. If you're out there, she was saying, I shall find you. The distance between us is getting less with every mile. Just hang on.

After a while, she got up stiffly and went back to her cabin to try to sleep. But it was no good. The minute she was lying down on that swaying bunk, the vertigo came back and she was gripped by waves of nausea. Once or twice she was actually sick. To her shame, Charlie came to her rescue, holding her waist and bringing her water.

The hours dragged by. But by the time nightfall came, the wind had dropped a little and they opened the promised bottle of champagne.

'Sorry we couldn't manage a hammock,' Charlie said as the three of them collapsed round the table in the saloon. 'Here's to you, Laura.' He raised one of the pewter mugs that were usually kept for beer. 'And to all you hope for.' Their eyes met and they smiled.

'To beautiful Funafuti,' said Meli, who had a girlfriend there and was looking forward to a brief but blissful reunion.

After the champagne, Laura felt able to face the galley again, and put together some soup and sandwiches. The sea was calmer now.

Charlie turned in while Meli took first watch. Laura slept well too, exhausted after the last twenty-four hours.

To her disappointment the next morning was still grey and drizzly. As the island of Funafuti came into view on the horizon it had a desolate look about it, like a spar of driftwood floating with the tide. It was Laura's first glimpse of a true atoll. She was amazed at how low it lay in the water, not much more than a sandbar, until the thatched roofs of a village came into view with palm trees clustered behind.

'It may look small,' Charlie told her as they tied up at the jetty. 'But it's the Port of London as far as the Ellice are concerned. And a damn good anchorage too!'

Laura was searching in vain for a familiar face amongst the little crowd that had gathered to watch their arrival. Somehow she had expected Ratu Edwin to be there to meet them. Nor could she spot an official launch, just a scattering of island boats and a few upturned canoes on the beach. Small naked boys wet from the sea came scampering round them, shouting and laughing. But there was no sign of her friend.

Laura's heart sank. 'Do you think we've missed him?'

But Charlie had spotted a jeep parked under the trees.

'That's probably him. Come on. Meli's got your bags.'

A young islander in police khaki scrambled out to salute them. Ratu Edwin was waiting at the airstrip, he told them.

'The airstrip?' Laura was confused.

'Plane to the Gilberts takes off in ten minutes. The Ratu say he will explain when he sees you.'

'Well, that's better than another sea journey,' Charlie told her cheerfully.

Laura put her hand on his arm.

'You're not coming, then? Just to the airfield?'

'No point, angel. You're in good hands with the orderly here. And I don't think you'll have any traffic problems.' He indicated the number plate EL1. 'The only four-wheeled vehicle in the Ellice Islands.'

They both laughed as she climbed up into the front seat.

'Besides,' he added, 'Meli and I have to get some supplies on board, take a look round for some likely passengers.'

'No blue-rinse widows here?' she teased.

'Not here, no.' His eyes were very blue as he smiled at her. The engine was starting up. 'Keep in touch, Laura. I want to know what happens, don't forget.'

She leaned down quickly and kissed him on the cheek. Then the jeep was rattling away. Turning, she saw the two figures waving at the end of the lane, the one so tall and fair in his crumpled whites, next to him the burly familiar shape of Meli in his luridly patterned sulu and shirt. Then the jeep rounded a bend and they were gone.

She felt a mounting sense of edgy anticipation trying to imagine what lay ahead. Quickly she began to talk to the young man next to her. Did he come from the Ellice group? The orderly turned on her one of those dazzling island smiles.

'No, I am from Fiji, like Ratu Edwin. Ratu sends apologies for not meeting,' he went on. 'Says it is best he wait by the plane.'

'Of course. Is it far to the airfield?'

'Only one mile.' He shrugged. 'And that is the end of Funafuti.'

As they jolted along the sandy road the sun came out, glinting on the puddles between the ruts and the creamy white flowers of the frangipani trees on either side. The faces of the people they passed, old and young, seemed to Laura beautiful, with their serene expressions and bright eyes. The Ellice greeting sounded like the cooing of pigeons. Outside the tiny trellised houses, hens were pecking at upturned coconut shells. A child was sweeping a path with a broom of twigs. Two stout women stood beaming at them from the verge, huge bunches of green bananas clutched to their bosoms. Fiji had been mostly Melanesian, Laura thought, dark and brooding. Ahead were the unknown Micronesians. But Funafuti was a piece of pure Polynesia.

Now and then the wind blew the trees apart. Just beyond them the sea was always there, always so close. It seemed incredible to her how carefree people could be living out their lives on a mere thread of land like this, often more than a hundred miles from the next inhabited atoll.

Just ahead, through one of the gaps, she caught a glimpse of the airfield, a small white plane standing on a strip of green, a tin-roofed building alongside. As they drove up the clearing, she could see the figure of Ratu Edwin towering over the group of people who were standing together in the shade. The moment he came forward to greet her, she felt calmer. Whatever lay ahead, he was in charge and she knew he was her good friend.

'Laura.' He took both her hands, his dark eyes studying her intently. 'You got my message? It was a shock?'

She nodded. And then the words came tumbling out together.

'You've heard something about her, my mother? Was it Timu who told you? Where is he? It's so hard to believe.'

She was aware of the eyes of the other passengers, and felt Ratu Edwin's hand beneath her elbow.

'He had to go back to Taparua. I told him you would see him there.' He led her towards the boarding steps. 'The pilot's waiting for us. We can talk on the way.'

The heat inside the tiny Fiji Airways plane was stifling. It was like climbing into an oven. Eight other passengers crammed in behind them with their bags and bundles. Everyone was silent as the plane launched itself into a bumpy takeoff, the tops of the palm trees tilting just below, and then the sea so very close, it seemed.

Laura pressed her sweating palms against her skirt. Next to her, Ratu Edwin exuded only a faint scent of eau de cologne as he delicately dabbed his forehead with a spotted silk handkerchief. As the plane rose and straightened out, people began talking, noisy with relief. The seats behind them had been left empty, except for the police orderly who was already fast asleep. She found herself thinking of that other flight she had shared with Edwin. Already it seemed like a different life, totally separate from everything that was happening to her now.

He turned to her as if reading her thoughts.

'It seems we're destined to meet on the wing. Flying back and forth over the Pacific like a pair of sea birds.' A smile came and went over the smooth brown face, almost Oriental with its broad cheekbones and long-lidded eyes. 'That first encounter of ours, that was when you told me all about yourself, about your mother. Since then you've found out quite a bit more?'

'Mostly about how she died.' Laura broke off, willing herself to wait.

'This is different, Laura. The old man Timu, who worked for your father, his story is of how she did *not* die.'

'What did he say?' Her heart was beating painfully.

'That when your father escaped from the island, your mother was alive and in fairly good health. He simply left her behind. Timu was with her when the Japanese came. Later, they took her away, perhaps to one of their prison camps on the other islands.'

'And then?'

'It was the last time he saw her. Since then he has heard nothing of her. She seems to have just disappeared.'

'But I thought . . .' A terrible disappointment was dragging at her. She looked at him pleadingly. 'I thought there might be real news of her, recent news.'

He shook his head. 'I'm afraid not. But then nobody's been trying to find out, have they? At least it means there's a faint hope. She could have survived the war, be living somewhere in the Pacific area, in Japan even.'

'But it doesn't make sense,' Laura protested. 'Why wouldn't she have tried to make contact with someone?' She stared out of the window. 'Tried to find me again,' she said in a low voice.

She felt Edwin's hand on her arm. 'There may be reasons we can't imagine. After your father's treatment of her, who knows?' He leaned closer. 'And Laura, my dear. This Timu. He says there is something else he has to tell you. About how your mother came to the islands in the first place.'

Something seemed to jump inside her. She turned back to him.

'Before I was born?'

'Presumably, yes. Timu was sworn by your father never to talk about this to anyone. But now he is old, a sick man, he feels he must tell you.'

'He heard my broadcast?'

Edwin nodded. 'He asked me what he should do. He is still very frightened of your father. But I told him there was no need to be. Not any longer.'

Briefly Laura felt a scent of that fear herself, coupled with outrage at what her father had done. His face with its cruel lines appeared clearly in her mind. 'Poor Timu,' she whispered.

'So you see, Laura, why I thought you should come? You may still have to search for the end of the story. But at least you will have the beginning.'

Impulsively Laura reached over and took Edwin's hand, that long slender hand with the upturned fingers and the mysterious blue ring.

'I'm so much in your debt, Edwin. You've gone to all this trouble to help me. Why?'

'Let us just say I felt a responsibility. We became friends so very quickly, as people sometimes do on plane trips. And there was something else. Trust? A sort of affinity?'

She felt a quick pressure before the hand was withdrawn.

'Besides,' he went on, 'it is the worst of misfortunes among my people to lose one's line of descent. Not to know where one has come from, on the maternal side especially. That would be unthinkable for us. Even the poorest commoner can recite his family tree for five generations back at least.' Then he stopped and gave her one of his sardonic smiles.

'Sorry. I'm beginning to sound like one of those terrible anthropologists.'

But Laura's mind was running ahead. 'Would it be possible, do you think?' She hesitated. 'For you to come with me to Taparua?'

'I have already made arrangements to do so. I thought it would help.'

'Jack would have come,' she said awkwardly. She found it quite painful to say his name. 'He had this appointment in Canberra. He wanted me to go with him.'

Edwin's expression was diplomatically neutral. 'His father said something about it when he telephoned to let me know you were on your way.'

At that moment the cabin door in front of them swung open. In the cockpit they could see the pilot's face turned round to them with a grin.

'How would the BBC lady like to join me?'

Laura looked at Edwin uncertainly.

'Go on,' Edwin urged. 'It's a Fiji Airways tradition to invite the VIP up front.'

Taking a deep breath, she got up and climbed through the hatchway.

'Good girl.' The broad-shouldered Australian patted the seat at his side, wiped the sweat off his balding head. 'Bit of a scorcher up here but the view's too good to miss.'

As she squeezed herself in behind the control panel, Laura was aware of a strange thing happening. She felt immediately at home in that tiny glassed-in cabin, floating like a gull through the glittering blue air. Elation seized her, as if she had discovered her true element. It was the exact opposite of the instinctive fear she felt for water. There was even something heady about the smell of fuel oil and hot leather.

'It's marvellous!' She had to shout above the roar of the engines.

'You've done it before?' He was obviously surprised at her confidence.

'Not like this.' She peered at the needles on the dials in front of her. 'It's as if you're actually flying the thing yourself!'

A cross-current of air jolted them sideways for a moment. 'Whoops!'

She grabbed hold of one of the side props until they were level again. There was something hypnotic about the silvery blur of the propellers. It was so different from being in an airliner, so high up you were cut off from reality. Here, you could actually see the waves crawling across the shimmering expanse of sea, the underwater layers of coral around a sandbank, a ship on the horizon like a toy. You could watch the shadow of your wings, crossing the water just ahead as if you were racing one another.

'When I was little I used to think that the equator was something you could actually see,' she said. 'Tied round the middle of the world like a string.'

'If it was, you'd see it right now, just below us. And somewhere out there's the international dateline. If we turned right we could hop from Wednesday back to Tuesday, just like that. How's that for a lark?'

Time itself could melt up here so close to the sun, Laura thought. The idea excited her and once again she felt the adrenalin of hope run through her.

'And there's the Gilberts.' His gloved hand pointed in front of her. The shape of an island had appeared, then another, and soon a third, stretching ahead like stepping stones from nowhere to nowhere.

'Can we see Taparua?'

'Taparua?' He looked doubtful. 'Bit off our track, that one. Tarawa's where we're heading, right below us.' He pulled out a seatbelt. 'Better fasten this if you want to stick around for the landing.'

They were dropping down now towards shiny roofs, a network of narrow causeways, a dockside busy with shipping. A runway slanted up to meet them surrounded by sea. Laura caught her breath. One of the engines was coughing like an old sheep. She heard the pilot curse. Then the wheels grazed the rough surface, jumped a little, and came down again. With a squeal of brakes the little plane rolled slowly to a halt, shaking all over with the effort of achievement.

Ratu Edwin was looking amused as she climbed back to join him. 'You must have been enjoying it.'

'I was.' Still exhilarated, she collected her things and followed him down the aisle.

'There'll be a few formalities here,' he told her. 'Tarawa sees itself as the seat of colonial government in these far-flung parts. Ah, yes.' He peered out through the door. 'There's young Simpson, the new Commissioner.'

As he stepped out, he raised his hand towards the little group of officials waiting outside the airport building. A limp Union Jack drooped from a bamboo pole. Bairiki International Airport, the sign over the doorway announced.

'They know we're travelling on to Taparua?' Laura asked, suddenly apprehensive.

'Of course. I told them it was part of your BBC itinerary. They should have booked us on to one of the copra boats.'

A thin young man in knee-length shorts and safari jacket was coming towards them.

'David Simpson, isn't it?' Ratu Edwin held out his hand.

'It's a great privilege to have you with us, sir,' Simpson replied rather nervously. Laura was introduced. Another young man, part-European, came forward, clutching a file, followed by a police officer in khaki. Ratu Edwin's orderly hovered behind, carrying his briefcase and bags. The sun beat down on them, almost directly overhead.

'Shall we move inside?' Edwin suggested smoothly.

The reception office with its corrugated iron roof seemed even hotter. The word deafening came to Laura's mind. Could heat be deafening? Or was it the effect of the air pressure inside the plane? She felt her head would burst. Her ears were painfully congested and the sounds around her were muffled and distorted. She jumped as an alarm clock went off on the desk nearby. No doubt it was to remind the sleepy clerk that the flight from Fiji had arrived on time.

Ratu Edwin was asking Mr Simpson about a boat to Taparua. The young man's face, shiny with sunburn and perspiration, wore an expression of extreme anxiety.

'I'm afraid that particular visit may have to be cancelled, sir.'

'Cancelled?' Edwin was frowning. 'I don't understand.'

'The message just came through this morning.' The Commissioner was stammering a little. 'From Suva, the Director of Medical Services. Taparua has been put under quarantine. All contact with shipping is forbidden until further notice.'

'For heaven's sake, what kind of quarantine?'

'An outbreak of typhus, Ratu Edwin.' The clerk stepped forward with his file of papers. 'As you know, sir, the threat of contagion is a real one.'

'Fifty years ago, perhaps.' Edwin looked bewildered. 'Not nowadays, surely. At least not to my knowledge.'

'The fear is it may spread to the other islands if there is any outside contact. But I'm a bit out of the picture,' Mr Simpson said in a dejected tone. 'I only arrived to take up this appointment a couple of weeks ago.'

Laura was sorry for him. But like Ratu Edwin, she could hardly believe what she was being told. The elation of the flight had evaporated. Instead, she felt frustration building up, as well as a growing thirst.

'Any chance of a glass of water?' she remarked to no one in particular.

'Of course. Forgive me, Miss Harrington, I should have thought.' The Commissioner moved across to her. 'We'll go up to the house straight away. Sort things out there.'

'Just one minute.' Ratu Edwin had put on his glasses and was studying the cable handed to him by the clerk. 'Is this the only communiqué you've had?'

Simpson nodded.

'Signed by the Director,' Edwin went on. 'But no mention of the source of this information.' Folding the paper, he put it in his pocket and drew himself up to his full height. 'I'm sorry, but as it stands I don't accept this order. I need confirmation from the Governor. You have a telephone at the house, David?'

'Of course. We'll get through right away.'

Grandly known as the Residency, the house turned out to be a rambling bungalow set at the end of a dusty lane. It had a fine view of the bay and several cracks in the verandah floorboards. Inside, the phone itself was covered in the fine coral dust that seemed to filter through everywhere.

There was no trouble in getting the local operator to book a call to Government House in Suva. But the hour spent waiting for the connection seemed to Laura one of the longest hours in her life. Even when the call came back it was simply a message to say His Excellency would not be available until later. Meanwhile, his office said, the matter was being looked into by the Chief Secretary.

'At least you'll have time to look around Tarawa,' Mrs Simpson told her over lunch, a peculiar chicken curry handed round by a nervous orderly in squeaking boots. The Commissioner's wife was a fair-haired young woman with a new baby who was howling his head off on the back verandah, despite the ministrations of his Gilbertese nurse.

'It's the prickly heat,' explained Mrs Simpson. 'There's really nothing you can do about it. Look at me.'

She indicated the rashes on her arms and neck. Laura thought how pale and tired she looked, her English prettiness already fading at the edges. 'So little fresh food here, you see, so no vitamins.' She sighed, looking around at the packing cases still piled up on every side. 'Actually we had been hoping for a posting to Fiji. Perhaps next time.'

'Are there any other English here?'

She smiled wanly. 'Enough for a couple of bridge fours. I don't play myself.' She lowered her voice. 'The two other wives seem quite batty and one of them smells of gin at ten o'clock in the morning.'

Lunch over, she led Laura through to a spare room at the other end of the house.

'You must be dying for a lie-down.' She closed the shutters against the afternoon glare. 'What an interesting life you must have, travelling the world for the BBC.'

It was a familiar remark. Her own response was equally familiar. 'It has its ups and downs.'

'And Ratu Edwin will certainly tell you all you need to know about the Pacific. What a charmer! Reminds me of Omar Sharif! But why are you so keen to get to Taparua?' Mrs Simpson was looking at her with some curiosity as she smoothed out the faded cotton bedspread.

'I was born there,' Laura replied simply. 'My father was a doctor there.'

'Good heavens! How extraordinary!'

She seemed at a loss for words.

'It's very kind of you to look after us like this,' Laura said.

'We'd have liked to put you up here, but you can see what a mess we're in. But I gather the rest-house is not bad at all. They even have a decent cook, which is more than you can say for us.'

'I had thought we'd be travelling straight on.' Laura was trying to hide her dismay at the thought of an enforced stay on Tarawa.

'Never mind. I'm sure things will sort themselves out.'

The door closed behind her. Left to herself, Laura found herself trying to puzzle out the mysterious tabu on Taparua. It obviously caused Edwin deep disquiet. When they were on their own again he'd be able to explain.

That was not to be for some time. First came the obligatory tour of the settlement, with David Simpson at the wheel of the ramshackle office jeep. Everything about the place looked makeshift and out of place, as if perched in the middle of a moonscape – the weatherboard government offices, the ugly stores and shipping offices. Then something attracted Laura's attention.

'What's that?' She pointed to a wooden cross overlooking the bay. The enclosure around it had been marked out with whitewashed stones.

'It's a war memorial,' Simpson said. 'Do you want to look?'

'There was an execution here,' Edwin told her.

As they got out, he stood close to her and touched her elbow as if to prepare her. 'Towards the end of 1942 the Japanese rounded up all their European prisoners and beheaded them.'

'Who were they?' Her voice sounded faint.

'Local traders mostly, old men, some New Zealand wireless operators, a young missionary. Their names are all there.'

'No women?'

'No women. They were all evacuated.'

It was an unnecessary question. Laura knew her mother's name could not be among those inscribed on the cross. But still she stood there staring at the list, sickened to imagine her at the mercy of such captors. That awful time was suddenly very close. It made any hope of individual survival seem foolish.

'I believe it was an act of retaliation,' Edwin was saying. 'There had just been a bombardment by one of the Allied ships. In the outer islands the war had less impact, of course. They say some of the people there were not so badly treated.'

'Tarawa was a famous victory.' Simpson might have been talking about Waterloo. 'Terrible losses for the Americans, but the real turning point of the Pacific war.' He took her arm. 'I say, are you feeling all right?'

'I'm okay.' What else could she say? She had no intention of going into family history with a stranger. 'I was only thinking of all the blood that must have been spilt on this beach.'

'Perhaps it's time we were getting back.' With a protective gesture Edwin ushered her back into the jeep. 'The ship we were booked on,' he said to Simpson. 'Can you check with the captain in case he's heard anything about this quarantine order?'

'Of course, sir. We'll probably find him at the club.'

As they drove round to the waterfront, Laura was expecting the usual genteel retreat for stranded expatriates. Through the open door she glimpsed something very different – a smoke-filled barroom noisy with island voices, swarthy men in battered straw hats, wharfees in oily overalls, grizzled characters out of Conrad. In the background someone was playing an out-of-tune piano.

Men only was the rule, Mr Simpson had said. While he and Ratu Edwin went inside, Laura was content to absorb the scene from the open window of the jeep. On the jetty beyond, cargo was being hauled to and fro. A couple of ancient trucks revved and roared in the dust. She could see masts and rigging bobbing on the waterline. So this strange place did have a heart after all, she thought, and it lay here, where all the flotsam and jetsam of the islands came together, a sort of colony of castaways from every corner of the western Pacific.

Something stirred in her mind, a faint memory of other ports like this. The ship she was taken away on as a small child must have stopped at such places on the way to New Zealand. All at once she was seized with a desperate impatience to be on one of those cargo boats making for home, for Taparua and Timu, whatever the hazards.

'Did you find him?' she asked the two men as they reappeared. Simpson nodded. 'Captain Bentley, a good man. He says he'll wait till first tide tomorrow in case we get an okay by then.'

Edwin was looking preoccupied.

'The strange thing is he knows nothing of a typhus outbreak, nothing of any quarantine ban. The mystery deepens, as Mr Sherlock Holmes would say.'

'Perhaps there'll be a message from Suva waiting for us,' Simpson said as they drove back to the Residency.

But there was no message for them, no alternative for Laura and Edwin but to pick up their belongings and move on to the government rest-house.

'What on earth's it all about?' Laura asked as soon as they were alone.

Simpson had dropped them off at the rest-house and a servant had taken their bags inside. She and Edwin were still standing on the verandah steps of the sprawling old bungalow on the edge of the beach. Darkness was falling now, and a squall had blown up. Laura felt rain on her shoulders but she hardly noticed.

'What's happening?' she went on.

Next to her, Edwin was staring out to sea. 'I don't know anything for certain. It's just that it seems so unlikely, a quarantine order like this, out of the blue. It makes me think there's someone who wants to stop you getting to Taparua.' He turned back to her, his face grim. 'Your father?'

It was a question, but at first Laura was too astonished to respond.

'You mean, he's behind the whole thing?' she asked after a moment. 'There's no such thing as a typhus epidemic?'

'The thought came to my mind straight away.'

'But how could he set it up, make an order on his own authority?'

'Remember, he was once Director of Medical Services himself. He still has huge influence with the department. No doubt the present Director is one of his protégés.'

'But what possible grounds could he give him?'

Edwin shrugged. 'Perhaps he'd say someone had come to his house with the disease. Someone from Taparua. Everyone knows he still has links with the Gilberts, writing about them and so on. Besides, his own housekeeper comes from the island.'

'How could he have heard I was coming?'

'Word travels fast in these parts.'

Laura shivered. All at once she had a powerful sense of invisible malice, the shadow of her father pulling strings like a puppet-master from that solitary house on the headland.

Edwin's voice came to her like the breath of sanity. 'You're cold, dear girl.'

He pushed open the door with its rusty mosquito screen. It banged to behind them and they found themselves in a cavernous sitting room lit by a single oil lamp.

She looked at him helplessly. 'I know it,' she said. 'He'll do anything to stop me.'

She broke off. There was a movement in the doorway at the back of the room. It was not the boy who had taken their luggage but a wrinkled little Chinese man, obviously the cook Mrs Simpson had mentioned. An appetizing smell of something spicy wafted in behind him as he put down an extra lamp.

'Dinner nearly ready,' he told them.

'There's no hurry,' Edwin said. 'We'll wait for the others.'

'Others? No others staying here now.' He grinned widely. 'Young men get marry, go away.'

'Who usually stays here?'

'Oh, any bachelors posted here. Government officials on tour. That kind of thing.' Edwin was looking uncharacteristically ruffled, she thought.

'Want to see rooms, Ratu?' The old man indicated a side passage behind another mosquito door.

'I think we'll have a drink first. Is that all right with you, Laura?' She nodded, and he moved across to an ancient sideboard, opened the cupboard door and brought out a bottle of whisky, half full. 'That's a spot of luck.'

He poured a generous measure into a couple of glasses, added a dash of soda from the siphon. Handing one to Laura, he frowned. 'But you're going to catch cold. You got quite wet out there. You'd better have a hot shower first, get changed.'

She smiled. 'I'd rather have the whisky.'

'Then put this on.'

Edwin took off his Harris tweed jacket that never remotely succeeded in making him look English. As he slipped it over her shoulders, she felt its warmth against her bare skin and caught the faint scent of tobacco and sandalwood. Treacherously, a picture of Jack slid into her mind. In a place like this, they would be sharing one of their stupid ongoing jokes. At that moment, she missed him so keenly it was like losing her balance, putting her foot on a stair that was not there.

She saw Edwin's eyes on her, watchfully, as if he knew. They sat down at either end of the large, sagging sofa, and sipped their drinks. Outside, the rain had set up a rhythm of its own, steady as a heartbeat as it dripped from the eaves of the thatched roof on to the verandah.

'I thought it never rained in the Gilberts,' Laura said. She could feel the whisky spreading a glow at the back of her throat.

'It does occasionally. They say in the Ellice it brings good fortune. They have poems about it.'

Sitting curled up in the corner of the sofa she had taken off her shoes and was nursing her right ankle.

'What have you done to yourself?' Edwin asked.

'Nothing much. Just a scratch. I caught it on the rocks at Sawai.'

'A coral scratch. That can be nasty.'

'I know. I had one once when I was a child. About three or four, I must have been. No older anyway, because that was when I left.'

She found herself talking quickly. But Edwin wasn't listening. He'd taken her foot between his hands to examine it. Unconsciously perhaps, he was pressing down gently around the swelling, with a slow circular movement of finger and thumb.

'The famous Tongan massage?' She said it jokingly, partly to conceal the faint brush of arousal she felt at his touch.

He raised his eyes and they looked at each other.

'I think it's healing.' He got up quickly. 'But you'd better take a couple of these, just in case.'

He brought out a small bottle from his briefcase. 'I always carry these round with me when I'm travelling. Just ordinary antibiotics.'

He put two pills in her hand.

'Water would be better than whisky,' he said. 'Cookie will bring some.'

There was a jug already set out, Cookie told them. With an air of professional pride he led them into an adjoining room. Places for two had been formally laid out at each end of the long table. Candles had been produced from some storeroom and now stood in saucers, flaring and guttering in the breeze that crept in through the bamboo blinds. Deftly the old man pattered around them with trays and dishes. Steaming noodle soup was followed by an excellent fish soufflé and the pineapple fritters which were obviously his speciality. There was no wine. Instead two large cans of Pepsi Cola were produced, and a pot of china tea.

'What will happen if the ban is the real thing?' Laura asked as they ate. For the first time she felt an awkwardness between them, as if they had to make conversation. 'I mean, there's nothing I can do out here without seeing Timu first. And I know you have your own commitments. Mr Simpson's expecting you to go on tour with him the day after tomorrow.'

'I know that,' Edwin said. 'I'd take you with us but it would be useless from your point of view. Taparua is where you have to go, come what may.'

'It's not fair to be stopped now.' She put her head in her hands, suddenly overcome by anger. 'So near and yet so far.'

'Just trust me,' she heard Edwin say. 'Trust me, Laura. There will be a way, you'll see.'

When she looked up again, he was gazing at her down the length of the table. His face was half in shadow. Only his eyes were caught by the candlelight, pinpoints of silver that seemed to hold hers with a special intensity.

'So far, and yet so near,' he said quietly.

They got up from the table. Cookie was waiting with candles to show them to their quarters, on opposite sides of the corridor.

Later that night he came into her room.

'Did you know you cry in your sleep?'

'Do I?' She was half-awake, disoriented by a memory of utter desolation. The candle in the corner had almost burned away.

'It was unbearable,' he said. 'Like a child with a nightmare.'

Very gently he lay down beside her and took her in his arms. It was a moment that was both unpremeditated and inevitable.

'You wish this?' he asked softly.

'I wish it,' she replied in a whisper.

'You know it may never happen again?'

'I know.'

It was not making love in any way she knew, she thought afterwards. Rather it was a single long embrace or sequence of embraces that seemed to have no beginning and no end. Through the hours they lay together, she gave herself up to learning this new language. They were lessons in a tender and comforting sensuality, a kind of languid innocence that Europeans had perhaps lost for ever, or had never even known. As she concentrated on these discoveries, fear and loneliness slipped away. She knew that later the recollection of this time together, minute by minute, would be something she would wear in her mind like a charm, drawing only good fortune and turning away the bad.

The word 'love' was not spoken and nor did Laura expect it. Only at dawn, just before leaving her, Edwin told her the words of the Ellice poem about the rain.

'O wind that brings rain,
O rain that delivers the love of lovers,
Let us go and seek that wind
Wherever it may fan us, let us go.'

The next morning, a message from Suva was brought down to the resthouse. They were free to travel on to Taparua that day.

CHAPTER SEVEN

'No government office in the world will ever admit it's made a mistake,' Edwin said. 'The way they put it in the cable was that the "risk of an epidemic had been over-estimated".'

'And my father was definitely behind it?'

It was the first thing she had wanted to know, the first thing he had told her. But even now, aboard the MV *Island Star* on their way to Taparua, she needed to hear him say it again. To satisfy her, Edwin brought out the cable from his pocket.

'Alert was issued by Dr Harrington re typhoid suspect arrived Suva from Taparua,' he read. 'Further examination revealed negative results.'

'Why did he back down, do you think?'

'Because he couldn't produce the evidence. My call was to ask the Governor himself to look into it, which he obviously did. Old Sir Clifford's a good friend of mine and a stickler for detail.'

Laura felt a childish pleasure in outwitting her father. But there was still one thought that chilled her.

'He knows that I'm on my way there now, of course.'

'Laura, there's nothing more he can do about it, believe me. Besides, he must also know that I'm with you. I think that must have some effect, don't you?'

Laura smiled. 'It's had an effect on me,' she said in an undertone.

He frowned at her teasingly and shook his head. She had half expected to feel awkward in his company today. Instead there was a new kind of closeness as they leaned side by side against the rails, an ease that flowed between them, needing no words.

'Tarapua's not far now,' he said.

The day was fine and the journey had been a smooth one, though hardly luxurious. The deck around them was packed with fellow passengers on their way to other destinations up and down the island chain. Mothers and babies sheltered from the sun under ancient black umbrellas. A bevy of old ladies sat propped against sacks of copra, fat legs outstretched, fanning themselves and gossiping. At the other end the men were concentrating on their tobacco and games of cards. Wide-mouthed Gilbertese laughter punctuated a dozen shrill conversations. Rolls of straw mats were stacked everywhere, with brightly-coloured bundles of clothing and baskets of cooked food for the journey. Someone had brought two small pigs aboard, shiny black specimens that rolled to and fro on their tethering ropes like a pair of seals.

At one level, Laura was totally absorbed by it all, and she had recorded five minutes to use as background sound in the programme. As the little ship churned through the blue, a breeze sprang up, wonderfully cooling through the thin layers of her long muslin skirt and Indian blouse. Her face was shaded by the straw hat she had bought from some women selling at the quayside. The sun brought out the dry, grassy smell of it as she pulled the brim down over her eyes.

Here and now I would be almost happy, she thought, were it not for the thought of my father. There was also a growing edge of suspense in her mind about the meeting with Timu that lay ahead. Why would her father go to such lengths to try to prevent it? And what would be her own memories, returning to the island where she had spent those first strange years of her life?

For a second she was back in her father's study at Suva Point as he reached out to touch her. The old, half-buried memory that his touch had sprung in her still had the power to sicken her.

'Missus!'

A small girl was tugging at her skirt. Huge black eyes stared up at her from beneath a glossy black fringe as the child held out a piece of orange.

'You like?'

'Thank you. I like very much.'

She slipped it into her mouth. How strange! The taste of it on her tongue combined with the shipboard smells and movements produced a quite different snapshot in her mind. She was a small girl too, on board the ship that was taking her away from her mother, being given a piece of fruit to stop her crying. She had never seen an orange before and had no idea how to eat it.

Now, Laura squatted down by her new friend and helped her to peel the rest of it. Edwin had gone to check their baggage. Not for the first time since the trauma of the abortion, she found herself wondering what it would be like to have a child of her own, a daughter especially.

The little girl put a sticky hand on Laura's wrist, examining her old silver bracelet. They exchanged a conspiratorial smile. How hard it must have been for my mother to part with me, Laura thought, all those years ago.

'Like kids, do you?'

Captain Bentley was standing in front of her, his cap over his eyes, hands in his pockets. His shirt sleeves were rolled up, displaying lavish tattoos of serpents and anchors and other more mysterious emblems. Part German, part Gilbertese, he was a genial man who had already assured her she was welcome to stay on board for as long as she liked.

Yes, she liked kids, she told him.

'Any of your own?' His eyes were on her hand, looking for a ring that wasn't there.

'Not yet.'

He turned away. 'There's Taparua for you, just coming up.'

She got to her feet and stared out over the water. All of a sudden the name was a reality, a thin green sliver caught between the blue of the sky and the deeper turquoise of the lagoon. Distance framed it like a postcard someone had pinned to the horizon. Laura tightened her hands around the rail. As the ship got closer, she could see a line of surf stretched out ahead of them, the finishing tape at journey's end.

Captain Bentley was frowning, studying it through his glasses.

'Landing's a bit tricky here. No break in the reef, you see. We have to anchor outside and you do the last bit by boat.'

'Shooting the reef!' Back at her side, Edwin sounded exhilarated. 'You're not a real islander, Laura, till you've done that.'

He pointed to the canoe that was being paddled out from the shore towards them. 'Don't worry. These people are experts.'

Laura watched mesmerized as the little craft seemed to explode through the wall of white foam and re-emerge without effort on the other side. Within minutes, the canoe was circling the bows of the ship. Half a dozen faces squinted up at them, upraised paddles dripping and glinting in the sun.

Voices called back and forth and everyone lined the rails to watch. Edwin and Laura were the only ones to disembark. Captain Bentley was taking the *Island Star* round to the other side to load copra and house thatch.

'Sailing at noon,' he called down to her. 'If you want to travel on with us. Okay?'

'Fine,' she called, waving back.

She looked round at Edwin, sitting low in the stern close behind her.

'We have to wait for the right wave,' he said in her ear. 'To take us over the reef.'

Just ahead the rollers were curling and crashing onto the hidden coral. Then came the big one. There was a sudden yell from the rowers. Laura felt the canoe rise in the air like a horse going over a fence, saw the straining backs of the men as they dug their blades into the churning cascade of water. Crouching forward, she seemed to be half submerged. There was a roaring in her ears. For a moment they were held fast by the undertow, then as suddenly released, shooting out onto the glassy surface of the lagoon.

She wiped the water from her face and turned to see Edwin grinning back at her.

'You see what I mean!'

Laura closed her eyes, her face raised to the sun. Smoothly, the canoe came to rest on the edge of the beach. Edwin leapt out into the shallows, talking to the rowers and making them laugh. With his black Tongan kilt tucked up between his knees, he could have been a boatman himself, except for that elegant bearing which marked him out wherever he went. She thought again how strange it was that he should be the one who had brought her back to Taparua, someone she had met simply because his seat on a plane was next to hers.

Stepping onto the sand, she stared around her, hungry for some reminder of the past. Surely she should have some sense of coming home again, however faint. Instead, she felt completely at a loss. The beach was deserted, chalk white in the glare of the sun. Perhaps Timu had gone to meet the ship at the loading bay. Perhaps the village itself was round the other side of the island.

Suddenly, she saw a small group of people making their way through the coconut palms. A white-haired lady in ragged black was advancing towards her, nodding and smiling.

'Timu,' she called to Laura. 'Come, I show you Timu.'

Laura found herself taken by the hand and led up the beach like a child. Beside her, Edwin was accompanied on either side by two equally dignified old men. The little procession made its way along the path through the trees. As they walked, Gilbertese conversation crackled around her, some of it translated by Edwin.

'This lady is Timu's sister. He is waiting for us at his house.'

'Tell her I was born here,' Laura said. Her companion was inspecting her with discreet glances.

'She knows. She was living on another island at that time. But Timu has been telling her about you.'

Laura was still carrying her shoes. She wanted to feel the sandy track hot and powdery under her feet. Even the wind was hot, tinged with the smell of salt and dried fish.

The village houses they were passing, like baskets on stilts, jogged something else in her memory. She was holding on to another hand above her head, hearing another voice telling her softly, in broken English, that she must never walk between two people who were holding a conversation on either side of the path. It was bad manners, remember?

But today there were no people on the path. Everyone had gone round to the landing beach. Even at Timu's house further along, proudly modern with its wooden frame and green tin roof, there was no one to be seen.

Then in the doorway a man appeared, a small bent figure leaning on a stick. As Laura came up to him, he seemed to sway a little, holding on to the doorpost with his other hand. He stared back at her, his face wrinkled up in disbelief.

'Lora,' he said, speaking the name in the island way. 'It is Lora. That small girl . . .'

He was unable to go on. Without taking his eyes off her, he sat down slowly on the step. Laura bent over him and very gently put her arms around his shoulders. As clearly as he remembered her, so she remembered him, except that age had masked the familiar face, crumpling up the broad, square-cut features like brown paper. But the darting gaze, so intensely bright and dark at the same time, was unchanged.

'Please don't upset yourself, Timu. We should be happy that we're able to meet again, after all these years.'

'Right. Right, Miss Lora.'

He wiped quickly at his cheek with an upturned palm. Then, fastening up the buttons of what had once been his khaki uniform jacket, he got to his feet to greet Ratu Edwin.

It was cooler inside the little front room with its four shabby cane chairs. There was also a low table made from a packing case, a ship's chest with brass locks, and a shelf for the old man's textbooks. Timu's wife, Maria, a stout little woman in a muumuu, brought in a tray of tea. She touched Laura's arm for a moment, shaking her head in affectionate disbelief. She did not sit with them but retreated shyly to the doorway again, next to Timu's sister.

For a while they were able to talk of general things, the journey, last year's drought, Timu's trouble with his circulation. Edwin told him of the typhoid rumour. The old man looked amazed. There had been no such thing in his time, though he remembered many years ago Dr Harrington had gone on board a mission ship to treat one such case. Laura and Edwin exchanged glances. Perhaps that had given him the idea.

All the time Laura knew that Timu was rehearsing in his head what he had to tell her. There was no hurrying such things. In Timu's world the unfolding of the past was a solemn ritual. It must be properly laid out, with due attention to detail. She saw the anxious lines on his forehead and bent to touch his hand.

'Don't worry, Timu. We can go through it bit by bit.'

Edwin leaned forward. 'Perhaps you could tell your side first, Laura? What Dr Harrington told you in Suva.'

On an impulse, Laura reached for her canvas bag. 'Timu can hear it for himself.'

She brought out the little black recording machine. The tape was already on the spool. She pressed the playback button, waiting for the faint whirring sound, a muffled crackle before the conversation began.

The editing at the broadcasting station had sharpened the words, but she could see Timu was not taking them in. At the first sound of Harrington's voice, that unmistakable drawl, thin and high-pitched, he had started forward in his chair. He pressed his hands to either side of his grey head. His face was aghast.

'It is him, Harrington. Dr Harrington.'

Seeing his distress, Laura switched off the machine. 'You would rather not hear?'

'It is only like the wireless, Timu,' Edwin put in, trying to reassure him. 'But this one keeps the messages inside.'

'He spoke into it when I went to see him in Suva,' Laura explained. She paused. 'I asked him what had happened to my mother.'

Timu sat up straight again. His eyes were fixed on the recorder as if confronting a snake.

'Then I must hear that man's words.'

For the next few minutes he listened in silence. Laura too had to nerve herself to hear it again. Edwin's expression was tightly controlled. He did not look at her. Only when Harrington came to the point of describing his escape so soon after Millie's death, was the silence broken.

'No!'

It was a cry of outrage. Timu was on his feet, pointing to the machine with a trembling hand.

'It is lies, all lies! How can he say these things?'

The voice had come to an end. The tape flickered loose on the spool.

Maria was crouched at Timu's feet, trying to calm him. Edwin and Laura got up from their chairs and stood on either side of him. Timu turned first to one and then the other.

'My wife was there when the boat came for Harrington.' His voice was shaking with passion. 'She and the other women. They were with your mother, Lora, in the house.' He shook his head despairingly. 'That poor lady, Missis Millie.'

At the sound of the name, Laura felt pity surge up inside her. She drew Timu down on to the pile of mats against the wall and sat facing him, holding his hands in hers.

'Someone told me my mother had killed herself,' she said.

Timu stared at her. 'How could that be? She was alive, in his house.'

Timu's sister, the old lady in black, had brought in glasses of palm toddy, brown and syrupy. As the old man sipped, he became quiet again.

'You were there too that day?' Edwin asked. He was sitting just behind Laura, watching Timu carefully.

The old man shook his head. He had gone round to the village on the other side. One of the elders had died and he had to attend the mourning ceremonies. Everyone was fearful that the Japanese might soon be landing. The mission church had already been bombarded. Stories had come down from the Marshall Islands of the terrible things the soldiers did to the local people when they invaded.

'This was why your mother sent you away.' He looked at Laura with an expression of tenderness. 'I it was who carried you on to the mission ship, did you know? You had a label tied to your dress with string, like a parcel. But you did not cry.' He smiled. 'You never cried with Timu. Not even when you cut your foot on the coral and I put the medicine on it, special leaves. A vein had been opened, but next day it was healed.'

Laura saw Edwin glance at her ankle.

'She still cuts herself on the coral,' he said.

Timu's wife was talking to him now, urgently, with quick movements of her hands. She wanted to describe how things had happened that day. Timu told them she understood a little English, but was wary of speaking it.

'She says the doctor had packed some belongings in a bag, as if he was expecting to leave at any moment. My wife went to the house as she often did, to help your mother. Your mother was in bed.'

'She was sick?' Laura asked.

'Sometimes the doctor gave her injections that made her sleepy. This was how she was that night. Someone came to tell the doctor a schooner was anchored off the reef. He took his bag and ran to the beach. A boat was coming off to meet him.'

'And my mother?'

Again Maria spoke. This time she was even more agitated.

'She says Missis Millie had been tied to the bed. The doctor had done this with such skill it was taking too long to free her. My wife ran down to the beach with some of the others. They waded out to try to catch hold of the boat to tell the men the doctor's wife was still in the house. They must wait and take her with them.'

Maria could contain herself no longer. Her face was contorted with distress as she seized Laura's arm.

'Was no good,' she broke out. 'Doctor say wife die ten days before. He say we crazy people. Say we talk about *teanti*.' She faltered. 'Ghosts.'

Timu came to her rescue. 'We Gilbertese believe the spirit of a dead person stays in the house until it is time to make its journey on to the other world. Dr Harrington told the Europeans on the boat that this was what the women were crying about. They are still pagan people, he said. Take no notice of them. And so they rowed away. We did not see Dr Harrington again.'

There was a silence which nobody could break, not even Laura.

'So Mrs Harrington was left to the Japanese,' Edwin said finally. 'I'm sure you did your best for her.'

Timu sat clasping and unclasping his hands, his eyes lowered.

'There was little we could do. The soldiers treated us like slaves. They kept Missis Millie separate. They knew she was an American. I think they treated her worse than the rest of us.'

'How long was she a prisoner?' Laura had to force herself to ask the question.

'Two, maybe three months.' He looked up at her and began to speak quickly. 'But then a new commander came. One day soon after, we saw your mother taken away on a boat, with two of the guards. We believe she was put on a ship with some other European prisoners, sent up to a camp on one of the Japanese islands. Saipan maybe.'

Laura felt a shudder run through her. 'Perhaps she was taken there to be executed.' She turned away.

'I told you, Laura,' Edwin said gently. 'This means there might still be hope. Not everyone died in these camps. There were survivors. When you go back to London, there are organizations that will help you find out what happened to her.'

'I do not believe she was to be killed. If so, it could have been done here, with no one to know. I think that officer had another plan for her.' Timu touched Laura's arm. 'Your mother was very beautiful, even though she was so pale and thin. She had strength inside her too.' He laid his hand on his chest. 'Here. In her spirit.'

'Picture?' Maria asked Laura softly. 'You have picture?'

Laura moved away, trying to compose herself. Very carefully she brought the wallet out of her bag and took from it the tiny creased snapshot.

'Aiya! Aiya.' Timu was rocking to and fro, holding it close to his eyes. 'That is she. The poor lady we knew.'

He passed it to his wife who had begun to cry, tears rolling down her plump cheeks. She murmured to Timu.

'She says you are so like her. That lady is still living in your own face.' He looked at Laura thoughtfully. 'But I think your mother's hair was not your colour. Something lighter.'

Laura hesitated. Her hand was on the shell locket under her shirt. It was such a private thing. She had not even shown it to Edwin. But now, on impulse, she took it off and gently opened it, laying it on the mat between them.

'My mother gave me this before I left.'

Just as gently, Timu reached out to touch the curl of her hair. He drew a quick breath.

'I remember it. So bright, like the sun we used to say.' Then he closed the shell and handed it back to her. 'Be careful with this, Lora. Some people use magic on such things. Bad magic, good magic.' His voice died away.

'The house the doctor lived in?' Edwin asked. 'Is it still here?'

'We will walk there,' Timu said. 'I will show you.'

'But your legs?'

'It is not far. It is good for the circulation, to walk. Also, I have my stick.'

He got up, putting his hand on Lora's shoulder. 'And my friend here!'

As they went out, she turned to him. 'Ratu Edwin says there is something else you want to tell me. About my mother.'

Timu nodded. 'When we get to the house, I will tell you.'

The path to the house took them away from the village. Laura was glad. She didn't feel she could talk to other people just yet. As she walked between the two men, she told Timu about meeting his daughter at the house at Suva Point. But his face was closed and he asked no questions.

'She was foolish. She let herself fall into that man's hands. There is nothing I can do.'

It was all he said. They had come to a clearing on the other side of the island, half a mile away. The afternoon shadows were lengthening and the wind had dropped. This was the side that was open to the sea, close to the reef with no lagoon for protection. The surf pounded with a rhythmic, never-ending vibration that seemed to roll in from the edge of the world. Laura thought it was a noise that could drive you mad.

Now she could see the shore itself, a desert of stones thrown up by the waves. In the old days, Timu said, this part of the island was tabu, a place where people came to make prayers to the gods, sacrifices too perhaps. He showed them a cairn of small boulders where gifts of tobacco were still left from time to time. Otherwise people rarely came this way. No landing was possible and it was far too rough for fishing. Robert Louis Stevenson's words came into Laura's mind. 'Accursed ocean side . . .'

She repeated them half to herself, then turned, startled by a harsh cry from the trees behind. A huge frigate bird had come flapping down from the branches in pursuit of the unwary gannets feeding among the rocks. Through the trees, she could glimpse a broken concrete wall and the remains of some fortifications.

'Japanese bunkers,' Timu said. 'Many soldiers were killed when the Americans landed. Afterwards the bodies were burned. But there is still death in this place. It is a bad place.'

Where was her mother then, Laura asked herself? Suddenly cold, she drew back from the steps that twisted away underground, overgrown with creepers. They reminded her of those dungeon entrances in English castles, ruins that still smelled of brutality and despair.

Edwin had moved away. He was examining the remains of a field gun, a rusty funnel tilted sideways in the long grass.

'They left this behind?'

Something like a smile appeared on the old man's face. 'Our people say it is the reason the Japanese were defeated. This is the most sacred spot on Taparua. It is where our ancestors are buried, facing west according to custom. When the soldiers put the gun here, these old spirits were very angry. So they took revenge. Thanks to them our enemies were wiped out, every one of them.'

Laura was walking ahead, glad to be out in the sunlight again. Once more, she was almost remembering things, the narrow path with the rustling pandanus bushes on either side, a bright blue butterfly that seemed to be leading the way ahead, and then the glimpse of a rooftop, painted a dingy red.

'I see the house,' she called back.

She hurried on. But she was unprepared for the rush of emotion when she reached what remained of it, a broken framework of rafters and walls, greenery thrusting through the bamboo partitions. She climbed the verandah steps. The floorboards inside had been torn up, but tucked away in the crack was a piece of brown matting, so old it was almost unrecognizable. Just for a moment there was a chink in time and, through it, the past slipped back, a tiny fragment of it. In that moment, it was the four-year-old Laura on the verandah, watching that matting being made, the coarse feel of the dried reeds as one of the women showed her how they were woven into patterns. Her mother was sitting next to her. Between them was a baby turtle in a bowl of water. It was to be her pet. Her mother held it up to show her, but suddenly it was knocked from her hands. Her father was standing behind them. Water flew over the matting as the bowl was kicked aside. His high voicc raging at her mother was the last thing Laura remembered as she was picked up and taken away, that and the sight of the turtle lying on its back on the verandah, legs waving feebly like a run-down toy.

She closed her eyes to turn off the scene. She could hear Edwin and Timu on the path.

'Be careful,' Timu called. 'It's not safe to walk inside. The white ants eat the woodwork.'

Then Edwin was standing beside her, watching her face. 'You remember it, Laura?'

'Yes,' she said, with an effort. 'A little.'

The three of them sat down on the verandah steps.

'In the war, the Japanese used it as a hospital,' Timu told them. 'But I remember it being built. It was the 1920s. Dr Harrington had just been posted here and he wanted a house on the ocean side, away from the village. No one could understand it. The district officer before was happy to live near us, by the lagoon. He was a good man, taught us cricket on the beach.' He shook his head. 'Harrington. Even then he was a secret person. Also the loneliest one I ever knew.'

'And you were appointed his assistant?' Edwin asked.

'I had just come back from medical school in Fiji. I knew nothing of him, except that I was always frightened of him.'

The old man had settled himself against the verandah post, his stick between his knees.

'But the time I want to tell you about was later on. In 1937. I remember because that was the year other strange things happened too. There was a new English king. There was also the day the sun went dark. The total eclipse they called it. People here thought the world was going to end.' He cleared his throat. 'And then there was the finding of the European woman on Nikumaroro.'

'Nikumaroro.' Edwin looked puzzled. 'That's the one the English call Gardner Island, in the Phoenix group, two or three hundred miles away?'

Timu nodded. Laura had a sense of the world suddenly standing still. She waited for his voice again.

'The Phoenix Islands were uninhabited. Ours were becoming too crowded. Government had a scheme to settle some of our people there, so they sent an expedition to make a survey. Dr Harrington was in charge. He took me with him and six other Gilbertese.'

The lines on his face deepened. 'I did not know what that journey would bring. We spent a week going around the different islands, seeing if food could be grown, if there was water. On the last day, we stopped at Gardner, just Harrington and myself. There was a bird there he wanted for his collection. So he sent the other boats back to the Gilberts and we landed alone, just the two of us.'

He paused, leaning his head back against the post, looking away from them. Laura sat motionless, her eyes fixed on his face. This time the gap between the words seemed unending. But the old man was simply ordering the pictures in his mind, one by one.

'Doctor had gone ahead, on down the beach. I was walking slowly because of my foot. I had been stung by a stone-fish the day before, in one of the lagoons. When I caught up with him he was standing in a patch of thick bush, higher up. I heard him speaking, but that was not unusual. Doctor often talked to himself. He was looking down at something on the ground. I went up close and could not believe what I saw. There was a woman lying unconscious, a European woman. She was wearing trousers like a man. I thought she was only half-alive. Her head was bleeding and her clothing all torn about as if she had been thrown up by the sea. Her eyes were closed. But as I stood in front of her, she opened them. They were bright blue.'

He put his hand out to Laura.

'Your colour, Lora. That woman was your mother.'

The words hung in the air. Laura held on to Timu's hand as if it was the only way through the maze.

As if from a distance, she heard Edwin's question. There was no sign of another boat? Or any other survivors?

Timu shook his head.

'Wreckage gets washed down over the reef at high tide. All we could do was wait until she could tell us herself what happened. Harrington sent me back to the boat to get my first-aid bag and something to make a stretcher.'

Laura bent closer. 'And when you got back?'

'When I got back, she had come round. I gave her some water but her lips were so burned it was hard for her to swallow. Harrington was crouched down beside her, asking many questions. But I could see that everything that happened to her was wiped away. She was struggling, trying so hard but it was no good. I had seen this before, with other injured people. All she could tell us was finding herself alive on the beach, crawling under some branches for shade. She had water in a bottle on a belt but that was soon finished. Two, maybe three days had gone by. She could say no more. She closed her eyes again. I told Harrington, this woman has lost her memory. Or her mind, he said. That is a good thing, he said.'

Timu had begun to tremble, holding closer onto his stick.

'Then I knew that he it was who was mad.'

The old man wiped his mouth with the back of his hand. All at once he looked exhausted.

'Wait,' Edwin said, getting up quickly. Close by some coconuts lay fallen under the palms. Laura watched him pick one up and open a knife from his pocket. The operation took only a moment. Timu drank gratefully, the clear liquid trickling over his chin.

'Rest for a moment,' Laura urged him. But he was in the grip of his tale, which would not wait.

'While I was dressing the woman's injuries, Harrington was doing something very strange. Some of her belongings were scattered around, shoes, a scarf, a piece of a map. These things he was burying under a bush. Then he said that no one must know we had found this castaway. He would take her back to his house and keep her there. The people would be told that she was his wife, that she had come out to the Gilberts from Fiji where he had first met her.' He turned to Laura. 'This was the story he told you?'

She nodded. 'But how would he explain her condition?'

'He had an answer to that. A swimming accident at one of the islands on the way out. Doctor's face was very white and his eyes were staring. No one must know, he kept saying. And then, something I did not understand. Findings keepings. He said that over and over, talking to himself.'

The old man was sitting huddled up now, his head in his hands. 'I did wrong,' they heard him say. 'I should have spoken to the government people in Tarawa. But he said if I told anyone, even my family, I would lose my job and never get another one. It was to be our secret. It was an easy one to keep,' he went on. 'That poor lady did not even know who she was.'

'But she remembered her name?' Edwin asked.

'That came all of a sudden,' Timu said. 'She spoke it like a child, just Millie, as if it was a nickname, something her family called her, not a proper name. Then everything seemed to go blank for her again. I wondered . . .' He broke off.

'Wondered?' Laura prompted him.

'It was just that Harrington seemed to look pleased. As if he had an idea of who she might be, as if it was a good thing that she could remember no more. When we were back on the boat, he told me again, no one will know. No one from outside comes to my house. No one comes to my island. Those words frightened me. After that, he never spoke again of that day.'

Laura's mouth was dry. 'So all the time she was my father's prisoner.' She took a deep breath and was glad of Edwin's hand on her arm.

'Lora,' Timu said quietly. 'There is something else. You speak of your father.' He had his eyes fixed on hers, their expression solemn. 'But you should know that Dr Harrington is not your father.'

Laura felt a sensation like falling. 'What do you mean?'

'As we lifted your mother on to the stretcher, I saw she had begun to bleed, from the inside. I laid my hand on her. This woman is pregnant, I told Harrington. Maybe just two months or so. Then let her miscarry, he said. It will save trouble.'

Timu's eyes were shining now, as he looked at her.

'But Missis Millie did not lose her baby. I looked after her and seven months later I delivered it.' He smiled. 'It was a girl. Your mother had a name all ready. She called you Lora.'

CHAPTER EIGHT

It was an effort to move. She had no idea how long she had been sitting there. She had lost awareness of everything outside the flow of Timu's voice. But now she felt an overpowering need to be alone.

'Just for a few moments,' she murmured to the others.

She got to her feet and almost ran down the steps, round to the garden at the back. It was a wilderness of vine and scrub, but the old banyan tree was still there, leaning crookedly against the wall. She flung herself down beneath it, her knees drawn up, her head buried in her arms.

She had been holding back tears for so long that to cry was to release a passion that encompassed everything. But mostly she was crying with gratitude. It was as though a life sentence had been lifted. Or as if someone had told her that a diagnosis of terminal illness had been a mistake after all.

'I am not Harrington's daughter.'

Over and over again, Laura repeated the words in her mind. Until this moment she had not realized the torment it had been to think of such a man as her father, to think of his genes in her blood. Now she was free, free to wonder who her real father had been. Somewhere in the world, she thought suddenly, he might still be alive, not even knowing of her existence. It would be more than she could hope for to find him. She knew that – for the present at least. Slowly all her thoughts were focusing again on her mother. As she lay there, her imagination was flooded with pictures of Millie fighting for survival on that deserted beach. Everything that had happened in her life had somehow been locked away in her head and the key thrown away. All she could know was that she had been cruelly robbed of her most precious possession, her own identity. Then someone had appeared to save her from dying. But how long would it have taken her to realize that she owed her life to a madman?

Laura raised her head. Vaguely she could hear voices from the front of the house. It seemed that people had arrived to fetch Edwin, who came hurrying towards her as she got to her feet.

'I'm afraid Captain Bentley is expecting me back. I'd forgotten. The elders are waiting on board for a ceremony.'

'Of course.' She was in control of herself again. 'And tomorrow you go on tour.'

'The government launch is picking me up at ten. I'd take you with us but there's really no point.' He took her hand. 'You must go back to Timu's for the night. Then tomorrow you can travel on with Captain Bentley.'

'You think that's best?'

He nodded. 'On the other islands you may find people who can tell you more. Maybe people who shared your mother's experiences when the Japanese took her away.'

'I shall see you in the morning, before you go?'

'I would not leave without saying goodbye.' He had released her hand but still stood close to her, his eyes on hers. 'My dear Laura,' he said gently. 'It will take time for you to take in all we've just been told. Such extraordinary things.'

'It was suddenly hearing I was not Harrington's child,' she broke out. 'You can't imagine . . .'

'I can. I do. Now I must go. Till tomorrow.'

She waited a moment, then walked round to the front of the house. Timu was waiting for her.

'Now we will both go home and rest. Your room is ready for you there.'

They went along in silence for a while, his hand on her arm. The sun had gone down and it was quickly growing dark.

'Is it hard to believe what you have just heard?' he asked her when they were nearing the house.

'Some of it is good news,' she said quietly. 'The rest . . .' She dropped her head. 'My poor mother.'

'You have some more questions? I will do my best.'

Again she shook her head. There were so many questions about her mother's life with Harrington, most of them too painful even to frame. Besides, Timu would not know the answers.

'There is something,' she said. 'How did Harrington react to the baby when it came? He pretended to the people I was his child, of course. Perhaps he even pretended to himself?'

'It could have been so. It was hard to tell. It did not stop him treating the child badly. By that time his mind was becoming so . . .'

He searched for the English word, wringing his hands to illustrate.

'Twisted?' Laura suggested.

'Twisted, yes. It was hard to make sense of anything he did.'

They had stopped to rest for a moment.

'And was my mother not even allowed outside the house?'

'At first he let the village women take her walking on the beach each day, towards sunset.' The old man screwed up his eyes, fixing them on the last glimmer of the sea. 'Then one day she tried to write some words on the sand. It was a message in case strangers might land and see them. So Missis Millie went walking no more.'

He took her arm and pointed to Maria standing on the path with a lamp.

'See, she is waiting for us. Food will be ready.'

After supper, Laura was glad to go to the little room they had prepared for her. The truckle bed in the corner was piled high with soft mats and Maria had hung a mosquito net above it. On the walls were faded family photographs strung around with shell necklaces, a picture of the Queen in her Coronation crown pinned up in place of honour in the centre. By the side of the bed Timu had left a shabby morocco-bound volume, a much-treasured history of the islands by some anthropologist of the early 1900s who prided himself on his poetry translations. Opening it sleepily, Laura came across a 'Song of the Drowned Islanders'. The tiny lamp threw a flickering light across the page:

> 'We pluck at the living present,
> Cry the ghosts,
> But we cannot reach it.
> A wall comes before us
> And we flutter against it like moths . . .'

Quickly she pulled the tapa quilt across her shoulders and blew out the flame. It was reassuring to hear the homely sounds of pots clattering faintly from the kitchen, the low voices of Timu and Maria, the occasional bark of a village dog, before sleep came.

In the morning she woke late. Timu had already gone to the loading beach where the *Island Star* would be taking on copra. Maria gave her breakfast – strong tea with tinned milk and, unbelievably, doughnuts.

'In the war,' Maria said haltingly, 'the Americans show us.' She laughed, revealing her few remaining teeth. Then she led Laura out on to the path and pointed the way.

'You all right? I come too?'
'No need, dear Maria. You've been so kind to me already.'
'Good luck, Lora.' The stout little woman produced the phrase with some pride as she squeezed her in a motherly embrace. Fifty yards along the path, Laura turned and saw she was standing with folded arms, still watching, until the trees hid her from sight.

She met few people on her way. An elderly couple gathering brushwood gave her the usual morning greeting. A young fisherman with a net across his shoulders stepped back, smiling shyly, to let her pass. Then the path widened out on to a stretch of beach where the sand was dark and smooth. The sea was out, leaving the surface ribbed and gleaming in the sun. A small solitary bird like a sandpiper hopped along the tideline looking for worms, whistling to itself as it went.

Laura stopped for a moment. She looked back towards the village. Through the palm trees the thatched roofs were clearly visible, with the smoke of cooking fires hanging above them in a thin blue haze. It was a scene of perfect stillness and peace. Why then was she aware of something else, a sense of danger that seemed to come from inside her head, making the skin prickle at the back of her neck?

Of course. She knew it at once. This was the beach she had first seen in her dream on the journey out, where Harrington had stood with the bird in the net. Perhaps it was the same beach where her mother had walked each evening, where more than once perhaps she had written her message in the sand. What words would she write, Laura wondered. Just 'Help Me'?

She walked on, seeing in her mind her mother's footprints stretching ahead of her. Soon the tide would wipe them out as surely as the message itself. As she walked, hundreds of tiny crabs stirred and scattered around her, so that the surface of the sand seemed to ripple like grass in the wind. Perhaps her mother had used shells to mark out the letters, she found herself thinking, these small white cowries that lay everywhere. That way, they might even be seen from the air. But what plane would ever have flown this way thirty years ago, and fly so low?

Once again, she asked herself why such an episode from her mother's life should suddenly be so vivid in her own mind. Perhaps the place itself had the power to transmit a picture from the past. Or it could be simply a case of telepathy between mother and daughter. It was something Laura had experienced before with close friends. Did that mean that her mother was alive, turning the memory over in her mind perhaps, wherever she was?

Or dead, trying to make contact from some afterlife?

The thought caught her off-balance, piercing her to the heart, swift and cold as steel. Stumbling a little, she turned back to the path. The sun was in her eyes, dazzling her, as she fought down the idea. In the distance she could see the *Island Star* at anchor. There was a white motor launch alongside flying the Union Jack, the government vessel come to pick up Ratu Edwin. He would be waiting to see her before he left.

She began to hurry. The sight of a crowd of islanders gathered on the beach lifted her spirits. She wanted to lose herself among those chattering figures, the men with bright cloths tied round their heads like pirates as they hauled the sacks of copra down to the boats, the children running to and fro, the women lounging in the shade of the meeting-house, the maneapa.

She saw Captain Bentley in his battered white topee, and Edwin bareheaded with his back towards her conferring with him. Bentley waved to her and Edwin turned round eagerly.

'Laura! I was just leaving. The launch came early.'

She could see there was no chance to talk alone with him. Had it been helpful seeing Timu, was all he asked her. Of course, she replied. She was so grateful that the meeting had been arranged.

She turned to Captain Bentley. 'I expect Ratu Edwin's been telling you I'm trying to find out anything I can about my mother. It seems she was taken away by the Japanese. Are there still some Europeans around who might remember that time, do you think?'

Bentley looked doubtful.

'Not in the Gilberts, I shouldn't think. Most of them were executed at Tarawa. The rest left long ago. Still.' He scratched the stubble on his plump chin thoughtfully. 'Might be worth talking to the Catholic Fathers up at Abaiang. They've been longer in these parts than most.'

'Are you calling in there?'

He nodded. 'Sure. We always go up to the northern islands.'

'And I alas shall be travelling south,' Edwin put in. He held out his hand to Laura. 'But we shall meet again in Fiji.'

Laura felt the quick pressure of his smooth long fingers as his eyes rested on hers.

'See she gets some rest on the journey,' he told Bentley. 'And feed her up a bit with some of your curries. She looks a bit under the weather to me.'

He began to walk away towards the boat waiting at the edge of the lagoon, then turned.

'I'll check on a few things when I'm back in Suva – the shipping records for '37, just in case there's any mention of some kind of accident at sea.'

'One more thing, Ratu Edwin.' She hurried across to him. 'Could you get word to Jack's father?' She was speaking in a lowered voice, trying not to show emotion. 'Just to say I got here all right and I'm travelling on. In confidence, of course.'

She caught a wry smile before he turned away again.

'Of course. And I'm sure the message will get safely through to Jack.' He raised his hand in farewell.

She watched the little boat take him out to the launch, then looked around for Timu.

'Here's your friend,' Captain Bentley told her. A familiar bent figure was coming towards them, with the aid of his stick. 'He'll take you into the maneapa. Best place to wait till we're ready to go.'

He was right. The shade of the long thatched interior was refreshingly cool after the heat and dust outside. Dark eyes inspected her as she followed Timu through the groups of people sitting and lying on their mats. Gauguin faces gleaming in the dusty light turned from their conversation as here and there Timu put in a word of introduction.

'This is where everyone comes,' Timu told her. 'Everything happens here, dancing, singing, important meetings. Sometimes it is just sitting and chatting, waiting for the boat. Everyone has their place according to their family, you see. It is the custom.'

Through Timu, Laura began to talk to some of the women near her. Where had she come from? Where was she going to, they wanted to know, all alone without husband or child?

She was from England, she replied, travelling north to visit the rest of the Gilberts, to take back some stories about them to the people at home. Was it true that she had been born in Taparua, someone asked? She nodded, amidst sounds of wonderment and much amazed shaking of heads. But nobody around her seemed to remember that time. Either they were too young or the war had uprooted all continuity, scattering people to other islands, other lives.

Laura felt a touch on her shoulder. It was Timu's sister, the lady in black whose name it seemed was Elenoa. Crouched behind her, she told Laura in a private whisper that a friend of hers from the Ellice Islands would like to greet the visitor before she left. She was sitting in the corner, her legs were too bad for walking. Elenoa added some words in Gilbertese.

'She is what is called a wise woman,' Timu explained. 'One of those people I was telling you about,' he added in an undertone. 'One of those who can make contact with someone by magic, if they have some small possession of that person.'

But Elenoa had already taken her by the hand and was leading her to the far side of the maneapa.

'I tell her you lose your mother,' she said in Laura's ear. 'Maybe she can say how she pass away.'

The same chill Laura had felt on the beach came over her again. Was this then the final dead end? A message from a ghost?

But the old lady in the corner was already holding out a hand to her. The moonlike face lifted up to her was impassive, the eyes filmy, as she leaned back against the pillar with her legs stuck out in front of her like a discarded doll. Laura sat down with Elenoa opposite her, careful to avoid the various small objects laid out around her on the mat, a bottle of oil containing leaves and a scrap of cloth, cowrie shells in an open box, a knot of palm fronds. Her eyes still on Laura's, the woman muttered something in Gilbertese.

'She speaks to the dead people,' Elenoa explained in a matter-of-fact way. 'But she need something first. Something of your mother.'

The old woman's gaze focused on the locket round Laura's neck, as if she knew what it contained. Obediently Laura took it off and placed it in her outstretched hand, watching with beating heart as she prised it open carefully and brought out the wisp of hair. Still holding it between wrinkled thumb and forefinger, the woman closed her eyes and bent her head.

Laura felt sweat trickle down under her shirt. Elenoa touched her arm comfortingly.

Suddenly the wise woman gave a cluck of irritation. Shaking her head, she replaced the hair inside the shell and handed it back to Laura with a dismissive gesture. She spoke sharply to Elenoa.

'She says no good,' Elenoa murmured. 'She can do nothing.'

'Something is wrong?' Laura asked. Her fingers were shaking as she slipped the cord back round her neck. She wished she had never met this woman with her hooded eyes and low grumbling voice.

'She is not there.' Elenoa translated. 'Your mother is not there.'

'Where?' Laura was confused now, as well as distressed. 'I don't understand.'

'The place where the dead must go.' Elenoa patted her arm again, the expression patient. She was choosing her words with some difficulty. 'Maybe she is still on her journey there. It is a long way across the sea far out to the west.'

Laura reached across to take the old woman's hands. They felt scaly, like snakeskin, with a queer life of their own.

'Please ask her to try,' she said to Elenoa. 'Ask her to tell me something more.'

She saw the old woman shrug as she released her hands, gesturing to Elenoa as she talked.

'How can she?' Elenoa explained. 'It is the hair. It is the wrong colour. She says it is the hair of a young woman. It no longer has power.'

All at once Laura felt suffocated in that crowded place heavy with the smell of coconut oil and tobacco smoke. As she stood up, she realized that something else was expected. With a quick word of thanks, she handed over a packet of cigarettes and saw the old woman's face soften. Bending towards her, Laura caught some final words, spoken quickly with a faint smile. Elenoa's face was solemn.

'She says maybe it mean your mother still alive.'

Timu had come back to them.

'It is not a good thing to deal with people like this,' he told her disapprovingly. 'Besides, you have to go, Miss Lora. Message come from Captain Bentley. The ship is ready to sail.'

The small bent figure of Timu watching from the shore was Laura's last memory of Taparua. Aboard the *Island Star*, Captain Bentley had kindly set aside a tiny cabin for her. She was glad of the privacy, something that never seemed to matter to the throng of passengers on deck. But when she closed the porthole, it was abominably hot. If she left it open, there was the problem of the flies who had followed the boat out to sea, mainly because of the pigs. There were now five grunters tethered together on the forward hatch-top, permanently upwind of her cabin it seemed, adding their own particular stench to the rich smells of the humans and their cooking.

In spite of the heat she slept a good deal over the next three days. The irrational joy she had felt at the wise woman's last words had soon worn off. Sometimes she was fighting off nightmares of her mother in some forgotten Saipan prison, starving and in rags. Sometimes she was dreaming of Jack, searching for him in the empty house in Vailima, and by the pool where they had swum on that idyllic morning in another world, another time. These dreams were stained with the violent colours of jealousy. Nearly always, Kim had a part to play, sometimes coiled in a sexual embrace with Jack that was so vivid, so painfully humiliating that Laura woke gasping for breath, choked with anger and frustration.

Existing in some vacuum, between one hope and the next, she was at the mercy of such visitations. It was a relief, in the cool of early morning, to make some sense of recent events by jotting them down in a journal, otherwise it seemed possible that reality might be lost altogether.

Once or twice, she wondered about using her machine to record her thoughts. But there were only three tapes left and these might be more urgently needed in the days to come. From time to time her small friend with the orange would seek her out to play some game or other. Laura had caught sight of the little girl weaving between her fingers the string figures like cat's cradles that all the island children made, and at once she remembered her own efforts at making them, taught by Katua all those years ago.

In the evenings Captain Bentley invited her to share supper with him and the Gilbertese mate, pungent fish curries washed down with much whisky in his smoky little cabin with the lantern swinging just above their heads. As the ship steamed northwards they tried to teach her the names of the different islands. Marakei meant Fish-trap, Abemama Light of the Moon, Beru was named after the lizard whose shape it resembled. Butaritari was translated as Smelling of the Sea because it had been pulled up from the depths by Naureau, the creator of the world.

In the full glare of noon, each landfall seemed the same to Laura, a tawny smudge on the horizon spiked with green, the close-up of running figures coming to greet them down the beach, cargo and passengers loaded and unloaded. She began to feel like a Bedouin crossing an endless expanse of blue desert in search of these sandy waterholes.

On the fourth day something quite different came into view, Abaiang. It was early morning and in that silvery light the island reminded her, unbelievably, of an English village. The massed palm trees could have been oaks or elms among the thatch of the village houses, and out of them rose the turrets of a church complete with clock tower.

'The biggest in the Gilberts,' Captain Bentley told her. 'The Sacred Heart Mission are very proud of it.'

Laura was standing with her bags at her feet, ready to disembark. The *Island Star* was to continue round to the other side.

'It's Sunday,' Bentley reminded her. 'So that's where you'll find everyone, including Father Pierre. Terrific old guy. Knows everything about the Pacific. You'll like him.'

'They won't mind my arriving out of the blue like this?' Laura asked, suddenly doubtful. 'I mean, I'm not even a Catholic.'

He laughed. 'Out of the blue is the way everyone arrives in this part of the world.' He gave her a salute as she got down into the boat. 'I'll be round at the next village. Just send a message if you're planning to stay on a day or two. We can always pick you up on the way down again.'

Her little friend waved to her from the rails. Everyone else seemed to be going round to the other village too. Laura found herself stepping onto the little jetty alone, though soon enough the usual reception committee of excited children had gathered around her, squabbling as to who was to carry her bags. A few English words were tried, on both sides. In the end, Laura said simply, 'The church,' and everyone seemed happy to take her there.

Staring up at the extraordinary edifice, she was reminded of a giant wedding cake. Every inch of the façade was plastered with a thick white coating of crushed coral and lime gleaming in the sun. White-painted stones lined the steps leading up to the arched doorway with its carving of the symbols of the Order of the Sacred Heart entwined with an anchor. From inside came a low murmuring, like a hive of bees.

At this point, her escort fell respectfully back. The bags were deposited inside the door and Laura found herself alone again. A childhood memory came over her. At her Catholic boarding-school in Yorkshire, she had become used to making the sign of the cross at church services, and she did the same thing now. The holy water inside the huge conch shell was cool to the touch. The scent of incense seemed at once familiar yet oddly tinged with something else – the heady perfume of tiaré flowers.

She had been rehearsing how she would introduce herself, but as yet there was no need. A white-haired priest who had to be Father Pierre moved around the altar at the far end. In front of her stretched a rustling sea of figures seated on mats on either side of the long, shadowy nave.

A bell tolled from somewhere overhead and the low chanting of responses began again.

Against the wall behind her there was a single empty bench. She sat down unnoticed. All at once her spirit felt curiously rested. The strangeness of the scene entranced her, with the quiet intensity of feeling it contained.

In fact, half the congregation were far from quiet. Babies wailed from time to time, rolling about on their backs, while toddlers staggered to and fro clutching at rosaries and trying on discarded straw hats. Dogs came sniffing eagerly in and out of the open doors. But most people took no notice of all this, their black heads bent in prayer. And when the hymns began, the flood of voices, male and female richly intertwined, swept away all distractions.

Up in the steeple a bell rang again, and a kind of general confession began. Father Pierre simply took his seat behind the rails, facing sideways, and one by one the people filed forward to kneel and whisper in his ear. Last of all went the children, small girls in neat cotton frocks with flowers behind their ears, thin little boys in clean white shirts and bright sulus clutching their prayer books to their chests. Laura wondered what sins they had to tell the priest as they filed back with broad grins on their faces.

Then the service was over. Everyone streamed out through a side door. To Laura, the empty church seemed suddenly larger and barer than she had imagined. The only decorations were the patterns of faded gold fleur-de-lys on the blue-painted walls, and the inscriptions of the Stations of the Cross, interwined with the names of the islands. Father Pierrc disappeared into the vestry.

Laura paused, hesitating to disturb his Sunday rituals. The next minute she turned to find him at her side, transformed into a shabby old man in rumpled trousers and a frayed blue shirt. The pendulous face lit up with a smile as he held out his hand.

'You are travelling round on the *Island Star*?' His accent was strong, almost rough. 'Your first visit to the Gilberts?'

Laura found herself at once at ease in this calm presence.

'The first for many years, Father.'

Was this the moment to explain a little more? But Father Pierre was energetically striding towards a small door at the side.

'I expect you'll want to see the clock. Visitors usually do.'

Dutifully Laura followed him up a steep flight of steps and then another. At the top, inside a glass case, various mechanisms were whirring and wheezing away. From the clock face on the other side of the wall came a loud ticking, regular as a heartbeat. Father Pierre's heart was obviously just as steady. Only Laura was out of breath.

'A famous French maker,' he told her proudly. He checked the time on his pocket watch. 'You can imagine what a work it is, keeping it in order in a climate like this.'

'Actually, Father,' Laura began. She caught up with him as he galloped down to the bottom of the steps.

'Actually, Father, I came to ask you about the war.'

'Ah, the war. You are a journalist?'

Standing there in the quiet of the nave, Laura found she was able to explain things more simply than she had imagined. Her family had been living in the Gilberts when the Japanese invaded, she told him. Her father escaped to Fiji but her mother had not been heard of since. There was a story that she might have been taken away on a Japanese boat.

'And you, my child?' Behind the thick glasses, the old man's eyes were sharp and searching.

'I was evacuated earlier with the women and children. First to New Zealand, then back to England.'

'Surely your mother should have gone with you?'

'She was sick, too sick to travel.' Laura fell silent. Father Pierre watched her face carefully.

'This sounds a sad story.' He led her over to the bench at the back. Laura sat down but he remained standing, his hands clasped in front of him.

'And so long ago. You are not still hopeful, are you?'

'Sometimes I am, sometimes I'm not.' She paused. 'You were in the Gilberts yourself at that time, Father?'

'Yes, in one of the furthest islands, right up at the northern end.' He shook his head. 'So I fear I can be of little help to you.'

Laura felt the familiar plunge of disappointment. Father Pierre was pacing slowly to and fro now, head bent, hands behind his back.

'My own experience was rather strange,' he went on. 'Not typical, perhaps. There was a Japanese trader on the island, a friend of the mission. When war broke out the Japanese became the enemy. So we invited him to the house to be our prisoner. Then when the island was invaded, he asked us to move in with him to be his prisoners.' He smiled faintly. 'But we were lucky in having a Japanese officer who went along with these arrangements. He was an unusual man, an educated man. He treated us with some sympathy and we survived.' He stood up in front of her, looking down at her gently. 'Perhaps your mother was also fortunate. And did not suffer, at least.'

'You were a Frenchman, Father. Your country had surrendered.'

'Your mother was English?'

'American.' There was a silence. 'Do you remember the name of your Japanese officer?' she asked.

Once again, the priest shook his head. 'Too long ago,' he sighed. He seemed to be searching his mind. 'I heard there were some Europeans actually sent away to Japan. Perhaps when you go back to London, some organization like the Red Cross would have records.'

'Perhaps,' Laura said dully. 'Someone has suggested it.'

Father Pierre put his hand on her shoulder. 'I think a glass of wine is needed. You'll come to the house for lunch?'

'Thank you, Father. That's very kind of you.' On the way out she paused. 'I'd like to light a candle, if I may.'

'But of course, my child.'

Half a dozen were already burning on the little iron tray near the altar. As she added her own flame to the rest, Laura felt a kind of resigned calm flow through her. The smell of melting wax mingled with the last whiff of incense. Kneeling with her head in her hands, she wondered at this new self that had begun to emerge since leaving England, as if layer after layer of protective packaging had been stripped away. Before, she had prayed for her mother. Now she prayed for herself and for the strength to face failure, not just the failure of the search but the failure of love. At the end of the journey she might have to go home empty-handed and alone. But it wouldn't be a return to the old life. Of that, at least, she was sure. Most of the old Laura had gone, broken up into a hundred worthless fragments. What was to replace it would have to be something that had grown of its own accord, like a plant with roots rather than a carefully fashioned piece of china.

When she stood up, she was touched to find Father Pierre on his knees behind her. He got to his feet awkwardly, stuffing his rosary into his pocket.

'I hope it's chicken,' he said, leading the way towards the tall shuttered house at the back of the church. 'Wati does that quite well!'

It was indeed chicken, nicely roasted though rather tough, and accompanied by a mountain of baked yams and plantains. It was served by two demure girls with flowered aprons and long glossy plaits. Father Pierre wagged his finger at them as he toddled to and fro with a jug of red wine, looking for glasses.

'They are naughty children, these servants of mine. Everything is so untidy. I have to apologize.'

Laura surveyed the large jumbled room that had an air of shipwreck about it. Books and papers lay everywhere alongside cardboard boxes crammed with dusty files. Native rush mats lined the floors, and the only furnishings were a sagging horsehair couch, a couple of frayed deckchairs, and an immense mahogany desk covered with an ancient rug.

'Imagine,' he said, pouring out the wine into two rather musty-looking glasses. 'It takes months for mail and newspapers to get to us from France. Not that we're ever short of anything to read.' He waved a hand towards the shelves that lined the walls. 'Mostly exploration and theology. The Mission also equipped us well with reference books, mostly out of date now. Oh yes.' He beamed. 'We're quite well known for our library at the back of beyond.'

Halfway through the meal there was the unexpected sound of a motorbike.

'That will be Father Rogé. He's been doing baptisms in the next village.'

A young man with bristly hair and a round red face walked in, brushing dust from his soutane. He shook hands shyly with Laura, glancing sideways at her as he joined them at the table. He came from the Savoy region, he told her. He'd only been in the Gilberts since 1965. It was nothing compared to Father Pierre's thirty-five years, or the whole lifetimes spent in the islands by the first mission fathers back in the nineteenth century.

The young priest turned his attention to the chicken and ate hungrily. Father Pierre continued to talk with the single-minded energy of one who rarely saw a new face. They were good people, the Gilbertese, he explained. They tried. But the pagan beliefs died hard, witchcraft, possession by spirits, the old tabus.

'Not long ago they still kept the skulls of their ancestors in their houses. Kept them nicely polished too.' He drew on his Gauloise with a chuckle, and passed one across to Father Rogé to smoke with his coffee. 'Somehow we all live together, different as we are.'

'What happens if you become ill?' Laura asked them. 'Tarawa is days away.'

'If it is serious, one of the sisters comes down by boat,' Father Pierre said. 'You'll be going to see the sisters, of course?' He saw her look of surprise. 'You did not know about the mission convent and the school up at the far end of the island? They would welcome a visit from you. When does the *Island Star* leave again?'

'Not till tomorrow.'

'Reverend Mother would be happy to give you a bed for the night. Whereas for us.' He spread out his hands with another of those chuckles of his. 'It would be difficult.'

The old man got up and began to bustle about again. 'You can leave your bags here. No need for a boat. Wati will lend you her bicycle. You like to cycle? Many people in the villages have bicycles. Bicycles and sewing machines, the two best gifts of civilization.'

Suddenly he stopped and struck his forehead with the palm of his hand. 'How strange! The name of that Japanese officer has just come back to me. It is always the same, the minute one stops trying. Tanizaki. It was Captain Tanizaki.'

Without quite knowing why, Laura brought out her notebook and scribbled it down.

Father Rogé bent down to fasten on the large black sandals he'd slipped off under the table while he was having his meal.

'I think it will be too tiring for her to cycle,' he said quietly to Father Pierre. 'It's quite a long way and she's not used to this climate.' He turned to Laura with a sketchy bow and the same shy smile. 'If you do not mind riding pillion on a motorcycle?'

It was something Laura had never done before, but in this part of the world nothing seemed strange. Or rather, everything was so strange that one more new experience was lost among so many. Within minutes Father Pierre was giving her his blessing, Father Rogé was donning his goggles and they were off.

As they roared away through the village people waved and called out to them. Further along, they slowed down to cross a shaky little bridge and a gaggle of girls came fluttering and chirping towards them like a flock of tropical birds. One, more daring than the rest and with a garland of frangipani tilted over her eyes, performed an impromptu dance in honour of the priest, arms extended, hips twirling.

Hastening on again Father Rogé turned to Laura to laugh, his face more red than ever.

'They only do it to tease! A man without a woman is still a complete puzzle to them!'

The track ahead was empty, eerily still in the glittering afternoon, with the sea flats stretching away on either side. This was the new causeway built by government to link the atolls together, he told her, so that people could cross the length of the island even at high tide. It was like travelling through the landscape of a Chinese drawing, Laura thought. The harsh light bleached out all colour, reduced things to outline – the sparse trees, the occasional figure on a bicycle, the fragile wooden jetties with their thatched latrines perched out over the shallows on stilts, like storks.

'Are you okay?' Father Rogé shouted to her from time to time above the noise of the engine.

'Fine, thanks!'

At the end of the causeway, the coral track seemed more bumpy than ever. Laura simply hung on, battered but exhilarated, grateful for Father Rogé's muscular solidity. She only hoped this sweaty embrace was not embarrassing him. But he was calling to her to look ahead. Just round the next bend she would see the convent.

A fresh cloud of dust swarmed round them as they rattled up to the tall iron gate. Through it she could see a long white building with a crenellated skyline that reminded her of old movies about the Foreign Legion. As she got off stiffly, Father Rogé pulled on a bell that hung from the wall.

'I shall just hand you over, if you don't mind,' he told her. 'There's an old man on his deathbed in the next village. They'll be waiting for me.' He smiled at her, suddenly looking little more than a student. 'Besides, this is Mother Superior's territory. We don't exactly exchange social visits.'

Laura took off her dark glasses.

'That was fun,' she began, when the gate was opened by a very young, very dark little nun in grey.

'You have a visitor,' Father Rogé told her. 'A Miss Harrington from England. Could you take her to Reverend Mother? I'm sorry I have to hurry away.'

With wide eyes the little nun nodded. As Father Rogé disappeared, she led the way up the path then turned to Laura and put her finger to her lips.

'The children are practising for their Christmas concert,' she whispered. 'You will come and watch?'

Christmas! In this nomadic existence she had entirely forgotten about such a thing. It made her sad somehow to think she could forget.

They had come to a large shaded verandah. Inside she could see about fifty small girls and boys seated cross-legged in orderly rows. Some singing had just come to an end and there was a burst of applause. She had a glimpse of white-veiled figures ensconced in cane chairs at the far end. Laura watched from the back as the little nun crept up to one of them and spoke into her ear.

A face was turned in her direction, weatherbeaten against the white of the veil. A pair of sharp eyes surveyed her. A hand was raised to beckon her over.

Other heads turned now as Laura made her way forward. All at once she was the nervous schoolgirl of twenty years ago.

'I'm sorry, Reverend Mother,' she whispered. The courtesy form of address had come back like magic. 'Please don't let me interrupt. I'm travelling through and the Fathers suggested I visit you.'

The veiled faces on either side were also inspecting her, smiling and nodding. A space was made and a chair was pushed forward.

'You're very welcome, Miss Harrington.' Reverend Mother's voice was harsh and broadly Australian. 'Just in time for the rest of the programme.' She clapped her hands together briskly. 'Children! Please continue! A visitor has come to see your concert.'

Behind them, the hissing crescendo of whispers died away. From a side door a troop of tiny girls emerged looking like elves in their skirts and garlands of croton leaves. Their arms were stiffly outstretched in front of them, ready for the dance, and Laura saw that on the back of each hand was balanced a small shell. They began a high-pitched chanting, keeping time with their bodies, ritual swaying movements with heads held high, bare feet circling and cupping the wooden floor. All the time the shells remained in place on the outstretched hands. Laura was mesmerized, drawn into the intensity of the performance.

'It is the traditional Gilbertese dance-form,' Reverend Mother told her. 'When they are older, they will not need the shells to keep their postures correct.' She glanced at Laura. 'I suppose you've been told the missions destroyed all the old customs?'

'I had heard it said.'

'Well, not us, Miss Harrington. Not us!' She shot Laura another of those quick looks, twinkling between sandy eyebrows and mottled cheeks. 'Are you a Catholic?'

'I'm afraid not, Reverend Mother. Church of England is how I was brought up, apart from a couple of years at a convent school.'

Mother Superior surprised her with a gruff chuckle. 'Never mind! We can't all be lucky.'

The dancers had been replaced by the older children. A handsome boy in a white shirt and shorts stepped forward and began beating time with a small wooden clapper. At the same instant a flood of singing was released, rich and rhythmic like the voices in the church.

'Our Christmas carol,' Mother Superior whispered. 'Sister Angelica composed it specially.' She nodded towards the little nun in grey who was pointing out the words on a blackboard, line by line, in Gilbertese and in English.

'In the place for the animals
Lying among the feeding stuff
We shall see the Christ child
Shivering with cold . . .'

The clear voices rose and fell. Outside the heat was almost visible, making the air quiver over the huge flamboyant tree, burning off the scarlet petals like an English frost. Laura watched a lizard scuttle between tinsel chains on the opposite wall. It froze and cocked its head as if listening to the sound of the singing.

There was a lump in her throat as the last words died away. The children stood to attention, a sea of smiling faces turned towards the front row.

'Happy Christmas, Sisters and Miss.'

A very pretty nun had appeared from the far end of the verandah. 'Tea's ready, Mother,' Laura heard her say in a soft Irish voice. 'The children are having theirs in the compound.'

Moving around the tea table with its embroidered cloth and flowered china, Laura studied the faces of the other nuns as she was introduced. The Irish one with the heart-shaped face and the long black eyelashes was Sister Bernadette. There was a New Zealander with spectacles and a toothy grin called Sister Clarissa, and two

Gilbertese novices in their grey habits, little Angelica and an older one, Sister Maria.

'We could do with twice as many,' Sister Clarissa told her, earnestly pushing the glasses back on her nose. 'We run a dispensary as well as a school, you see. And there's the kitchen garden to look after and a couple of goats for our milk.'

'We lost Sister Philomena just a few weeks ago,' Sister Angelica said in a low murmur, handing round home-made biscuits. 'She was the last of the old-timers. So now there are just the four of us.' She dipped her head politely. 'And Reverend Mother, of course.'

'Oh, and Sister Kiri,' the Irish nun put in.

She turned to look down at the beach which curved away directly beneath the convent grounds. 'That's where you'll find her. She's great on collecting shells, for the necklaces the children make. Not one for the social occasion is Sister Kiri.'

'Poor Kiri.' Reverend Mother's harsh voice was suddenly gentler, Laura noticed. 'Always a loner. She's been with the mission so long nobody remembers how she came here in the first place.' She touched her forehead significantly.

'She's not quite with it up here, if you take my meaning.' She picked up the teapot. 'So you're travelling for the BBC, you were saying. More tea?'

But Laura was looking down at the beach, watching the woman in the distance who was making her way back towards the convent. She walked slowly, a thin, stooping figure wearing not the white of the order but a shorter robe of a brownish colour. A brown scarf was tied low over her head. Kiri must be a lay sister of some kind, Laura thought, most likely a Gilbertese from her name.

She put down her cup. 'Excuse me a moment, Reverend Mother.'

Something made her move away from the verandah, out towards the steps that led down to the beach. Sister Kiri was bending to pick up some shells at the edge of the sea, where the waves crept in with barely a ripple. Carefully she put the shells into the basket she was carrying. Then she stopped and looked up, directly at Laura who was halfway down the steps. Laura stopped too. She felt her heart turn over.

It was a European face. The first sight of it struck Laura with a shock of recognition so piercing it was like terror. Dear God, she remembered thinking. Could joy be like this?

At that moment she thought she would fall. But the woman had come up to her and with a gentle movement had taken hold of her arm. She was smiling at her.

'Laura,' she said, almost dreamily. 'Little Laura. Why have you taken so long?'

PART THREE

8 DECEMBER 1969
VIA CABLE AND WIRELESS LTD SOUTHWEST PACIFIC
MESSAGE FROM SACRED HEART MISSION ABAIANG GILBERT AND ELLICE ISLANDS COLONY
TO MR MAX RENFREY NAILANGI PLANTATION VANUA LEVU FIJI
URGENT AND CONFIDENTIAL

CAN YOU CONTACT JACK REPORT SUCCESSFUL OUTCOME OF SEARCH STOP MISSING PERSON SAFE THOUGH FRAIL SUFFERING CHRONIC AMNESIA STOP TAPE RECORDING ALL RECALL POSSIBLE EVIDENCE CRIMINAL CHARGES STOP LOVE LAURA

CHAPTER ONE

How to begin, I ask myself? It's all very well you putting this recording machine in front of me, here in my little room, and then telling me now it's my turn to talk. Everything I can remember, you say. Well, before that, one simple thing you wanted to know. A small thing. Why am I called Kiri? It's a nickname really, the island name for that little sandpiper bird that likes to walk along the edge of the sea, just as I do. The sisters gave it me ages ago and it's kind of stuck. It seems more my name than Millie nowadays.

Something like that is easy. But Laura, dearest Laura, have you any idea how difficult it is to go back to all the rest, back to those terrible early days with Harrington on Taparua? You've seen him as he is today. For myself I could never bear to set eyes on the man again any more than I could bear to hear his voice. What you've told me is enough. Let him think of me as dead. At least you know the most important thing, that he is not your father at all. I only wish to God I could tell you who your real father was, maybe even *is*. But that part of my life is gone and buried, like so much else.

As you can see, even now my mind is not as strong as it should be. A miracle like this is kind of a shock to the system, you know! And it was a miracle seeing you coming towards me on the beach down there, still my little daughter even after all these years. At the same time, can you believe it, it was no surprise at all. More like the most natural thing in the world that you should find your way back to me. It had to be your search, not mine. It was my bargain with Harrington, you see, to let you go for ever. Otherwise . . .

But that part comes later. What you need to know is how I survived at all, right from the start. You say you don't want to interrupt me with questions, so this will be like writing you a letter, the letter I was never able to send you. A kind of diary of my heart.

In one sense it's easy to start because there's only one starting-point

– that moment when I found myself alive. Everything before that is a blank. I was lying face down on a beach, still half in the water. All I was aware of was pain, pain everywhere but especially in my head. And the sense of being absolutely – what would the word be? – bereft? Something terrible had happened, something so terrible that my mind refused to remember it.

That was the most awful thing of all, Laura. To have no memory, not just of what had brought me to that place, but of who I actually was.

Later on, very slowly, I was able to come to grips with this. I had to accept the fact that I had been robbed of all my previous life – what I now look on as the first half of my life. I must be about seventy, mustn't I? At the time I was anything between thirty-five and forty, I suppose. But it was like being a newborn baby, emerging from darkness and water into a world I couldn't begin to make sense of.

I was as weak as a baby too, and with no human presence to turn to. Until the Englishman appeared, and the coloured man with the kind hands and the soft voice. That was Timu.

But for days on end I had to try to survive alone. However often I scanned that reef there was never a glimpse of a boat, or a single sign of any wreckage on the beach either. There was no clue to any disaster at all – only myself. I remember telling myself that I was a castaway: washed up on a desert island. It sounded so unreal, something that belonged to an adventure book. In the stories the solitary survivor had to exercise ingenuity to stay alive. I would have to do the same. And for good reason too. Not memory, not rational thought of any kind but pure instinct told me I was pregnant. It was just something I knew. I had an unborn child to protect. And somewhere out there my husband, the father of the child, might still be alive, searching, waiting for news. I touched the wedding ring I was wearing. It said nothing to me. I made a great effort to turn over. I put my hand on my body where my trousers were torn. My stomach seemed quite flat. But how sick I felt, how terribly sick. And now I could see bloodstains, and feel blood trickling very slowly down my legs. How could such an early pregnancy survive, I asked myself. But I vowed I would do my best to keep that invisible scrap of life going. It seemed it was all I had in the world.

In the books, castaways light fires and send up smoke signals, don't they? All I could do was use my last ounce of strength to drag myself up the beach to where I could see scrub and bushes growing. I knew I needed shade. The sun was almost directly overhead, striking bare skin through my rags of clothing. My head was bare too. My hair seemed to be cut very short. I felt blood caked to it like dried mud and my mouth was dry too, so dry it was difficult to open my lips. Then the pain cut through everything else. I passed out.

When I came to, the sun had moved round. It was coming at me sideways now, like a sword. I managed to pull some branches over me to make a kind of bivouac. Strange the way that jolly camping word came to mind. Not that I had much of a mind for the next forty-eight hours, just a reeling blankness.

There were some lucid patches. I remembered to ration out the bottle of water that was fastened to my belt – another strange thing. I took a small sip every few hours. I was guessing time. My watch had stopped because of the water, I suppose. It said twenty minutes past nine o'clock. I took stock of what else I had with me – a soaked map in my jacket pocket, one shoe still left on. A few yards away I saw a small tin case, very battered. I tried to open it but the lock was stuck. For the first time I noticed I couldn't move one of my legs properly. I must have fractured something. It was dark again and I drifted into sleep.

When the sun came up for the third time my water was finished. I could no longer move at all. I thought, now I will surely die. No one will come by to such a forgotten speck of land as this. I only hoped to be able to sink into oblivion, rather than suffer. I cried then, I remember, wishing I had someone to send my last thoughts to. But who? I prayed anyway. Somehow I was sure I had always done that.

Harrington's voice was the thing I remember next, that thin cold drawl. I didn't take in what he said. I couldn't answer anyway, until Timu brought me some water. But I could never forget the expression on his face. It was a kind of amazed excitement, and it frightened me. The kindness came from Timu. With Harrington, it was as if he had stumbled on something of great value, like treasure trove. So I knew I would be taken care of. But I would not be returned to my rightful owner, not yet anyway. My mind might be damaged, but it was something I sensed right away. I was barely alive, remember. Just grateful for a rescuer, whoever he was. And now, I thought, my baby may live too.

It was the chance of keeping you alive, Laura, that kept me alive through the next few months. Otherwise I would certainly have killed myself. I had to turn myself into someone I was never meant to be in that other, unknown life of mine. That woman had been strong, determined, used to having her own way. I don't know how I knew this. I just did. Now I had to be a stranger to myself just to survive. I had to be acquiescent, devious, humble, as befitted a broken piece of humanity washed up like driftwood from God knows where.

I began to realize this that very first night, back at Harrington's bungalow. That awful dark barn of a place with the rats running along the rafters and cockroaches scuttling in every corner! The sea was so close that I thought the sound of the surf on the reef would drive me mad. It seemed to be inside my head, in, out, in, out, never-ending night and day as long as I was there to hear it. I didn't share Harrington's room. It might have been better if I had. At least I would have seen him at close quarters, sleeping like an ordinary human being. I might have found out more about the secrets he carried with him, the things that made him the terrible man he is.

I was given my own room. It was quite small, partitioned off with thin bamboo walls. There was no glass in the window, just wooden shutters. He said I was to keep them closed while I slept in spite of the heat. He had a mania for locks and security, like everything else. But who would break in on me, I wondered?

The only furniture in the room, apart from a chest and an old canvas chair, was a truckle bed in the corner. Harrington coming towards me as I lay on that bed, regularly, every night, was the most fearful thing I knew. That first night I had been given food and drink, sweet biscuit broken up into warm tinned milk. Timu's daughter brought it to me, Katua, a gentle girl about ten or eleven years old. She and her mother helped in the house. It was their kindness that got me through so many things. They wanted to change my clothes and bathe me. But Harrington had given me some kind of medication that made me drop into sleep like a stone. He told me I had been delirious on the boat journey back. We would talk the next day about what could be done for me.

As the medication took effect I felt calm, almost hopeful. The ordeal on the beach was beginning to fade. I thought maybe my first reactions to Harrington were disturbed. Obviously he'd be looking for a way to get me back to the outside world, to find out what had happened to me.

I must have slept for two or three hours. But then something woke me. A lamp had been brought in, placed on the chest by the bed. Harrington's face bending over me looked for the first time truly evil. Deranged, even. A pair of scissors glinted in his hand, the large kind doctors use. The sheet that covered me had been pulled away. Very neatly and methodically he was cutting away the remains of my clothes, the stained trousers, the torn shirt.

I closed my eyes again quickly and lay absolutely still. Harrington was stripping me with as much care as if he was unwrapping a precious parcel. When I was naked he stepped back, and I knew he was staring down at me. If he had simply pulled the clothes off of me or told me to undress I would not have felt such terror. But this was madness.

'You're awake,' he said. 'Only pretending to sleep.'

I said nothing.

He asked me if I had heard what he had said to Timu back there on the beach. I told him no, how could I? I had passed out by then.

'Listen now,' he said. 'I've brought you back here to stay with me. I need a wife, you see.'

He said it in a perfectly reasonable way. That's what I remember about it. He told me he'd never had a woman with him in all the time he'd been on the island, posted there by government five years before. And he still had another two years to serve before his leave was due.

'Then my luck turns and you arrive.' He touched the wedding ring on my hand. 'I noticed that straight away. Another piece of luck.'

He smiled at me then. There was a charm about his smile that was totally unreal. It was like a pantomime mask, suddenly put on, and suddenly taken off again.

'It's a nuisance about your pregnancy. If you are actually pregnant, that is. Still, I shouldn't think it'll last long, one way or another.'

He might have been talking about an infection. Then he ordered me to speak to no one now I had been found. The local people would be told we were married in Fiji and I'd come out to join him like any good colonial wife. I must swear not to try to run away. Again that smile. 'There's nowhere to run away to.'

Why should I agree to this, I asked him, trying to sound equally reasonable.

'It's quite simple,' he told me. 'I have given you back your life. Now you owe me something by way of payment. You belong to me, Millie.'

The way he spoke my name so softly, so greedily! Yet with such a natural air of ownership. That told me how completely helpless I was. That, and what followed.

Laura, please don't ask me to speak again of it, not now or ever. Yes, it was rape, but worse, more vicious, more callous. He had no idea of any normal human responses. So I was treated as an animal, violated, humiliated. I tremble now even thinking about it. And all the time I knew I must not resist, could not resist, trying to keep my precious pregnancy intact.

Afterwards I was sick.

In the morning Maria brought me breakfast – flat bread and tea with a piece of pawpaw and also some clothes, one of those smock-like cotton dresses the Victorian missionaries had decreed that the women should wear. I managed to get to what passed for a bathroom in

Harrington's bungalow. It had a 'thunder box' lavatory and a tin bath and a jug filled with water from the well. On my way back to my bed I could smell burning. I opened the shutters and saw that Harrington had made a bonfire. He was raking the embers together with his back to me. I could see the remains of my clothes, and other things wrapped in newspaper. I knew he was destroying all trace of the possessions I had come ashore with, the map, the shoe, the wristwatch. When I asked him about the other things, the box and the water bottle, he just shrugged.

'Gone and buried. What would you want them for?'

I was lying on the bed again, too weak to move. He was in the doorway, looking at me with that awful smile. I spoke without thinking.

'You know who I am, don't you?'

Again the shrug. 'Don't be absurd. How could I?'

Of course. How could he? Yet I knew he was lying. I studied his face. The features were handsome, like a marble statue, but pitted with the scars of some tropical skin disease. The pale eyes didn't even bother to meet mine. He was cleaning the dirt from under his fingernails. How I hated those hands – the narrow shape of them, the yellow marks from his cigarettes.

I screamed at him. 'For God's sake, who am I? Why won't you tell me?'

I broke down and actually went on my knees before him, beating at his legs like a child. It was the first of many scenes like that. His reaction was always the same. I would be left alone without food or drink, the key turned in the lock, the shutters bolted from the outside. The footsteps went away. Much later he would come back to ask if I was sorry for the trouble I'd caused.

Since then, over and over I've pondered it. If he did know who I was, why was it so important to him to keep my identity a secret, even from me? I suppose the answer was that a nameless person could never be claimed, like left luggage without a label. Even if he had been informed that there had been an accident at sea and that he was to keep a lookout for bodies or survivors, the authorities couldn't check, not with so many specks of land in these millions of square miles of ocean. So he was quite safe in keeping me for himself. Findings keepings, as he put it, like some gloating schoolboy.

It's hard to believe but he even tried to keep the names of the islands from me. Timu told me, of course. The one where I'd been found was part of the Phoenix group. I liked that – the phoenix rising reborn from the ashes. It seemed a good sign and I clung to it.

From then on I would go through his study when he was out, looking for a map. But he locked his atlases in the glass cupboards behind his desk, along with his specimen cases of moths and butterflies and the notebooks he was forever writing up in his tangled, microscopic handwriting. He'd even destroyed his stack of old newspapers, the ones that came with the mail boat every six months. I'd seen him burning them in the Dover stove in the kitchen late one night after Maria had cleared up and gone home.

For a while he'd even locked away his precious wireless, his only other link with the outside world. Why he did that I never knew. Unless he thought I might catch something that would jog my memory. He had to avoid that. While my past was a blank, I was helpless. And being helpless, I was his slave. What else could I be?

Most days, of course, he had his duties as district officer to attend to. He was medical officer too, and magistrate. He seemed to relish this absurd power over a few hundred people. Simple, easy-going souls they seemed on the surface, but who knows what went on in their minds about him? The ritual was always the same. Every morning a tattered awning would be set up outside the hut that was his dispensary-cum-office. Slowly a queue of silent people would file past for injections or medicines, while he sat bolt upright at his table in his starched whites and hateful khaki topee.

Watching from the verandah where I spent most of the day I noted he hardly ever smiled, and neither did anyone else. He liked to speak the language but I saw the natives look back at him dumbly, not understanding the Gilbertese he learned from books. Timu would stand behind him and translate. There were endless scraps of paper to be signed. Taxes, fines, stamp duties, were the words I heard.

Sometimes a prisoner was brought before him. The most frequent offence was adultery, it seemed, with the occasional crime of passion after a bout of sour toddy drinking, rarely theft, but once or twice indulgence in manual labour on the Sabbath – something the old Methodist missionaries had strictly forbidden.

The prison was a thatched lock-up nearby with a compound for exercise. It looked like a friendly place with relatives coming and going with food, and no stigma attached to the person sentenced. Harrington hated the laxness of this system but it was traditional, and he was powerless to change it. That was why he introduced beatings, he told me. Corporal punishment had done him no harm at school, and what were the natives after all but wilful children?

Every day the Union Jack flew from a bamboo flagstaff. At sunset it would be lowered by the old police orderly from the village, standing to attention in his ragged lava-lava and brass belt. Then Harrington would come inside, take a bath and change into a pair of white duck trousers and a dinner jacket from his university days, which had gone green with the tropical damp. We would sit down to eat dinner in silence, one at each end of a battered wooden table. Harrington told me with relish that it had been used as an operating table by his predecessor in the Gilberts, before the new folding kind had been introduced.

'I don't expect you can cook,' he said. It was soon after that first night. 'American women aren't brought up to it, are they? But at least you can open cans, I suppose.'

It was the first time I had consciously thought of myself as an American. I was pathetically grateful for that tiny piece of information. It was like being given the first piece of a jigsaw or a word in a crossword puzzle.

But I did cook. I seemed to know how and managed to concoct a few dishes out of the limited stores that came out once a year on a government ship from Australia. Anything was better than the endless local diet of strange root vegetables, coconuts and fish. Now I was over the sick part of my pregnancy I was ravenous, with cravings that could not be satisfied. Once I came across some canned raspberries and devoured them like a child, burying the empty tin in the sand so that Harrington wouldn't know. Sometimes Timu's wife would smuggle me in a delicacy, a small guava or a kind of shellfish that pregnant women liked. When she had swept out my room, she would sometimes give me a massage with scented oil. When she saw the bruises Harrington had inflicted on me, she used to cluck with dismay to herself.

'But baby all right,' she would reassure me. Her hands on my stomach were especially gentle. She was with me the day I felt the baby move for the first time. She hugged me and we both cried for the joy of it.

CHAPTER TWO

That was September 1937. I knew the date from the calendar on Harrington's desk. I had to wait until early '38 for the baby's birth. Time dragged, like the kind of bad dream where you keep thinking you've woken up but you haven't, and so it goes on.

Some things helped, like the thought that he was due for home leave in just two years. He would be given a passage on a government ship and come what may I and my child would be on that ship too, or on any other vessel that came by Taparua, wherever it was bound. There was also an ancient sewing machine that was discovered in one of the storerooms, which I was allowed to use once I had managed to get it working again. Maria and the other women gave me some odd lengths of flowered calico and I was able to make up a few Mother Hubbard dresses for myself. I wanted trousers, like the ones I had been wearing. So I took a pair of khaki cotton ones Harrington had thrown away and altered them for myself.

At least I was able to see myself. I couldn't find a mirror in the house. Harrington must have kept his own out of sight for some reason. But Maria secretly brought me a fragment which I kept under my bed. My face looked like a boy's despite the lines around the eyes and the drawn cheeks. I had a snub nose with freckles, clear blue wide-apart eyes, a square jaw with a mouth that seemed meant to smile but was painfully cracked and dragged down at the corners. My hair was longer now as Harrington decreed it, wiry to the touch and bleached like straw by the sun. It was a desperate face, the face of a prisoner in solitary. But at least it proved that I existed, whoever I was.

There was other proof too – endless photographs that Harrington produced of me. They were the result of long sessions when I had to smile, pose, sometimes strip myself bare for his satisfaction. He had an obsession with his camera. He'd set up a darkroom where he produced a succession of these tiny brown snapshots to be pasted in albums alongside his pictures of Pacific islanders. These were meant to represent the different physical types, Melanesian, Polynesian, Micronesian. All I saw were sad pictures of naked men and women, facing the camera as if it were a firing squad.

Otherwise the albums were empty. Harrington's whole life seemed to me empty, even though in the evenings he would talk on hour after hour about his past, circular, repetitive reminiscences that often made no sense. It was as if he was pouring out all the talk that had been locked up inside his head for all those years on his own. As if, during that time, everything that was stored there had become cramped and distorted, and somehow rotten.

In his memories Harrington was always the victim. He said he had been the most outstanding medical student of his year at Cambridge. But his tutors had a grudge against him, accused him (rightly no doubt) of cheating at exams, gave him only a pass degree. Everyone was jealous of his brilliance. His father had disowned him because of some legal trouble over a forged signature.

'Quite a clever signature too,' he said in that reasonable way of his. 'And I had to have the money for drugs, do you see.'

Then there was something about killing a family dog which apparently they'd 'held against him'. 'I only wish I'd killed my father too,' he told me.

He'd got into the Colonial Service somehow by volunteering for the Pacific outposts no one else wanted.

'But really I'm what you call a remittance man,' was how he put it, quite proudly. 'The family paid me an allowance, in addition to the CO's salary and fare, just to make sure I didn't go back.'

There was a job in the government medical department in Tarawa and then the post at Taparua came up, which not surprisingly had been empty for some time. 'That's what I like about the life, despite the conditions. You can do what you like, be what you like in a place like this,' he told me. But he didn't expect to be here for much longer. He planned to move on to an academic post in Australia, publish books, establish his name as a Pacific authority – which, you tell me, is almost exactly what he has done.

I remember asking him if he had any other relatives in the world. Apparently there was an unmarried sister working as a missionary teacher in New Zealand. But she wanted nothing to do with him, nor he with her. They didn't even share the same name. Harrington was a name he'd taken for himself after a master he'd admired at school, one of Oswald Mosley's followers. So that too was just another piece of fantasy. It struck me as a supreme irony that here was I who would give anything to know my real identity, forced to live with someone who had been only too anxious to throw his away at the first opportunity.

All this he used to tell me sitting on the verandah, stretched out on one of those long planter's chairs drinking whisky after whisky, surrounded by a haze of cigarette smoke. Does he still use menthol with his cigarettes, I wonder? I had a particular loathing for that smell. It seemed to suffuse everything about him. At least the smoke helped to keep the mosquitoes away. But the moths and the flying beetles were immune to it, knocking themselves senselessly against the glass of the hurricane lamp until they died. He used to put the bodies carefully into a jar on the table that was full of preserving fluid. The next day he arranged them in cases with the rest of his specimens.

As for me, I was given a mat to sit on, and I would lean my back against one of the verandah posts. I had to be near enough for him to stretch out a foot in its black mosquito boot to touch me from time to time, like a favoured dog. This was when he was pleased with me, for reading aloud to him for instance. He liked the Russian novels best, especially Dostoyevsky's *The Idiot*. Then, strangely, a month or so later it was Proust, which had pages in it that made me want to weep. *Remembrance of Things Past* was a cruel book for someone who had no recollection of either youth or childhood, and I think that amused him. Sometimes I had to go on with the reading for hours on end, until I could hardly keep my eyes open. 'Too slow,' he'd say. Or, 'Not enough expression.'

Soon enough, though, he'd grow bored and turn to some other entertainment. The gramophone, for instance. He had an old Victrola he'd brought out from England. It was my task to keep it wound up and change the records, dusty stacks of Wagner and Brahms, Verdi and Puccini operas that he kept in old cardboard boxes. The speed seemed to run down in no time at all. I can hear it now, that dreaded sound of the music beginning to drag and flatten before I could get to the machine. He used to put out his cigarette on my arm when I let that happen. Once I was shaking so much I let the head with the needle drop out of my hand – it scratched right across his favourite side of *The Meistersingers*.

I was thrown against the wall for that, beaten across the head and locked in my room. But he had to get me back again because he was too drunk to operate the thing himself. So on it went – the *Rigoletto* arias of grief and passion that touched every nerve in my body, the tender scenes from *Bohème* that were even harder to bear because they were so terribly at odds with what was happening to me. I would look up at the tropical stars so brilliant yet so cold, and think of all that glorious music soaring out into the velvety dark with only two lost souls to hear it, each locked into a private hell without escape.

I think Harrington was using drugs even then, something he injected to numb thought and heighten sensation. But the whisky was my real enemy. After just half a bottle he would be out of control, and in the living-room cupboard there were cases of the stuff. They were sent out by an Australian firm with his food stocks. I remember one night when he'd finished off almost a whole bottle, he made me put on a record of *Carmen* and dance to it, over and over, tied to the end of a rope like a performing animal until I fell down and couldn't get up again. I was six months pregnant then. Despair made me wild. When I thought he was asleep, I went to the cupboard and took out the last three bottles and poured them down the sink.

It's a strange thing but the courage I'd summoned up seemed to be mine by right, as if it was part of my real self, if you know what I mean. It stayed with me for quite a while too, even when he came to find me and struck at me with a broken end of one of the bottles. Luckily he was barely able to stand himself. There was a bad cut down the side of my face, but nothing more. It healed, but you can still see the scar.

I managed to get the key from the other side of the door and locked myself in. But all the time I was dressing the wound with a strip of sheeting, I was thinking of something else. Some tiny scrap of recollection had surfaced in my mind and I scrabbled away at it, trying to retrieve it. Somewhere a long time ago, I had done exactly the same thing. I closed my eyes. I was emptying a bottle of whisky down a kitchen sink. My father's whisky. And my father? I waited, but no picture clicked into place. All I could remember was the fear I'd felt then too, and the desperation that had driven me.

Another time, just once, it was a physical image that pricked my memory. The year before I came, Harrington had an electrical generator set up by an engineer from a government supply ship. He'd been too lazy to keep it in order and let the thing run down. It was housed in a lean-to at the back of the house. He was furious when he found me looking at it one day. It was curious, but that piece of machinery was something I felt instantly at home with. Not that exact piece, but just mechanical workings of any kind. It was as if I had once been taught how to handle such things. Then there was the smell of it, the engine grease and the oil and the dirty rags.

Timu came in and we did some simple repair work together. Harrington stood back in silence watching, biting his lip. But he didn't let me in there again.

But it was the fan that was the real trigger. Nothing definite, just something that stirred the nerve-endings inside my head, as if it was trying to remind me of something else. The fan itself was one of those antiquated models on a stand, wired into a corner of the living room. Apart from a primitive fridge and the sterilizer in the dispensary, it was the only piece of electrical equipment in the place, brought ashore by the same engineer. Now the generator was working Harrington switched it on one evening when it was more airless than usual, the middle of the hot season when the sweat sprang off you at the slightest movement. I heard the humming noise, watched the blades begin to turn. The spinning movement became a blur. I moved towards it, unable to take my eyes away, until I almost reached out to touch it. Then I must have blacked out.

Harrington was standing over me when I came to. 'It's the heat,' was all he said.

But I knew it was something else, something intensely personal and actually thrilling. Every evening the sight of that whirring fan drew me like a magnet. I watched it, hypnotized almost. What was the fascination, I kept asking myself. But it was no good. The link was too hard to make. I can only describe it as a sort of twinge of association, perhaps a bit like the itch they say you still feel when a limb's been amputated. Then the fan stopped turning. The generator had broken down again and this time nobody bothered to fix it.

I hope these tiny episodes don't sound completely meaningless to you, Laura. But they stand out in my mind alongside the big things that happened, and so I'm passing them on to you with the rest of the story.

Now another day comes to my mind, the day when I wrote my message. For weeks I had begged Harrington to let me go out walking, just for a short time each day. My room was so stifling. Besides, I needed the exercise as well as the fresh air now it was only a couple of months before the baby was due. The actual birth was something I tried to keep at the back of my mind. All Harrington had said was that he wanted nothing more to do with it. Timu would deliver me, Timu and Maria. I had already made sure of this with Timu, and I had complete trust in them. They said it would be best to have the baby in the makeshift little operating room at the back of the dispensary. It was just a thatched hut like all the others, but at least it was clean and had medical equipment of a kind.

In the meantime I longed to escape from the house, if only for an hour towards evening, when it was fractionally cooler. Finally he agreed that I could go for a short walk at sunset each day along the north end of the lagoon beach, but only in the company of Timu's wife and some of the other women, and never anywhere near the village. Even so, that hour of late afternoon was the time I longed for. Then at least I had company, other women around me and space to breathe, strolling along the edge of the sea as the sun went down over the horizon and the sky turned from blue to that wonderful luminous green, so still and so empty.

Then came a morning when Harrington was out early in his boat, visiting a settlement on the other side of the island with some of the elders. Maria and her friends were going to the beach looking for shellfish while the tide was out. Daringly, I went with them. It was only an hour or so after daybreak and not too hot yet. Maria took me by the hand as she always did. It was a protective gesture as well as an affectionate one. That simple human touch meant more to me than any words could have said, though I knew some of the women believed I wasn't quite right in the head and needed to be looked after like a child.

We went by way of the point, a troupe of six or seven chattering together, the women with their baskets, me carrying an old sunshade I had found in the cupboard. It was a mouldering white silk affair that must have been left behind by some administrator's wife years ago, but at least it kept the sun off my face. It was beautiful along that path. The freedom of it went to my head. I remember the rustle of the trade wind through the pandanus leaves, the scent of some small white flower growing in the bush, a wonderful butterfly that fluttered ahead of us, copper and violet-coloured like a chip of stained glass.

It was eerie there too in such a lonely place with the sea breaking so close all around us. Even though they were laughing the women were telling stories to frighten each other, and me. I'd been learning some Gilbertese from Harrington's books, and from Timu too, but I still needed Maria to translate most of the time. 'Teanti', the spirits, were everywhere, especially the spirits of the dead, they were saying. A being called Naka caught the ghosts in a net on the ocean side as they tried to fly past to the afterworld. Not far from where we were walking was the wall one of the village men had been building when he was washed away by the sea. Now he came back every day as darkness fell to try to finish it.

'He turns human beings into stone for it,' Maria told me, rolling her eyes.

At the end of the path we came to a strangely-shaped rock, humpbacked like a human figure. Maria's daughter drew me to one side so that I did not walk past it. The women's faces were serious now. It was a place where they used to wash their clothes, they told me. Until one of them died there, giving birth. Her spirit inhabited the rock and she could put a spell on any pregnant woman who passed too close. What would happen to the woman, I asked? Not to the woman herself, one of them began. But then they bustled me on and refused to say any more.

We came to the beach. Pure coral sand, rosy pink in the sunshine, and quite deserted. Maria told me it was the best place on the island for boats to come in. I thought she meant the local fishing canoes, but apparently they liked to use the village side. This was the landing used by the big boats, a government ship or the mission schooner, the *John Williams*, maybe two or three times a year.

She turned away with the other women for a few minutes, looking among the rock pools for shellfish. I walked on until I was standing alone, looking out at the sea. All the time I pictured in my mind a boat at anchor and visitors coming ashore. Something strange happened to me, an impulse so naive it was ridiculous. And yet real despair was what made me do it.

Just above the tideline where the sand was still firm, I began tracing some letters with the point of my parasol. They were large letters which slowly spelt out two words. Help Me. When I had finished, I gathered up some of the small white shells that lay around everywhere. Then I began marking the outlines of the letters with the shells so that they stood out even more clearly.

I was so absorbed in my task that I didn't even hear Maria call out to me. I saw nothing except my message, until a shadow fell across it.

Harrington was standing behind me. He must have come back early, walking across the beach from the other side while I had my back to him. I didn't even turn to look at him, just watched as his polished boot slowly rubbed out the final E.

'You really are crazy,' he said. I turned to face him, and his expression of cold malice made me shiver. 'Who do you think will see this? And even if someone did, what would they think it meant?'

He reached out suddenly and pushed me so that I fell on the sand. Maria and the other women came and helped me up, leading me back to the house.

Harrington didn't follow at once. When I stopped to look back he was pacing slowly along the length of the message. His head was bent, and he was removing with his boot every line of lettering until all my work was gone.

I don't know why, but this particular episode has been running through my mind over and over lately. I've even been dreaming about it. That's why I'm able to remember it so clearly. I suppose it was a kind of turning point, a symbol of how hopeless my situation was, for the time being anyway.

When I was let out of my room again I went into Harrington's study to fetch something for him and I saw he had been adding to his collection of specimens. There was a new victim in the glass butterfly case, the purple and copper beauty that had flown up in front of me along the path to the point – or if not the same one, one of its species. I don't know why but that was when the tears came, just at the sight of it pinned down, its colours already fading, the edges of the wings frayed from handling against the black velvet lining. My own tiny bit of freedom had gone on the same day, you see.

I knew I would never be allowed to walk on the beach again. After a few weeks it didn't seem to matter so much. My every thought became concentrated on the baby. I could feel you kicking strongly, and you felt huge. I knew nothing about the process of having a baby. I began to be terrified. I was also afraid of Harrington's reactions to the birth. So far he had refused to even discuss it. But Timu had told me what to do. For the rest, I hoped my instincts would come to my rescue. They had before.

It was early one evening when the pains began. I was lying down in my room with just a sulu wrapped around me. I measured the time between them by counting. I had neither watch nor clock. When they came closer together, I got up and went into the study. Harrington was there writing, no more than a dark shape behind the white folds of the mosquito net he always had hanging over the desk while he worked. When I told him what was happening, he just got up and went out to call Timu. Luckily he was still in the dispensary. He helped me walk the few yards across while Harrington went back into the house.

'Don't make too much noise about it,' he called after me. 'I want to get some sleep tonight.'

In fact, I didn't call out at all for the first few hours. I was determined to be brave, and I knew I could be. But can you imagine the strangeness of it all? You haven't had a baby yet, Laura, but whenever and wherever it happens, it will be nothing like your own arrival into the world. It was such a forbidding place, that little dispensary. I was lying on a tin table which Timu used to fold up when he took it round the islands for emergency operations. He'd covered it with towels to make it more comfortable, and he'd hung an old sheet across the rafters so that insects wouldn't drop down on me from the thatch. There were two pressure lamps hissing away. Timu had laid out his precious set of surgical instruments in their leather folder. I could see no other equipment except a couple of enamel bowls, cotton dressings, and the rows of labelled bottles along the shelves. A kettle was steaming on a primus stove in the corner – it was like a touch of home, and it reassured me.

Rolling up his sleeves, Timu had put on his rubber apron and said I must not be shy with him. He had done this kind of thing many times and I must trust him. He told me my waters had broken, which meant nothing to me. But when he examined me he was almost too gentle. He was so frightened of hurting me, so sorry for me, I knew. I could see the beads of sweat across his forehead, and his dark eyes wrinkled up with concentration.

When the grinding pain of it all became too terrible he gave me something to help. All he had was chloroform. He put a mask over my face and dropped the anaesthetic on it very slowly, a bit at a time. Every now and then I felt his finger raise one of my eyelids to see the effect. At first I was just drowsy, the smell of it sickly-sweet and suffocating. I was coming in and out of a half-sleep, full of awful dreams.

Then in the middle of the night, just when I felt my whole body was going out of control, everything changed. I opened my eyes and saw Maria had come in. She was whispering to Timu. Others seemed to be crouched in the doorway, faces I remembered, among them a very old woman with long grey hair. I was aware of being helped down from the table and supported outside into another place, a few yards away at the back. It seemed to be an ordinary native hut, close-smelling with the reed blinds let down and a few wicks flickering in coconut shells. Shadowy figures drew me inside.

'The women will look after you,' Timu said. 'This part they do best.'

Next I was crouching down in the midst of them. There was a rope hanging from a beam. I must hang on to that, they told me, push as hard so I could. Someone behind me was rubbing my back, her strong hands easing the bands of pain. A small fire had been lit. The smoke had an aromatic scent and they were fanning it towards me. Every now and then Maria wiped my face gently with a wet cloth.

I didn't mind calling out any more. The women were joining in, chanting together, making a rhythm for the efforts of my body.

Then all at once, you were there. Just when I felt I would be torn apart came the sudden miracle of delivery. It's a good word, a deliverance in fact, the slippery bundle safely out in the world, taken up by friendly hands, slapped and rubbed clean and put into my arms as I leaned back against the soft mats. I felt as I had when I crawled out of the sea that day.

There was such excitement and such pleasure in the ring of faces that surrounded me, and cries of delight too at the first cries you gave. But somehow, in that precious moment, I felt that you and I were alone, studying each other.

'You are my life now,' is what I said to you. I remember so clearly staring into your tiny pointed face, your hazy blue eyes with long black lashes.

Maria was examining your body, every inch of it. She pronounced you perfect, and as she said it I was struck by the relief in her voice. Then I suddenly thought of the humpbacked rock on the beach. If she passed too close to it a pregnant woman could give birth to a deformed baby. That was the spell they wouldn't speak about. And Maria was happy to see I'd escaped it.

As for me, Timu had been to check that all was well and the old midwife had completed her ministrations. I had a good strong body, she told me, patting it like a horse. Not so young, though, to be a mother for the first time. That startled me. I looked at my bony hips and long thin legs as she bathed me. How old exactly was this woman with no name, I wondered? Late thirties, I would guess, but in good condition like someone used to physical training, though made a little soft by six months without exercise.

She was talking about my breasts now, pinching them scornfully. Too much like a boy's, she said. And yet they were full of milk and you were sucking already.

I was so glad you were a girl. It was as if I had a friend for life. I had an identity too, at last – Laura's mother. The name was already in my head. I don't know where it came from, but I liked it. The women liked it too, rolling it round their tongues and making it sound like an island name. Lora.

Maria's daughter Katua brought me a garland of creamy yellow frangipani and hung it round my neck. That sharp fragrance always brings the moment back to me. They had laid an old cotton quilt over me. Someone had rolled the shutters up on one side and I realized it was almost light. The air felt cool and clean after the stuffiness inside. Slowly I could see the first gleam of sunshine catching the huge glossy leaves of the babai plants in the food gardens, the size and shape of elephants' ears. Everything looked larger than life and innocent like the jungle in one of those naive paintings. I could hear the clatter of buckets as people began to go to the well, the birds calling in the bush.

'They will know already in the village about the baby,' Maria said. Hadn't I heard the tanguoua bird?

At the exact moment of birth it had called out twice. This was something it always did, just to tell everyone that a new child had arrived in the world.

She went out with the other women to fetch fresh water for tea. In the silence I heard singing. I'd heard it before, but never like this. Every morning at first light, the toddy-cutters go out to climb the palm trees. They're collecting the juice that comes from the newest growth right at the top. And as they work they sing. But what songs! Have you heard them yet? So old and mysterious, nobody knows the words. But the voice I heard close to the little house seemed to be speaking to me. Then faintly from the other treetops came other voices, the strangest high-pitched warbling, like a cricket's chant or a new kind of bird. There was something solemn and pure about it too, that reminded me of worship.

Timu had just come in with a pitcher of juice for me from the lime tree that grew in his garden, the only one on the island.

'What do the toddy-cutters sing about?' I asked him. I was almost asleep.

'It is a song of thanks,' he told me. 'Thanks for what God has given them this day.'

And now I'm feeling a bit weary myself, Laura. Telling you all this has been like going through the whole thing again. I'll sleep well, I think, the kind of sleep I haven't known for so many years. That's what happiness does for you, dear Laura. And the rest tomorrow, maybe.

10 DECEMBER 1969

CABLE AND WIRELESS CO CANBERRA

MESSAGE TO MISS LAURA HARRINGTON C/O SACRED HEART MISSION ABAIANG GILBERT AND ELLICE ISLAND COLONY SW PACIFIC

AMAZED TO RECEIVE YOUR NEWS OF DISCOVERY STOP RETURNING FIJI TOMORROW PLANTATION BADLY DAMAGED BY HURRICANE STOP WILL MAKE RADIO CONTACT WITH YOU AT MISSION STOP JACK

CHAPTER THREE

This is the part of the story it still breaks my heart to remember, the time I had to let you go, Laura, and try to accept the fact that I might never see you again. Are you so certain you want to hear it?

Going back to the house, the day after you were born, that was a moment I was dreading. How would Harrington react to the presence of a baby that wasn't even his? His mood swings were completely unpredictable. I agonized over what might happen to both of us, but you especially, so tiny, so vulnerable, with only me to protect you. Whatever happened, I knew I would defend you like a tiger, with my life if need be.

As usual, everything was different from the way I imagined it, at the beginning at least. The next afternoon I was still resting in that little shanty house behind the dispensary. I kept putting off the moment when I would have to go back to Harrington, happy to be nursing my baby in peace, with Maria and Katua to look after me. And then towards sunset he appeared, stooping through the narrow doorway, carrying a bottle of what looked like brandy. He was smiling, almost relaxed. It was rare for him to seem relaxed. Obviously, he'd decided he'd been given a new role, and he was playing it with his characteristic attention to detail.

'Timu tells me I have a fine, healthy daughter,' were his opening words. 'I've come to inspect her, and congratulate the mother.'

He sat down cross-legged beside me in the approved island fashion and proceeded to open the bottle. The women around me murmured approval, relieved to see his change of heart. But I was looking into his eyes, and I could see a glint of cold amusement at the game he was playing. That pretence of affectionate husband and proud father didn't deceive me for an instant. But it was odd. Somehow it was more than play-acting. Maybe it was becoming another of the fantasies he lived in, something he would actually bring himself to believe as time went by.

So I smiled back at him. I think I was grateful just for the pretence of normality, no matter how brief it might be. He poured brandy into the two glasses he'd brought with him. As I took a sip, I watched him gazing at the tiny bundle beside me wrapped in tapa cloth.

'More like me than you, I'd say.' He delivered it like a verdict as if for public consumption. I held my breath as he touched your cheek with the rim of his glass. You whimpered faintly and he frowned. 'I hope she's not going to be temperamental like her mother,' he said.

I told him I'd let you settle down a bit before I brought you over to the house. Maria nodded. I should rest where I was for a little longer. Her voice was soft but her face was determined. She knew what I would have to endure when I went back.

Harrington shrugged. If I wanted to stay on in this smoky little hole of a place, that was my business. So I had another night of peace and went back to the house the following morning.

Maria had made my room as welcoming as she could, with new mats and a patchwork coverlet she and Katua had been sewing for me. Luckily you were a quiet baby, because I worried that bouts of crying would rouse his temper. The women asked if they could make a feast for us on the third day after the birth, which was a local custom. I was amazed that Harrington agreed. So they arrived in a procession in their best lava-lavas, carrying baskets of fish boiled in coconut milk, a kind of spinach called taro, and baked bananas with toddy boiled up to make a syrup like molasses. Everything was set out on leaves on the verandah. For the baby they had brought a Moses cradle woven out of softened pandanus reeds and lined with oiled matting to make it waterproof.

Of course Harrington saw the whole occasion as a fine chance to present himself as the father figure of the island community, wise and all-powerful, the absolute authority on local custom and ceremonial. His speech of thanks for the gifts was bizarre. As far as I could gather, he talked almost entirely about his own achievements as a colonial administrator, how fortunate the people were to have their future in his hands.

When it was over, the women took me outside to bathe me in sea-water. That was another of the third-day rituals. He didn't allow me to walk to the shore any more, but they had brought two full cans up from the beach. It was poured all over me, from head to toe, as I sat wrapped in a length of cotton under the banyan tree at the back of the house.

It was a carefree feeling, like being a child again. But I worried how Harrington would react to the noise and laughter. When I went inside I saw immediately that he was in one of his rages. It was as if a wind inside his head was blowing from a completely different direction. You were crying without stopping, a relentless shrill wail I've heard other newborn infants give way to since.

Couldn't I see you were starving, he demanded? How could I expect to satisfy you with breasts like mine, any more than I was able to satisfy him physically in any other way? He was stammering, almost incoherent, like usual when he was in a rage, with his face working and his neck jerking to and fro. Still, the next words came out clear enough. From now on the baby would be fed by a wet-nurse.

I went to pick you up from the basket. But he got there before me, and he held you out like a piece of clothing he wanted to get rid of. A stout young woman came forward, but unwillingly, when he called her name. She had given birth a month ago before and had plenty for two, he said roughly. I could see a red patch on your face where I was certain he had hit you while I was outside. If I tried to take you out of his hands he would do worse, I knew that.

So the young woman carried you away to nurse, and from then on she took you every morning and every evening. I was miserable, physically as well as mentally. I used to bathe my breasts at nighttime in warm water to try to relieve the tenderness caused by the accumulated milk. It gave him a sadistic pleasure to see that. One night as he was watching me dry myself, the candle he was carrying dripped a spot of hot wax onto me. I suppose I shouldn't have let him see the pain I felt, because from then on it was a regular sport of his. He would corner me against the wall and make sure that the wax dropped onto the nipples, that was his subtle refinement. I tried not to scream because I could see the extra pleasure that gave him. It didn't last long, but I can only tell you it was worse than the pain of labour. You probably find this part hard to believe. But it's how he was, Laura, how other perverted men may be too, as long as women keep silent.

Somewhere out there, away from Taparua, the real world went on with its everyday business. Just a few months later, a rare message came from out of the blue for the District Officer, Taparua. The District Commissioner, a Mr McAlister, was to pay the island an official visit. Once a year the DC made a tour of the whole territory and Taparua was last on his schedule. The usual government ship was under repair so he would be travelling on the *John Williams*, the flagship of the London Missionary Society. With him would be the Reverend David Hunter, whose parish covered this part of the Gilberts.

Harrington made no attempt to keep this piece of news from me. On the contrary, I had duties to perform. They would be coming to lunch at the house, and I was to be the hostess.

'Show them what a devoted wife I've found for myself,' was the way he put it. Naturally there was a warning. Not for one moment would I be left alone with them, so there would be no chance for a 'heart-to-heart' about how I came to Taparua. 'Accusing me of kidnap and assault and all those other wild fancies of yours,' he would say. 'Begging to be taken away, and so on. So you needn't think any more about it.'

But of course I did. The scenario became an obsession with me. Over and over in my mind I rehearsed what I would say if I had only the space of two minutes to tell the truth. I don't know who I really am, I'd begin. There must have been an accident at sea. I landed up on an island called Gardner in the Phoenix group. I'd lost my memory. Harrington found me there and now he's keeping me here against my will, like a hostage except there's no price on my head. He's mad, and violent. Please help me.

Even as I went through it, I realized how crazy it sounded. I would need more than a couple of minutes to tell them the kind of details that would convince them that this was real, desperately real. And I knew I had to be calm, not rant as if I was hysterical or neurotic. But I was certain there would be a chance to be alone with one of the men. There had to be. Perhaps the missionary, while McAlister was doing his official rounds with Harrington.

I thought of writing it all down in a letter that I could pass to either the Commissioner or the Reverend, but there was no way of being sure they wouldn't put it straight into Harrington's hands. They couldn't possibly know how dangerous he was, and I did. Only hours before the boat arrived, I found him shaking you, hard, with an awful controlled kind of violence, so that your head lolled helplessly back and forth. Your tiny hands were clutching at the air in terror, and then your screaming turned to choking.

I snatched you from him and stroked your little head.

'Worse will happen if you betray me today,' he said. 'It's right that you should see.'

And I believed him. The man was capable of anything. What if I did manage to tell my story, even then how could they possibly take me away without his permission? They would have to ask him if what I told them was true, and he would scornfully dismiss the whole thing. Then you and I would be left at his mercy. As it was, I often wondered why he kept me alive. Finally I understood that I had become as essential to him as his morphine injections. And he was also afraid of discovery, don't forget. Timu was bound to silence about how I had been found in the first place, but Harrington knew he wouldn't hesitate to give evidence against a murderer.

There was one other fantasy running through my mind. Maybe I could board the boat without anyone noticing I had gone. The idea of a mother and child escaping as stowaways was probably ludicrous, looking back on it. But still I tied my things up in a bundle, just in case I got the chance.

It all seemed totally unreal as the four of us sat around the table for lunch. That morning I had watched from the verandah as the tall schooner glided in to anchor across the bay. At first I didn't notice, but then I realized I had tears in my eyes. It was a sight I'd seen so often in my dreams, it was hard to believe it was actually happening. I caught a glimpse of the landing party being rowed ashore. It seemed like hours, but finally two men came walking up through the trees towards the house. One had grey hair, the other was younger.

Over lunch I saw how very different they were. McAlister was a broad-shouldered Scot in his fifties, who'd spent all his life in the Colonial Service in the Pacific. He had an air of severe concentration about him, and he put on his spectacles to attack the plate of roast chicken and yams that Maria put down in front of him. I tried to imagine how he would react to my story, but I couldn't. The Reverend Hunter was altogether more approachable, a teacher from a theological college in England, not more than thirty or so, with a round face, a bristly moustache and a breezy manner. He was balding early and already had false teeth 'thanks to this wretched native diet', as he told me cheerfully. He'd been setting up his Methodist Mission schools in some of the most remote islands for the last ten years or so, and obviously loved the life. Meanwhile Harrington was impressing the Commissioner with his grasp of native affairs and the deep loyalty the local people showed him.

I felt both men had already summed me up as yet another dutiful colonial wife, facing hardship without complaint in some remote corner of Empire for the sake of her husband's career. I'd done my best with my appearance, and I tried to seem composed. I had on a cotton skirt and blouse instead of the Mother Hubbard smocks. My hair was growing wild, so I'd tied it back with a treasured piece of ribbon that came from the native store on the next island. More than anything I longed for proper shoes. The white nursing plimsolls Timu had once bought in Fiji for Maria had been her kindest present to me, but by this time they were almost worn out.

Secretly it was all I could do to hold myself together. It wasn't just the tension of waiting for my chance – maybe McAlister would go across to the office with Harrington immediately after lunch? – but it was also a shock to be confronted with normal human company again. I'd been cut off from the outside world for nearly a year. Harrington so dominated everything I thought, did and said, that I'd almost forgotten how to speak to anyone else. And obviously he was watching me like a hawk, ready to pounce on any dangerous turn in the conversation.

'So you're an American, Mrs Harrington?' McAlister said. 'How did you come to meet your husband?'

I looked across at him, but he was already replying for me.

'Rather romantic, really. Millie was on one of those world cruises. We met in Fiji and she decided that life in a South Sea paradise was just what she was looking for. So she accepted my proposal there and then.'

McAlister gave an approving nod. 'Good for you, Harrington. Just what you needed, a spot of looking-after. One can't exist as a bachelor, even in paradise.'

'Except that it isn't really paradise, is it?' The missionary was looking at me. He had bright blue eyes, big and bulbous like marbles, and they had a way of seeing through to your real thoughts. For the first time he dropped his professional jolly manner and spoke to me gently. 'How is your health standing up to this strange way of life? The diet, and so on? Can leave you feeling a bit washed out, especially after the baby.'

I told him I was in quite good shape. Physically, I added carefully. I went on holding his gaze, maybe trying to prepare him to believe what I was going to tell him. If I had the chance.

'Lucky you have a doctor for a husband.' I had begun to hate that rasping, no-nonsense Scots accent of McAlister's. 'And he was a first-class midwife too, I'll be bound.'

I looked down and made my voice as steady as I could. 'Timu attended me. He and his wife have been kindness itself. My husband preferred not to be present.'

There was an awkward silence, one of many. Then McAlister broke in to say, well, at least it wasn't long now until our leave came round. All being well, of course. There was this growing possibility of Britain going to war with Germany. If that happened, there would be a national state of emergency, repercussions right across the globe. Government officials would have to stay at their posts, wherever they were.

I thought all three of them must have heard my heart thudding. I felt the blood drain from my face. The prospect of time stretching out forever on Taparua was suddenly more than I could bear. That decided it. More than ever, I had to grasp this one-in-a-thousand chance of escape.

'I expect you've picked up some of the news on your wireless,' McAlister was saying. 'The Nazi hounding of the Jews in Germany, for example . . .'

Harrington started tapping the table with his knife, frowning. 'Actually, many people believe the Jews need controlling, don't they, sir? They've been getting far too powerful for my liking, I must say, in our own country especially.'

I could see the hatred in his face, breaking through the smooth façade just for an instant, and I think the others saw it too. The Reverend Hunter changed the subject. Where was the baby? He was rather good with infants, he said cheerfully. He'd just christened three at their last port of call.

So he turned to me, beaming. 'Perhaps you'd like me to do the same for yours? I know there's no church on Taparua. But perhaps just an informal naming and a blessing, here in the house?'

'I would like that very much,' I said.

I stood up, trembling. This might be my chance, maybe my only chance. Harrington hated any kind of religious observance.

'The baby's just in the next room, Mr Hunter. We needn't disturb Mr McAlister and my husband. I know they have business to do.'

But the Commissioner was on his feet, protesting. It would be a pleasure to be in attendance at such an important event. He even said he would be happy to act as godfather. And Harrington himself led the way through the door. He gave me a cold smile.

'Perhaps my study would be the more appropriate place?'

So it was taken out of my hands. For a few minutes I was in despair. But surprisingly enough, the little ceremony wiped away everything else from my mind. You were still asleep. As I held you close to me, your calm breathing calmed me too. I concentrated on the innocence of that small face of yours, perfect as a flower.

Maria and Katua had slipped in behind us, Timu too. He cleared the papers off a side table and poured water into a pottery bowl from Fiji that Mr Hunter had noticed on the shelf. Harrington simply nodded agreement to all this. But his face was a mask, betraying nothing, as we gathered round. Mr Hunter spoke the words of the christening service softly and simply, such old and potent words, in this forgotten corner of the world. Even the Commissioner seemed moved, leading the Amens. He took a step forward when he made his promises.

Now you had a name in the world. Now you were Laura. I saw you flinch a little as the water touched your head with its sprig of dark hair. There was the faintest wail, but your eyes were still closed. So were Mr Hunter's, his round pink face all at once transformed in prayer. I was praying too, praying for God's intervention in my life and yours, to somehow release us unharmed or at least give us some ray of hope for the future.

Then Mr Hunter opened the Bible he had with him in the pocket of his jacket, a worn little volume whose leather cover was stained with sea-water. He would finish with a short reading, he said. It was a passage from the Psalms that meant a great deal to him, to us also perhaps in a place so far from home.

I will never forget that reading. I can hear the verses as clearly now as when he spoke them that long-ago afternoon on Taparua with the sun's rays catching the glass of the butterfly cases, the savage carvings on the walls, the dank-smelling books lined up on every side like bars.

'Whither shall I go from Thy spirit? Whither shall I flee from Thy presence? If I ascend into heaven, Thou art there. If I make my bed in hell, behold thou art there . . .'

Through the open shutters I could see in the distance the familiar rise and fall of the surf against the horizon. Then came the words that pierced me to the quick, as if they were meant for me alone.

'If I take the wings of the morning and dwell in the uttermost parts of the sea, even there shall Thy hand lead me and thy right hand shall hold me . . . Amen.'

Hunter's voice died away, and he made the sign of the final blessing. His eyes rested on mine in the silence as McAlister put his hand on Harrington's shoulder as a sort of congratulation, and they started back into the next room. Hunter still held the Bible. He put his other hand on my arm, the arm which was holding you.

'Are you all right, Mrs Harrington?' he asked me.

I couldn't help but clutch you tighter, and maybe he noticed. I knew I had to force everything into that moment, but luckily the ship was not sailing till the following day.

I kept my voice so low he had to bend close to hear me. 'Tomorrow. While my husband is taking the Commissioner to the village, I have to speak to you.' I didn't dare take my eyes off the door. 'Please, for God's sake, help me.'

It was a struggle not to break down, but I couldn't afford to. Hunter was looking alarmed, but also concerned. Of course he'd call in the morning to see me, 'drop in for a chat', as he put it. He knew what it was like to feel so isolated. I think he thought he was going to hear some kind of confession. Especially when I begged him not to tell my husband he was coming.

That was the moment when Harrington turned back to see if we were following. He must have guessed what I was up to, though Hunter said nothing.

He was very clever. When they had gone, there was no punishment. In fact, he said nothing at all about what he suspected me of having done. All I know is that I never saw the Reverend Hunter again. Oh, yes, he came to the house the next day as he'd promised, while the other two were away on the far side of the island. But Maria couldn't wake me.

'I explained the problem,' Harrington told me later. 'I let him know you'd had rather a bad nervous breakdown during your pregnancy. You still suffer occasional lapses, and this was just one of those occasions. You had to be given calming medication. The excitement of visitors was obviously a bit too much for you. After a couple of days' rest, I told him, you'd be back to normal again.'

In fact, he gave me a very powerful bromide. Timu said it was used to treat lunatics! Every Gilbertese island has cases of dementia, especially at the full moon. The people believe bad spirits take possession of the unwary. Relatives bring them to the doctor to be 'put to sleep' until the spell passes. That was the injection Harrington gave me early in the morning. He repeated it many other times when he wanted to keep me quiet and out of sight.

I screamed and fought against it that first time, but it was useless. He was good at injections. The needle went in fast and deep, and within minutes I felt the darkness come down. I almost welcomed it. I knew my chance had gone, you see, and I felt such a terrible sense of hopelessness – you can imagine it. Oblivion was a relief.

I must have been unconscious for several hours. When I came to it was sunset and the *John Williams* had sailed. Then Maria came in, carrying you. Inside your shawl she had tucked a note from Mr Hunter. He must have suspected that Harrington was ill-treating me, to have given the note to her. All it said was that he was sorry to hear I was unwell, sorry not to have been able to see me again. But he was certain that home leave and a change of climate would make all the difference to the way I felt. Meanwhile I had my beautiful daughter Laura to care for. Next year, when the mission ship was on a return visit to these parts, there would no doubt be a chance for us to meet again.

There was no such chance, of course. The following year the war in

Europe broke out. Timu told me Mr Hunter had been transferred to another part of the Gilberts. Later on, when the Japanese invaded, I heard he was murdered at Tarawa. He was rounded up and beheaded with twenty or more other European prisoners. He had shown great bravery, apparently. He had refused to leave his mission post, and kept up the spirits of the others right till the end.

But I'm moving on too fast. First came the official communiqué cancelling all leave, as McAlister had predicted. The Western Pacific High Commission in Fiji had ordered that all government officers were to remain at their stations until further notice. If the war spread to the Pacific, emergency measures would be announced regarding defence, evacuation of civilians, and so on.

The word evacuation planted a fresh seed of hope in my mind. But it would only work if the Japanese declared war. So far they were keeping quiet. Harrington listened to the wireless now every evening out on the verandah, smoking his interminable, horrible cigarettes. He was more concerned than anything about how his supplies of drink and drugs would get through from Australia. We only got the vaguest rumours through the crackles and fades as the batteries ran down. There was a build-up of Japanese naval forces in the area. But it was the war in Europe that occupied the bulletins. As I sat listening inside, I prayed that the Japanese would come. A year later, I couldn't admit that to anyone.

All my life was focused on you. You were walking well and talking in a weird mixture of local and English words. You were pale because I kept you out of that burning sun but you looked pretty healthy.

Luckily it didn't worry me that our stocks of powdered milk were also getting low. Like the islanders you hated cows' milk in any form, and there was always coconut milk, which would never run out. Also other Gilbertese food – babai, bananas, fish and sometimes homemade bread.

Mr Hunter had left behind with us one of his pupils, Joseph, who'd become quite a good cook-boy. He was a gangling, eager kid, maybe fourteen or fifteen years old. He spoke English well but he was a bit careless in the kitchen about keeping the stores tidy. It was this that gave me the idea, when the worst time came.

There was a new development, you see. Harrington was getting dangerous, and now you were to be the victim. You'd become his latest obsession, a sort of prize in his collection. As far as he was concerned, you belonged to him by right. You were three then, going on four, a beautiful child, so bright and intelligent, longing for friends your own age to play with, but Harrington had forbidden me to let you go outside the garden. Maria and Katua wanted to take you to visit the village, but it was absolutely out of bounds, and so was the beach. Sometimes they would bring little children to the house while they were working, but Harrington soon put a stop to that too.

Obviously he wanted you to develop exactly along the lines he planned. He tried to make you read at a ridiculously early age, he explained his collections to you, and then he'd strike you in a fury if you broke something by accident. There was not a grain of affection in him. He studied you almost like an anthropologist, measuring your rate of growth, the proportions of your body, the shape of your head, and especially your quickness of response to his instructions.

I know all this because I did my best to never let you out of my sight. But it wasn't always possible. He was cunning, as I knew only too well. Sometimes he even deceived me into thinking that he was genuinely concerned for your welfare, he was so careful in his attentions. And he had his own way of keeping me to my own regime. The days had always been filled with small cruelties and humiliations, and they never stopped during all this time.

I think he had blotted out in his mind any thought of your real father, whoever he was, wherever he was. I hadn't, of course. Not a day passed without me wondering which features you had inherited from him. Was it your dark hair? Or your pale skin? Or perhaps your determination when you carried out small tasks, like arranging shells and pebbles into different patterns every day. And the way you never cried when you fell, but picked yourself up and kept climbing the steps or the fallen tree or whatever it was. Timu gave you pieces of charcoal to draw with, so that you wouldn't use Harrington's coloured pencils. There were no toys or dolls, but Katua brought you a tiny pet turtle which you loved passionately. I remember Harrington throwing it out in a fit of temper. It was a terrible moment, but even then you refused to let him see what you were feeling. Only later, when we were alone together, did you give way and cry.

Why couldn't you have told me what your real fear of him was? Maybe you just couldn't put it into words. I'm not surprised – it was grotesque. I was only confronted with it by accident, and it was the one thing that truly broke my heart.

By now you had a room of your own. Harrington had set it up with the kind of geographical pictures and charts he thought were instructional. Nothing else was allowed. Then one night you woke up screaming. I ran in to you and found you in a sweat of panic, trembling all over like a puppy. It was a dream, you said, a bad dream. Someone was trying to hurt you.

I knew who that someone was, even before he appeared in the doorway. The lamp in his hand threw a crooked shadow on the wall, and lit up his face from below with that wolf-like expression I recognized. It was exactly the way he had appeared to me in my room that first night.

When you saw him you cowered down under the sheet, pretending to close your eyes. He took something out of his pocket, the leather razor strap he kept in the bathroom.

'This will see off the nightmares,' he said.

I put myself between you and that strap as well as I could. Then suddenly he stopped and reached into the other pocket. It was a piece of chocolate, a treat from some private stock or other.

'This tastes better than the strap,' he said to you. 'Doesn't it?' He put it on your pillow and went away.

Immediately I pushed the bed against the door. That night I slept with you, and every night after that. In the morning I bathed you myself, something Maria liked to do, usually just a splash with a sponge and a bucket. But I wanted to examine you carefully. I had to see it for myself, that what I dreaded was true – the traces that showed what he had tried to do to you, small half-hidden bruises you insisted to Maria were from climbing the banyan tree. You even tried to hide them from me until you finally broke down. 'No more,' you cried as you clung to me. 'Tell him not to do that game again. I get frightened.'

'How many times did it happen?' I asked you.

'One, maybe two,' you said.

'Did he use the strap then?' I asked.

'No,' you said. 'Only if I told. And now he will use it on you too.'

Harrington was always 'he' or 'him'. He had never been able to get you to call him a name, let alone a name for 'father'.

I'm sorry to bring such horrors into the light again, Laura. It would be nice to think I'm burying them for ever, here in this black tape box of yours. Anyway, you've probably already guessed them for yourself. Maybe you even remember them, heaven forbid.

That was the day I went to the store cupboard in the kitchen. No one else was around. I had a memory at the back of my mind of the little blue bag labelled 'Arsenic' which was kept in a rack behind the door with the disinfectants. They used it to keep down the rats, which were everywhere.

That morning, it was as if God himself was showing me what to do. Carelessly Joseph had replaced it not on its rack, but on a shelf directly above the food provisions. The bag had tipped over and I could see a bit of powder scattered on the container of flour just below. If the lid had been left off, the flour would have been contaminated without anyone knowing.

Any other day I might have called Joseph to scold him. But today was different. Harrington had ordered fish pie for the evening meal and I was making the sauce to mix in with the other ingredients. As I measured the arsenic into the flour I felt no remorse. The only trouble was, how much? It had to be enough to kill, but not to make the whole thing inedible. I remember feeling quite calm, as if I was following a recipe. Fate had shown me the way, and I was grateful.

I was careful to put away the blue packet in its proper place afterwards. I would make sure to give Joseph a strict telling-off another time.

There was no problem about avoiding the dish myself. Often enough I excused myself from sitting down to dinner with him. It was more than I could bear to face him across the table every single evening. I would have something earlier on in my room. That evening I could eat nothing anyway as I waited for the hours to pass with you safely asleep in the corner.

Harrington had finished his dinner. It was around midnight and he was sitting on the verandah as usual, listening to the wireless. I could just make out the Australian news bulletin, something about a Japanese air attack on a place called Pearl Harbor. All of a sudden the broadcast was blotted out by a sort of choking sound and then violent retching like a dog.

It went on for what seemed to be hours, though it must have been only minutes, while I lay on my bed, rigid. I was willing myself not to move, even when I heard his footsteps dragging towards my room. Not even when he pushed open the door and stared at me, bent over on the floor. His face was green and his mouth was hanging open. He seemed to be locked in a kind of spasm, with his arms wrapped tight across his stomach. A rasping noise came from the back of his throat, but it was a moment before I made out the words.

'Fish poisoning. The key. The dispensary key.'

I knew where the key was. Normally it hung on a hook on the verandah. Now it was under my mattress.

I shook my head as if I was still half-asleep. I'd worked out that he'd go looking for an emetic as soon as the pangs came on. Certain poisonous fish were well-known. Just a couple of mouthfuls and you could die in agony. The only chance was to make yourself sick, immediately.

I didn't know if it was the same with arsenic.

The wireless was playing dance music now and a girl sang 'Over The Rainbow' in some studio, far away.

Half disbelieving, I watched him make a huge effort to straighten up. Just for a second he seemed to recover himself, long enough to turn and stumble towards the kitchen. As I followed him I realized I had reckoned without that demonic willpower of his. There was a tin of mustard powder on the table. Mustard was his favourite, he had it with every meal. From the doorway I saw him empty the whole tin into a glass of water and swallow it back in one gulp. He never did anything by halves, did he?

He dropped the glass and it broke at his feet. His eyes were closed tight and sweat was streaming off his face. He stood there, shaking violently. Then he pushed past me. The next minute he was out on the verandah, half-falling down the steps into the garden. In the distance I heard him begin to vomit. On and on it went until finally there was silence. He was groaning as he came in again and slowly made his way back to his room. But I knew it was the sound of survival. Against all the odds, he would live.

I was sick myself then, sick with frustration at failing so narrowly. If I had only added another measure . . . If I had only remembered the kitchen . . . Now, if I tried again, he would be too clever not to suspect me. I didn't dare take the risk.

He was in bed for twenty-four hours. The day after that he was up again, shaky but basically unaffected. Joseph was thrashed and then dismissed for his negligence in catching and cooking fish that was unfit for human consumption. There was no proof that it was his fault, but he protested his innocence in vain. When I tried to intervene, the boy himself stopped me. Later he told me why.

'Doctor is very bad person,' he said. He tapped his head. 'Crazy up here, I think.'

In fact I'm sure he was only too glad to leave. He had already suffered more than he could take in the way of 'disciplinary measures'. Besides, he wanted to get back to his own island. Now that America had joined the war, there would be fighting in the Pacific. The bombing of Pearl Harbor was only the beginning.

As for myself, I found it impossible to imagine anything more dreadful than what I'd already endured. But I looked at you and I shuddered. Daily the rumours grew more horrific, drifting down from other islands to the north where the Japanese were already in occupation. It seemed they showed no mercy, either to captured Europeans or to the local population. Women were raped, prisoners tortured or killed with a bayonet, and children left to starve.

I still believed then that the British would defend the Gilberts. After all, the islands were part of the Empire. The inhabitants had been British subjects since Queen Victoria's reign, Timu told me.

When I said this to Harrington he laughed. 'The British defend these little specks of sand? You must be joking.'

'And the Americans?'

He hardly bothered to answer. 'Those precious fellow countrymen of yours? Hardly famous fighters. Bound to make a mess of whatever they try.'

The next day a message was brought by fishing boat from one of the larger islands, where they had a primitive wireless station. All European women and children must prepare to be evacuated. A government supply ship from Fiji, the *Viti Levu*, was being sent to pick up every family in the group. Colonial officers would be given the opportunity to leave later.

I can see the yellow slip of paper now with the smudged words printed in pencil. I was out on the verandah steps when Harrington came across from the office with it in his hand. It was tea-time, that cosy-sounding word so loved by the British. On Taparua it was just another charade. When Harrington had finished his work for the day he expected the tea tray to be ready on the wicker table – the tarnished teapot, the cracked china, the weevily biscuits – with the household dutifully gathered round. I guess it probably looked like one of those sepia snapshots from a colonial family album, complete with the native servant sitting respectfully in the shadows. In a photograph you wouldn't see the hateful atmosphere that Harrington brought with him or the way the little girl in the sun-bonnet shrank back against her mother as her 'father' stood looking at them from the verandah rails.

With the mocking smile I knew so well, he passed me the slip of paper. My hands shook as I studied it. The *Viti Levu* would be off Taparua in twenty-four hours. Mrs Harrington and one child would be expected aboard. There would be about forty other passengers, including a number of missionary workers. Mrs McAlister, wife of the District Commissioner, would be in charge of their welfare. The destination was first Fiji, then New Zealand, where the authorities in Auckland were making arrangements to receive and accommodate the evacuees.

I felt suddenly dizzy. It was like a door opening inside my head. Within days, we would be out of Harrington's grasp for ever. I was so overwhelmed at the very thought of it I hardly heard what he was saying. Then, more loudly, he repeated himself.

'Aren't you listening? I've sent a message back with Timu. The ship will not be calling here.'

I couldn't speak. I just stared at him, waiting for his next words.

'You can't honestly imagine I'd let you go? Free to tell whoever would listen your crazy fantasies. Then I suppose you'd get treatment for this so-called amnesia of yours.'

Speechlessly I shook my head. Then I took a deep breath. I had to try to get through to him, try to convince him that if necessary I wouldn't do anything that he didn't want me to do. All I wanted was to get away with my child and live a normal life.

The word 'normal' was a mistake. When he heard it I saw a flicker run over his face. How vindictive his expression could be!

'And in this new, normal life of yours, what exactly would you exist on? Or do you have your own resources tucked away somewhere?'

I knew I had nothing in the world except what I stood up in. But I went on talking desperately. The American Consul in Auckland would help me, I told him. There were refugees like myself all over the world now there was a war. Help would be given to anyone made homeless like myself, especially a mother with a small child. I would not involve him in any way.

He laughed at that. 'You and your promises! Do you think I would trust you not to open your mouth even for one instant, after what happened with the Reverend Hunter? No, here you are and here you'll stay for as long as is necessary.'

There was a chilling sound about these last words. But now I was begging for something else. It was my last resort. I begged that at least you could be allowed to go. You would be looked after by Mrs McAlister and the other women on board. In Auckland, his sister could take you. Who could refuse a little girl like Laura? I knew she was still stationed there. A letter had come with the *John Williams* mailbag, though he'd been careful to keep it away from my eyes. In a mocking voice he'd read a few lines aloud to me – how she was willing to bury their differences with this threat of invasion – and then he'd destroyed it.

My voice began to break as I pleaded with him. Finally he snatched the slip of paper from me.

'You're hysterical, as usual. I've told you, my reply has already gone back. I've told them you're not well enough to travel and you're staying here with me. The *Viti Levu* will be turning back for Fiji before it gets anywhere near Taparua. So you can forget about it.'

It was his smile that goaded me. I sprang at him, trying to claw the paper back, running my nails down his arms. In my hatred of him, I'd lost all control.

I felt him take me by the shoulder and force me backwards to the edge of the steps. Then he caught sight of Timu standing silently, watching, just a few yards away. Timu also had a piece of paper in his hand. He spoke very quietly.

'Your message cannot get through, Doctor. The transmitter is broken down, so ship's course cannot be changed.' Then he turned to me and his eyes were fixed on mine. '*Viti Levu* be here tomorrow morning first thing, Missus Harrington.'

CHAPTER FOUR

It was Timu who took you to the ship the next day. Who else would have been able to persuade you to go without me, walking away down the path with your hand in his?

He'd wanted to carry you. But you had insisted on walking, or rather trotting, because you were in a hurry, so excited at the prospect of going on a boat for the first time. But why wasn't I coming too, you kept asking?

For me, the lying was almost the worst part. Or not so much lying as diverting you from the truth. It was a boat for children, I told you, taking you on a holiday to a place called New Zealand. You'd be staying with an aunt who was a teacher. So you'd be able to go to school with other children. You'd have friends to play with – much better than staying at home on your own on Taparua.

As I talked I was buttoning up the blue cotton frock I'd made for you. Katua had put too much starch in it so that it almost stood up on its own, which made us laugh, just for a minute.

'And you come soon?' That was the next question.

'Very soon, I hope,' I said. 'If there's another boat.' Then I tried to get a little nearer to the truth. 'There's a war now,' I said, 'people fighting. It's best for children to go somewhere else. Harrington wants me to stay here with him. You know how bad he can make things if he gets cross.'

A shadow crossed your face and you gave that grim little smile it was so painful to see.

'I know,' you said.

Then Harrington came in and pinned the envelope on to your dress. In it was the name and address of your aunt and a note asking her to look after you. He wouldn't let me see the note, or the one he sent on board with Timu to give to Mrs McAlister. So I don't know what he wrote about me, why it was that I was unable to go with my daughter. I expect it was the same story he told the Reverend Hunter, about his wife being a sick woman confined to her bed, needing his medical care, and so on. I didn't really mind any longer. All that mattered was that you would be away from him and away from the Japanese, and safely looked after from now on.

As he pinned on the note, he saw you put up your hand to cover the locket that was tied round your neck with my last piece of ribbon. It wasn't really a locket but a little double shell. The lock of my hair inside was for good luck, and I'd fastened it up safely with sealing wax.

'What's this?' he asked. He'd taken hold of it roughly between his finger and thumb, and I thought he was going to wrench it off. Rage suddenly flared up in me.

'Don't you dare!'

He drew back, startled for once.

'I suppose you know the *Viti Levu*'s out there,' was all he said. 'I want this child on board before anyone comes ashore looking for you.'

That was part of the bargain. I'd bought your freedom with a promise, you see, a promise that I'd meet no one from the ship when it called. More than that, I'd pledged never to try to leave Taparua nor to tell my story to anyone. Above all, I was to make no attempt to follow you, or to attempt to reclaim you in the future. If I did, he said, 'the girl would suffer'.

It was the threat of a madman, of course. I didn't ask how he would carry it out, or what his plans were for me in the meantime. I knew too well the consequences of crossing a man like Harrington. It was enough, for the moment, to have won my bargain after all the hours of pleading with him that evening.

I won another concession too. He'd not give me the injection that would have kept me asleep that morning so that I could say goodbye to you.

Now you were ready to go, I almost wished I'd not been granted this last favour. It was almost unbearable to stand in the doorway and look at you for the last time. I wanted to print that picture of you on my mind. Like a photograph. That small, determined figure in a stiff blue dress, barefoot as you always were. Where could I have got a child's shoes on Taparua? The soles of your feet were hard to the touch, I remember, like an island child's. Your few precious belongings – a scarlet seed necklace from Katua, a cotton shift for nighttime, towel and comb – were packed into a native straw holdall with some guava fruit. It hung from your shoulder and weighed you down a little on one side. I'd cut your hair in a fringe that hung in a thick dark line above those remarkable eyes of yours. Looking back at me, you were half frowning, half smiling, resolved to behave well, as I was.

I held my breath, hardly daring to move lest tears break through.

'Goodbye,' you said.

I replied in the island way, 'Ko-na-mauri' – blessings upon you. Then I flew down the steps of the verandah to take you in my arms, feel the never-again softness of your cheek against mine. With an effort I stood up to let you go. The next minute you were gone, disappearing into the pale early-morning light, hurrying away under the trees with Timu at your side.

The landing beach where I had written my message all those years ago couldn't be seen from the house. It was screened by bush and trees that grew all round the northern point of the island. But I waited at the window of my room a long half an hour before the *Viti Levu* sailed away. Harrington had gone to his office and I was alone. I wanted to see the little steamer move safely out into the bay. Finally, there it was, a cut-out shape like a cardboard boat against the glitter of the sea. I watched until it vanished over the horizon. Then everything blurred as I broke down at last and let the tears come, leaning my back against the shutters. When I turned around Timu was standing in the doorway. I saw him try to smile.

'Miss Lora is quite all right,' he said. 'She went straight to play with the other children on the deck. Mrs McAlister says to tell you she will see she does not fret. And she says she is very sorry about your sickness.'

There was something else I had to ask him. 'Yesterday, Timu. Was the radio transmitter really broken down?'

He shook his head, laid a finger across his mouth. 'I could not send that message.' He spoke under his breath, glancing over his shoulder. 'How could we have got the child away if no ship came? If only you too could have gone, Missus Millie.' Then he shrugged and turned to go.

'Doctor waiting,' he said dully.

Over and over afterwards, I told myself that I must look upon this separation as if I had given you up for adoption. Lots of mothers had to do it. Of course, their children were usually taken away as infants. But all over the world then, parents were being parted from children of all ages by the war. Kind Maria tried to help me by telling me it was an old custom in the islands to hand over an extra child to be brought up by a relative.

But, dearest Laura, you were not extra. You were all I had in the world. Perhaps that's why, underneath my brave effort to think of you as gone for ever, I never really felt I'd lost you. I always had a strange sense of being with you, through all the rest of your childhood, and the growing-up years too, even with the Laura who was a woman. And I never really lost the certainty that I'd see you again, that fate would somehow draw you back to me, however long it took.

But those first few days after you'd gone were terrible. It was almost the worst time of my life – that part of my life that I was aware of, at least. I comforted myself thinking of you as moving out of the danger zone, in all senses. You'd be going into the real world to learn what a normal existence was like, not just in New Zealand but later in England. I knew Harrington's sister planned to go back there as soon as possible. He'd told me that bit too, reading aloud from the letter with his twisted smile. In a strange way, it actually made it easier for me to think of you being so far away, somewhere on the other side of the world, totally cut off from me. After all, who was your mother? Someone whose existence was as unreal and as unhappy as a ghost's.

In the weeks that followed, thank God, Harrington was preoccupied with the progress of the war. He had put up a map of the Pacific on the wall of his study, and now it was dotted with red stickers marking the possible advance of the Japanese through the different island territories – the Solomons, the New Hebrides, Papua New Guinea. The Gilberts were in the front line, and news was already coming through of bombing attacks on the outlying atolls.

But I never heard anything about any further evacuation ships. Until one day I found a note from the nearest radio station, crumpled up in his waste-paper basket. It was a message from the government in Fiji. The High Commissioner, Western Pacific, had arranged for a flotilla of small private boats to travel in secret to the Gilbert and Ellice Colony to pick up all remaining British officers and get them back to Suva before the Japanese made their first landings.

Now I knew why Harrington had been sorting out and packing his things together. Two canvas bags stood ready in his room. I looked through them quickly while he was out and found them crammed with a few clothes, some prized books and papers and even – so ridiculous – a small case of his favourite specimens.

It was clear that he had no intention of letting me leave with him. I didn't know whether to be thankful or outraged. My first thought was that, with him gone, I'd be free to try to leave Taparua anyway. Timu would help me, maybe, and some of the other people. Then I realized that once the Japanese invaded I'd be far from free, a prisoner in an internment camp at best, at worst tortured and possibly executed. A lone white woman, especially an American, would be a prize captive from their point of view. Besides, I never lost that primitive fear of what Harrington might do to me, or you, if I did get away, even after the war was over.

The only thing I could do was get down to the beach and try to board the boat with him. Obviously I would come to no harm so long as I was with our rescuers. But once we got to Fiji, would he try to keep me with him as he had done on Taparua? Would he force me into the same kind of slavery, isolated on some remote government station, with his stories of a wife who was mentally ill and had to be kept away from other people?

It was worth the risk, I decided finally. An inner voice gave me the courage to try, maybe the voice of the Millie I had once been. I told myself that Suva, where the boat would take us, was a busy port, a civilized capital. Once there, who knows what I could manage, with a little ingenuity? Surely somehow I could give Harrington the slip and find help to get myself on to New Zealand. A madman's rule could have no power once we were back in the real world.

The rescue party, for instance. They'd be European settlers of some kind, maybe a planter with his own launch and a list of names of people to be picked up. My name would be on that list – Harrington and wife, a sick woman who'd been too ill to travel on the *Viti Levu* when her daughter was evacuated. I'd be expected on board on this final round-up, however sick I was.

I told Timu my plan. He checked the dispensary for me and found the bromide bottle was empty. Supplies of morphia and even chloroform had also run out now that the Australian shipments had stopped. So Harrington would not be able to give me the usual sedative to keep me out of the way. It was bad luck that Timu himself had to travel to the far end of the island to attend the funeral ceremonies of the island's chief elder. But he would see that Maria and some of the other women kept close watch on the house, even though Harrington refused to let them in now you were gone.

Only Harrington knew when the boat was due to arrive. I watched his movements carefully and kept a lookout from the house as well as I could. Then came the night when, just as I was going to sleep, he dragged me from my room out on to the verandah. At the far end there was an Indian-type string bed that had sometimes been used by the woman who was nursing you, or Katua would rest in it with you in the daytime.

'You sleep there tonight,' he said. He pushed me down on it, then left me.

I took it as one of his whims. He was always looking for new ways to humiliate me. Sleep was difficult anyway because of the mosquitoes, which whined and circled incessantly. I had snatched up the sheet from my bed, so at least I was able to cover myself from head to foot. An hour or so later I was half dozing when I was aware of movements close by.

Till then I'd forgotten that on the outside wall, just below the bed, there was an old chain where Harrington had once kept a dog. The next moment there was a faint clicking sound. I felt something grazing my leg. I sat up and saw Harrington bending over me. He'd pulled the sheet away and was fastening the chain around my ankle. I recognized the small padlock from the dispensary door. In the lamplight I saw the glint of the key in his hand as he straightened up again. With a casual gesture he tossed it over the rails far into the undergrowth of scrub and vine beyond the fence. He looked down at me.

'Bitches need to be tied up,' he said.

He was breathing hard, and obviously hurrying to get away. I felt a terrible weariness. What was the point of struggling?

'Why don't you simply shoot me?' I asked him. 'Like you shot your dog?'

He shook his head with that cunning look.

'I don't have to bother. The Japanese will take care of that.'

He stared at me, reflectively almost. 'I'm sorry to have to do this. But you do see I have no alternative. And after all I gave you a few years. A chance to bring that wretched child of yours into the world.' He shook his head. 'Just to think, if it hadn't been for me you'd have died on the beach alone. At least on Taparua you'll have company at the end.'

He put his hand in his pocket and I saw him frown as if he hadn't quite made up his mind. Then he fished something out and dropped it on to the bed. It was a very small package, wrapped in blue paper.

'Just in case. Call it a farewell present – something I shan't be needing now.'

Without another word he picked up his bags, took the lantern in his other hand and turned for the steps. My last glimpse of him was of a running figure silhouetted against the circle of light, as he disappeared under the trees.

When he'd gone, the darkness seemed even more intense. The chain felt cold and heavy, lying across my leg like a dead snake. I still had the package in my hand. I tore away the paper and took off the lid of the box. There was something smooth inside, like a tiny pebble – a capsule of some kind, poison obviously. I shivered just at the touch of it. Then carefully I secured the box again and felt with my fingers for a chink in the latticed wall next to me, where it would be safe and hidden. Perhaps such a thing was standard issue for British officers. Or was it Harrington's own private way out? It had his macabre touch about it, that was for sure.

It suddenly struck me as comic that I should have been experimenting with arsenic when all the time Harrington had his own means for doing away with himself. Lying there in the dark, I wanted to laugh. But I knew that would sound like real madness to anyone who might come, and of course people would come at any moment, I told myself. The noise of a boat's engine, lights and movement on the beach, would bring the whole village running.

Almost at once I heard the sound of people, women's voices calling to one another that there were lights around the jetty. Maybe it was the Japanese. I called back to them and saw figures with flare torches coming towards the house, cautiously at first, then hurrying up on to the verandah. Maria and Katua were the first and soon I was surrounded by familiar faces, exclaiming in horror and pity when they saw what he had done. Hands struggled to free me, but the chain was locked around my ankle and the key would probably never be found again.

The men from the village were all away at the funeral, Maria explained. But the old man, the one who had been a policeman, he was still at home. He would have something to cut the chain.

Katua and another young woman went off to find him. But Maria was going after Harrington and the boat, determined to stop them from leaving without me. Most of the others ran after her.

The old midwife stayed with me. I could hear her cursing Harrington as she went into the kitchen to bring me something to drink – the remains of a pot of tea from his last meal. Then she sat by my side, smoothing my hair and rubbing my legs, still talking to herself indignantly. Her touch was so soothing I almost found myself drifting off to sleep. You see, I knew there was nothing that could be done, even if they made it to the beach in time. No one on board the launch would take any notice of a party of hysterical native women. Harrington would see to that. And strangely enough, I'd almost stopped caring. As I visualized the boat turning back to Fiji and the distance between us widening, I felt a curious calm descend on me. Just to be rid of that malignant presence was like a spell being lifted. Inside my head there was the kind of lightness you feel when a fever has gone, almost like euphoria.

I tried to explain this to Maria and the others when they returned. But they were so full of anger and disbelief at what had happened, it wasn't possible.

'I hear everything. The three white men on the boat, he tell them you be dead,' Maria burst out. 'Long time you are sick. Then you die, three, four days ago. You buried here, on the island, out at the point.'

He was even crying, they told me. All the white men had sad faces. Take no notice of these women, he was telling them. They are speaking of the spirit of my wife. You know these Gilbertese people, the things they believe. So the boat went away.

And now the Japanese will kill you when they come, they wailed. That's not true, I told them. I shall survive, we'll all survive. If we obey them they'll spare us, you'll see. We'll help each other. And it won't be long before the British and the Americans get here. Then there'll be no more Japanese.

But they kept on wailing, pulling at their long hair, crouched around my bed. Only the arrival of the old man, Beni, put a stop to it. Hobbling forward on his stick, he began apologizing in his usual courteous way as if the situation was quite normal. It had taken him a long time to get here because he walked so slowly. And then there was the difficulty of finding the hacksaw in the stores. Somehow or other it had got lost, but he did have a blade.

Carefully he unwrapped it from its oily rag. The chain was not thick but it was coated with rust. The hook that held it to the wall had been reinforced with plaster.

How Harrington must have hated that dog to make so sure he could not break loose! Eventually, though, in Beni's knotted old hands, the blade worked through the metal and the chain fell away. The women embraced me with tears in their eyes and put me back in my own bed. Maria and Katua slept on mats in my room that night.

In the morning I remember walking out beyond the garden to see if I could find the key. A stupid thought, really, and not important any longer. But I could find no trace of it. It was only weeks later, when the whole garden had been burned flat, that I came across it behind a stone. As I picked it up I thought I could feel Harrington's touch still on it, like something unclean. I had to force myself to slip it into my pocket. But that was a time when a thing like a padlock and key was a gift from the gods, a treasure beyond price, a guarantee of safety that could make the difference between life and death.

When the Japanese first came, I don't recall feeling real fear, not the kind I had felt with Harrington. The morning of the invasion I was standing on the verandah, looking out to the line of the sea in the distance.

After months of drought it was raining, an unnatural-seeming event with the sky leaden-coloured instead of the inevitable blue and the downpour making a steady drumbeat on the iron roof. Even the coolness was alien, and the smell of parched ground lapping up the wet. I remember thinking that it might just save the banana crop and the breadfruit that was shrivelling on the trees.

When it stopped a mist hung everywhere, like giant cobwebs. Slowly it lifted and out in the bay I saw the grey shape of a warship of some kind, a destroyer perhaps, with two smaller vessels, one on each side. In that setting they looked totally unreal. They were too far away for me to make out the markings and I cursed Harrington for having taken his field-glasses with him.

I needn't have wasted time wondering. The next minute there was a series of long whistling sounds, then the crunch of shells exploding. Not far away I saw a strange sight, the tops of several palm trees sliced off as if a huge sword had gone through them. Smoke singed the air and hung in trails through the branches.

For a moment I stood without moving, until the adrenalin began to work. I ran inside, and I found myself crouched under the table before I'd even thought about it. I couldn't understand what the Japanese thought was worth destroying on a place like Taparua. The answer, of course, was the morale of the people. The bombardment was an announcement that the enemy was taking us over, also a warning of what they could do to us if we didn't submit.

A humming silence followed. I wondered where everyone was. Beni had made his usual early-morning call to put up the flag on its bamboo pole in the compound. I'd told him there was no need now that the island was without a government officer. But raising the bleached and tattered Union Jack and lowering it at sunset was obviously an all-important ritual in his life, and I hadn't the heart to stop it. Perhaps it meant something to the rest of the people too, a sign that, in name anyway, these were still King George's islands.

I went to the back of the house. The office and the dispensary were deserted. There was no sign of life in the nearby huts either. Perhaps there had already been a landing and the whole village had been rounded up somewhere, Timu and his family with them?

Well, now that Harrington had abandoned his post, the house at least was mine, I thought. So here I would stay. I went back to the front verandah and sat down with the cup of tea I had been drinking. It was absurd, an American woman in the role of the solitary memsahib holding the fort, as it were. But what else could I do?

It was eerie, waiting there on my own. Everything was so still. Even the birds seemed frightened into silence. The rain had come on again and seemed to be closing in around the house. I tried to imagine what the Japanese would be like and what they would do to me. The first sight of them was a bit of an anticlimax. Dwarfed by the palm trees, a small formation of soldiers in sodden khaki green came into view, carrying their rifles before them with bayonets fixed. At the front in a more imposing uniform was a short squat figure who was obviously the commanding officer. The wet sand made it difficult for them to keep up a brisk march but they were doing their best in their soaking canvas boots. The officer called out to me in some kind of mongrel English that I was not to move.

'I'm not moving,' I told him.

'Stand up then!'

I thought it best to obey at once. His response was to stride up the steps, pick up the wicker chair and hurl it into the garden. The soldiers stood around in a circle, bayonets poking towards me, while the officer commenced a ferocious cross-examination. What was I doing here? Why was the government officer not here to surrender to him? Where was he hiding?

He was an unprepossessing figure, several inches shorter than me, with a face that reminded me of a toad and a toad's habit of blinking and puffing as he surveyed me. He was so obviously disconcerted to find a white woman there at all, I almost felt sorry for him.

And so I had been left behind! He was sneering at this, enjoying the amusement of the soldiers. Well, I was a memsahib no longer, he told me. Now I was in the hands of the Japanese armed forces, a personal prisoner of the Admiral himself, he went on, tapping his chest. This was so obviously an exaggeration of his rank I almost smiled.

But then he wrenched at my arm to lead me inside and I caught a gleam of pleasure on his face that reminded me of Harrington. One thing these five awful years had taught me was that resistance, even passive resistence, only brought more pain in the end. And I had had enough of pain.

'Also, when I speak, you bow,' shouted the Admiral in his silly high-pitched voice.

I bowed and was given five minutes to collect my belongings together. This was a great kindness, I was told. Be grateful. The house and the office was now Japanese property. It would be the headquarters of high-ranking personnel such as himself. Meanwhile I was to be taken to the village meeting-house where all the people of the island were gathered, awaiting the orders of their new rulers.

I took only the necessities – washing things, a towel, a change of clothing, a mat and a quilt for sleeping. The quilt was a new one Maria had made for your bed on your fourth birthday. It was the only thing that caught me unawares, that picture of you as you slept next to me, one thin arm thrown out towards me. It took a moment to regain control of myself before I went back to the Japanese. At the same time, a great feeling of gladness came over me at the thought of leaving that horrible house with its daily reminders of Harrington.

Perhaps the Admiral was aware of this somehow. At any rate, when I reappeared he hit me hard across the face with the back of his hand. Then he noticed the mosquito net that I'd rolled up to take with me. With a scornful grunt he plucked it out of my bundle and handed it to one of his aides.

'This you do not need. Now you are one of the peasants.' He laughed.

All around us the soldiers were dragging the shelves of books on to the floor, kicking and treading on them enthusiastically. Harrington's precious display cases were smashed into pieces, along with his various Pacific curios. From the office more soldiers were dragging stacks of government files and official papers, most of them dusty with age and rotten with insect droppings.

'What these mean?' the Admiral kept demanding. 'British plans for war? You tell, you tell.'

I held up my hands. How would a woman know such things?

'And safe. Where key? Where? Where?'

Harrington had lost it long ago, I told him wearily. There was nothing of value to keep in it anyway, apart from his collection of pornography which I saw him burning a week before.

Now the Admiral was ordering his own bonfire. Soon, with the help of a drum of kerosene, books and documents were burning outside the verandah, until the drizzle descended again and reduced them to a smouldering heap. Meanwhile, in the compound the Union Jack had been hauled down to be replaced by the Rising Sun. The British flag was about to be flung on the fire with the rest of the debris, but the Admiral held up his hand. It was to be taken to the village, he ordered. I only realized why when we got there.

It seemed a long walk in the rain. One of the soldiers had taken pity on me and found an old handcart for me to push along with my belongings stacked inside. The Admiral had agreed to this, as long as I kept up with the soldiers. The funny thing was that, with my long legs, I always seemed to be walking ahead of the Japanese, who were all short men. Someone had produced a bicycle for the Admiral so he was able to take the lead, striving to keep his dignity as he swivelled between the ruts, his sword sticking out behind him.

No further words were exchanged till we got there. That was the moment of real shock, to see the hundred or so islanders herded together and squatting in rows, so cowed and downcast-looking it was hard to recognize them. You could feel the fear inside the long dark maneapa, with the soldiers lining the walls and fixed bayonets pointing at the mass of men, women and children. I saw Timu and his family in the front, but I was careful to look away from them quickly.

I knew the Admiral's main intention would be to humiliate me. First I was put to stand in a corner while we were lectured on our new future under Japanese rule. The forces of Nippon would soon be in command of the entire Gilbertese group, and then all the other British territories of the Pacific. Our masters had deserted us, just as they had fled from Singapore. The great battleships of the British Empire already lay at the bottom of the ocean – the *Prince of Wales*, the *Repulse* and many more.

The Admiral's voice rose higher as his excitement grew. Now we were all part of something called the Greater East Asia Co-Prosperity Sphere. But the new subjects of Imperial Japan must obey orders without question, must work night and day to bring about final victory. And disloyalty would be met by a sentence of death. All information about the enemy must be passed on without fail. The white government officer Harrington – where was he hiding? His eyes fell on Timu.

'If we find him, it will be so much the worse for you.'

'He left by boat,' Timu said. 'He left his wife behind because she was sick.'

'And so the day of British rule is gone for ever.' He turned and made a signal to the soldier with the Union Jack, who threw it to the ground where it lay spread open at my feet. All around me I heard an intake of breath.

'Walk then, English woman,' the Admiral announced. 'Tread British flag into dust where it belong.'

He stared at me, waiting, his hand on his sword.

Even then it seemed to me an absurd ritual, so theatrical and out of place. So why was it hard to obey? Perhaps it was because I knew all those eyes were on me, waiting to see what I would do.

'Walk. Or you too will be beaten to the ground.'

I stood still, trying to control my shivering. Physical bullying was nothing new for me, I told myself. And I too could play charades. I shook my head.

The Admiral took a step closer.

'You love flag too much?'

'Pardon me, Admiral.' I made a deep bow. 'I think there is a mistake here.'

'Mistake?' He raised a finger, and I felt the prod of a bayonet on my back.

'This is not my flag, Admiral,' I said slowly. 'I am not a British subject. If you have a Stars and Stripes, that would be different.'

'Stars and Stripes.' The Admiral was spluttering now, trying to hide his confusion.

I bowed again. 'I am an American citizen.'

I heard the hiss of surprise among the Japanese. There was silence. All eyes were now fixed on the Admiral. I could see him struggling to save face, tugging at his bristly little moustache, at the same time as he must have seen me as an even more valuable prisoner.

'To say so is not enough. Show papers!'

I spread out my hands. 'The soldiers at the house have destroyed them with everything else.'

His eyes bulged. He jerked round on his heel and threw a question at the adjutant. Where was there an American flag, he was demanding, no doubt. The man looked doubtful. He issued more orders. A frantic running to and fro began among the ranks. It seemed a Stars and Stripes was not to be produced. But something must be done to resolve the situation.

With a sudden gesture he unsheathed his sword, hooked the flag on the end of it and tossed it over his shoulder through the open side of the maneapa. It landed in the mud where a pack of village dogs were fighting over scraps of food. In the rows of faces watching I caught sight of Beni, stiff and impassive, except for the tears that were streaking through the white stubble on his cheeks.

Inside the maneapa, the Japanese flag was being hoisted across the main beam, and a portrait of Emperor Hirohito was pinned up beside it. Led by the Admiral, the soldiers sang their national anthem, standing stiffly to attention.

Like Beni, I was careful to let no expression show. I had won a minor victory, but it was a short-lived one. I had spoilt an important ceremony and I was to pay for it.

CHAPTER FIVE

The isolation was the worst part of what followed. For the next few weeks I was shut up in what had been the island jail. It was not a forbidding place, that little bamboo shack under the ivi tree. I had seen it so often from the outside, but it was very different to be shut inside, with no windows, a bare earth floor and only a rough sleeping bench.

Normally prisoners would have the company of a friendly jailer. They'd be given a few tasks around the place and visited by friends and relatives who brought food in daily. But me, I was in solitary confinement. My jailers were two particularly mean guards, who took it in turn to cuff me and kick me and generally ill-treat me. More than once, my daily dish of mouldy rice was turned over 'accidentally' by a boot as it was placed in front of me. Still, what I really feared was being raped after one of their drinking sessions. I had the padlock and key to lock myself in at night, and that helped me rest easier. But I think the Admiral had made it clear that sex was an entertainment he reserved for himself. When the time came.

For the moment, he had moved on to supervise the occupation of the next atoll. While he was away, his second-in-command decreed that I should be allowed to join the villagers in the labour lines. So at least I got out of jail each day, and normally I managed to work next to Maria. We were digging and planting to raise crops for the troops. Other times the women were rounded up with the men to load up the coral that was mixed with lime to make concrete for the Japanese bunkers.

The rains had gone now and the sun beat down relentlessly every day. Sometimes my hands were raw and my face was covered in a mask of stinging white dust. Water was rationed by the guards to a few mouthfuls so that our throats became almost too parched to swallow.

'Timu is sick,' Maria told me one day. We were not allowed to talk, so she had to whisper. 'Sick in the stomach.'

There was nothing I could do to help. Dysentery was spreading because of the insanitary conditions of the soldiers' camp and because the people were being starved of their normal diet. Already small children were suffering the most. I only thanked God my own child had been spared. Everything went to the Japanese. Because of their stupidity, even fishing was restricted. The canoe sheds had been burned to the ground with most of the boats inside them. 'To stop escape,' as the Admiral had announced.

But where was there to escape to? The soldiers had settled over the island like a swarm of locusts, small wiry figures in their green uniforms and those strange caps with the flapping neck bands. It seemed that little Taparua was in the front line of defence for full-scale war when it came. Rickety watchtowers had been erected and wireless cable was strung from one end of the island to the other. From a little hut just inside my compound a single operator, sweating like a coolie, pedalled away to provide the power for the batteries. A system of loudspeakers, fixed to the tallest palm trees, relayed messages and orders. I hated those disembodied voices that boomed out like mad giants from the highest branches, where the toddy-cutters used to sing their hymns to the spirits of the trees.

We knew that if and when the Americans came, there would be far worse ordeals, bloody reprisals by the Japanese, wholesale slaughter on both sides. The likelihood that I would survive any of this seemed remote. 'Head off! Head off!' the guards screeched at me like the Queen in *Alice in Wonderland*, for the most trivial infractions. Maybe I would fail to bow deeply enough, or to scrub down every last inch of the jailers' quarters to their satisfaction.

Ono and Taito they were called – I'll never forget those two names. One was very fat, the other very thin. I cheered myself up by thinking of them as Laurel and Hardy. Little Laurel was actually given to strange impulses of compassion from time to time, like slipping me the remains of a tin of condensed milk from his rations. That was on a day when I was almost too weak to get up and follow the work line.

The so-called cell I occupied was more like a large birdcage. The walls were of split bamboo and at nighttime I would look out through the chinks and wonder if the rest of the world still existed. There was a strict blackout because of the threat of air attacks. One night I was terrified by the sight of strange lights quite close by. Sometimes they were motionless, sometimes they seemed to move towards me. The next day I discovered the explanation, a fungus growing on some ancient trees that gave off a phosphorescent glow in the dark. Somehow I found that comforting. Not everything followed the orders of the invaders.

Soon there came the turning point that changed everything. Late one evening a message was brought that I was to be taken to the government bungalow. A new commanding officer had arrived and I was summoned to appear before him at once.

Pushed and prodded by rifles in the usual way, I was taken by the guards along the lane to the house I still thought of as Harrington's. I hadn't been back there since my capture. As the official Japanese headquarters, it was tabu to the local people, myself included.

As we got nearer I felt the familiar thrill of dread at the sight of that lighted verandah. In my mind, I could see Harrington in silhouette sprawled in his chair, the whisky bottle on the table at his side, the wisp of smoke from his cigarette hanging over his head.

The sound of the cicadas in the undergrowth rose up on either side of the garden path. That low, shrilling vibration seemed like an echo of my own nerve endings. What kind of encounter was this to be? How next was I to be threatened and humiliated?

At the verandah steps, the guards came to a halt. Standing between them, I could hardly believe my ears. Inside the gramophone was playing and into the night air came floating the music of flute and harp, so beautiful and so ethereal after the hell of the last few weeks that I almost felt faint.

Then for one ghastly moment, there came another thought, like a hallucination. What if Harrington himself was there? What if it was some trick by the Japanese to bring him back to Taparua?

But then I remembered – Mozart. Harrington always hated Mozart. He had bought the flute and harp concerto by mistake and hardly ever played it.

Next to me the guards were conferring in whispers. Suddenly, in the open doorway above us, a tall figure appeared. An order was given, but not with the usual bark of command. Perhaps it was the music behind it that softened the voice and made it sound almost conversational. I was pushed forward up the steps. The guards fell back into the shadows and I was face to face with the new Japanese officer.

I was aware at once of a personality that was totally different from any of the Japanese I'd met so far. It wasn't just that he looked different – a dark blue silk tunic instead of his uniform jacket, and a long thin face with a high forehead and horn-rimmed glasses. Somehow his whole manner seemed to belong to a world outside the war. Even at that first meeting he seemed to be approaching me on human terms, summing me up with a short-sighted, sidelong look as if he were genuinely curious about me.

'I am Colonel Tanizaki,' he said. 'Your name?'

'Millie,' I told him. 'It's what I'm always called.' The words Mrs Harrington always stuck in my throat, now more than ever.

'Mili.' He was frowning, obviously puzzled. 'Your husband was the district officer here. The runaway?'

I nodded. It was the easiest thing to do. I was struck by the ease with which he spoke English, almost without an accent.

'And left you behind?'

'Yes.'

Behind us, the Mozart rasped to a halt. With a start, the Colonel went to the machine and switched it off.

'Strange man. I like his taste in music. I found the gramophone in a cupboard. The soldiers must have missed it when they were cleaning out. Also a few records that were not smashed.' He glanced at the shelf behind him. 'Some books were also left. Poetry, for the most part.'

I was finding it hard to adjust to his kind of conversation, I suppose, because the room seemed to be spinning around me. Also, the summons to the house had meant I'd missed my usual supper-time gruel. Forgetting for a moment that I was a prisoner, I felt for the chair behind me.

Colonel Tanizaki pushed it towards me, then sat down at the desk. There was a pressure lamp on one side and he moved it closer to me. All at once his manner became more peremptory. He had brought me in for interrogation, he told me. There must be information I could give about British policy in the island territories, their plans for a counter-attack, for instance. My contact with America was also of value. The letters I was getting from home. From what I was told, how was the morale of the civilian population?

'I'm told nothing,' I replied. 'I get no letters.'

He looked irritable. 'I don't understand.' He looked at me more closely, his eyes narrowed. Then he leaned back again with an air of puzzlement.

'What on earth are you doing here?' he asked me next. And then, when I was silent, 'Where in the States do you come from?'

'I don't know,' I told him.

'You don't know?' This time he sounded not so much exasperated as incredulous. 'That's odd, is it not?'

Again he peered at me owlishly against the glare of the lamp. He reminded me of a schoolmaster losing patience with a difficult pupil. Because of his forbearance so far, I decided the Colonel deserved the truth.

'I lost my memory,' I began.

My story seemed to go on for some time, partly because of the number of questions he asked me as I told it. At the end he called for tea from the kitchen. A servant poured two cups and we sat in silence for a moment. He was still looking at me, shaking his head.

'It's hard to believe. But why should you lie?' He seemed to have given up the call of an official interrogation and began asking me about my daughter.

'I also have a daughter, the same age,' he said.

He brought out a photograph from his wallet of a family group. His wife was a diplomat's daughter, he told me. His own father had also been in the Japanese foreign service, ambassador to Austria. So he'd been brought up with foreign languages and European customs and gone on to follow the same profession. He'd just been given his first posting in San Francisco when the war came and he found himself back in Tokyo as an army officer. A square peg in a round hole, was how he put it. Was that the correct idiom?

I told him it was, and he permitted himself a smile. 'But it is all in the service of his Imperial Majesty, the Emperor,' he added. He had become stiff and solemn again, as if remembering his proper role.

'I wish to know what the local people are saying about the Japanese. What will be their allegiance if there is an Allied landing? You know them well. You will be able to find out and tell me.' He stood up. It was time for me to be dismissed. I was to be brought to him at the same time tomorrow evening to report back.

I made the appropriate bow and was taken away.

From then on I spent an hour in the Colonel's company every evening. They were strange encounters, seemingly polite, but I was always on edge for a change of tone. Usually, if Japanese NCOs or servants were in and out, I would be asked questions relating to the war, to which I would give my usual noncommittal replies. From the officers' mess nearby I could hear loud voices and laughter. But I always felt protected in Colonel Tanizaki's presence. After the interrogation, he liked to expound on world politics, waving his hand elegantly as he talked. One of his favourite subjects was the difference between the Japanese and British views of Empire. Then he would move the conversation on to a lighter level, to poetry and music and the strange rituals of Japanese theatre.

My own responses were limited because I had no personal point of reference before 1937. This was something that especially intrigued him. He treated my amnesia like a fascinating crossword puzzle, firing off all kinds of suggestions that might bring back my memory and fill in the empty spaces.

For example, he asked me if I remembered knowing any Japanese people in my American days. He had noticed that I seemed to be familiar with various Japanese phrases. Also that I seemed to be, as he put it, 'at ease with our peculiar race'.

'Perhaps you spent time in Hawaii,' he suggested, 'or even on the West Coast.' He raised an eyebrow. 'Many well-to-do families in those parts used to have Japanese servants. So silent and discreet, it was said of them.'

I focused all my concentration on the idea. Just as I gave up, a name slid into my mind. I seem to remember it was Talio. But beyond the name, nothing else surfaced. It was like the picture of me pouring away my father's whisky. The briefest of flashes – subliminal, would you call it? – then the familiar blankness descended again.

Colonel Tanizaki told me a strange thing, that he felt sure he had seen my face somewhere before. A newspaper photograph, he thought, a younger face maybe, but still the resemblance was there. 'You are in your forties now, I suppose?' he asked me.

Your guess is as good as mine, is what I felt like saying. But underneath the flippancy I felt the tremor of hope that still gets through to me from time to time.

'Maybe I'm a famous person then.'

He looked at me from the chair opposite, his head tilted consideringly. 'It could have been Katharine Hepburn. There is a likeness.'

It was strange. I knew the name, of course, and yet I could not attach it to any personal memory. I turned back to the board on the table between us. He had introduced me to a game called Chinese checkers – more relaxing, he said, than chess, but it uses the same parts of the brain, and more interesting than playing alone. For myself, nervousness made it difficult to concentrate, but I was trying.

'When I write home next,' he said, 'I shall ask my wife to send me my old cuttings album. I always kept newspaper pieces that caught my interest. I'm sure that's where the photograph is.'

He must have seen the tension on my face because he suddenly said, consolingly, 'One day, everything will come back to you. I'm certain of it. Now you must return to quarters.'

I was dismissed when he looked at his watch. This time he stood up with a kind of half-bow.

'I regret very much that you are being kept under lock and key,' he said. 'This is not necessary. But it was the Admiral's idea – he has a peculiar view of war.' He smiled wryly. 'I can hardly invite you back to your home to live, as I'm sure you appreciate.'

'I appreciate,' I replied.

These brief attempts at civilized exchanges were a sort of lifeline for both of us, I think. It was a curious friendship, if friendship isn't too strong a word. There was no sexual undercurrent to it at all. I thought of the Colonel as a shy man, as well as a courteous one. But both of us were exiles in an alien land, isolated from normal life for one reason or another, and perhaps it was this that made the real bond between us.

The room itself was full of reminders of a Japan that had nothing to do with the madness of world war – the long scroll of painted characters pinned across the main wall ('A line from one of our philosophers, I forget the exact translation'), the great bronze gong, shaped like a bowl, which he used to summon his meals. Of course I could never be invited to share in them. But I was sometimes given a small parcel of food to take away which I passed on to Timu's family whenever I could.

Perhaps it also helped that I was able to remonstrate with him when I saw some of the injustices being inflicted on the people by the soldiers. Some of them were stopped. But I had to be very careful not to overstep the mark, or to let it be known to anyone else that the protests came directly from me. I was also getting better treatment in the jail.

As far as the other Japanese were concerned, I was the classic Western traitor, willing to exchange whatever information I had in return for the Colonel's protection. But all this was about to change. A week later Colonel Tanizaki summoned me to tell me to have my belongings ready to travel with him the following day. He was leaving for the main island of Tarawa, where the Japanese had established their base.

I began to protest but he stopped me.

'You will be with other European women. The Catholic mission has a convent there for the nuns of the Sacred Heart order. They will take you in. You will be safe there.'

Then he told me that the Admiral was returning to take command of Taparua. If I stayed I would be entirely at his mercy. Conversations between the guards had been reported to him. Once he was gone there would be sexual assaults as well as the everyday hardships of being in jail.

'At Tarawa, at least you will be treated according to international rules. Besides,' he drew himself up, 'our people do not imprison women in holy orders.'

'Do I have to take my vows?' I said, trying to joke. The Colonel frowned, and it suddenly occurred to me that he might be Catholic himself.

'Are you a Catholic?' I asked him.

'Yes, my family became converts two generations ago. But it is best not referred to at times like this.'

The next day I was taken on board the vessel that was bound for Tarawa. It was a twenty-four-hour journey, and although I was officially under guard as a prisoner in transit I was allowed on to the foredeck from time to time. Here Colonel Tanizaki was ensconced in a canvas chair with various plans and papers spread out in front of him. But there was little opportunity for our normal conversations. The dark glasses he was wearing were like a mask and they put up a barrier between us.

We were now on a war footing, circling around islands which were either already occupied by the enemy or, at least, under threat of invasion. There were rumours of an imminent assault on this part of the Pacific by the Americans. The map spread out in front of the Colonel reminded me of the one in Harrington's study, with its miniature flags and arrows running from one dot of land to another. The whole area was to become a battleground, he explained, a chaotic melting pot of attack and counter-attack between East and West. Huge fleets were on the move everywhere, carrying the kind of weaponry that the native populations couldn't even begin to imagine.

Every now and then we could see smoke on the horizon. Occasionally I felt the vibration of a distant bombardment. And then there were the planes, Japanese planes, some of them flying solo on reconnaissance missions, some of them in formation, preparing to drop their bombs on some helpless native population. But whatever the plane, I felt the same weird sense of dread, an uncontrollable panic that couldn't be logically explained away. After all, we were travelling in Japanese-occupied waters, under the flag of the Rising Sun, so we ourselves were in no danger from the air. But it was enough to make me shiver and turn away.

Standing next to me at the rails, Colonel Tanizaki noticed this.

'You are like the natives. Just the sight of a plane and you're terrified, as if you'd never seen one before. Surely America was full of the things – weren't they all the rage back in the twenties and thirties?'

'But these are not aeroplanes. These are killing machines.'

I remember that was my answer, my attempt to explain feelings that rose deep inside me whenever I saw the shadow of wings overhead. The drone of the engines seemed to cut right through me so that I had to cover my ears. It was an irrational, instinctive fear, like a child's. I recall actually going below to be sick once or twice. After the war, of course, hardly any planes flew over the islands, not in this part of the Gilberts at least. So it's a trauma I've almost forgotten, buried in the past like so many other things. But just remembering these times has brought it back, for a moment. I suppose everyone has a secret fear of some kind, and that was mine.

But some things can never be forgotten. The sight of the outrigger canoe on the second day, for example, suddenly appearing out of nowhere with its strange load of passengers. At first we thought it was a fishing party from Tarawa. We were not far from landfall. But when the Colonel raised his glasses, he gave an exclamation of disbelief.

'They're Europeans! And some of them look like women!'

It was hard to tell because the figures in the boat seemed to be covered in black drapes of some kind. Then from the stern a white cloth was waved. It was only when our vessel drew alongside that we saw they were nuns, all of them in their tropical white habits which they'd covered up with a strange assortment of dark materials – curtains, spreads, anything they could lay their hands on.

'So that we shouldn't be spotted from the air,' they explained. That was later, when the four of them had been got on board, along with the two Gilbertese men who were with them.

But first there was a scene of panic and confusion. Terrified faces looked up at us from the canoe and Colonel Tanizaki gave orders to the captain to shut off the engines. One of the women looked badly wounded. Another one, much younger, held up her hands.

'Don't shoot us! For God's sake don't shoot!'

'There'll be no shooting,' Colonel Tanizaki called back. Then, to me, he said, 'Tell them they needn't fear to come on board – they'll believe you. Then they can explain who they are and what exactly they're doing in mid-ocean.'

Explanations didn't take long. They scrambled up on to the deck, but at first they were too frightened and too exhausted to speak. They'd put out from Tarawa to try to get to the island of Abaiang, they said. They thought our launch was pursuing them, sent to pick them up and take them back for punishment.

'Why did you try to escape from Tarawa?' Colonel Tanizaki asked them sternly. 'You know it's forbidden to travel between the islands.'

It was the youngest nun, a fresh-faced Australian girl, who told the story, how, two days before, American planes had bombarded the harbour. An ammunition dump next to the convent had exploded. There were many casualties among them, such as the French sister Mary Clothilde whose leg wound I was trying to dress from the first-aid box. Jacob their interpreter had overheard the Japanese planning to execute all remaining Europeans on Tarawa as retribution. He volunteered to take as many of the nuns as he could fit in his canoe to make for Abaiang, where there was also a large Catholic mission.

'I would have got them there safely,' Jacob protested. 'But we picked up a shark. It scented blood in the water from Sister's bandages when we were trying to wash the wound. After that it never left us alone. A few minutes ago it nearly overturned us. That is why we made the signal for help – even from a Japanese boat.'

The little French sister was crying now, huddled under her blanket, saying it was all her fault.

Colonel Tanizaki was looking down at the empty canoe. I made myself look too and caught a glimpse of a circling grey shape nudging at the tiny craft like a dog with a bone. He turned to the other man, a skeletal figure who sat rocking to and fro, his head in his hands, mumbling to himself.

'And who is he?'

The last patient from the hospital asylum, one of the other nuns told us in a soft Irish voice. The Japanese had murdered all the other inmates a week ago.

I saw Colonel Tanizaki's face tighten.

'How were they executed?'

'They were lined up blindfold along the edge of the cliff and bayoneted from behind,' she told him. 'That way there was no need to dispose of the bodies. The sea took care of them.'

'This man ran away and hid in a cave,' Jacob went on. 'How could I leave him behind? His family are my family.'

There was silence for a moment. Colonel Tanizaki turned away to the bridge.

'I must go to Tarawa. But I shall direct the Captain to make for Abaiang first.' He looked back at me, then at the Irish nun. 'This American lady is also seeking refuge. You will see she is taken care of at the convent there, Sister.'

The sister bowed her head in reply. I saw her fingers move along the rosary hanging from her waist as if making a silent prayer of thanks for unexpected mercies.

CHAPTER SIX

It was the note that Colonel Tanizaki gave us as we went ashore that was our chief protection over the next few months. It was addressed to the officer in charge at Abaiang, Major Otaka. A good-looking man in his fifties, he was very much the traditional soldier of the old school, formal in manner but fair-minded in his way and not given to the Admiral's excesses of rage. Colonel Tanizaki had told me that he had stipulated in the note that neither the nuns nor the Gilbertese should be punished for trying to get away from Tarawa. For no reason they had been put under threat of death there, and now they deserved better treatment. He added that he expected to be in Abaiang himself before long, depending on the progress of the war.

And so there began a new way of life for me, one which has supported and comforted me ever since. The fine convent you see here now, Laura, is nothing like the place it was when I first came all those years ago. The sisters lived in two long huts, partitioned off for prayers and privacy. On the other side of the compound there was just a thatched chapel and a weatherboard schoolroom. Even those had been ransacked by the Japanese when they first invaded. The windows were broken, the mosquito-proof ceiling of perforated zinc was torn and cut and most of the furniture was gone. Some of the holy pictures on the walls had been slashed with bayonets but they still hung there, repaired with tape as well as possible.

That little band of nuns who ran the mission were amazing women. The first evening I was shown with the other newcomers to a place at the long supper table – one of the few things the Japanese had left them – as if all was normal. Few questions had been asked of me. I was simply Millie, a refugee who'd been left behind when the evacuation ship made its round of the islands. Too ill to travel, separated from my husband and child, these were the shorthand reasons for my situation, and they were given and accepted without cross-examination.

Prayers were said by the Mother Superior, a tiny wrinkled lady in her eighties, who was the aunt of a bishop serving in Melanesia. The meal was shared out from a huge bowl of watery rice and beans and green kumala tops. There was also something salty mixed in it that might have been meat.

'It's the Major,' said one of the Irish nuns. I can see her now, sitting across the table from me, laughing at my expression. It was the first time for so long since I'd seen anyone laugh. 'The commanding officer sent a pig over for us when a cargo of livestock arrived for the camp. So we decided to name the creature in his honour.'

'We tried to feed him up,' said someone else further down. 'But he was far too old and thin, with all those black bristles sticking out of his ears.'

'Just like the Major's!'

Everyone was laughing now, and they told me that all they could do with him was kill him off, salt him and mince him up for rations.

'This is the last of him, praise God,' Reverend Mother piped up.

Those first few days at Abaiang – I wish I could describe the effect they had on me, how much it meant to me simply to have just a curtained-off corner in the dormitory that I could call my own. And then, the company! How wonderful it was to be accepted into that community, to begin to feel some respect for myself again. Even though I didn't know that self by name, I knew it in my heart. It was a strange thing that with the soldiers so close, their practice gunfire and the noise of building work going on every day, I had never felt so much at peace.

The sisters, of course, wanted to know if I was a Catholic. I tried to explain to them that for someone without a past that was an impossible question to answer. But every day I couldn't help being moved by their devotion to their faith, their absolute certainty that God hadn't abandoned them. They saw His hand in so many things. The breadfruit trees, for instance. Normally they produce a crop only once every six months. Here they were bearing fruit all the year round.

And then there was what they called, after the Bible, 'the miraculous draught of fishes'. This was at the time of the full moon. Traps were usually set inside the reef by the nuns and their helpers and they would get a modest catch, a few dozen fish of different kinds. But that night there was a haul of several thousand – a fantastical sight, huge shining shoals piled up in the nets. There were so many that all the people of the village came to help dry and store them. The Japanese took more than their share, of course. But even so, every day for months there was a decent portion for everyone, with enough left over to be ground up for the chickens. They were very precious, the mission chickens.

There was a special Mass of thanks after that. The church was almost bare, but the little altar and the tabernacle were intact.

'Please take the Sacrament with us,' Mother Superior said to me that morning. 'You're no longer a stranger in our midst, and only God knows what your suffering has been.' She said no more but laid her hand on mine for a moment before she led the way in.

I didn't know it then, but the Hosts were especially treasured by the nuns. The flour to make them had been sent by the Catholic Women's Guild of Australia at the outbreak of the war, and now the contents of the tin were dwindling fast. The flask of sacramental wine was also nearly finished, so each of us would take just the smallest drop to moisten our lips, as a token.

Once or twice we'd find a couple of the guards sitting at the back to watch us out of curiosity. But the only time a service was actually interrupted was the Sunday when the Major himself arrived with an official scribe in tow. There was a long string of questions to be checked – names, ages, nationalities and so on.

More important, though, was how long did we spend in prayer each day? What was the subject of our prayers? He had been told that one of the Methodist pastors on another island had told the people to pray that the British and Americans might win the war.

'That man was tied to a tree for three days without food or water,' he told us grimly.

I made the usual bow and dared to ask him if it was he who had given the order.

The Major looked embarrassed.

'I was not in that place. But it is not your business to ask questions, Christa Ona – Christian Lady. Colonel Tanizaki will be strict with such behaviour too.'

Apparently the Colonel was shortly to replace the Major on Abaiang, in time to organize troop movements for the 'total victory' against the Americans.

That 'total victory' was to be the terrible battle for Tarawa beachhead, when thousands on both sides were slaughtered at low tide. Already we could see the preparations building up, Japanese warships crossing the horizon daily to Tarawa, carrying the amphibious landing craft and tanks. Even on our own island, Abaiang, extra bunkers and trenches were being put in along the sea-front, and from time to time Jacob brought us secret information he'd overheard at the wireless station and the officers' quarters.

Like the rest of the sisters, I managed to shut most of it out of my mind. We were too busy just trying to survive from day to day. We had a primitive hospital at the mission, really nothing more than a quarantine hut, stocked with the very few medical supplies the Japanese had not requisitioned. Typhoid and dysentery were spreading, especially among the children of the village we were looking after. Two of the sisters died within days of one another. Sister Mary Clothilde's horrible shrapnel wounds refused to heal, although I changed the dressings daily and did my best to keep off the swarms of flies and mosquitoes.

'I think you must havc had nursing experience, Millie,' one of the sisters said, watching me.

I said nothing. But I was aware of the same feeling that had come over me once before – the time when I was helping Timu with the generator on Taparua. It was a skill that seemed to belong to a previous life, a strange sort of familiarity as if I had performed such tasks before.

People often talk about déjà vu. But it was more real than that, as real as some of the deep-rooted convictions I held without quite knowing why. A passionate belief in pacifism, for instance, which made me sometimes sit down and scribble lines that hung together like poetry. Perhaps they were even lines I'd written before in my young days. I don't know. I only know they would surface out of nowhere from time to time, images of courage and freedom, the splendour of clouds and the enduring stars. The origin of these thoughts was always a mystery. But I held on to them because they were the only relics of my past that I had.

As well as the nursing, and work in the kitchen and the laundry which we all shared, there was also the school. About twenty children still came in for lessons, however hard the Japanese tried to stop them. Most of the time there was a guard in attendance questioning Jacob to see whether we were teaching the children anything subversive about the great Japanese Empire.

But Mother Superior was more than a match for our masters in all kinds of ways. I shall never forget the time a bullying corporal tried to walk off with our only remaining bucket. The saintly little lady hung on to her side of the handle with such determination that in the end he had to admit defeat and pretend he hadn't really wanted it in the first place.

Dear Laura, I expect you're wondering how often I thought about you all this time. The answer is, every single day that passed. But especially when I was teaching my group of five- and six-year-olds.

There was a small girl in that class called Miriama. She'd sit cross-legged on the mat in line with the others, her head bent over her slate, and as I passed I could never resist touching the thin little nape of her neck, beneath the braids of black hair. It was so like yours as you used to sit on the verandah step, absorbed in your patterns of shells and stones.

It was hard to keep back the sadness, the terrible sense of loss, wondering where you were learning your lessons now, and if the unknown aunt put her arms around you at bedtime. I had told the sisters about you, of course, and they mentioned your name from time to time, which somehow made it even harder.

Occasionally fragments of news would come through from the outside world about the progress of the war. Each time I would steel myself to hear reports of attacks on New Zealand. Then, looking at the map, I would realise that several thousand miles of empty Pacific lay between you and the Japanese advance into the Gilberts. The firm black lines of the Equator and the Tropic of Capricorn ran across the blue like lines of defence. It was a childish thought, but it comforted me.

I liked to go into the church on my own sometimes. It was where I felt closest to you, where I could concentrate in peace on the pictures of you in my mind.

One day I'd taken a bunch of white hibiscus to put on the altar. I was arranging them in the discarded brass shell-case we used as a vase when I heard a movement from behind. I turned and saw the figure of Colonel Tanizaki in the shadows at the back. He was standing very straight, his arms at his side. But his head was bent and his eyes were closed as if he were praying.

I walked towards him. He looked up at me and gave me his usual half-bow. We were alone, otherwise such a gesture would have been unthinkable. I bowed in return, and a smile passed between us. Just for a moment we were outside the war zone again, the same two friends who had listened to a scratchy Mozart recording and played Chinese checkers back on Taparua.

'How are conditions at the mission?' he asked me.

We talked for a moment, and then he told me the crisis was very near. The American fleet had been sighted and he had come to Abaiang to supervise the movements of troop reinforcements across to Tarawa. While he was speaking I noticed how thin he had become. He was unshaven and there were deep lines on either side of his mouth.

'It will be a long, bloody battle,' he said. 'I must tell you I have little hope my own people will win. Then for Japan worse will lie ahead, I think.' He stared past me at the tabernacle. 'I thought I should offer up a prayer. The troops will do the same to their own gods when the time comes.' He turned back to me. 'Who knows what is to become of any of us?'

'The war won't last long,' I said. 'Then you'll be able to live your own life again, as we all shall.'

He shook his head. 'You don't understand. I may be no great soldier, but I am a true Japanese. The shame of defeat will be mine too. I shall be partly to blame. This is what we are trained to believe. We all must pay.'

A barrier had come down between us. I felt he was almost talking to himself.

'I'll leave you, Colonel Tanizaki. I'm sure you would like to be alone.' I moved away and then stopped. There was something else I needed to say. 'I would like to thank you. For getting me away from Taparua. For being kind to me, although we are enemies.'

I was at the door when he called me back.

'Perhaps now is not the best moment to speak about it. But I have some news for you.'

'News?' I was suddenly afraid. What news could be good news for me? I stood facing him, a few yards between us.

'You remember I was writing to my wife to ask for my file of cuttings to be sent out to me? It arrived at Tarawa with the rest of my mail from home, just a couple of weeks ago.'

'Yes?' My heart began to beat very fast.

'There is indeed a photograph of the woman I was telling you about. The one that looks like you. A report about her also. The date is 1937.' He hesitated, staring back at me. 'But if you are that woman, no one else can know. Not now, not here. It is too dangerous.'

'I don't understand,' I said.

'You would become a pawn between our two countries. A hostage, or worse. An execution could be ordered.' He took off his glasses and pressed his hand to his eyes, as if he saw something there he wanted to erase. 'They would take your head. It would be proof.'

He stopped. We heard someone move in the porchway behind us. A guard looked in, then snapped to attention. Colonel Tanizaki spoke to him sharply. When he had gone he turned to me again.

'I have a conference with the Major before he leaves. The day after tomorrow, if you are here at the same time, I will bring the cutting.'

He had put on his glasses again. He was looking at me in a way that made me feel a stranger to myself.

'I am not certain, of course.' He paused. 'If it is true, your life would change. After the war.'

'It has already changed,' I told him. 'Just by being here, and I am grateful.'

It was the last thing I ever said to him. I stood in the porch and watched him climb into the truck that was waiting outside. The next day the battle of Tarawa began.

At the convent we had just finished supper. Suddenly there came the rumble of explosions, far away, different from anything we had ever heard before.

'The Americans,' Mother Superior said. 'The Americans are landing at Tarawa.'

I felt myself shiver. For a moment we sat totally still, in a circle of suspense and fear. Then we began to move about frantically, putting up the hurricane shutters, getting medical supplies together. Long after dark, crash after crash of the distant battle went echoing on. From the verandah we could see flames leaping up across the horizon like sheet lightning.

'We cannot sleep,' Mother Superior said. 'Let us go to pray.'

Dawn was breaking as we made our way across to the church. The drum roll of the bombardment was constant now, louder than ever. The ground was vibrating under our feet as if the whole world was coming to an end. I felt safer on my knees, I don't know why, with the rosary held tight between my fingers.

When we came out all we could see, looking across to Tarawa, was a huge pall of black smoke. But the strangest thing was that our Japanese soldiers were nowhere to be seen, and the camp looked deserted. The day before we had watched them gathering up from the village anything that could be used as weapons – spades, picks, shovels and so on. Rifles and bayonets were polished, amidst the sounds of marching orders and much shouting and running to and fro. There was no sign of Colonel Tanizaki. The troops were positioning themselves along the fortifications at the far point of the island, ready for an American assault from Tarawa.

As we walked back to the convent we heard voices overhead. The boys from the village had climbed to the tops of the tallest palms. They called down to us that they could see ships – hundreds of them, moving in all directions. The next minute some of the children came running after us to say the Americans were landing on the beach on the opposite side of the island. Huge iron boxes were floating on the water, with machines inside like trucks with guns.

They meant tanks, of course. We could hear the chattering of machine-gun fire clearly, shellbursts exploding very close. Finally there was silence.

By now Jacob had disappeared to try to find out what was happening. Inside the convent, everyone was jubilant at the thought of the Allied liberators actually on our soil at last. The hated Japanese would be pushed back into the sea, the way they had come. But I couldn't put Colonel Tanizaki out of my mind. For me, the Japanese meant one man, someone who had concerned himself with my own fate at a time when death threatened all of us. And now?

It felt like forever until Jacob returned. He told us that the far end of the island was a battleground. His face was smeared with ash from the fires still burning there and, close to, I could see he was shaking all over. The fighting was almost over. But he had seen terrible things, one thing more terrible than all the rest. The last party of Japanese to survive had retreated to one of the bunkers on the beach with their machine guns, firing out through the slits in the walls. In spite of their numbers, the Americans couldn't reach them. Shells from their submarines, rifles and cannon were all useless. Then the Japanese ran out of ammunition. The Americans waited for them to come out and surrender. But everything was silent. So the Americans stormed the trenches and went in. Jacob went with them to be an interpreter with the prisoners. But there were no prisoners to be taken.

'All were dead.' His face was rigid with shock, his eyes darting from side to side, the scene in the bunker still imprinted on them. 'All the soldiers were sitting against the walls, straight up, shot with their own pistols.' He swallowed. 'All but one man.'

'Colonel Tanizaki.' I spoke the name in a whisper as one does of the dead.

'Yes, the Colonel. A good man. He hadn't used a gun. He killed himself on his sword. There was much blood but his face was not marked. Not like the others.'

His voice died away. He held his head in his hands so that we shouldn't see what he was feeling.

One of the sisters took him into the kitchen to give him some tea. I went to my corner of the dormitory to be alone. I was glad to think that the face of my friend had not been disfigured. Those gentle, scholarly features were not meant for violence. Closing my eyes as I lay on my bed, I saw it clearly again and felt sadness at the waste, rage at the pointlessness of the whole war. At the same time another picture came into my mind, the devastation of the Japanese camp now burning to the ground, leaving no trace of personal belongings,

Tanizaki's or anyone else's. The scrapbook with the photograph from a Japanese newspaper was something I would never see.

Strangely enough, I hardly ever thought about it again. Loss and destruction had been part of my life for as long as I could remember. Besides, Colonel Tanizaki could well have been mistaken, thinking he'd solved my mystery in the same way he solved a crossword puzzle. It seemed so unlikely, a report about me, unless it was an account of the accident at sea that had brought me to the Gilberts in the first place. This possibility did haunt me a little, I have to admit.

Then it all faded from my mind. That was the time I fell ill, you see. The presence of the American troops on the island before they moved on to their next battle is something I hardly remember. Most of the next few weeks I hardly left the dormitory. I suppose I had what you would call a severe nervous breakdown. Not surprising, really, considering what I'd been through.

My physical condition has never been the same since. I seemed to have some kind of heart trouble, fainting fits, dizzy spells and so on, and occasionally the most awful migraines. I had to stay in bed most days. But the nuns were kindness itself, especially Mother Superior, whom I came to love dearly. She died soon after the war.

Because I was so weak I cried a great deal, something I never did much of before, and still don't. However hard I tried to forget, you were in my mind continually, Laura. I found myself wondering, in a wild kind of way, if I couldn't get you back to the islands when peace came, so that I could bring you up here, have you with me forever. Even if Harrington knew, what could he do about it, now that I had a home at the convent and the protection of the nuns? I would still keep my side of the bargain not to leave the Gilberts, nor to tell the true story to anyone else.

Well, the war did come to an end, and I sent off a letter to Auckland. Harrington had seen to it that I was never told his sister's name, which was not his, of course. You remember I told you he'd changed his name to Harrington when he was a young man. So I simply addressed it to the English teacher at the Methodist mission school.

I held out little hope, and when the envelope came back marked simply 'forwarding address not known', I wasn't surprised. She'd obviously gone back to England and taken you with her. I remembered the account of my death that Harrington gave to the rescue party from Fiji. No doubt he reported the same story to his sister who would then break the news, gently I hoped, to you. So now little Laura Harrington was not just a refugee but an orphan, and the lifelong responsibility of her appointed guardian.

That was the end of that particular dream. Who could subject a child to further traumas, when she had settled into a new way of life, with all the adaptability of the very young? Besides, a search for you in England was out of the question, without resources of any kind or a single clue where you might be.

The one person I was determined not to think about was Harrington. My horror of him, and the hatred I felt, was so intense I could have become a woman possessed if I had allowed myself to dwell on what he had done to me. No, I had to put that nightmare time behind me, and try to live for whatever future lay ahead.

Soon after the Japanese surrender, a visiting bishop came to the convent. He himself was the survivor of a cruel spell of imprisonment in Saipan. Two of the other Fathers had died under torture.

'None of us who've been through the war in the Pacific will ever be the same again,' he said to me. I had been taking instruction from Mother Superior in the Catholic faith, and it was the bishop who received me as a convert. Afterwards he took confession in the tiny cell next to the altar.

'What do you want to do with your life now, Millie?' he asked me.

'Live in peace,' I told him. 'Find myself. I don't know how.' I took a deep breath. 'I once tried to kill a man, Father. I was living in hell.'

'And now?' His voice was calm.

'Abaiang seems like a glimpse of heaven,' I said. 'My place of refuge.'

'Then you will stay on here, work here?'

'If it could be arranged, Father.'

And so it was arranged. I became what's known as a lay sister, wearing the working brown robe you see me in now, nursing, gardening, mostly teaching, as I still do today if I'm feeling strong enough. Can you understand how I've come to love this world of islands? Its remoteness and its calm and those endless horizons, they seem to hold me safe. It was this Pacific Ocean that delivered me up out of nowhere, remember, and I must be grateful to it for the rest of my life.

One more thing I mentioned to the bishop that day. I asked him if it was wrong to long so much for the return of a child I'd given up for good. I remember his answer well.

'Who knows what is "for good"?' he said. 'Only God, I think.'

I said that to myself many times. And after twenty-five years here you are. Somehow you knew I was still alive and you found your own way back to me from the other side of the world.

Laura, I'm tired now, so very tired. Shall we finish the recording? It's the end of the story, isn't it?

PART FOUR

CHAPTER ONE

Laura switched off the machine. Very gently she leaned across the bed and moved the pillow more comfortably beneath her mother's head.

'Not quite the end,' she told herself. 'Not yet.' Then to her mother she said softly, 'You just sleep, Mama. It's late. I'm sorry I've made you talk so long this time.'

The thin brown face smiled up at her, eyes half-closed. 'See you in the morning, honey.'

The Americanism took Laura by surprise. The accent itself was so faint now that you could almost forget her original nationality. And yet, as her mother had told her story, it was as if, beneath the surface, a very different personality could be glimpsed. Laura was able to imagine her in her thirties, the adventurous young woman who had grown up in the America of Scott Fitzgerald and the Jazz Age, looking for new horizons and the excitements of travelling the world. The elderly nun in the patched habit was a kind of camouflage, someone she'd grown into over the years. Even now Laura was still overcome by the strangeness and the cruelty of her mother's life. More than anything else, she was struck by this chameleon-like ability of hers to adapt and survive. There was an extraordinary spirit of endurance about her that surely few women could claim.

At the door Laura turned to look back at the sleeping figure on the bed and felt a wave of protective love for her. Now she can let go and turn to me, she thought. I'm the only person who can give her that new hold on life. She'll come away with me. Together we can try to make up for all the missing years.

The little convent guest-room where she was to sleep was next to her mother's. One of the nuns had turned down the narrow white bed for her and placed an oil lamp on the table next to it. There was a Victorian neatness about the lace-edged cloth and the sampler on the wall embroidered with the order's insignia of the Sacred Heart and

Anchor. Laura felt as secure as a child as she slipped under the mosquito net.

Lying there, she had a sudden picture of her room at the flat, with its William Morris chintzes and Cézanne prints, the air-freshener smell blotting out the fumes of the traffic below. Home is where the heart is, people always said. But strangely heartless was the way it seemed to her now, like a stage set for someone else's play.

She tried to reassure herself. Imagine how her mother would enjoy the sheer comfort of the place, the mod cons of kitchen and bathroom, the shelves of books everywhere, and the soft bed in her own room. Round the corner in Harley Street was the medical carc her mother would need. A first-class psychiatrist might work wonders on that damaged brain. Laura visualized the small, choice meals she would cook for her in the evenings, when she got back from Broadcasting House. She'd bring home recordings for her to listen to, and the occasional congenial visitor from time to time.

She turned out the lamp. But in the darkness she found herself grappling with other thoughts. Back in Fiji, so many hazards awaited her before she could be free to go back to England. Harrington first. All through the last twenty-four hours a slow-burning rage against him had been gathering. Now he must be confronted with the evidence of Millie's survival. She thought of this encounter continually, sharpening herself to a razor edge for whatever it would bring.

Then legal action must be set in motion, listing every one of the crimes he must pay for. How did one even begin to classify them, the terrible injustices of thirty years ago? Here she would have to rely on Jack, Jack who was no doubt back in Fiji already, out at Nailangi estate helping his father deal with the disaster of the hurricane.

She tried to think of him calmly, but detachment was difficult. Why had he not been in touch? Ever since the cable had come, she had been subconsciously waiting for a message of some kind. So many things could have happened. He could still be in Canberra, prevented from leaving for one reason or another. And then, of course, Kim came into the equation. Perhaps she was with Jack at Nailangi with the rest of the family, including his awful mother. Whatever the situation, he'd now have enough on his mind without taking on the dilemmas of someone else's life.

How silent the mission was at night! Turning on to her side, she was on the edge of sleep now, her thoughts fragmenting, one image chasing another. The wartime scenes her mother had been describing flooded again through her mind. Yet she knew that, if she dreamed at all that night, it would be a dream of Jack. For weeks now, she had successfully banished him from this inner theatre of her life. He was a daylight ghost, flicking in and out of mundane experiences, conversations, journeys, things she had seen and done since they parted.

I'm not even sure I'm in love with him any more, she said to herself as sleep came finally down. Yet here she was, almost instantly locked into the same old heartbreak, the distorting-mirror scenes at Vailima, the search through an empty garden, the sight of him waiting on the steps where the dark pool glimmered through the ferns. She felt again the touch of his skin and the agonizing haste of an embrace that always foreshadowed some imminent tragedy.

'Ships that pass,' she heard him say clearly, just as the dream ended.

She felt bereft when she awoke and remembered it, disturbed by the ache of longing it left behind. At least the wretched Kim had no part in it this time, she told herself, trying to make light of the dream. But why dream of the past when the most important discovery of her life was happening here and now?

She hurried to dress and was brushing her hair when there was a tap on the door. The pretty Irish nun stood there with a cup of tea on a tray. Sister Kiri was still sleeping, she said.

'I mean Millie.' She smiled. 'We still can't believe she has a daughter come all this way to find her.'

'I can't quite believe it myself,' Laura said.

'Reverend Mother would like to see you for a few minutes when you've had your tea. It's just a few yards down the corridor.'

The door at the end of the passage stood open. Inside, the Mother Superior was sitting at her desk, an iron bed behind her, a carved wooden crucifix on the wall. The only splash of colour in the white room with the white-robed nun was the screen in the corner covered with bright photographs.

'Some are our schoolchildren,' she told Laura. 'Taken by a visiting American priest a few years ago. Some are my family, friends back in Queensland. I shan't be seeing them for another five years,' she went on in her matter-of-fact way. 'So it's good to have them around me.'

She looked up with the weather-worn grin that contrasted so sharply with her saintly white veil.

'That Sister Kiri of ours. Or rather yours. I shouldn't think she's talked so much for the last twenty years put together.' She chuckled. 'Something of a miracle, I reckon, the whole thing. You've given her back her grip on life.'

'But sadly, not the rest of her memory,' Laura said.

'Does a name really matter? I left mine behind when I first came here. Glad to get rid of it too.'

Laura couldn't resist the question. 'What was it?'

'Daisy May Connelly.' She barked a sudden laugh. 'Quite a turn-up for the books when I swapped it for Sister Benignus, I can tell you.'

'About my mother,' Laura began.

'Yes, your mother.' She leaned across the desk, suddenly authoritative, her hands clasped in front of her, red capable hands with a plain gold ring that gave them the look of a hardworking housewife. 'What's going to happen to her now, Laura?'

'I want her to come with me.' Then, in case that sounded ungrateful, she added, 'It's not that she hasn't been happy here. But now that we've found one another . . .'

'I understand that. And I'm sure she'll want it too. But the point is, where? You haven't discussed it yet?'

'Not yet. But I have a place in London, where I work. Big and very comfortable.'

Reverend Mother looked doubtful. 'She'd never cope with that, you know. Imagine the shock to the system. She's had such a sheltered life. And her health these days is a bit precarious, heart trouble, you know.' She looked at Laura thoughtfully. 'Somewhere not too far away, perhaps with the same kind of climate. Could you settle back in the Gilberts, do you think?'

'How could I?' Laura was suddenly impatient. 'I have to keep my career going. I don't have a private income to support me.' She felt a stab of conscience. 'As a matter of fact, I should have been back at the BBC a week ago. My Pacific programmes are due to go out next month and I haven't been in touch for ages.'

'You mustn't think of taking your mother with you, Laura.' The Mother Superior's face was grave. 'It might even be the death of her. And you know,' she placed her hand over Laura's, 'she has a home with us for as long as she needs it.'

Laura sat silent for a moment. 'It will be hard, leaving her.'

Reverend Mother watched the frustration on her face. 'But you'll be coming back, won't you? When you've had time to work out some plans. You might even think about Fiji? There'd be broadcasting work, good medical care. You have contacts there, surely.'

'Ratu Edwin Vunilau, the government minister. He's a good friend.' She paused. 'One of the settler families, the Renfreys.'

'Well then.'

But Laura broke in. She was trying to find words for a situation she couldn't hope to explain in the bright morning light of the mission office.

'It's just not possible, Reverend Mother. Millie's husband, the one who treated her so terribly, he's still living in Fiji. There's this violence in him, this cruelty. He's mad. Quite mad. If he heard she was back in Fiji, heard she was still alive even, I know he'd stop at nothing to harm her.' She took a deep breath. 'It's an old story. So many twists and turns, so many lies.'

'This is your father you're talking about, Laura?'

'No. He is not my father.' She stood up slowly, feeling the weight of her mother's past like something she would have to carry with her always. 'I wish I could tell you more, but it takes too long. Besides, some of it is still too dangerous. One day, perhaps, you can hear the tapes I have been recording.'

Reverend Mother got up from her desk. She came round to Laura and put her arm round her shoulder.

'I had no idea of any of this.' The sharp blue eyes with the sandy lashes could be surprisingly kind. 'But things change, don't they? God sees to that.' She walked with her to the door. 'Anyway, you won't have to hurry away. The next ship's not due for another week. Or perhaps you could stay for Christmas?'

'Alas, that's just not possible. I should have been on my way already. But can't I do anything to help while I'm here? I seem to have done nothing so far but sit and talk.'

'Maybe you could go over to the school and chat to the children. Tell them about London,' Reverend Mother said briskly. 'Instead of your mother's class. I think she should rest today.'

'I'd like that. And thanks for your advice.'

In the passage, Laura turned again. 'Oh, Reverend Mother, I forgot to ask. There's been no message for me? No word from Fiji?'

'Afraid not, my dear. The wireless station's closed today. Maybe tomorrow.'

'Maybe.'

It was idiotic to feel disappointment. It was just that, once she knew Jack was back, she'd be able to make plans to meet him and decide what should be done about Harrington. She didn't feel she could take the next step alone. You needed to know the people in authority, the Public Prosecutions Office, the police department. There was Ratu Edwin, of course. He'd supported her from the start. She'd have to see him and tell him the whole story as soon as she got back to Fiji. He deserved that, at least, and he'd be waiting to hear from her.

Before she walked over to the schoolhouse, Laura went to look in on Millie. She was still sleeping, lying on her side, the long narrow body outlined under the sheet, knees drawn up, hands folded beneath her chin. As always, Laura felt the mystery of her mother's secret life.

How young and vulnerable she looked, her small haggard face softened by the mosquito netting. The cropped head on the pillow could have been a boy's. To Laura she seemed like some piece of driftwood thrown up by the sea, bleached and worn away but somehow indestructible. She wanted to reach out and touch her. But she stopped herself, as a mother would hesitate to disturb a sleeping child.

Whatever happens, we'll be together, she thought. Fate must allow that much.

Very gently, she closed the door. She went into her own room and pulled on the wide straw hat that travelled with her everywhere. Crossing the compound, Laura was glad of it. It was nearly midday and the sun was almost directly overhead, the heat intense. The hum of high-pitched voices drifted out from the open-sided bamboo buildings, the three-times table and then the four. An iron bell clanged and the hum changed to a babble of excitement as she found herself surrounded by a swarm of children.

'Dinnertime! Dinnertime!'

The cry went up on every side. One small girl took her by the hand, leading the way to the shade of a giant ivi tree on the edge of the field. Hurrying in their wake came Sister Bernadette, fluttering to and fro like a cabbage butterfly in her white habit.

'You'll join us, won't you, Laura?' she called.

For the next thirty minutes, lunchboxes of breadfruit and fish curry were shared among the chattering throng. Bottles of lime juice and water were produced, while Bernadette talked to Laura about her four brothers on their family farm in Derry, and the one who was a priest in Liverpool. Then it was the children's turn. How many rooms were there in the Queen's house in London? Had she ever seen the lady? How many islands were there in Great Britain? And please, could Miss Lora write down her name for them?

A slate and chalk was brought out by the small girl who was only about the age Laura had been when she left Taparua. The circle of faces pressed around her. As she printed the letters a breathless silence fell, broken only by the squeak of the chalk.

Then, very faintly, there came another sound, a low vibrating drone that floated towards them out of the distance. The children were puzzled, scrambling to their feet and staring around them.

'A plane?' Sister Bernadette's eyes were round with disbelief. 'They never come as far over as this.'

'Sounds like it.' Laura's voice sounded calm but her heart was in her mouth. She pointed towards the horizon. 'There it is.'

All eyes followed the moving dot that glinted in the sun. Now it was the size of a bird, losing height and coming in towards the land. Then it was close enough for Laura to be sure. There was only one yellow plane like that, small and shiny as a toy. But was Jack flying it? Or was someone else bringing it over from Nailangi, perhaps with a message?

She didn't really have to ask herself the question. As the aircraft circled over the field, directly above their heads, she had the strangest sensation. It was as if there was an invisible wire connecting her to the figure in the pilot's seat. She could feel a current running between them like electricity.

An arm appeared out of the cockpit window, waving. She caught a glimpse of a face behind goggles and raised her hand high above her head.

'I think it's a friend of mine from Fiji,' she heard herself say conversationally to Sister Bernadette. Inwardly she was aware of rising panic. Jack's arrival out of the blue was the last thing she had expected. She began to prepare herself for the encounter, and then gave up. A rational scenario seemed unlikely.

The children were shrieking with excitement now, running from all directions with people from the village to where the plane had made its landing on the far side of the field. Sister Bernadette ran with them, lifting her skirt above white-stockinged ankles as she tried to get them under control.

But Laura stood where she was. She wanted to see Jack at a distance first to give herself time before they were face to face. For a second the sun flashed on the familiar copper-coloured hair as he swung himself down to the ground. The crowd of children and villagers engulfed him almost completely. Then it was he who had to make the walk over to her, loping across the field with that long stride of his.

'Hello, Laura,' he said quietly. His face was serious.

'Hello, Jack.'

For one absurd moment she thought they were about to shake hands. Then he reached out to take off her hat.

'Can't really see you under that thing.'

He was smiling now as they studied each other. Perhaps beneath the surface he was struggling for composure too.

'I didn't expect you to come out here,' she said. 'How are things at Nailangi?'

'Not too good. It's been a bad time.'

He handed her back her hat. They were aware of Sister Bernadette waiting to be introduced.

'I must apologize for landing without permission,' Jack told her.

Laura saw Bernadette's shyness dissolve at that smile, her green eyes darting up at him under the long black lashes.

'You'd best see Reverend Mother,' she replied demurely.

She turned and began to shoo the children back to the schoolhouse. At the same time Laura could see the other nuns hurrying towards them from the convent verandah, Reverend Mother leading the way. For a moment she and Jack were standing alone.

'I had to come,' he said. 'I felt you deserved an apology.'

'What for?'

'For being such a cynic. Trying to put you off the whole idea of finding your mother alive.'

'It doesn't matter now.'

He shook his head. 'I should have backed you all the way.'

'It was difficult at the time. There were . . .' She hesitated. 'Other complications.'

He frowned.

'There must be something I can do to help now. You're pretty well stranded out here until the next boat.' He was beginning to stammer a little. 'It's all so incredible.' He waited for a second, his eyes searching hers. 'I thought you might need me.'

It was hard to break away from that steady gaze. But Mother Superior was just a few yards away.

'G'day!' she called. There was an abrasive edge to the greeting. 'Didn't think we'd ever have a plane dropping in on us without warning.'

This time Jack was the penitent schoolboy. 'You must forgive me, Reverend Mother. If I've done any damage to your field you must hold me entirely responsible and send me the bill.'

Laura came to the rescue. 'You remember I mentioned the Renfrey family, Reverend Mother? This is Jack Renfrey, a friend of mine. He's come to see if I need a lift back to Fiji. Actually,' she went on, 'I think he wants to see if this long-lost mother of mine really exists.'

Then she remembered.

'The plane! Did she hear it coming down, do you think? If so, she'll be terrified. She has this phobia.'

From the house one of the lay workers was coming towards them. She looked worried.

'Your mother's still in her room. I think she needs you.'

Laura turned to Jack. 'Come with me?'

'Of course.'

As they hurried inside she felt his hand on her arm with a quick, reassuring squeeze. It was something he always did when she was anxious and she was grateful for it.

'Perhaps it's been too much for her,' she said. 'Going over everything again. Harrington's story was a total lie about meeting her in Fiji. He found her washed up on Gardner Island. She was his prisoner for five years and then the Japanese came.' At the bedroom door she said quickly, 'Don't ask her about it now. It's all on the tapes.'

'Laura? Is that you?'

The voice from inside was tremulous. Laura opened the door.

The first sight of her mother shocked her. She was crouched in the corner of the bed, her legs tucked beneath her, as if she was getting as far away from the outside world as she could. Her eyes were staring, her expression fearful.

'I'm so sorry, Laura.' Her voice had sunk to a whisper. 'I'm afraid I've got myself into rather a state.'

Then she caught sight of Jack. Laura could see her making a tremendous effort to regain some kind of self-possession.

'This is Jack Renfrey, Mother. You remember me telling you about him – we met in London a year ago.'

Millie managed a smile, though her face was still very white.

'It was your plane then, Mr Renfrey. You must forgive me. It must have been the war, I think. Just to hear one overhead seems to bring on this stupid panic. Not that we often catch sight of one these days.'

She sat up against the pillows, pushing her fingers through her hair. The unconscious gesture was a shadowy reminder of a once-magnetic charm.

'Well, this one's landed safely, Mrs Harrington,' Jack replied.

They saw her flinch a little. 'Millie, please.'

'I'm not surprised you get panicky remembering those Japanese bombings,' he went on easily.

'Oh, that,' she said, half to herself. 'I was only glad to have got my little girl away before it all started.'

Jack sat down on the bed and took her hand. 'The wonderful thing is that she found her way back to you after all these years.'

'Yes, it is wonderful,' she said huskily. 'It's almost more than I deserve.'

Her eyes rested on them both. Laura thought she saw the shine of unshed tears. 'I'm better now,' Millie went on. 'You mustn't worry about me. It's just sometimes, well – it seems quite a lot to take in.' She looked away, towards the window. 'Where is your plane, now, Jack?'

'Still on the field. But there's an old copra shed nearby. I'll get some of the village people to help me park it inside. It'll be out of the way there, in case the children start playing around with it.' He got up and touched Laura's shoulder lightly. 'See you soon.'

When he'd gone, Laura helped her mother to wash and dress. There was colour in her face again and a touch of some old animation.

'You didn't tell me he was so striking-looking, that young man of yours.'

'He's hardly my young man, Mama. But yes, he is handsome, I suppose.'

'Not exactly handsome,' Millie said consideringly, her head on one side. 'Sex appeal is hard to define, isn't it?'

Laura was startled. She found herself laughing. 'Well, yes.'

But her mother was looking at her coolly, fastening the cord on her robe. 'I imagine that's part of the trouble. That other women find him so attractive.'

'One in particular.' Laura glanced away.

'I wouldn't know about that,' her mother said. 'I only saw the way he was looking at you.'

Laura was tidying the bed. 'He's only here because he feels guilty about leaving me in the lurch. Also, he knows I'm in a hurry to get back to Fiji.'

'Is there such a hurry?' There was a wistful note in Millie's voice.

Laura turned to her. 'Mama, you must understand. Before I do anything else, I have to see Harrington. Face him with the truth. That you are alive and that he has to pay for what he did to you, and to me. Everyone has to know what sort of man he really is.'

Her mother sat down on the little rush chair in front of the chest of drawers. Her face was tense. Laura saw, even after all the years, the look of fear.

'As long as you don't involve me, Laura. I've tried so hard to blot him out of mind. I can't go through all that again.'

Laura crouched down by her and took her hands. 'But don't you feel any anger, any bitterness at all? Just to think of him in that house, the great Dr Harrington writing his books, giving his interviews, making his speeches. While you . . .'

'While I?'

'Have just been broken and thrown away as if you never existed.'

'Don't.'

Laura felt her mother's fingers tighten against hers, so that the nails drove into her skin.

'Don't tell me. Just hearing about his life brings it all back to me. It makes me want to . . .'

Laura looked into her mother's eyes and saw a flash of such hatred there that she shivered.

'You mustn't distress yourself any more,' she said. 'It's all there on the tapes.'

'It's like an infection.' Her mother's voice was so low she had to strain to hear it. 'The man is like a plague. He can still destroy. I have to keep myself hidden away from him. My life is precious to me now, because of you.'

'It's precious to me, too,' Laura said. 'If I do nothing, he'll always have this power over you, over both of us. Remember the worst lie of all? That I am Laura Harrington, his daughter?'

She got up and stood behind her mother, stroking her thin shoulders. 'My father is the man you married. Someone who may still be alive.' She touched the wedding ring on her mother's hand. 'Do you ever think of that?'

'Often. Especially these last few days, looking at you.' The eyes of the two women met in the little mirrorr above the chest. 'That dark hair, those cheekbones, they must be his.' She hesitated. 'There's something in your character too that's different. There's an openness, a drive to make contact, to draw response and make things happen. I've seen it in just these few days.'

'And you?'

Millie sighed. 'Someone who pretended, maybe. Underneath, I was always a loner at heart.'

'This man,' Laura said slowly. 'If I ever found him. If there was some way of knowing what happened to him. Would you change everything for that?'

'I'd go to the ends of the earth for that.' Millie closed her eyes for a moment, as if willing back some tiny fragment of recollection. When she opened them again they were curiously blank. With a swift movement she got to her feet and stood very straight, facing Laura. 'But there is no way of knowing. There never will be. I've given up trying long ago. It's best not to even think of it.'

'You know I have to go away anyway, Mama, don't you? Back to London. Just for a little while.'

'I know that, dearest. My life goes on here. I'm part of the mission furniture, after all this time.'

She looked down at herself ruefully, plucking at the faded brown folds of her smock. When she turned to Laura there was a gleam in her eyes that was almost mischievous.

'You don't suppose I could borrow something of yours to put on? Just for a change. It's so long since I've worn anything different.'

'Of course, I never thought of it,' Laura said eagerly. 'I haven't got much with me, but you're welcome to pick anything you like.'

There was a tap on the door and Jack reappeared. Laura noticed that he'd shaved and changed into a fresh shirt.

'I thought I'd better make myself respectable now I'm under holy orders. Reverend Mother says I may spend the night in the sleep-out. Very nice it is too, just like an old-fashioned English summerhouse.'

'That's where we put the visiting priests,' Millie said teasingly. 'You'd better be careful. It's well and truly haunted by a learned French bishop who used to work there on his Gilbertese translations.'

'You got the plane put away?' Laura asked.

Jack nodded. 'And now the people from the village want us to go to a welcome party at the maneapa. The usual song-and-dance affair for distinguished visitors. That includes you, of course.'

Laura looked doubtful. 'Perhaps not, Jack. My mother and I . . .'

But Millie interrupted. She must go. Gilbertese dancing was famous and the people would be offended if Laura didn't accept the invitation.

'Come on, Laura,' Jack said. 'They'll be waiting for us.'

The brief Pacific dusk was already dissolving into darkness as they made their way towards the lights of the village.

A young man had come to lead them there with a lantern, chattering as they went in his careful mission English. Even though he was walking between them, Laura had a heightened awareness of Jack's physical presence. As they crossed the path to the first houses she felt his shoulder brush against hers. The current was still there, powerful and unmistakable, fixing everything that happened that evening indelibly on her mind.

They could hear the drumming from a hundred yards away, a swift, pulsing throb that came from the meeting-house at the end of the village. Their guide began to hurry, and they hurried too. They heard an old man's voice, high-pitched like the call of a muezzin.

'He is calling any people still in their houses,' the young man told them. 'Then the dancing will begin.'

Under the long thatched roof of the maneapa a crowd of onlookers sat silent and waiting in the amber glow of the lanterns strung from the beams. The dancers also waited, men and women in two separate rows, brilliant in their finery of flower garlands and leafy skirts. The air was heavy with the scent of coconut oil and frangipani, and the sweat of suspense.

Laura and Jack were shown to the two upright chairs placed in their honour at the front. But Jack explained they would prefer to sit with the elders on their mats. There were the usual speeches of welcome. Then a stout master of ceremonies beat out a brisk tattoo on the long wooden drum across his knees.

There was a rustling sound like the onset of a tropical storm and the dancers were on their feet. The chanting and the drumming had all at once transformed them into a corps de ballet, arms weaving, bodies swinging, hands gesticulating to the thudding rhythms and counter-rhythms. Their faces shone with concentration as the story took hold of them. Teeth gleamed, eyes flashed. Fat girls had become beautiful and haggard men leapt and spun with the grace of fauns. As she sat watching, Laura felt that tingling of the blood that Stevenson had described when he and his wife saw just such a dance a hundred years ago.

She turned to Jack. There was no need for words. Their glance exchanged the same message of delight. An old man was dancing now, alone. There was a sense of the sacred in those stiff, hierarchical poses, as the refrain around him rose and fell hypnotically and the people watched entranced.

Then the mood lightened. The women began a warbling song, softly suggestive like the cooing of doves. A handsome young man began a pas-de-deux with one of the prettiest girls, circling one another, hips rolling, but never touching.

'This is the Polynesian style,' Jack murmured. 'Something different.'

The others joined in and the next minute Jack himself was pulled to his feet by one of the older women, plump and wickedly smiling as she lured him into the centre of the circle.

Oh God, Laura thought. She bent her head. She had seen Europeans attempt this kind of thing before and cringed.

But she had forgotten Jack's Tongan blood. An admiring silence fell. When she looked up she saw a different Jack. He had slipped off his shoes and was moving with his partner to the manner born, indifferent to the audience. Completely absorbed in the spell of the dance, together they generated a rising charge of excitement. Soon the other dancers were urging him on, clapping faster against the beat, voices soaring to an ecstatic pitch. Jack was smiling now, head flung back and eyes half-closed, his arms outstretched, legs flexed apart in the stealthy, almost catlike movements of the man's part.

Watching him, Laura felt her heart turn over. The way he danced had a raptness about it that reminded her, so very sharply, of the way he made love. In that instant he was holding her fast, moving against her in the water, willing her to lose herself in that final oblivion.

Damn you, Jack Renfrey, she said to herself.

The crescendo of sound rose and broke. To wild applause, the dancers retreated into the shadows. Jack was at her side again, panting slightly.

'Sorry about that,' he said under his breath. 'Couldn't very well refuse.'

She moved away from him slightly. 'You're very good at it.'

The closing speeches were made, and then it was time for the exchange of gifts. Jack had brought bundles of stick tobacco for the men. Laura got up and sprinkled highly-scented talcum powder from the store over the bare shoulders of the women. On an impulse she tied the silk scarf she was wearing around the neck of Jack's partner and received her garland in return.

'Your man can dance,' the woman told her approvingly. The broad grin revealed a number of missing teeth, though she was probably no more than thirty.

Laura's mind was on the walk back to the convent. This time they were to be alone.

'We know the way now,' Jack had said, taking the lantern as they made their farewells.

Outside the maneapa the shapes of other couples detached themselves from the stream of departing villagers. The talk faded away amidst the snatches of laughter. The lane stretched ahead, powdery white in the starlight. Someone on a bicycle went weaving past them, singing softly to himself, still wearing his coronet of gardenias.

The village houses were open-sided and as they walked along Laura could see figures preparing for sleep, shrouded in mosquito nets. The life of the village was following its unchanging pattern so familiar to her mother, so strange to herself, the outsider who was already preparing to leave again.

'What time do you plan to take off tomorrow?' she heard herself ask Jack, almost harshly.

'Quite early, if that's all right,' he said in an offhand way. 'I have to be back at Nailangi by lunchtime. The insurance people are coming to assess the damage. Agricultural inspectors and so on.'

'It must be a relief to your father to have you there.'

'He's certainly been a bit shattered by it all.'

At the end of the lane, he turned to her and said in a different voice, 'I'd have come back from Australia anyway. Even if there'd been no hurricane.'

'Would you?' She tried her best to sound neutral.

'I want to help you sort things out with that bastard Harrington, for a start. You know that.'

'He's not my real father, by the way. But you'll hear all that on the tapes.'

'God, Laura!' He stopped and looked at her, trying to see her expression. 'Then who is?'

'That's something I have to find out.'

She heard him catch his breath. 'So much has happened to your life. I should have been with you. It was wrong to let you go on alone.'

'I wasn't alone,' she reminded him. 'Charlie brought me over, remember?'

'Oh yes, Charlie.' Abruptly he began to walk on, slightly ahead of her along the narrow path through the bush. 'And then there was Ratu Edwin. I gather from what my father tells me that he's been especially helpful.'

'I could never have made it without him. He's someone I trust completely.'

There was an edge to this remark she hadn't intended.

'That's not altogether fair, is it?' He flung the words over his shoulder. 'I did have a job at Canberra to go to. Also, you were supposed to come with me. Or had you forgotten?'

'I expect Kim made up for that.'

The moment she said it, she felt regret. This conversation was turning into something cheap, not worthy of either of them.

'Can we leave Kim out of it?' he said coldly. 'That's something else.'

'And the job?'

He shrugged his shoulders. 'That's something else too.'

He fell into one of his silences. She walked at his heels, keeping up with the pool of light from the lantern. They were not far from the convent now, she could see the white shape of it against the sky. The roll and hiss of the surf were clearer too, but the sea itself was still screened by the thickets of palm and fern.

At one point she stumbled slightly where the path took a sudden turn through the undergrowth. He stopped and held up the lamp for her to see. 'Be careful.'

They were standing beneath some tall mango trees, a few yards from the mission gates. The fruit was almost ripe, giving off the strange, tarry fragrance that for Laura would always be linked to this particular turning-point in her life. The lamplight had aroused a fluttering in the branches overhead. There was a clapping of wings that was almost violent in the dark stillness. Taken unawares, Laura gasped. Jack put down the lamp and pulled her to him.

'Still frightened of fruit-bats, then?' His voice had a mocking tenderness.

'Not really.' She took a deep breath. 'Please let go of me, Jack.'

He continued to hold her, his arms wrapped close around her, his face against hers. Their bodies seemed to have come together in a familiar, casual way that had nothing to do with her intentions. In the same way, as he kissed her, she opened her mouth to his hungrily. She drew back to say his name, this time in a whisper, as if it was hard to believe.

'So you do remember who I am.' Jack cupped his hands round her face. 'Who we both are, you and I. What we've been to each other, right from the start.'

'Everything's different now.'

'Everything except we two.'

The lamp at their feet threw his features into vivid relief. His eyes were shadowy sockets, pupils gleaming beneath that well-remembered, impatient frown. He took her by the shoulders, shook her gently and would have kissed her again. But both of them heard someone calling.

'Sir! Sir!'

A small boy was running through the gates towards them.

'What is it?' Jack put his hand out to the child. 'Who are you?'

'Watchboy, sir. I look out by the gate at night.' His face was wrinkled in distress as he pointed across the field where Jack's plane had come down, to the copra shed beyond. 'That place where the airship stay, I just see one person go into that place, sir. I come straight way to find you.'

'You did well,' Jack said. 'Probably only someone from the village taking a closer look,' he added to Laura as they made their way quickly across the field. 'As long as he's not fiddling around with my fuel tanks.'

The boy trotted at their side. Getting closer, they could see a chink of light coming from inside the shed, which loomed up ahead almost the size of a small hangar. One of the tall double doors stood a little ajar. Inside there was the flicker of an oil lamp.

Jack ran the last few yards. 'Anyone in there?' he called.

There was no reply. At the door, he stepped inside and looked round warily. Laura was just behind him.

'The plane's okay. Can't see a soul.'

But someone had carefully hung a lantern on a nail in the wall. The wings of the plane threw huge shadows up to the iron roof and over the piled-up sacks of copra at the back. The air was thick with the musky smell of dried coconuts.

Standing quite still, Laura heard a rustling sound. 'Rats,' she said. Instinctively she stepped back.

Jack had gone round to the far end of the plane, peering into the half-light as he went.

'Hello?' she heard him say. 'Who's that?'

As she followed him round, Laura thought her heart would stop beating. The slender figure in the borrowed slacks and shirt on top of the cockpit steps was familiar yet unrecognizable. Then Laura remembered Harrington's snapshot of the young woman in trousers.

Her mother was sitting in just the same pose, her arms wrapped round her knees, her head cocked to one side. Laura could see there was no fear on her face, only a kind of radiance. She didn't seem to know they were there. It was as if she were listening to some voice inside her head.

'Be careful,' Laura whispered to Jack.

He stepped forward out of the shadows. 'So you decided to take a look at it after all,' he said in a soft voice.

Millie turned round to them almost dreamily.

'I knew they'd be looking for me,' she said. 'But you didn't tell me it was my plane they were sending.'

'Your plane, Mama?' Laura slowly approached her mother.

'My little yellow plane,' Millie replied with a touch of impatience. 'The first one I ever had.'

'Tell us more,' Jack said. He motioned to Laura to stay where she was as he went over and leaned against the wing. He looked up at Millie calmly. 'What happened after we'd gone?'

Millie closed her eyes tightly, as if trying to knit together two separate strands of thought. Opening them again, she said, 'It was quite simple. I had supper with the others. Then back in my room I got to thinking about the plane, here in the shed like you said. It was so close. Why be frightened of it, I said to myself? Now it's safe on the ground, it'll be all right. I had to come and see for myself.'

With a sudden movement she stood up. She seemed to sway a little. Quickly Jack reached up to her. But she turned away, not looking at them any more but at the plane itself.

'It was as though it was pulling me here. Something was going to happen, something I already knew, as though time was turned inside out. I wasn't in control. Like sleepwalking, maybe.' She placed the palms of her hands against the casing of the fuselage, as if caressing it. They saw her shaking a little. 'But this is for real all right,' they heard her whisper.

There was a coating of dust where the sand had blown against the damp surface of the bodywork. Quickly, with her forefinger, Millie traced some letters. She turned with a little grin of triumph.

'That's what I always wrote for them when I came down.' All at once she slumped forward a little. Her hands went up to her head.

'Oh, what a pain,' she said in a wondering way.

Jack caught her as she fell. Her eyes were closed. She felt as light as a leaf as they lifted her between them on to some sacking. Laura knelt beside her, cradling her head in her lap and loosening her clothing. Millie was breathing in a strangely irregular way. Was she still smiling, or was it some sideways quirk of the muscles around her mouth?

'Could be a stroke,' Jack muttered. He turned to the boy. 'Run quickly to Reverend Mother. Tell her to get a stretcher.'

Above their heads, the lamp picked out the tracing in the dust. Just two words, a name roughly scrawled. 'Amelia Earhart.'

Laura read it out half to herself, trying to grasp the reality of it. She stared across at Jack. Then, bending over her mother, she repeated the name urgently, as if she was calling her back from some unreachable place of darkness and danger.

But the woman lying between them did not stir. Very lightly, Jack touched the pulse in her throat.

'For God's sake don't die on us now, Amelia,' he whispered.

CHAPTER TWO

Some instinct made Laura wary when, back at the convent, Reverend Mother wanted to know what exactly had happened.

'Going out to the plane in the middle of the night! What on earth possessed her? Did she tell you?'

'Not really,' Laura said. 'I think it was sleepwalking. She must have been overexcited by all that's happened the last few days.'

They were speaking in whispers, one on either side of the bed where Millie lay. Her breathing was quiet now and her expression calm. Sister Clarissa, who was a trained nurse, had declared it to be a slight stroke. A sedative injection had produced what seemed to be normal sleep. In the morning they would be better able to see how she might have been affected.

'Jack will take her by plane to Tarawa if she needs to see a doctor,' Laura said. 'He'll help in any way he can.'

Even at this moment she missed his presence. The crisis over, he'd gone to his quarters, taking the tapes and machine with him.

'I won't be able to sleep anyway,' he told her. 'And I need to know exactly what she told you, just to try and make sense of it all.'

In her own mind too, Laura was struggling to absorb the meaning of that extraordinary moment of recall by the plane. Was it the opening of the floodgates, or no more than a freak trigger of the mind?

She was suddenly aware of how exhausted she was. But nothing would make her leave her mother's bedside.

'Please don't stay any longer,' she told Reverend Mother. 'I'll stay with her. I'll put my mattress on the floor next to her.'

'If you're sure.' She got up and to Laura's surprise kissed her briskly as she left. 'You're a good daughter, Laura. Your mother's a lucky woman.'

Lucky, Laura thought, as she lay down at Millie's side. Is that how the world would see her, this mysterious survivor from aviation history? Her journalist's memory was racing, turning over a mental card index. Amelia Earhart. The name was clearly stamped, but the details were blurred, a vague mix of the kind of newspaper references that kept cropping up about famous women fliers of the twenties and thirties. Earhart had crashed over the Pacific and never been heard of again. She remembered that much.

And was this really her? Moving the candle closer Laura turned to study the woman on the bed, the person she called simply Mama, or Millie. Fame made her a stranger in a way, someone Laura would have regarded with awe. But what if the whole thing was a delusion, a stray image thrown up by a mind that was fragmented beyond mending?

Her mother's face was a mask. Laura imagined the brain behind it fighting its way back to the chink of light that had broken through the darkness. Blowing out the candle, she pulled up the sheet and fell into an uneasy sleep.

Around dawn, she felt her mother's hand reach out for hers. In the pale glow from the window, she saw that Millie's eyes were open and that she was trying to smile.

'It's happening, you know,' she whispered. 'It truly is.'

Laura sat up. Gently she stroked her mother's arm. 'What's happening, darling?'

'The past is coming back. Not just the name, but everything else.' The voice was slurred but understandable. She turned to Laura urgently. 'It is *my* past, you know, not somebody else's.'

It was as if her mother was claiming a piece of lost luggage at a railway station. Laura felt a lump in her throat.

'I know it is. But try to go slowly.'

'I thought it was a dream at first. But now I'm awake, I know it's real.' She gave a shaky little laugh. 'It's going on now. Frightening. And painful. A bit like having a baby.'

Laura sat on the bed beside her, holding her close. 'What are you remembering? Can you tell me?'

'It's hard to keep up with the pictures. They come and go so fast. Back in the shed, I was remembering the flying, my little yellow plane and all the others. But now I'm right back at the beginning. There's this little girl, myself, always wanting to do something dangerous, horseback riding, jumping fences I wasn't supposed to at my grandmother's place. She was the one who called me Millie. Coasting downhill on a sled on my stomach, far too fast, ending up between a horse's legs. Shooting rats in the barn. There are quiet bits, too. Like reading in my grandfather's library, leather bindings that smelt wonderful.'

Laura settled her back against the pillows and drew a shawl over her shoulders.

'What about the rest of the family?'

'There's my mother, who loves me so much. And a sister we call Pidge.' She closed her eyes for a moment, frowning. 'My father, looking for the whisky bottles we tried to hide. Moving house. Kansas, Des Moines, Chicago. Then high school. There was a class photograph. I see it clearly. Underneath my photograph someone wrote, "The girl in brown who walks alone".'

Now Laura was caught up with her in this pursuit of the past. 'The flying, Mama? How did the flying begin? Is there a picture there?'

But she was too impatient. Her mother shook her head.

'Not yet, not yet. There was the war, wasn't there? The First World War. Soldiers sent home, walking wounded at Toronto. There's a military hospital and I'm scrubbing floors, washing bedpans.'

Her face lit up again. 'Yes, of course. That was when I saw planes close up, when the officers were training.' She was straining to catch at that long-ago excitement. 'The planes took off on skis. The snow was blown back from the propellers. I felt the sting of it on my face, the thrill of the takeoff. I knew I had to go up myself one day. There was an air circus at Los Angeles. You paid for a ride. As soon as we left the ground, my heart was flying too. We called it "going upstairs". Did you know that? Isn't that quaint? But I knew it would be my life.'

'And the family?' Laura prompted. 'What did they say?'

Her mother hardly heard. 'It was a bug, you see, a craze. Lots of people got it. The girls that flew were called all sorts of things. Ladybirds. Angels. Flying Flappers. But I was serious. I worked to get money for lessons with some company. What was it? A telephone company, that's right.'

Her voice was quickening now, her eyes searching ahead of her for the next pictures. Laura was afraid she would collapse again.

'Don't hurry it,' she said soothingly. 'There's all the time in the world.'

Millie shook her head. 'Maybe not, Laura. I want to tell it fast, so that you'll remember too. It's the little things that bring it back. Oil on my hands, from the engines. And the smell of my first flying suit. I tried to make the leather look old, rubbing dust into it.' She smiled to herself. 'My hair was a problem. I cut it secretly, week by week, so no one would notice. But it was the helmet and the goggles that really changed you. Your face got burned up there in the open cockpit, and you ended up with great white rings round your eyes – just like those horny toads we used to keep as children.'

'Weren't you ever frightened?' Laura whispered. They were both talking in undertones lest they should be overheard and disturbed. 'Does that come back to you at all?'

'It was a drug.' Her mother's face quivered. Laura could glimpse in her expression the faint reflection of ecstasy. 'To be alone up there in that huge solitude. On the long flights you looked down on deserts and seas like a bird. Clouds like icebergs. Mirages at sunset . . .'

She turned to Laura. 'I flew the world, you know.' There was youthful pride in her voice. 'I broke all the records. But the publicity, the interviews, the crowds – George took care of all that.'

'George?' Laura seized on the name, every sense alert.

'My husband.'

It was said in such a matter-of-fact way that Laura could hardly believe what she had heard. She felt her heart race. Suddenly Millie's face crumpled. It was the first time she had cried since she'd come round. Holding her head in her hands, she began rocking to and fro against the pillows, the sobs shaking her whole body.

'Where are you?' Laura heard her whisper. She caught her breath. 'Why didn't you come looking for me?'

Laura was struggling with her own tears. It was her father Millie was talking to.

'George?' She was waiting for the other name, scarcely daring to hope.

But her mother was drifting away again. 'I can't – just George.'

'Was he a flier too?'

Through her tears, her mother gave a little laugh. 'Only with words. George was business, big business. He ran my life. He almost invented me.' She reached for Laura's hand. 'I nearly didn't marry him, you know. I wanted my freedom. But he had such charm, such persistence.'

Laura pressed her mother's hand. She was on the edge of it now.

'That last flight,' she said softly. 'Did he arrange that too?'

'He wanted me to do it solo. The last leg, anyway. Said it would make a better story.' She had become very pale as the words came jerking out. 'But I knew I'd never do it without Fred. Even then . . .'

Her voice tailed off. She was staring straight ahead, at the window. Sunrise was just breaking through.

'I was so tired. I felt so sick. Maybe I got careless. The radio contact, that side of it.' She buried her face in her hands. 'But how could I miss it?'

'Miss it?' Laura felt fear. To have brought Millie to this point could have been a terrible mistake.

'Howland Island. It must have been so near. Then it was too late. Time ran out, fuel ran out. I had to go down. Down, down, down.'

With a sudden movement she flung herself out of the bed and ran to the window. The sight of her long thin legs beneath the nightgown struck pity into Laura's heart more than anything else. Before Laura could stop her, Millie was beating at the pane with the palms of her hands.

'Glass all around us, trapping us in. I caught hold of Fred, but I knew he was dead already.' She turned to Laura, clutching at her. 'There was so much blood.'

But Laura had hold of her and was drawing her back to the bed. 'Hush now, hush darling. All that's over a long time ago.'

Her mother's eyes were closed.

'But how did I do it?' she whispered between dry lips. 'How did I get the strength to pull myself out onto that reef? Then Harrington . . .' She shuddered. Laura saw a single last tear roll from one closed eyelid. She had to lean forward to catch the words.

'Dear Fred. I'm so sorry.'

Her head was turning from one side to the other on the pillow. Laura reached for the rest of the sleeping draught left on the bedside table. Gently she brought the glass to her mother's mouth.

'Just a sip,' she told her. 'It will help.'

Obediently her mother drank. For a moment her eyes were wide open, staring up at Laura.

'Say nothing to the sisters,' she whispered. 'Not yet.'

'Of course not,' Laura replied softly. 'You need time. We all do.'

Millie turned her head away again. She was breathing more quietly, and soon Laura saw that she slept.

'How exactly did she describe it?' Jack asked over his shoulder. 'The last part, when she came down?'

Sitting behind him in the plane, Laura found conversation difficult. For a moment or two she tried to reply, but the noise and vibration made it too tiring to go on.

Even before they took off, there had been little chance of talking alone, apart from a few minutes together on the verandah. Leaving her mother to sleep, Laura had been far too restless to return to her room. Instead, she had slipped outside for fresh air. There she'd found him, perched on the verandah rail with his knees drawn up in front of him, his head tilted back against the wall. She was instantly reminded of their first meeting in Fiji, when she had come upon him relaxed as a cat on the terrace outside her hotel room.

He hadn't seen her and she stood for a moment without speaking. The early morning air struck cool against her skin under the thin dressing gown. She wanted to go over and lean against him, feel his arms around her. But people were already beginning to move around the compound. He turned his head.

'Laura,' he said quietly. 'You must be exhausted.'

He got up and they stood against the rail side by side. He hadn't slept either, he told her. He'd listened to the tapes, magnetized, unable to switch off the machine. All the time he'd been matching in his mind the bizarre sequence of events on Taparua with the revelation of Millie's identity.

'It all fits in,' he said in a low voice. 'I wasn't born at the time, but in the forties I remember people on the islands still talked about it – the Earhart disaster. How could the plane have just vanished into thin air? I was only a small boy but I collected model planes. This woman pilot became one of my heroines. Your mother. It's incredible.'

Laura was aware that he was looking at her differently somehow, as if she was someone else.

'You do realize,' he went on, 'what this news will mean to the rest of the world?'

'And you realize, don't you, that it can't be told to the world until she's ready for it?'

Jack looked irritated. 'Do you think I'm stupid? Do you think I'd breathe a word to anyone while she's in her present state?' He shook his head. 'The extraordinary thing is how close to the surface her memory was at times. Remember the electric fan? At the back of her mind she was seeing a propeller, but she just couldn't make the connection. There must have been so many moments like that.'

'So what do we do next?'

'You have to read up everything you can about Earhart. Family, husband and so on.'

'My father,' Laura said quietly. 'I have his first name from her. A few things about him she remembers.'

Jack touched her hand. 'He may still be alive.'

'I know.'

'And then we get Harrington.'

'Do you think he knew all along who she was?'

'I'm certain of it. Government officers were alerted on every island.'

Packing her things after breakfast, a sense of outrage had seethed through her again. But she was careful to conceal it when they went in to say goodbye to her mother. It would do little good to stir up the hatred she had seen in her mother's eyes the day before. This morning her condition was better, Sister Clarissa reported. All she needed now was complete rest.

Propped up on her pillows, Millie leaned forward to kiss her, smiling. She looked fragile but mysteriously younger, Laura thought, refreshed as if she had been away on a visit. She sat down on the bed, holding Millie's hands.

'I'll be back again after Christmas. I'll be flying to London in a day or two. But there's something I have to see to in Suva first.' She hesitated. 'Something we talked about yesterday.'

She saw her mother look at her intently. 'Jack will be with you?'

Laura wrapped her arms tightly around her. She could feel her mother tremble.

'Don't worry. Jack will be with me.'

'That's all right then,' she heard her murmur, half to herself.

Gently Laura released her and got up to make way for Jack. Millie took his hand as he bent to kiss her.

'Perhaps next time you'll let me take you flying,' he said with a conspiratorial smile. Laura saw her mother's face light up.

'It would be the most tremendous thrill.'

'Now now, Millie,' Reverend Mother put in from the doorway. 'One thing at a time. You must get yourself well first.'

Laura turned to take one last look at the woman on the bed. The wrench of leaving her was a fierce physical pain. She raised her hand. 'Goodbye, Mama. I'm thinking about you always.'

Then she was hurrying away down the passage and out through the verandah. Reverend Mother was waiting for her.

'Can I keep in touch with you from Fiji?' Laura asked her as they walked across the field together. The plane had been pushed out and was standing ready for takeoff.

'Broadcasting House could probably fix up a link with the radio station here. You may need to arrange a time beforehand.'

'I'll do that. I'd like to check things before leaving for London. And thank you for everything, Reverend Mother. Not least for taking care of my mother.' The two smiled at one another with affection.

'Where's Jack?'

Looking around, they saw him running after them from the house.

'Your mother called me back,' he told Laura. 'Something she'd forgotten.'

Laura was remembering that incident now as they flew steadily on towards Fiji. The mission buildings and the tiny waving figures had been left far behind.

'What was it she wanted?' she asked Jack.

'Tell you later.'

He nodded down towards the shimmering expanse of blue. Far below a solitary atoll drifted by like a leaf on the tide. Ahead of them, unrolling endlessly, there was only sea and sky.

'Makes you feel like God, doesn't it?' He smiled round at her, his face alight. 'Doing his Creation bit.'

Laura felt the same rush of pure happiness. Flight itself was a miracle, she thought, remembering her mother's words. Sunlight poured into the little cabin, enclosing them in a bubble of gold that was almost too bright to bear. For that moment she and Jack were the only two people in the world, their Pacific world of secret landfalls and lost horizons.

Without speaking, Jack reached for her hand. He held it very tight. Leaning forward, she could feel the warmth of his back under the leather jacket, her head close to his.

They were flying lower now.

'Look! Quickly!' He pointed to where the surface of the sea was broken by a trail of foam. A shape broke out of it, an arc that flashed in the sun and was gone again. Another followed, and yet more.

Laura caught her breath. 'Dolphins!'

Then the surface closed over again. That secret life had returned to its own element. Now the only moving thing was the shadow of the little plane skimming the water like a butterfly, always just ahead of them as if pointing the way.

Over the skyline, Fiji came into view. This side of the island group had virtually escaped the hurricane, Jack told her. It was Vanua Levu, to the northwest, that had taken the full brunt of it. Viti Levu, the main island, appeared below them lush and unscarred, the white bays and beaches looping away beneath the purple shadows of the mountain forests, a lonely village in the distance and figures fishing in the shallows.

'Can it stay like this?' Laura said, almost to herself. 'So idyllic and unchanged?'

'Everything changes,' Jack replied. 'Even in the islands.'

Even as they looked, paradise was giving way to townships, sprawling suburbs and tourist blocks, and the concrete desert of the airport. They were coming down on it, rolling along one of the private runways, and as they did so Laura felt euphoria drain away. Rain clouds hung low. Coming down to earth was the most apt of metaphors. Countless anxieties crowded her mind again. So much was unresolved. So many possible outcomes would depend on her willpower and judgement. And overshadowing everything else was the inevitable confrontation with Harrington.

'I have to fly straight on to Nailangi, I'm afraid,' Jack was telling her as they climbed out and stood together on the wet tarmac. 'I don't have any alternative. There's this meeting with the assessors and my father will be waiting for me.' He looked around at the windswept gardens. 'Still a bit stormy, even here. It's the time of the year, of course.'

'When will you be back in Suva?' Laura was checking the baggage at her feet.

'Tomorrow at the latest. But Laura . . .' He took her arm. 'You mustn't do anything with Harrington until then. We'll go out to Suva Point together. You promise?'

She nodded, trying to collect her thoughts. The air of Suva, stifling and clammy at the same time, made clear thinking difficult.

'So I'll see you at Vailima around midday,' he went on.

'Vailima?'

'That's where you'll be, isn't it?'

She shook her head. 'I don't think so, Jack. I think I should book in at the Grand Pacific.'

He raised his eyebrows, taken off-guard. But this time she was certain. She had to be independent, her mind free and making her own decisions.

'I have to go to Broadcasting House, for a start. There'll be messages from the BBC. I have to get my programme material sorted out. And something else, too.'

'Something else?' Jack's voice was cold.

'Finding out about Millie – Amelia. They're bound to have reference files, newspaper cuttings, that kind of thing.' She broke off. 'About my father. It matters to her almost more than anything else.'

'Of course.' He beckoned over one of the airport workers. 'Can you take the lady's luggage? Get her a taxi to go to the GPH?'

He turned back to her, his expression carefully controlled. Quickly he reached out and ruffled her hair, something that brought back their first meetings in London.

'I'll see you at the hotel. Tomorrow.'

'Give my love to your father,' she said as he walked away. 'And Auntie Atu.'

He raised his hand, half-turning his head as he strode back to the plane. Watching him, a picture of him hurrying through the rain in the Strand came back to her, Jack through a wet taxi window, his yellow scarf blowing behind him, his hair flopping over his forehead. Goodbyes were what they seemed best at, she thought as she climbed into the waiting car.

On an impulse, she asked the driver to take her straight to

Broadcasting House. She could ring from there to book a room at the hotel.

She knew it was the right decision as soon as she walked into the foyer. At the desk, flanked by vases of red and yellow hibiscus, the wide smile of the Fijian receptionist was immediately reassuring.

'Miss Harrington! Gee, good to see you back!'

While the bags were stacked behind the counter, she handed Laura a letter. 'BBC. Says urgent.'

'Oh dear. I expect I'm in trouble.'

Laura sat down to read it in a quiet corner of the foyer. As she thought, her producer was panicking. He had given up trying to make contact on the phone. The programme had to be ready for transmission in a fortnight. Could she be back with the tapes by the end of the week and have some edits done by then and a draft script? Please cable back by return, the letter ended.

She went back to the desk with it.

'Could you be an angel and do that for me? Cable my producer just to say I'll be back in three days at the most and all is in hand?'

'Sure. Charge it to us?'

'Please.' She was running out of cash. Jack had offered her some money but she preferred to use her remaining traveller's cheques, just as soon as she could get to a bank. 'Oh, and could you possibly book me into the GPH?'

'Just the night?'

'Best leave it open.' She fished into her somewhat battered briefcase. 'Now I have to find Bob Curtis. Can you tell me where he is?'

The session with Bob in the control studio was curiously calming. For the next half hour Laura concentrated her mind on the cuts and cues of her recordings, interviews and impressions she'd almost forgotten about during the last week. Only when he asked about her mother did she have to check herself. She couldn't afford to risk any word of that meeting on Abaiang leaking out before she had seen Harrington.

'Did you pick up any traces of her?' Bob prompted. His round brown face was eager, black eyes sparkling. 'Did anyone hear that broadcast and get in touch with you?'

'I did pick up traces,' she said slowly. 'But things are a bit hush-hush at the moment, Bob.'

He nodded, seeing she didn't want to be pressed any further.

'I promise you'll be the first to know when anything develops.'

'Something to do with the war, I suppose?'

'It looks like it.'

'Bloody Japs,' he said, obviously satisfied. 'And now they're all over the place.'

All the time Laura was thinking impatiently of the hunt that lay ahead of her.

'What kind of information system do you have here?' she asked casually, when they had finished work on the tapes. 'Newspaper cuttings and so on?'

'What are you looking for?'

'Anything about the pre-war period in the Pacific. Background material about the heyday of Empire, contrasts with the present, that kind of thing.'

'I'll show you.'

The room where he left her was a small packed annexe in the basement, next to the news office. A solitary reporter sat hunched over an ancient file of the *Fiji Times*.

'Do you keep any overseas papers?' Laura asked him.

'A few. But only back to the 1950s.'

Seeing her look of disappointment, he pointed to the filing cabinets against the wall.

'The older cuttings are in there. Obits and all that.'

There was a dog-eared card index inside each drawer. Running her fingers too fast over the E section, she found she'd passed from 'Early Archaeology' to 'Easter Island' and had to start again. Suddenly there it was, the magic heading: 'Earhart Amelia, American aviator'.

Her hands were shaking as she extracted the file and sat down with it at the nearest table. Inside were about a dozen crumpled clippings, all dating back to the late 1920s and 1930s. The print was smudged and difficult to read. But it was the photograph that jumped out at her. A slender young woman in a flying suit sat perched on the wing of an early plane. The goggles, pushed back against the short blonde hair, framed a boyish face. In the wide-apart eyes and snub nose Laura could clearly see her mother's features of thirty-odd years later.

She felt a shiver of exhilaration at the back of her neck as she jumped from one report to another. It was 1928 and Earhart was 'First Woman to Fly Atlantic', making the crossing with the crew of the famous 'Friendship' flight. Four years later and she was doing it solo, crash-landing in a field in Ireland. In between she'd created a sensation by flying single-handed across America, then breaking the speed record in something called the Women's Air Derby. In 1935 it was 'Earhart Conquers Pacific' with a non-stop flight from Hawaii to the mainland.

The excitement behind the faded lines caught Laura's imagination.

All over the world it was the era of aviation mania and Amelia, it seemed, was its heroine, an international star. There were accounts of her meetings with the Pope, Mussolini, the King and Queen of Belgium. In England, she visited the Astors at Cliveden, danced with the Prince of Wales and signed a plate-glass window with a diamond-tipped pen at Selfridge's, where her plane was on display to the adoring crowds.

There was a separate batch of clippings about the final flight. Laura found it hard to control her emotions at the headlines that now stared up at her.

'Earhart Down At Sea'
'Disaster Ends Flight'
'Fliers Lost In Mid-Pacific, Gasoline Runs Out'

Here were the stories of the search by ship and plane that was sponsored by President Roosevelt, 'costing an estimated four million dollars and covering twenty-five thousand square miles of ocean'. Here was the line about the false radio signals, buoying up hopes that somewhere the plane was still afloat, maybe not far from the elusive Howland Island.

Then gradually it became evident that the world had given up on Amelia. There were the usual public eulogies, including one from Eleanor Roosevelt, a personal friend. From a sequence of later reports came the post-mortems and the theories. The searches had been made in the wrong area. Amelia had been a secret spy for the American government. She had been taken prisoner by the Japanese, kept hidden in a Saipan jail . . .

At last Laura came upon the name she had been looking for: George Putnam, Amelia's husband. To see it in print was a moment she knew she would never forget. But the references were sparse, mostly connected with his family publishing firm. There was mention of the money he'd raised to fund Earhart's flights, his brilliance as an entrepreneur on her behalf. 'Lady Lindy' he'd christened her, drawing on her likeness to the most famous aviator of all, Charles Lindbergh, to set the seal on her achievements. There was one interview with him after the crash, describing his desperate efforts to organize the searches and his grief at his failure.

That was all. The cuttings petered out with no word as to what had happened to him afterwards.

The frustration Laura felt produced a sigh that was louder than she had intended. The spectacled young man looked up from the table opposite.

'Having problems?'

'An American publisher called Putnam. I need some biographical details.'

He pointed to the shelves of reference books in the corner. 'There's an international directory of publishers and writers somewhere there. Might help.'

Of course. Why hadn't she thought of it? Jumping up, she went across to the row of dusty volumes. After a while she found the one she wanted, and turned the pages slowly this time.

At first she refused to believe the name wasn't there. Finally, in the appendix, she found the explanation.

'George Palmer Putnam. Publisher, writer, entrepreneur. Born New York 1887. Died 4 January 1950.'

She sat looking at the bald entry. Had he lived he would now be in his early eighties. She wondered why the sense of loss she felt was so painful. She had never known this man who was her father. Yet she felt his presence in her. Now she understood that restless, compulsive edge to her nature that was so hard to subdue. It was almost as if he himself had known about her search for Amelia and had driven her to complete it. More than anything, she longed to see his face in a photograph. But that would have to wait until there was time to explore the books and the biographies that must exist about the two of them, and perhaps find out about any family that might still be alive.

Now she was thinking about that other man, the psychopath who had cheated Putnam not only of the chance of finding his wife, but of giving her back her identity. The years had gone by and then it was too late, something Amelia had known instinctively as she retreated into the anonymity of mission life.

Abruptly Laura stood up and pushed back the chair.

'Any luck?' asked the young man.

'Sort of. Thanks for your help. Just one more thing. Is it possible to put through a radio-telephone call to the Gilberts from here?'

'Weather and Shipping should be able to help. The office next door. Might take a while to get through.'

In fact, it took no time at all. The Indian clerk at the switchboard told her there was a line to Abaiang already open. The operator at the wireless station would put her through to the mission in just a couple of minutes.

Laura could hardly believe it was the voice of Reverend Mother coming through the headphones, faint but clear. She sounded surprised. She had not expected to get a call so soon. There was no need for Laura to worry about her mother. She felt strong enough to get up and was taking a little walk on the beach with one of the sisters.

'There's a message I want you to give her, Reverend Mother.' Laura spoke slowly. 'Something I've just found out that I think she should know.'

'Yes?' The voice was a little wary.

'Just tell her that George died, twenty years ago.' She paused. 'That's her husband. My father. She was recalling him to me quite clearly. But the name she couldn't remember was Putnam. George Palmer Putnam.' She repeated it, raising her voice against a sudden wave of static. She was aware of the people at their desks on the other side of the room. She must be careful, she thought.

'I have that,' Reverend Mother said. 'But Laura, are you sure she needs to be told just now? It's bound to be a bit of a shock.'

'I promised her,' Laura said simply. 'So that she can think about the future. Besides, it might help her to know her mind hasn't been playing tricks on her again.'

'You may be right. I'll do it gently.'

'Perhaps I can talk to her myself next time.'

She heard Reverend Mother hesitate. 'Her power of speech isn't so good today. A letter would be best.'

'I'll write before I leave for London.'

They both heard the operator break in. Time was up, there were other callers waiting to use the line. Their goodbyes overlapped, fading away over the thousand miles of ocean between them.

As Laura handed back the headphones and turned to go, she remembered she had left the Earhart file open on the table next door. It was still there and the room was empty. As she folded it up to replace it in the filing cabinet, one of the cuttings slipped to the ground. It was the one with the photograph of her mother by the plane.

Swiftly, Laura picked it up and tucked it into her bag. All her journalistic instincts chided her as she did so. But it was an impulse from the heart, she told herself, something she simply couldn't deny.

Later, in her hotel room, she pinned the cutting to her dressing-table mirror. As she sat in front of it, her mother's face and her own were framed together in the glass, astonishingly similar despite the differences in colouring. It was, in fact, an obituary account of Amelia's career. Folded away in the final paragraph, Laura found that some lines had been quoted, apparently from a poem written by Earhart in the 1920s. Softly, she read them aloud.

'Courage is the price that Life exacts for granting peace.
The soul that knows it not, knows no release
From little things;
Knows not the livid loneliness of fear,
Nor mountain heights where bitter joy can hear
The sound of wings . . .'

CHAPTER THREE

'The loneliness of fear.' That was something her mother was to endure long after her flying days had ended, Laura thought. The words went running through her mind back at the hotel.

She had slept for an hour, then had dinner brought up to her room by a soft-footed Indian servant, immaculate in starched white uniform and scarlet turban. Now she was restless, moving out through the tall shuttered windows to the balcony overlooking the lights of the bay. The Grand Pacific spurned the anachronism of air conditioning, and the atmosphere was now unbearably sultry.

She was disturbed by what Reverend Mother had told her about her mother's failing power of speech. What if she became totally unable to speak, or even to write? The recordings Laura had made at Abaiang would become even more precious, the only weapon she might have against Harrington. Nor had there been time yet to copy them off. Perhaps tomorrow.

Tomorrow was the day she would be face to face with him again, she and Jack. She sat on the edge of the bed, her head in her hands. All she had been reading in the files that afternoon had stirred up once again that well of hatred deep inside her.

She had a clear picture of Harrington out at Suva Point, busy at his desk like a spider in its web, spinning and scheming. She saw the telephone by her bed, and instantly something rose up in her that could not be contained. Picking up the receiver, she asked the receptionist to put a call through to Dr Lawrence Harrington.

She could hear the phone ringing through the bungalow and waited, praying for him to be at home. There was the sound of a receiver being lifted, then a man's voice at the other end, an Indian voice.

'Dr Harrington's residence.'

Laura swallowed. 'Is Dr Harrington there?'

'Very sorry. Doctor cannot be disturbed. He has work to finish before he is leaving tomorrow, first thing.'

'Leaving?' It was the only word she could manage.

'He is travelling to New York.'

'When is he coming back?'

'After Christmas maybe.' There was a note of finality in the voice.

She tried again. 'Is Katua there?'

'Katua is gone back to Gilbert Islands, memsahib. I am Doctor's new bearer. There is message, memsahib?'

Laura put the phone down, feeling it slip against the sweat of her palm. She was very cold suddenly, with a heavy weight inside her like a stone. The bottle of red wine she had ordered with her dinner stood half-empty on the table. She poured out a glass and drained it, then picked up the phone again. She had to tell Jack.

But from Nailangi there only came a low-pitched buzz. Out of order, the operator told her, hurricane damage. Of course. On impulse she asked the girl if she could be put through to another Suva number, Ratu Edwin Vunilau's house.

For a moment she felt guilty. Edwin didn't even know yet that she'd found her mother. There had been no time to tell him. But he was the only person she could turn to.

A woman answered the phone. Laura felt an irrational flash of dismay at the softly accented voice. In the background she could hear children and laughter, the beat of island music from the radio. She had the sense of breaking in on a rich tangle of family life, a private world where she would always be the outsider.

'Yes, my husband is here,' the woman said. 'One moment.'

Shouted messages followed. There was an impression of different people in different rooms in a large crowded house. Finally Edwin was on the line.

'Laura! This is a pleasant surprise.'

At the sound of his voice the memory of Tarawa came back to her, the dreamlike strangeness of that night at the rest-house. Like a dream, it seemed curiously inconsequential. But instinct told her that the bond between them was still there. She was relying on it.

Quickly she told him of the meeting with her mother and the kind of life Millie had endured at Harrington's hands. She only wished she could confide in him the strangest revelation of all. Not yet, she told herself, not yet.

'But to have found her, Laura!' Edwin exclaimed. 'Fate was on your side in the end. Dear girl, I am so very happy for you. And only too glad to have been able to help you.'

Laura was impatient to cut through the courtesies.

'So now I have the evidence to fix Harrington for what he did to her. Will you come with me?'

'With you? Where?' He sounded puzzled.

'To see him at his house, to confront him with the truth.'

There was silence for a moment. 'Is Jack not with you?'

'Jack's at Nailangi. I have to see Harrington right away. He's leaving for New York tomorrow. I need you with me, Edwin, to back me up.'

She could hear him having to explain himself in Fijian. 'Laura, I'm afraid that's out of the question. I cannot be personally involved in such a serious matter. You understand that, surely? My position in government would make it quite impossible for me to interfere in any way.'

'But as a friend . . .' she broke in.

'But as a friend, I'll give you any advice I can. We can discuss the matter in private, of course. But this is a major scandal. The charges must be brought in the proper way. The case must be presented to the Public Prosecutor and go through the Attorney General's department.'

He was speaking in a rapid undertone. 'This is for a legal expert like Jack to deal with. When is he coming back?'

'Tomorrow. So he says. But that's too late. Don't you see?'

'Listen, Laura. It's taken thirty years for the whole appalling business to come to light. Surely it can wait until Harrington's back from America. It's a United Nations seminar. It can't last more than a couple of weeks.'

'You don't understand,' she said in a whisper. 'What it's like to know how he got away with it. It's not just my mother. It's me too. What he did to me . . .' She was unable to go on. She felt as if she were choking.

'Laura, for heaven's sake.' She could hear a note of alarm in Edwin's voice. 'This is for Jack to handle. You and Jack together. You musn't think of doing anything on your own. Harrington is dangerous. The situation is dangerous.'

He waited for her to speak, but she was silent.

'Laura, you promise?' Then he added gently, 'I worry about you, you know.' He paused. 'Tarawa is not forgotten.'

'I know,' she said in a low voice. 'I understand.'

Quickly she replaced the receiver. She sat quite still on the side of the bed, her arms folded tight as if to hold back the force of her emotions. But it was no good. The compulsion was overwhelming. Why did she need anyone with her? She had gone alone to face Harrington in the beginning. She had penetrated the maze of the past alone. Now she must find her own way out.

She looked at her watch. It was a quarter to eleven. From outside there came the sound of the storm returning with a surge of rain against the glass.

She got up and pulled on the jacket hanging on the door, and slipped the bag of tapes with the playback attachment over her shoulder. She caught a glimpse of herself in the mirror, looking very pale. She stopped to tie back her hair with a scarf, before locking the door behind her and running down the stairs two at a time. The elegant white reception hall with its tall palms and colonial pillars seemed to be almost deserted. Fans stirred languidly from the vaulted ceiling. In the cocktail bar at the far end, someone was strumming a chord or two on the grand piano and she could hear laughter from a few end-of-the-evening drinkers.

The Chinese manager in his sharkskin jacket raised surprised eyebrows from behind the desk. 'Going out?'

'I need a taxi right away.'

He snapped his fingers at the Fijian doorman, then turned back to her. 'Weather is bad to be out. You going far?'

'Just to Suva Point.'

While they waited for the taxi, he recited a familiar commentary. 'You know, many famous people have stayed at this hotel? Noël Coward. Somerset Maugham. Mr Maugham wrote that story here, the one called "Rain".' He nodded at the downpour. 'No wonder, eh?'

The taxi driver told her it was the tail end of the hurricane that had done so much damage on the other side of the island. A high wind was battering its way through the rain. In the headlights she could see that the beach road was strewn with fallen palm branches. At the turnoff to the Point, the way was partly blocked where the high tide had thrown piles of flotsam over the sea wall. The taxi slithered to a halt.

'Can't go no further, marama. The house is just over there.' He pointed to the shape of the gabled roof through the trees. The outside lights were glinting on wet tossing branches. 'Path up is over there.'

'I know.' She handed over some money.

'You be okay then, marama?'

'I'm okay. Thanks.'

Too late, Laura realized that she hadn't asked for his card so that she could ring for a lift back. She'd have to rely on a phone directory, which might mean problems. Meanwhile, she had to concentrate on keeping her footing, with the rain driving against her face and the track ahead lit only in patches.

She knew the way she would go, through the back gate and up through the garden where Katua had let her out that day. She was looking for a sign of the Indian bearer as she followed the overgrown path. But the servants' shack at the side of the house was in darkness.

She had reached the back verandah. All the windows were shuttered tight against the storm. She tried to be as silent as possible, making her way up the steps and treading carefully over the creaking boards. She wanted to see the look of shock on his face as he opened the door to her, and stood outside the nearest window, perfectly still, for a moment. There was a crack of light along the hinges. Through it she could glimpse the room inside, see the figure seated in profile at his desk with the pressure lamp next to him.

The glare from the light threw every feature into sharp relief, the dyed hair, the beaked nose and the deep hollows beneath the cheekbones. More than ever, Harrington looked like some bird of prey, hunched over the papers he was turning with his long crooked hands.

She remained there without moving, concentrating on the satisfaction of observing the man while he still thought himself alone. She waited until there was a lull in the roaring of the wind. Then she rapped sharply on the shutter.

She saw him spin round in his chair, startled. 'Who's there?'

She did not reply, but knocked again. She was standing motionless, half in shadow, when the door at the end of the verandah was flung open.

'Who is it?' he called.

Without speaking, Laura walked towards him until he could see her in the light. She heard him take a sharp breath.

'Laura! So you're back.' He held his hands stiffly at his sides. She could sense him striving to control his nerves. 'What a night to go calling!' He stood aside, staring at her. 'Come in.'

She moved into the room. Everything was just as she remembered – the chequered drapes, the musty bookshelves, the glass cases with their labelled exhibits. He was no more than a yard or two away from her, watching her in the shadows. She wished she could stop trembling. It was not fear she felt, but the thrill of the hunt.

'You'd better take off your wet things.'

Quickly she dropped her soaked jacket on to the nearest chair. 'I'm not staying.'

'Just as well. I have work to finish before I get on the boat tomorrow.' He shrugged. 'Cruise lectures, as well as my United Nations paper.'

The smugness of his tone goaded her on. 'There's something I think you should know before you go.'

'Oh yes?'

He moved across to the drinks trolley, deliberately offhand. She thought she detected a tremor in the measure of whisky he poured for himself. 'Something for you?'

She shook her head. He sat down in the chair behind the desk and lit a cigarette, with the usual ritual rolling of the tip against the menthol stick. The smell reminded her of her first visit. There was the whiff of hospital corridor about it and she recoiled.

'Sit down.' He nodded at the tape machine slung from her shoulder. 'Still lugging your little recorder around the Pacific, talking to the picturesque natives?'

'Not this time.' She had taken the chair on the opposite side of the desk, next to the door that led to the front of the house. 'This time I've been talking to my mother.'

She watched the way his face slowly froze. A smile flickered on and off like a fading battery.

'Going in for spiritualism now, are you?'

'My mother is alive.' She sat very straight and pressed her hands together in her lap. 'In spite of what you did to her, she lived.'

'And where did you track down this miracle of survival?'

'The mission at Abaiang. A Japanese officer took her there from Taparua. That hadn't occurred to you, obviously. That someone might want to protect her.'

He was pouring another whisky. Laura noticed a hairline crack in the glass where it had slipped against the decanter.

'There were rumours,' he said.

'That's why you tried to stop me going there, with that ridiculous quarantine story?'

Somewhere behind her a shutter banged loose. Harrington went over to fasten it. She noticed he was barefoot under the Chinese dressing gown, also that he'd begun to move like an old man.

'So the woman has survived.' He spoke with his back to her. 'What of it?'

Laura waited until he turned towards her again.

'Survived to tell me everything. On tape.' She touched the bag at her side. 'And there's a witness too. Timu has told me exactly how you found her, how you kept her a prisoner. You enjoyed being a jailer. Having total power over someone else's life, as well as the pleasure of inflicting pain, mental and physical.'

He sat down opposite her again, leaning back, his eyes moving around the room as if his thoughts were far away. Her mouth was painfully dry. For a second she wished she had taken the drink he had offered.

'The madness of it,' she continued, her voice steady. 'Because you're still mad you can't see it, isn't that right? But the law can, and will. Then it will be your turn to be a prisoner.'

'The law?' Harrington widened his eyes in mock wonderment. 'So my daughter's going to take her father to court for his treatment of her mother? How very bizarre!'

Laura leaned towards him. More than anything she longed to reach out and strip off that mask of unconcern, reveal the raw underside of his secret self.

'What daughter?' She spat the words at him. 'To find out you were not my father – that alone has made it all worthwhile. To be free of the horror of that!'

'I suppose Timu told you that as well.' He began sorting through the papers in front of him. 'All this is quite pointless. I'm off to the States tomorrow and after the seminar I'm thinking of taking up a permanent post with Unesco. So Fiji will be past history as far as I'm concerned, along with whatever happened in the Gilberts all those years ago.'

'The appointment has been confirmed?' Laura ordered her words carefully.

'It will be when I get there. So I'm afraid your role as avenging angel is mere fantasy, my dear Laura. All this rubbish about criminal charges! Do you honestly think anyone's going to believe the ramblings of some deranged woman going back to the 1930s? I rescued an unknown survivor from an unknown disaster and she stayed on to live with me. She did tell you she'd lost her memory, I suppose?'

'She told me.'

'The unfortunate creature doesn't even know who she is.'

'She *didn't*.' She saw his head lift at the correction. 'Until two days ago.'

'What do you mean?'

For the first time she saw real shock on his face, and relished it. She spoke with deliberate slowness.

'I rather think you'll find less of a welcome in America when they hear about Amelia Earhart. I'm sure the whole world will want to know about the man who kept her hidden, then left her to rot for the rest of her life.'

'If this is some new fantasy of yours.' His eyes were fixed on hers. She could see panic begin to stir in them.

'No fantasy. Just fact. I've been with my mother for the past three days. Just before I left she saw something that triggered her memory. She's had almost total recall of how she landed up on that beach.' She stared across at him, almost curious. Could one penetrate the dark recesses of that mind, even now, she wondered? 'You knew all along, didn't you?' she went on. 'You guessed from the start who she was.'

To her amazement she saw he was smiling, a kind of smirk of satisfaction. For the first time she noticed his false teeth, loose-fitting along the lower gums, giving the smile a hint of the skull beneath.

'Of course I knew who she was. Even the most stupid of district officers would have guessed. News of her disappearance was circulated right through the islands. Everyone was told to be on the lookout for any wreckage washed up. There were even American seaplanes searching the area.'

'And you had your own ways of keeping her out of sight,' she said bitterly.

'It was easy.' He put out his cigarette. For a moment a wisp of blue smoke hung between them. He peered through it almost playfully. She drew back. She found this kind of mood swing even more disturbing than what had gone on before. 'Just to think,' he murmured. 'Here you've been busy playing detective. And all the time I've had my own Earhart file, right here in my desk.'

He fished for a key from the bunch around his waist, then bent to open a drawer. What he brought out was something like an old-fashioned scrapbook, the leather binding mouldy and torn. He threw it across to her and as it fell open she saw pages covered with pictures and cuttings, each with its neatly written label.

'How's that for evidence? Fairly complete, I think.'

Laura felt a wave of nausea. 'But why? What was the point?'

'Secrets,' he said in a low voice. 'There's a power in secrets, knowing something nobody else can imagine. Keeping it all to yourself.'

'Did you have no feeling for her at all?'

He looked up, surprised. 'Of course I did. She was a woman, a white woman. I needed that. *What* she was, that was far more important than *who* she was. It meant I was no longer alone. Indeed I think it was her presence that saved me from going round the bend.'

Laura could see that he thought this was true. Suddenly, she'd had enough. She felt her hunger for that moment of retribution drain away. What was the point of letting him hear Amelia tell her story? None of it would really get through. The armour of delusion he'd built around himself was impenetrable. Looking at him sitting there, she could see for the first time that his eyes were dead, as dead as the moths on the wall behind him.

'I must go,' she said. 'You'll hear from the Public Prosecutor's office wherever you are. Perhaps you'll enjoy being really famous.'

She pushed back the chair and got up. She saw herself hurrying back along the coast road the way she had come, anything rather than wait for a taxi. In her haste to leave she made the mistake of moving away to pick up her coat. When she turned back, Harrington had the bag of tapes in his hand. He held it up with a smile.

'These will go where they belong. With the rest of my Earhart collection.'

Too late, she reached out to grab them back. But he had the bag strap over his shoulder and it was impossible to wrest it away. She tried again. This time he seized hold of her by the arms and forced her backwards towards the door, the door that opened into the front of the house. In a flash of terror, she realized how strong he was.

'So now there's just little Laura to be dealt with,' she heard him say. 'Something I've done before and will be happy to do again.'

She felt herself being pressed against the door. She smelt his breath on her face. Just for an instant she was back on her bed again as a child, caught in a wave of revulsion as he tightened his grip on her. She heard herself gasp and began to scream.

From another room came a strange echo of that scream, a shrill rasping cry that stopped as suddenly as it had begun. She had forgotten about the bird in the cage, the old mynah that Harrington loved to torment.

The sound seemed to electrify her. She found herself reaching up against the wall at the side of the door. A Gilbertese fishing knife hung there, edged with shark's teeth. She had hold of it for just long enough to draw it sharply against Harrington's face.

He drew back with a cry of pain, pressing his hand to the line of blood on his cheek.

There was a split second where she was free to pull open the door behind her. Half falling, she found herself outside. But directly in front of her were the steps, a long curving descent into the darkness below. She had wrapped her wrist around the strap of the tape bag to wrench it away. But Harrington held to it stubbornly, stumbling against her back, both of them braced against the rain which gusted around them in sheets.

'Such dangerous steps,' he said in her ear. 'So easy to slip and fall, especially for a visitor on a rainy night who doesn't know them.'

For a split second Laura closed her eyes. Opening them again, she could see lights, down below where the steps ended. Or rather, she told herself, she imagined she could see lights. The real thing was too much to hope for. So was the sound of a car's engine, revving and grinding in the mud.

Harrington was holding her steadily now, almost in a friendly way, his arm round her waist. But she could smell the sour sweat of his panic.

'Laura! Are you there?'

The voice came up through the wind and the rain. She tried to shout back, but it was like one of those nightmares in which you were mute as well as paralysed. Harrington called out before her.

'Jack! What a night!' He still had hold of Laura's arm. She heard the labouring of his breath as he fought for composure. 'We were just looking out to see if it was beginning to blow over.'

Out of the darkness a figure appeared, springing up the steps towards them. Jack's face was white as plaster in the light from the house. It was caught in a look of desperation that Laura would never forget.

'You bloody fool!' He pulled her away from Harrington. 'If the weather hadn't turned me back . . .'

'Yes, an impulsive creature,' Harrington drawled. He was leading the way the way inside, as if this was a normal social occasion. Laura shuddered, unable to move from the doorway. Jack caught hold of Harrington by the shoulder.

'You're mad, Dr Harrington. You'll plead insanity in court, of course. It'll be diminished responsibility. Her Majesty's pleasure and so on. The trouble is it's not actually true. I think you were aware of every cruel thing you did to that poor woman. You'd do the same to Laura if you could.'

As Harrington moved away, Laura saw the bag of tapes where it had fallen on the floor between them. Automatically she bent to retrieve it, numb from shock. Vaguely she saw Harrington slump back into his chair and reach for the whisky decanter. Jack, standing over him, seemed to be feeling for something in the pocket of his jacket.

If this was a film, Laura thought, he'd bring out a gun. But it looked like a package of some kind, something very small. 'Amelia asked me to give you this,' Jack said. 'She never had to use it. She thought you might like it back.'

He dropped it onto the desk. Laura saw Harrington's hand close over it.

'A kind thought.' Harrington cleared his throat, took a gulp of the whisky. Then he flashed at Laura a look of such malevolence that it struck her across the eyes like a stone.

'Now get out.' His voice sunk to a whisper. 'This is my house. My life,' they heard him add as he turned away from them.

That was how Laura would always remember him, a hunched figure in a soiled gold dressing gown, sitting with his head in his hand, alone in a room of shadows. Above the hiss of the pressure lamp she thought she heard him laugh. Then they got to the door, and the pounding of the wind swallowed up every other sound.

Jack's arm came around her shoulders. 'Don't look back,' he said.

CHAPTER FOUR

Laura's mind registered almost nothing of the drive back, except when she asked Jack about the package.

'Amelia said you would remember,' he replied.

'When Harrington left her to the Japanese? The capsule he gave her? She kept it all that time?'

He nodded, drawing her against him so that her head rested on his shoulder. 'With Harrington still alive maybe, wouldn't you?'

'That was what she called you back for.'

'She didn't want you to know. It was for me to judge, she said. It's cyanide.' He turned to look at her. 'Why didn't you wait for me? Didn't you trust me?'

'There was only tonight. How did I know you'd be back?' She felt her throat tightening. So much to be explained, she thought wearily. 'I'm sorry, Jack.' She shivered. 'Will he – will he use it?'

He put his hand on her knee. 'Don't talk now.'

The ache in her head made it difficult to think. Trees and road went spinning by. She wasn't sure where she was until they were driving up through the forest to the house at Vailima.

'But the hotel . . .' she heard herself start to say. She seemed to be too weak to move. Jack lifted her out of the Land Rover and carried her inside.

'This is where you're staying. You're in quite a bad state of shock. Here I can look after you.'

He lowered her onto the bed in the room where she had spent her first night at Vailima. Images of herself with Harrington kept flashing round in her mind, tormenting her. She took a little of the mixture Jack brought her, his mother's Valium, he told her, with some kind of headache powder. He held out the glass again.

'Finish it off. It'll do the trick.'

He leaned over her, frowning a little, tucking her in. She felt the brush of his body above her. In the light of the candle he'd put on the bedside table she saw him bite his lip in concentration, a glint of white teeth against the long full mouth. She pushed the glass away. There was a look of such intense tenderness in his eyes that she felt almost faint. She sighed his name once, and then again, pulling aside the sheet between them.

His hands went down over her and she heard him groan.

'Make love to me, Jack,' she said. 'Help me forget.'

A narrow shaft of sunlight woke her, striking across her face where the window curtains had fallen apart just an inch. Harrington is dead, she said to herself. She was still half asleep, but she knew it as clearly as if she had seen the body, thrown from the chair on to the floor in the convulsion of cyanide poisoning. With a little shiver she turned towards the warmth of Jack's body as he slept on, his back to her.

Lightly with her finger she traced the hint of freckles on his shoulder, which always reminded her of the markings on a bird's egg. She thought of the way they had taken possession of one another again, more completely than ever before, it seemed. The lovemaking had been swift and consuming. The old reproaches and misunderstandings might never have existed. But already the moment was ebbing away. There had been no word between them of what was to come. No commitments had been made, no promises exchanged in that embrace. Passion had a private language of its own. But that burned out too, leaving nothing behind, she thought.

She had the strange feeling that this short time together had the same kind of finality about it as her encounter with Harrington. Perhaps on Jack's part, it might even have been as much an act of kindness as an act of love.

Lying there in the patch of brightness, she saw for the first time his suitcases standing packed and labelled in the corner of the room. With Harrington dead, what was there to keep her any longer in Suva? The man's crimes would die with him, no doubt as her mother had intended. Even now the scenes at the bungalow seemed to be fading in her mind, like some tawdry piece of theatre. All that was real now was Amelia. And Jack, she told herself, hearing his breathing so close to her, soft and regular as a child's.

But that was an illusion. After a few days with his father at Nailangi, Canberra and his work were waiting for him. So, no doubt, was Kim.

That was when the idea of leaving immediately for London took hold of her. Why wait any longer? Just the thought of losing Jack all over again was unbearable, saying another goodbye and watching him go as if she didn't care. Ever since the night of the dancing at Abaiang, she'd known in her heart that there was no alternative. Unless they could change the course of their lives and take hold of a future together, she must cut off completely. Get away while the going was good.

It only needed the sight of the letter to finally convince her. Carefully sliding out of bed, so as not to wake Jack, she'd gone into the kitchen to make tea. In the mail bag hanging by the steps yesterday's delivery was clearly visible, still unopened. She drew out the bundle a little guiltily but without hesitation. Among the official envelopes was a large package from Canberra with Kim's name scrawled on the back. She laid it on top of the pile on Jack's desk, where he would know she had put it. Already opened in the tray alongside, neatly confirming everything, was an envelope with the Qantas logo. Inside was his return ticket.

She had to be quick now before he woke. Quick to get showered and dressed, quick so as not to think about things too precisely. Silently she closed the door of the house behind her. There mustn't be time to notice the scent of wild orchids nor the flash of a hummingbird through the trees as she hurried down the path.

First thing every morning there was a bus from the village that passed along the lane at the bottom. It was something Jack had told her. She didn't have to wait very long. So fate was on her side, she told herself as she found a seat among the crowd of Fijians bound for market, and let the gentle hubbub of talk wash over her.

From the marketplace it was only a short walk to the Grand Pacific. She had to collect her bags and then phone the airline. Yes, they had room on the London flight from Nandi that evening. The ticket would be held in her name. The connecting flight from Suva left in one hour.

The doorman already had a taxi waiting. Once again Laura had the sense of everything running on course. The fates were still showing their approval.

No, there were no messages for her, the clerk at the reception desk said as she paid her bill. She hated herself for asking, hated even more the inquisitive smile on his face as she turned away.

No doubt Jack was as grateful for the clean break as she was. By the time she returned to Fiji again he'd be settled in Australia. Then she could concentrate on making plans for her mother's future.

What those plans would be she couldn't yet begin to imagine. It was as if her mind was divided into two quite separate compartments. In one was the picture of her mother as she was now, the frail elderly woman known as Sister Kiri, the refugee who'd found a kind of peace in one of the remote corners of the earth. In the other was the world heroine, the flier whose survival would be one of the great news stories of the century.

This second image Laura found almost frightening. How would she be able to handle the announcement of the discovery of Earhart? How would she protect her mother from the avalanche of publicity, the crushing impact of the outside world after so many years as a recluse?

These were the questions that rose in her mind as the taxi neared the airport. She also found herself thinking of Harrington, and of how near she had come to death herself at that awful house. For the first time she began to consider the possibility that he was still alive. What if he had decided against suicide in the end? He might be arrogant enough, and deluded enough, to think that he could brazen his way out of the strongest prosecution case. Even the scandal of a Jekyll and Hyde past could be made to sound far-fetched by someone as clever as Harrington.

At the airport there was a newsstand selling the *Fiji Times*. She glanced quickly through it as she checked in with her baggage. There was nothing in it about Harrington. But how could there be, she reminded herself. The paper had probably been printed around midnight, far too early for any news to have been reported.

She joined the other passengers in the departure lounge, stout island ladies with bulging wicker baskets, Indian families in bright best clothes, a few tourists hung about with instamatic cameras and plastic garlands. Out on the runways she could see the little planes of the local airways waiting to take off to scattered destinations like the Gilberts.

Over the loudspeakers music from the Suva radio station was interrupted for an announcement – the Nandi flight would be delayed for thirty minutes. Laura remembered her promise to write to her mother, and brought out paper and pen. She wanted to tell her all she had learned about George in the reference library, and everything she could remember of Amelia's exploits. Her mother would like that, she thought.

From habit, Laura wrote fast, scribbling the address down on an envelope so that she could post it before the plane left. She decided to say nothing about Harrington yet. The time for that would come later.

Over the relay system, the music broke off again for the time signals and the BBC news from London. Reading through her letter, Laura was hardly listening when the local bulletin followed. Then she heard the name Harrington.

'. . . The body was discovered by a houseboy in the early hours. Foul play is not suspected . . .'

Somebody clattered a tea-tray at the next table. Laura leaned forward, straining to hear above the noise and the thumping of her heart. '. . . note found by the police. Harrington stated that a terminal illness had been diagnosed. The decision to take his own life will shock and sadden . . . the demise of an internationally respected figure on the eve of his departure for New York . . .'

The newsreader's voice was interrupted by another airline announcement. Boarding for the Nandi plane would be in ten minutes' time.

There was a tiny space at the bottom of Laura's letter. In it she wrote a few words in a shaky hand.

'News just come through that H committed suicide last night. You will understand.'

She sealed the letter, then stood up so awkwardly that she knocked over the cup of coffee she had been drinking. She was aware of people looking at her. Her face had begun to tremble. She could feel a flood of emotion coming to the surface so fast that it was all she could do to look round blindly for the ladies' room. Inside there was a solitary cleaning lady, humming to herself as she wielded her broom.

'You all right, dearie?'

Laura nodded and quickly locked herself in a cubicle. She surprised herself with the passion of this breakdown. It's delayed reaction, she kept telling herself. So many things coming at once, and all the time I've had to pretend I'm in control. The overpowering relief of knowing that Harrington was dead had opened the floodgates. Perhaps, too, the ordeal of a public trial had been weighing on her more heavily than she'd realized.

In the distance she heard the final call for the plane. In a flurry she let herself out and splashed her face at the basin. Hurrying through the door she remembered to her horror that she'd left her carry-on bag at the table. Worse still, there was someone sitting there, a man in a battered panama. The fact that the man was Jack Renfrey seemed difficult to absorb, even when he stood up and held out the bag to her.

'I can see you're still in the habit of leaving your belongings behind.' He wasn't smiling. 'You've heard the news? Still lying even at the end.'

She nodded. In her confusion she was searching through her bag for her boarding pass, unwilling to meet his eyes.

'So it's all over,' she heard him say.

'I'm sorry. It's what I've known all along.' She was trying to speak clearly, without much success. 'What we've both known.'

'I'm talking about Harrington,' he said irritably. 'What the hell are you talking about? And anyway, why the sudden dash for London?

Was there a call from the BBC or what? All they said at the hotel was that you'd left for the airport.'

'There was a spare seat on the flight.'

She'd found her pass and was half running now towards the disappearing queue at the boarding gate.

'You might at least have left a note.' He was keeping pace with those long strides of his. 'I'm getting a bit tired of having to catch up with you, one way and another.'

She stopped in her tracks and spun round to face him. 'And I'm a bit tired of having to say goodbye without knowing if or when I'm ever going to see you again.'

He stared at her. 'But why should you think . . . ?'

'I saw the letter from Kim, I saw the ticket. Not again. This time it's my turn to make an exit.'

Jack seemed to be on the verge of losing his temper, but he took a deep and careful breath. 'As a journalist, you should at least make sure of your facts.' He held up the Qantas envelope. 'If you'd taken the trouble to look properly you'd have seen a cancelled return. I'm just about to trade it in.'

'What for?' she asked idiotically.

'Cash, of course. I'm going to be a bit strapped without my Australian salary.'

'So you're not going back?'

'I have to be here now, don't I?' he said, exasperated. 'I was going to talk to you about it today.'

She was facing Jack now, standing very close. 'And Kim?'

Out of the corner of her eye Laura saw a Fiji Airways stewardess bearing down on them, clutching her clipboard. The other passengers had disappeared through the gate.

'Kim?' Jack's expression was weary. 'I suppose she might be allowed to send my mail on for me from time to time without being cast as my partner for life.'

'That's over?' Laura felt weak to the point of unsteadiness.

'It never even began, except inside your head.'

He took her by the arm and began to hustle her towards the barrier. 'You're going to miss the plane if you're not careful.' He drew back from her, surveying her with narrowed eyes. 'You look awful, by the way. You'd better catch some sleep on the trip. And this time, let me know the time of your flight back.'

'Okay,' she said faintly. 'Oh, by the way . . .' She held out the letter for her mother. 'Could you post this for me?'

'I may even drop in and see her while you're away.'

The stewardess took Laura's boarding pass and motioned her through. 'They're waiting,' she said.

The turnstile clicked behind her. Jack was out of reach now. Turning to wave, she saw him vault over the barrier and break into a run to catch up with her.

'That Jack Renfrey!' she heard the stewardess exclaim with a giggle.

'Laura! Something I forgot!' he called.

They were on the edge of the tarmac. The little plane was standing less than twenty yards away, the steps still down, waiting for her.

He took her hand tightly and drew her to a standstill. 'Something I need to know right away.'

Oh, God, she thought. Why does this have to happen here?

'Nailangi,' he said. 'Should we sell it, or try to get it going again?'

'Who's we?'

'You and me, of course. Father's opting out. My mother's back in Australia, which leaves us.'

'Honestly Jack, what a time . . .'

The words got muffled in a kiss, a long leisurely kiss watched with interest by all the faces at the windows, and by the pilot himself, sitting with the cockpit door still open.

'Would you like to live there?' the voice in her ear demanded.

She felt herself nodding, too out of breath to speak.

'And Laura. You gave me an awful fright this morning,' he whispered. 'Promise not to do it again?'

'I promise.'

She broke away and ran to the plane. 'Sorry,' she said to the girl waiting at the top of the steps.

Her seat was next to the window. She pressed her hand to the pane, saw him wave the panama with that mock salute of his, and then he was gone.

CHAPTER FIVE

Catching up on sleep as Jack had suggested was easier said than done. Too much had happened in the last few hours for Laura's mind to be able to switch off. Besides, the first part of the journey was just a short flight acrosss the island, and the little plane was crammed full with chattering local passengers.

Even when she was safely aboard the London-bound Qantas jet, she found it hard to relax. Euphoria was a far more powerful stimulant than fear had ever been. The horrors of the house at Suva Point, those last moments with Harrington, would soon be consigned to the past like a bad film or a half-remembered nightmare. Jack's arrival at the airport had overlaid everything. Even now, the scene ran back and forth through her mind, the heart-wrenching confusion of it all, the absurd way he had of assuming she knew as well as he did that there was no other future possible except a life together. In his mind, there couldn't be the faintest doubt about something that had been settled the moment they'd seen each other across the hall at Broadcasting House.

The kiss on the airstrip had said it all. She could still feel the exact physical print of it on her mouth. As the plane lifted above the clouds, she felt her elation rise with it, felt herself floating on it like a bird.

A Nat King Cole song was playing through the speakers. The words came filtering into her mind from memory, 'under my skin' and 'deep in the heart of me' – Silly words that caught so much. She closed her eyes and heard herself sigh.

'Tired?' asked the steward at her elbow, busy with the drinks trolley.

'Happy, actually,' she murmured. 'I've just got engaged.' The prim-sounding expression made her smile when she thought of Jack.

'Then you deserve this.' He handed her a courtesy glass of

Australian champagne. 'And congratulations,' he added over his shoulder with a wink.

Perhaps I do deserve happiness now, Laura thought. She was remembering her state of mind on the journey out, which seemed years rather than weeks ago, the unfocused anxiety and the sense of foreboding that seemed to hang over her. Ratu Edwin had been aware of it right from the start. Falling so deeply in love with Jack had, at the start, made her even more vulnerable. It was the search for the truth about her mother that had changed her. Every obstacle she had met, every blow she had suffered, as well as the kindnesses she had received along the way, had built up an inner strength she never knew existed. Somehow the whole extraordinary experience had defined her and given her her true identity. She knew she would never lose it now, whatever happened.

After all, she was Earhart's daughter That in itself was a source of pride. She must be careful to contain it of course. Even so, she couldn't stop herself telling the passport officer at Los Angleles airport, 'My mother's American.'

'Should have got yourself born in the States.' He grinned up at her as he stamped her documents. 'A darn sight more convenient than a South Sea atoll. Though perhaps there's not that much difference nowadays.' He rolled his eyes at the group of flower-decked hippies strumming guitars in the arrival lounge next door.

Even passing through, Laura felt she had a claim on the country. California was where Amelia had set off from with such hope on that abortive last flight around the world. When the Qantas plane came down at Idlewild, New York, Laura thought of her mother again and the huge tickertape parade that had greeted the heroine of the nation after her Atlantic crossing.

Someday I will come back again, she thought, find out everything I can about her early years. There might even be some family to track down, the sister she had mentioned, nephews and nieces, though that would be for Amelia to decide. Was it too much to hope that her mother might come with her, one day? New kinds of neurological treatment in the States might restore her completely to her old self. If and when her identity became known, the Americans would surely be the first to claim her, with celebrations on a grand scale.

How much more she will need my protection then, Laura reminded herself, mine and Jack's. Just the thought of it was disturbing. With her journalist's training, she found herself turning over in her mind her own records of Amelia, not just the tapes but the notes she'd started to make. There would be a book, several books, but hers would be the one that told the truth. But how much of the truth? How would she tell of the ordeals she had suffered with Harrington without inflicting further damage on her mother?

As she thought of the problems lying ahead, Laura felt the euphoric glow die down a little. She slept for an hour or so. To occupy her mind on the last leg of the journey she turned to the draft of the script she'd written for her programme.

She was still scribbling as the plane began to come down at Heathrow. It was dark again and the lights of London and its suburbs seemed to wheel by endlessly before touch-down. How cold it was outside, and how bleak it all seemed! Glum-looking officials, pallid in the fluorescent lighting, barely looked up as the weary passengers were ushered through the usual rituals. Even the taxi driver was a morose character, dispensing endless bad news about the state of the country.

'Strikes. Fights with the bloody unions. Real trouble in Ireland,' he recited with Cockney relish. 'That Harold Wilson's a disaster. Be out by spring if you ask me. Then it's the turn of the other lot to make a mess of things. Just wait and see.'

'I won't be here,' Laura said. The prospect of leaving consoled her already.

'Some people have all the luck.'

He turned his attention back to the snarling traffic. Wigmore Street at least seemed comparatively peaceful. As she climbed the stairs to her flat on the third floor, Laura thought she must be dreaming. Some kind of perfume, sweet and strong, came drifting down to her. It was impossible to identify at first, and yet it touched a chord of happiness that made her spirits rise.

Then as she turned the stairs, she remembered. Tiaré gardenias. And there they were, an enormous bouquet of them, waxy white and wonderfully incongruous, propped against her door where the delivery people had left them. As she touched the petals she saw the card. 'Jack' was all it said, and that was more than enough.

The delight of the moment took her breath away. At the same time the phone inside began to ring. Struggling with her keys, her luggage, and the flowers, it seemed she would never be in time to answer it. Snatching up the receiver, she heard the voice break in at the other end before she could speak.

'Laura! You've just got in?'

'Darling! The flowers! You don't know how much . . .' she began, but Jack was too fast for her.

'I wanted to know you were safely there. I wanted to say I love you.

We were in such a hurry. It wasn't much of a proposal.' She heard him hesitate. 'But you did say yes, didn't you?'

'Yes! I said yes!'

They both laughed.

'And you're okay?'

'I'm fine. Ears buzzing, head spinning, but maybe that's just the effect you have on me.' Now it was her turn to hesitate. 'Jack, I've been thinking about my mother . . .'

'I've been thinking about her too. When she's well enough, in a day or two maybe, I'd like to bring her over to Fiji. To Nailangi. Then she'll be here when you get back. It'll be Christmas, won't it?' There was a note of childish glee in his voice which touched her almost more than anything. 'Would you like that?'

'I'd like it very much.'

'It's where she should be from now on, don't you think? It's such a huge old house. And now we're getting things straight again, we could even fix her up a little place of her own, like Auntie Atu. Can't you just see the two of them getting on really well?'

Laura was laughing again. 'Nibbling raw fish together, swopping their island stories.'

'And Amelia herself,' Jack went on. 'Though I still think of her as Millie. If she has to be famous all over again, she couldn't have a better hideaway than Nailangi.'

His tone was half joking, but Laura could sense the serious undertone.

'I've been thinking about that too. How we'd handle it – how she'd handle it. Reverend Mother seemed to think her speech was not too good when I rang through from Suva.'

'Laura, you mustn't worry. We must let fate decide what happens. It's all too early yet. Remember malua?'

'I've forgotten the exact translation.'

' "Que sera, sera," kind of thing. Or "leave it till tomorrow". ' The line crackled and surged between them. Laura had a sudden picture of a globe with two tiny figures on either side of it connected by a single thread.

'Darling, I've got to go now. It's early morning here. Got work to do. Don't forget the plane times. I'll ring at the end of the week,' he said briskly. Then his voice was husky in her ear, plaintive-sounding, as if in protest. 'Laura, I'm missing you.'

'I'm missing you too, my darling.'

'Till Friday.'

The two phones went down together.

Laura sighed and leaned back in the chair, staring around at her flat. It felt like the home of a stranger. On the table lay a stack of dull-looking letters, left there by Gladys, her weekly cleaning lady. Dusting and hoovering had obviously been done. But the whole place felt dead, a piece of machinery without the batteries. There seemed to be nothing of herself in it any more, not in the pretty chintzes or the prints on the walls or the carefully assembled bits and pieces of Victorian furniture.

Quickly she went into the kitchen and put the gardenias in water. As if by magic, the lush scent from the two tall jugs of flowers swept away the staleness of the air. In the fridge was milk, butter, bread and ham, deposited there by the faithful Gladys. Laura made herself a sandwich and a mug of tea. After a bath, in a sudden trance of tiredness, she fell into bed and slept.

The next morning, work took over. There was a flurry of phone calls back and forth with her producer, Nigel Dawson, a volatile character of about her own age who still cultivated the undergraduate image, with his faded denims and flowing locks. They got on well together, and the editing sessions in his office over the next few days went smoothly as they played back the tapes and planned the shape of the programme.

For Laura, it was a strange experience hearing the sounds she'd captured, the fishermen calling and the roll of the surf, morning birdsong and the conversations of the old men in the villages, but most of all the elegant, measured tones of Ratu Edwin. These were the resonances that were real to her, while the English voices and the clatter of typewriters in the surrounding corridors seemed by contrast totally unnatural.

'Must have been marvellous out there,' the young secretary Sara enthused as she typed up Laura's script. 'What a place for a holiday! Really romantic, I should think.'

'Not always.' Laura was smiling. 'But sometimes, yes indeed.'

Nigel was pondering over the extra background music that was needed. The Archives sound library had most things, from Fijian tribal chants to Tongan nose flutes. But the Gilbertese singing Laura wanted seemed impossible to find.

'Never mind, we'll go on trying,' Nigel assured her the day before they were due to record the programme.

On the way home she called in at Selfridge's to buy Christmas presents. Inside, the surging crowds, the endless displays of scent and jewellery and cosmetics, had an overpowering effect on her. There was something greedy about the sheer scale of it all that repelled her.

And yet a childish pleasure in the glitter of the scene swept her along, on up the escalators to the clothing departments. Here after some searching she found what she wanted, a new panama for Jack and a cotton trouser suit, dark blue, which she knew her mother would love.

Back on the ground floor, she stood in a quiet space next to the information desk. She was remembering the reports in the 1930s' newspapers about her mother's visit to the store after her solo crossing of the Atlantic when, as usual, she'd been mobbed by the crowds. Apparently the plane itself had been on display, though Laura couldn't imagine how exactly it had been done.

Standing nearby was a silver-haired man in black pinstripes who looked like a department manager. On impulse Laura went up to him. She was a broadcaster involved in a programme about the pioneer flyer Amelia Earhart, she explained. Was it true that her plane had been put on display when she made an appearance at the store back in the early thirties?

The man's expression was startled at first. His face reddened with pleasure.

'Was it true?' he repeated. 'It certainly was. I was here myself that day!'

'You were?' As usual, her instinct had been right, Laura thought with delight.

Mr Simpson, as he introduced himself, had been a messenger boy at the time. He vowed he would never forget his brief glimpse of the great woman.

'We were lined up to greet her like a guard of honour, myself and the other juniors. "Hi!" was what she said when we made our bows. I always remember that.' He beamed. 'It was so typical, so friendly! So American, of course.'

'How did she look?'

'Some people were disappointed she wasn't in her flying gear. But she looked stunning, white suit, little white feathered hat.' Mr Simpson's eyes sparkled. 'Like something from another sphere, a beautiful bird who'd materialized out of thin air.'

'And the plane?'

'Oh, that was up there.' He pointed towards the chandeliers. 'Believe it or not, but they'd reassembled it to hang overhead where all the crowds could see it. Marvellous little thing it was, bright red and gold. A Vega, I think it was called. Then she signed autographs. I've still got mine somewhere or other.'

'Was she pretty?'

Mr Simpson paused, consideringly. 'Not film-star pretty. But tremendously attractive, with real magnetism. Very bright blue eyes she had, and a special kind of smile.' He was studying Laura now. 'Bit like yours actually. That little gap between the two front teeth. Excuse me for being personal. "Gamine" is the word I think,' he added gallantly.

'Well, thank you. That's such a vivid picture.' She was beginning to feel guilty. 'I hope I'll be able to talk to you again, record something perhaps.'

'It'll be a pleasure!' They shook hands. But he was still searching his memory. 'Didn't she disappear in the end, a crash landing at sea?'

'That's right. Over the Pacific.'

'Bit of a mystery, wasn't it? Or perhaps she just wanted to do a vanishing trick. Had enough of fame and all that. Some celebrities do that. And who can blame them?' As Laura turned to go, he was smiling. 'Whatever happened, I'm happy to remember her just the way she was,' he said.

Outside, the noise was deafening. Music came pounding out from the nearby shops, not the cheerful songs of the Beatles but the raucous beat of rock 'n' roll. Laura tried to imagine the response of her mother, brought up on the graceful melodies of Cole Porter. She could see her standing bemused, like Rip Van Winkle, waiting at the edge of a pavement while the stream of cars and buses poured past, surrounded by the stench of petrol fumes and fried food.

Hurrying home, Laura found herself in almost the same state of alienation. In just a few weeks, the peace and beauty of the Pacific had detribalized her. Her old habitat of the city jungle was now as strange to her as it was irrelevant.

Back at the flat, with her mother fresh in her mind, she tried to telephone through Fiji to the mission at Abaiang. But it was a bad time to call – the complications of the connection proved too much for the system and she had to give up.

To distract her thoughts she switched on the television, watching while she ate a quick supper of scrambled eggs. There was a chat show on, an interview with some once-famous actress who'd been lured out of retirement for a comeback. Laura found it profoundly painful. In her mind, the ruined features, desperately made up under the arc lights, became her mother's. The trivial banter of the conversation rang even more hollow when she tried to imagine Amelia subjected to the same process. She switched it off. But later she found it hard to sleep, as the distorted images of her mother pursued themselves round in her mind.

The next day she was glad to get up early, to be at Broadcasting

House for the final recording session. As she checked in at the desk, the receptionist handed her a letter. The airmail envelope was postmarked 'Fiji'. She knew at once that the childlike scrawl could only be her mother's. But there was no time to open it now. She was late already. Hastily she slipped it into her pocket and ran for the lift.

Two floors below the studio was surprisingly warm, almost stifling. The engineer apologized for the breakdown of the air-conditioning. But Nigel made the usual chaffing remarks.

'Don't bother about her, she's used to it! Just back from the South Seas, after all!'

There was time for a coffee before they started recording, Nigel told her. The two men retreated to the control room on the other side of the glass for the usual technical checks, leaving Laura with her script and her BBC cardboard cup.

At once, her fingers touched the letter in her pocket. She knew she should read it at home, where she could give it her undivided attention. But she couldn't wait till then. At least her mother was able to put pen to paper and order her thoughts, she thought as she tore it open, even though the handwriting was painfully shaky.

'My Darling Laura,' she read. 'I just want to let you know something important before I see you again. It was good of you to find out about George, your father. Now he has gone, I feel he has taken that other Amelia with him, the one he helped to create. And that's what I want. To let out the news that she's still alive would be asking too much of her, I guess, even with your help. So we shall keep silent, shall we? – for my lifetime at least.

'Let's face it, I'm a wreck of an elderly lady now. I've had to accept so many humiliations and hardships in order to survive, the original Earhart got changed out of all recognition. Can you blame me if I want the world to remember me as I was? I think in my way I did help to show other women that it was possible to break out of their everyday lives, to achieve a dream if they were determined enough.

'I was always a free spirit. Now I want the freedom to live my own life as I choose, what's left of it. I want to celebrate the miracle of the return of my daughter to me.

'In spite of everything, I've been so lucky to have you find your way to me again. The nightmare really is over now, with Harrington gone into the dark where he belongs. Did you think me wicked to send him on his way? Was it not poetic justice? I have no guilt about it. In fact, no guilt about anything, only happiness.

'With all my love,
Your Mother.'

'P.S. Jack is taking me to Fiji in his little yellow plane. I want him to fly over Howland, just to prove to me that it really exists. And that may be the end of the last mystery of all.'

Laura folded the letter away. There would be time later to take in the full impact of her mother's decision. All she felt now was relief, the lifting of a weight from her shoulders. She was aware of sadness, too, at what Amelia was denying herself. But she accepted the wisdom of it. That Earhart lived would be a secret well guarded from the world by just three people. Love would keep it safe.

Now Nigel was back again, sitting next to her with his copy of the script, and she tried to concentrate on what he was saying.

'The tapes are fine.' Laura could see him searching for one of his last-minute creative touches. 'There are one or two of your links that could do with something, though, something . . .' He faded off, waving a slim hand to and fro. 'Something a bit more personal, perhaps. After all, you were brought up in the islands. What about a mention or two of family?'

Laura was prepared for this. 'I think that's another kind of programme, don't you?'

'Perhaps so.'

The red pencil hovered over another page. 'And here. What about a line or two of historical background, a mention of some of the Europeans who're always associated with the Pacific?'

'Such as?' She wanted to get the programme under way, knowing all the technical stops and starts that lay ahead. And Jack was ringing her at six to check the time of the flight tomorrow.

'Oh, I don't know.' Nigel was in full flood again. 'Gauguin. Somerset Maugham. Robert Louis Stevenson. And the explorers, of course. Wasn't there a woman flier back in the thirties who disappeared over the Pacific?' He ruffled his hair. 'Amy Johnson, was it?'

Laura twisted a paper clip between her fingers. 'Amelia Earhart?' she suggested. Just to say the name gave her a small private thrill.

'That's it.'

'Actually, that's a story that has no proper ending. No one knows what happened to her.'

'Maybe that's another programme too?'

'I don't think so. Best left to the imagination.'

The green light flashed on in front of them. 'Ready when you are,' came the voice of the studio manager. Nigel got up to join him.

'Good luck, Laura.'

'Thanks.' She took a ritual swallow of the glass of stale water.

He put his head round the door for a final word. 'Hope you like the music we're using to lead in.'

It was the music that took her off-guard. The old recording of Gilbertese singing descended on her as swiftly as a spell, evoking instantly the night of the dancing at Abaiang. The drumming tingled through her veins. The voices swooped and soared. She smelled the tang of sandalwood on Jack's skin beside her.

In forty-eight hours I'll be over the Pacific again, flying westward, going home. Make the time hurry, she said to herself.

'On the green then,' came the voice through the headphones.

'On the green,' she replied and, taking a deep breath, started to read.